BLIND MAN'S LABYRINTH

A NOVEL

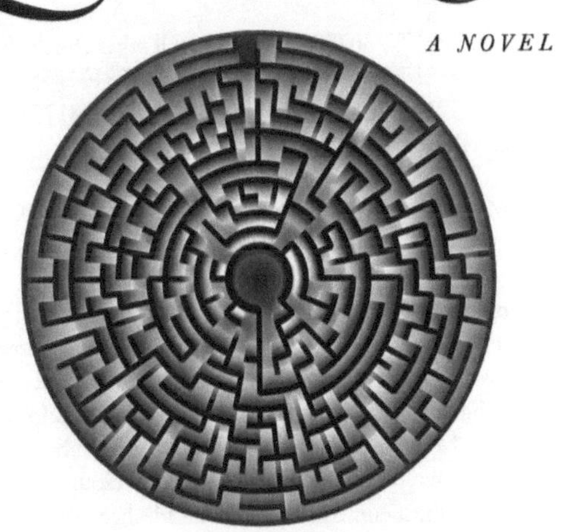

DARYL POTTER

PAPER STONE
PRESS

Paper Stone Press
Oakville, ON, Canada
www.paperstonepress.com
Published 2021

Paperback: 9781777307394
Hardcover: 9781777557805
Large Print: 9781777557812
Kindle eBook (KPF): 9781777557829

All other eBooks (ePUB):
9781777557836
Audio: 9781777557850

Blind Man's Labyrinth was first published in Canada. Canadian spelling conventions are maintained throughout.

The novel's epigraph is drawn from Lord Byron's epic poem, "Childe Harold's Pilgrimage," which first captured my imagination as a young boy reading from an old, dusty volume found in the Willows Public Library of Willows, California. My memory of this text was refreshed by referencing the following online resource: http://knarf.english.upenn.edu/Byron/charold1.html on January 1, 2021

Edited by Amelia Wiens
Proofread by S. Robin Larin of Robin Editorial
Map designed by Daryl Potter and Jackson Potter
Cover and typeset by Damonza

*For the Smiths
and the Loewens
and the Giesbrechts
of Fort St. John, British Columbia,
and Glenn, California.
I was the kid in the green parsonage.
Each of you made me feel like I belonged.
You changed a life
by how you lived your own.*

Through many a clime 'tis mine to go,
With many a retrospection curst;
And all my solace is to know,
Whate'er betides, I've known the worst.

What is that worst? Nay, do not ask—
In pity from the search forbear:
Smile on—nor venture to unmask
Man's heart, and view the hell that's there.

George Gordon, Lord Byron
Childe Harold's Pilgrimage

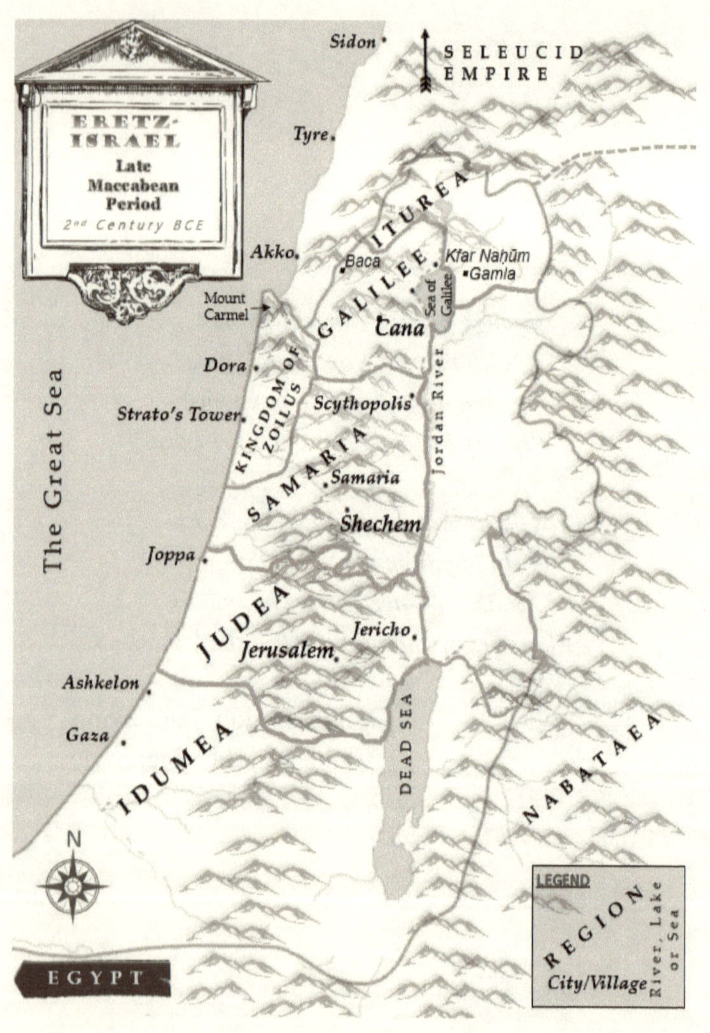

ERETZ-ISRAEL
Late Maccabean Period
2nd Century BCE
Sidon
Tyre
Akko
Baca
Kfar Naḥūm
Gamla
Mount Carmel
Cana
Sea of Galilee
ITUREA
GALILEE
Dora
Scythopolis
Strato's Tower
Jordan River
SAMARIA
Samaria
Shechem
KINGDOM OF ZOILUS
The Great Sea
Joppa
Jericho
Jerusalem
Ashkelon
JUDEA
Gaza
DEAD SEA
IDUMEA
NABATAEA
SELEUCID EMPIRE
N
EGYPT
LEGEND
REGION
River, Lake or Sea
City/Village

Blind Man's Labyrinth

1

92 BCE

THE BOY CROUCHES on thin legs before a black maw. His naked torso bears red and white and brown scars that writhe as he pokes frantically at flakes of darkness. The cavity before him admits only memories of heat. He sets the stick aside and reaches in, his bare hand disappearing into ash. He feels about and then, with barely a sound, he jerks his hand back, two fingers suddenly swelling. The look on the boy's face is not pain but joy, as though he were of some perverse type of human maladapted to survival.

"You let the fire go out," his oldest sister says. Her voice is quiet, but it enters him like thunder.

"No," he whispers, willing it to be so. His unburned hand holds a bundle of dried grass, a miniature broom that trembles of its own accord. He brushes the hot area clear of ash and exposes the previous night's coals. Holding the burned fingers away, he pokes the dried grass in, then adds curled brown leaves. Every curving rib shows as he inhales and blows. Smoke fills his eyes and he cannot see and it stings, but there is no crackle of fire to reward his efforts.

"He let the fire go out again," his sister reports.

The blow from his mother strikes the back of his head with no sound but the ringing in his ears. He absorbs the blow without overreacting and so avoids driving his forehead into the stone oven. He stays alert, engaging with the faint coals his fingers know lie hidden, bracing for a second strike.

His mother is of Jewish descent, an apostate who married a Phoenician from the Philistinian coast. The man had been a diver for sea snails, one who knew the secrets of the dye maker's trade. They had four children: two died in infancy, two daughters survived.

The boy, child of his mother, is not the son of the dye maker.

The boy adds more straw to his miniature broom and tries again with the hidden coals, resolute with his hands, cringing elsewhere.

In the days after the dye maker's death, the Tyrant of Dora discovered the woman and her isolated household and two young daughters, and so the woman in her widowhood became enslaved to the Tyrant. The Tyrant of Dora came with violence, violence that led to the boy's conception. The boy never met his father. The Egyptians or the Jews—the boy was never clear which—had killed the Tyrant before the boy was born, and the region became Jewish again, as did the boy's mother.

The boy hears movement. Perhaps his other sister has come to witness this failure and contribute to his discipline. He blinks away the sting of smoke. He again thrusts his dried-grass broom into the dark place where the coals should be. The straw seems to whither and shrinks without alighting. He moves his face in close to the ash and closes his eyes and blows again, and then he hears and feels the ignition. He does not need to see the tall spear of yellow flame to know it is there. He pulls back, grasping a handful of twigs with his burned fingers even as his mother smacks him across one ear. Just a smack. She has seen the flame and tempered her strike. He flinches appropriately and feeds twigs to the fragile fire, careful not to put the new flame out. He hears the joyful crackle of fire.

A hand takes hold of his hair and jerks his head back and around, and as he is pulled away from the fire, he sees his mother's legs and knows what will come next, but then a new voice speaks—an old man's voice.

"Come with me," the old scribe said.

His mother's fist immediately released his hair. The boy straightened and looked over at the old man. The man's thin white hair stood in its usual disarray, its energy contrasting with the limpness of his sparse beard.

The old man led the boy over to the ground where the boy had, on previous days, buried kitchen refuse and the last of the dye maker's empty snail shells. It was a great patch of weedless, well-worked soil, prepared according to the old scribe's meticulous directions.

"It's time to get the seeds," the old scribe said. He handed the boy a small coin and then pointed the boy back towards his mother.

She was calm now, serene even. The girls turned away to the fire and ignored him. His mother took the scribe's coin from the boy and put it into a pouch. The pouch came with a string, and she lifted the string over his head and around his neck. She tucked this gift into his shirt, and the boy felt her wrist brush against his skin. The brief warmth of her did not frighten him. In fact, he longed for it or some other sign of kindness. She exhaled as though she had been holding her breath, communicating detachment and resignation with only air. She turned away and walked back towards the house without a word.

"Go to Abram's farm," the old scribe said. "Demand a fair measure for your money, and don't drop any on the way back."

The boy walked for half the morning on this new mission. He had not eaten yet and was hungry. He was old enough to know that he was hungry for something more than food, for something that he could not name. But he was also hungry for the bread that his sisters would begin making in his absence.

As he walked along the road, he felt the pouch around his neck, confirming the coin's presence. He was determined to buy the best seed he could and plant it precisely according to the scribe's directions. He had dug the land diligently, just as the old scribe had directed. With the price of this coin, he would grow crops on that land that would supply the family's needs with such abundance that their goats would grow fat on the surplus. He was not distracted by the green of the land, the blue of the sky, or the whites and muted yellows of exposed rock around him, nor by the birds nor even by vain imaginations. He touched his coin, considered the seeds, and thought as specifically as he could about what he would grow and the good that would come from it.

At Abram's place, the boy approached the main house cautiously. When the man came to his door, he scowled and pointed to a small stool by the door where the boy should set down his coin. The farmer looked at it without touching it and then walked past the boy to a barn. He measured out a portion of seed and enclosed it in cloth. He carried the seed back out into the yard, looked to see that his coin still sat where he had left it, and then tossed the bag of seed in the boy's general direction. The boy caught the bag and held it against his chest with two hands. Two fingers still burned, but they held the bag as firmly as the others.

"Thank you," the boy said.

The farmer picked up his coin, holding it to one side as though it were unclean somehow, and returned to the house, closing the door behind him, never having said a word. The boy nodded to no one and began the long walk back home.

When he returned in the late morning with the bag of seeds, his mother was sleeping. The old scribe came and spoke to him and regarded the seeds carefully. He described their visible features and the wonder they would become. When the old man went out to the turned and fertilized soil, he carried the seeds. The bent-over scribe said a blessing there in which he called the seeds by name, and then he planted them himself. He moved on legs bowed with age and was severe in his work. The boy had carried the seeds many miles, but as the last one was closed up in the soil, it occurred to him that he had not touched a single one.

He felt something else within himself then, another thing he could not name. It was something like shame but went deeper. He followed the old scribe back to the house and could not look at his sisters. When he handed the pouch back to his mother in the afternoon, he hoped for something—a kind word or a touch from her perhaps—but it was a foolish hope. He felt that thing deeper than shame more strongly. His mother closing her hand over the pouch, her turning away, her disinterest, told him all that he needed to know. He was the Tyrant's son and no other's.

As dusk enveloped the farm, he went out to the pens. The usual nanny goat came to him as he sat on the ground with his back against a short stone wall. She butted his ribs with her head and then rested a hip against his shoulder in a gesture that was both rude and familiar. When her kid put a hoof against his stomach to nibble at his hair, the boy laughed. Though the hoof dug sharply, he was slow to move his hands beneath it, cradling the goat's foot so it could continue its mission of exploration, and the boy felt something else that he could not name. This was a feeling that made him smile.

As the moon rose high, lighting the small farm, the boy surrendered his time with the goats and made his way back towards the house. He was nearly there when he saw a shape lying in wait near the door of the house. The boy froze. The shape did not move. The boy approached slowly, trying not to make a sound, expecting what lay there to rise and flee or perhaps attack. As he moved around the shape, the light changed, and the boy saw that it was a man—the old scribe.

He ran then and knelt beside his protector and teacher, but when he dared to put his hand on the man and speak to him, the old scribe did not respond.

2
92 BCE

THE DEAD DO not rise, but the ill sometimes do. The widow helped the old man into the house in the dark. All through that night, the boy listened to the old scribe's laboured breathing and tried to read the future in its ragged sound.

The next morning, the old scribe stayed in bed.

The boy started the fire and then looked out over the field he had prepared and the old man had planted. He knelt and looked closely at the ground there, but no green shoots were rising yet from the dark soil.

He escaped his sisters' and mother's attention and went inside to look in on the old man.

"I'm fine, boy," the old man said, but his haggard face and grey complexion said differently.

The old scribe had come to this household after the Tyrant's death but before the boy's birth. He had come seeking aid. Bandits had set upon him on the road, and the mother had saved him and brought him back to the house and to as much health as old age would allow. Later, the mother and the old scribe supported one another. The boy grew up thinking of the aged man as his father, though the scribe and the mother had no relations. The old man lived in the house like a grandfather; he tutored the children and provided guidance on farming while the widowed mother cooked for them all. The scribe taught the mother how to be a Jew again and circumcised the boy, which some would have opposed since the boy was only half Jewish. The scribe did not interfere with the discipline of the children.

After inspecting the field once more, the boy took the goats from the pen, bringing them to a new place of full, lush grass within sight of the Great Sea. The sea frightened him. He was in awe of it and kept his distance as though the waters could reach out across dry land and snatch him away to a watery grave. How the dye maker had braved its depths to dive for the purple-dye shells, the boy could not imagine.

For the next two days, the boy continued in this way. The scribe's illness claimed his sisters' and mother's attention, so the boy escaped much of their scrutiny. It was a strange time of peace, and it occurred to him that even bedridden, the old man protected him.

On the fourth day, the boy visited the old scribe again, but the man gave no response. His gaunt face was stiff, and his head arched back as though struggling for breath. He did breathe. A raspy sound came from his throat, but no other sign of life appeared, and when the boy touched the man's arm, it felt cool to his touch. Only that dry hoarse breath assured him that the man still lived.

The boy bit his lip and prayed to no god that could hear him, for he could not be a real Jew due to his father, and raised in the widow's house, he knew of no other gods. The old scribe had certainly not taught him the ways of the Philistines or Phoenicians or Greeks.

Two more days passed, and the old scribe was little changed. He never saw his planted seeds sprout. On the sixth day of his illness, he died.

The boy and his mother were left alone in the house with the body. The girls had been sent with messages to the surrounding farms and would not return for some hours.

"Come with me," the mother said to the boy.

They went out of the house. The boy saw the garden's turned ground, and he felt a tightness within, for he did not know what to do with it now that the old scribe was gone. There would be insects and diseases, the remedies for which the boy did not know. He looked back at the house and considered its low walls and roof. He imagined that house with just his half-sisters and mother and without the old man, and the boy felt something that stole the colour from his face. This feeling he could name, but he would not say it out loud.

"We will prepare the funeral meal," his mother said.

The boy nodded.

"He was an important man," she said.

"Yes."

"At least, he used to be. A strange old man who came to us before you were born. He was from Joppa."

"I miss him already," the boy said. He felt a tear coming and tension in his chest. She put a hand on his arm, and the boy caught his breath. Her light fingers trailed down his arm and paused at his wrist. This affection was wholly new to him, and a tear of both grief and relief escaped and tracked down one cheek. Her hand tightened around his and lifted and pointed at an object in front of them.

"That one," she said.

He was unable at first to recognize her meaning.

"And that one." She pointed at the goats with his hand and hers together. "Its kid."

"No," he said. He said it quietly. He did not say it with defiance. He said it in surprise, denying his abrupt discovery of their mission, not comprehending the selection.

His mother looked at him and he looked up at her. He was still forming a question when her hand struck the side of his head, and he staggered back and stumbled to the ground, his hands and arms taking the abrasion of rubble there. Dust rose around him, and he stood quickly on thin legs even as two more blows caught him, one on either side of his face. He stood anyway, knowing it was what he should do. She stopped hitting him once he was erect.

"You do not say 'no' to me," she shouted at him. "These are not your goats. They are descendants of the miserable flock left to me by my husband, and if I choose two for the scribe's funeral meal, they are mine to choose."

The selection was without sense. The boy felt small stones in the skin of his forearms, but he did not risk brushing them away. The nanny goat was still in milk and the kid was very young. He felt the pain of the old scribe's death burrow deeper within. There were other goats and better choices, but the knowledge of who he was and what he deserved and all that was terrible about him made him powerless to intercede. The goats would die because he was worthless and his opinions were without merit.

A bleat came then from behind him, a nose and a rude mouth that pushed against the slack palm at his side, and then the shoulder nudge against the back of his thigh caught him by surprise. It made a difference. He did not alter his outer posture before the woman, but inside, within his chest, within his stomach, he felt a change. He grew still. The sloppiness of his insolent companion had set his dread aside, and he would have laughed if he had been alone.

He stayed still and gave no expression. A dimming and distance came over his mother's appearance, and he recognized what was happening. Her anger faded as he watched, and as it faded, so did she. She would go inside next and sleep, and he realized at that moment that he could read these moods as clearly as he could read the old scribe's texts. He understood something new then: he was fluent in this woman, and in realizing it, he understood what to do.

"I need to get the axe from the shed," he said. "And some rope. To keep the other from running away. And a bowl for the blood."

He did not think she had meant for him to carry out the slaughter on his own, but he stood firm before her as though that had been her original intent. She stood over him for a moment. She seemed to be losing will, slipping off into her regular darkness from which she would emerge later, either in kindness or in a rage. She said something tired and indiscernible and then walked away. He held still as she returned to the house. He studied her back boldly, testing the moment. His judgment did not betray him. She did not turn and catch him watching her but walked at a slow pace directly towards the house, not around the freshly planted ground but through it, bisecting the careful furrows and in doing so, leaving seeds unearthed and glinting in her wake. As she passed into the house, he brushed clean his arms and picked sharp grit from his skin.

He began to sweat and shiver. He gathered two small ropes and the hand-axe from the shed and set them beside the killing log. In the house, he retrieved the bowl only because he had mentioned it, and as he handled it, he realized he would need it after all. He walked about the house quietly. His legs were twitchy, and it was hard not to respond to them, hard not to hurry, not to make noise, not to sit down.

The boy emptied the old scribe's waxed canvas sack and carefully replaced the papyri and vellum pages with the bowl and some other items that came to mind. He looked at the old scribe's rolled texts left in a mound. The old Hebrew, Aramaic, and Greek letters, all of which the scribe had taught the boy to read, lay exposed before an indifferent world. The words were foreign to him now. Without the old scribe, they no longer mattered. The old man's body lay in the front room while his mother slept in the back.

Beside the oven were two loaves his oldest sister had baked that morning. He put them in the top of the sack and tied it closed. The straps were designed for the scribe's shoulders and were too long for the boy, but he found a way to cross and shorten them. In this way, the pack became his own.

In the yard, he tied the nanny goat and the kid to his waist. Carrying the hand-axe, he started down the road and then remembered a water skin tucked into a hollow place by the well. He returned to the house, filled the skin, and slipped it around his neck. He made it partway down the road again when another thought came to him. It was the bleating of the goats that gave him strength and imagination, and he returned to the yard. He went to the pen, opened it, and shooed the remaining goats into the yard. He gave the buck a sharp slap and it bounded away and into the rocky fields and the remaining goats followed.

With the nanny and kid still tied to him, the boy entered the road a third time, and this time did not look back.

3

92 BCE

Hours from the house, the boy stopped at the side of the road, milked the nanny goat into his small bowl, and drank the warm, sweet milk. There was no one to observe his theft. He drank without fear and trembled at the wonder of no one stopping him. He wondered if this was what it felt like to be drunk.

Later, in the shadow of an overhanging pine, he made a bed on a mound of needles fallen from years past. He had no way to make a fire and nothing to cook, but he decided that he was fine without a fire. The air was warm. His stomach felt good from the goat's milk.

The goats came uneasily to him under the pine, fearful of the dark and the overhang. They were used to a fenced enclosure and open skies above, and here was the opposite. He opened his pack and removed supplies by feeling their shape and then chewed pieces torn from the bread and drank from his water skin. He felt happiness he had never known before. Sorrow for the old scribe welled within, but also excitement. Before he slept, he tried to remember all he could from his already changing memories. The old man's death and his own departure made everything new, and the boy believed in the darkness under the pine that, through this flight, he was not just escaping the widow but the Tyrant's legacy as well.

He did not sleep long that night. Still, his sleep was more restful than that of many previous nights put together because he knew, even while sleeping, that he would wake excited.

In dim pre-morning light, he opened his eyes to cooler air. The sound of hooves on the road and men marching and wagons had combined to wake him. He sat up below drooping pine branches and saw a company of men passing by, marching five abreast. The ones who rode came on every breed of horse and donkey. The dimly lit men were the colour of yellow-tinged dust. The first two rows of riders carried bows, and their mounts bore great quivers that rattled with a strange sort of javelin. The men behind were on foot. They held long poles with over-sized spear points, giant weapons designed for monsters and not mere men. Those farther behind carried bows and quivers of every size, and behind them were slingers with bulging pockets and the telltale loops of braided wool and leather pouches. Among the company could be seen all sorts of swords, knives, and axes. It was a motley force of mismatched clothing and weaponry. They all looked like the road: hard, worn, and dusty.

The men went past with their wild beards in the early

light, hair matted, arms and faces like those who had slept on the ground, groomed in the smoke of wet fires. These were the faces of men who knew only days of terror and pillage. They wore no uniform but the road's dust and dried blood.

Two of the riders were soaked through as though they were weathering a hard fever. Sweat shone on their faces. Their hair stuck to the skin of their necks like dark mats of saltwater weeds clinging to rock.

A pair of wagons brought up the rear. The first appeared to contain the wounded, for some sat up and others were prone and all wore bandages or some other sign of injury. One of the seated men looked straight at the place where the boy hid, but the warrior's—or captive's—eyes betrayed nothing and he made no sign. The last wagon contained what the boy presumed were the dead, for they were all prone and piled one atop the other with rags trailing.

Following the last wagon and joined to it by a loose rope was a collection of rider-less horses and a mule. The trailing animals carried themselves with irregular movements and wildly rolling eyes, nostrils flared to the smell of death before them. Beyond them slunk a war dog. Canine jaws hung open and spilled drool. It seemed unaware of the boy. He guessed that the dust and stench, the direction of the wind, and the concealing overhang of pine branches were sufficient to hide both the boy and his goats.

After the men had passed, the boy ate the rest of the first loaf as the kid fed, butting his mother's side in a bobbing and aggressive manner. When the kid was through, the boy milked the other teat and drank the bowl dry, wallowing in the glut of unchecked consumption. He felt his blood surge on the sweet and the fat, and he was ready again for the road. Before departing, he emptied the rest of his water skin into the bowl, and the nanny goat drained it. Afterwards, the boy packed the bowl away and only then did the trio set out again, following the path of the bandits or irregular soldiers.

Much later in the morning, they came to a small stream that gurgled brightly in the sun. From a shallow pool in the stream, the nanny drank deeply as the boy refilled his water skin and washed out the bowl. The goat's kid stepped into the stream a few paces downstream where the flow was quicker and then pulled away in surprise at the water's force. After consulting its mother's posture and location, the kid moved upstream and re-entered the water in her quiet pool.

Back on the bank, the boy found a knife as long as his forearm. There was no sheath, but the boy found a way to slide it between the crossed straps at his chest. When the goats were ready, he set out again along the road, armed with the long knife and imagining himself to be a warrior—a warrior with goats. A rare smile crossed the boy's face, and it lingered. The kid occasionally tried to bite at the frayed cloth near his legs. The boy pushed it away. "Start eating grass, you stupid goat," he said, but his voice was kind, and the kid continued to bump into him and nibble at his legs.

Not long after midday, when the sun was hot and his head swam, they began to crest a low rise, and the boy did not notice that the company of the blood-encrusted ahead had halted. The men milled about on the road, bunching and spreading and talking. One man shouted at another, and the voices finally brought the boy to attention. There was another outburst, and two men walked from the group as horses and donkeys stepped sideways to make way. There was something in the air that left a coppery sensation in the boy's mouth. What he witnessed made the violence he had known until now seem small. He understood that his mother's hate had been a mere foreshadowing of what else there was in the world. He had never before witnessed violence between men.

The boy backed slowly down the slope. Once below the rise, he turned and hurried for nearly a quarter mile and then exited the road and climbed up into the woods with the goats struggling to stay with him. He eventually found a clearing not much larger than the goats' original pen. Dense trees surrounded the place, along with a thicket of low myrtle and vines. The central clearing was lightly grassed and twig rich and had just the one opening. It made the boy feel safe.

He set the knife into the ground where it stood tall and then unslung his pack.

"Now what?" the boy said to the nanny. The goat looked away and began to crop at thin greenery. The kid made preliminary attempts at the same before returning to its mother's teat.

The boy had no destination and no timeline now beyond the need to restock his nearly finished bread. He ate the last of it, drank from the skin, and then sat in the clearing and waited without knowing what else to do. As he sat there, he said he was sorry to the old scribe. The nanny started at the sound of his voice. Tears came to the boy's eyes, and he had no words to accompany the tears. This was just another thing he could not name.

The nanny's kid slept that night like a sack on a stick pile, its heaving torso atop a tangle of angular limbs. Before night came to the hillside, the boy was asleep as well, and the nanny kept watch in the dark and slept last and least of all.

❦

With morning came hunger. There was nothing left to eat and nothing further to give the nanny to drink. She approached him with the kid at her side and prodded his arm and nosed the empty bowl. He had nothing. He secured her to the thicket, the bowl upturned in the grass beside her. He trusted the kid to stay with the nanny. He left, and the empty water skin flapped at his leg in the morning light.

What came next was a time of slowness, a time of low movement across sloping ground and a circuitous path to the place of the marauders' camp. He used time as though its passage were its own reward. There came a moment, nearly at the camp, when the wind changed and a contrary breeze chilled him. He feared that he deceived only himself. He closed his eyes and kept his face down to the grass. His imagination overwhelmed him with the idea of some looming crag of a man reaching down and plucking him from his hiding place of bush shadows and grass. He nearly shouted out loud, his fear was so real, but he kept his face to the ground and did not move. He took in the smell of soil. He felt grass stalks bend against his cheek, and he focused on this sensation, willing away his imaginations. No assault came. He looked up. No stony deformation of a man stood over him. The chill passed.

He crept forwards again. Slowly. He began to feel his

thirst with more urgency and dared to lift his head and look. He had a clear view of the empty camp.

He suspected a trap and continued forwards cautiously. He could hear the small stream ahead, but he put thirst out of his mind. There were no men or horses or donkeys; still, he let a great deal of time pass in this game. Long after safety was certain, the boy finally stood and walked the open ground.

There were signs by the road of only a short stoppage; no one had spent the night here. The grass was unmatted. In a place where other travellers from days and years prior had made fires, there was only old compacted ash and an ambitious spider's web that transected the air over the pit as it joined a partially blackened branch to the ground, displaying an undisturbed dew shimmer.

The boy searched about and found nothing discarded that he could use, nothing to eat. He filled his water skin from the stream, drank deeply from it, refilled it, and then sat on the bank. He considered the way the men had gone, the violence of their passage, and whatever purpose held them together. His mind could not grasp any part of what he had witnessed, how the spearmen coordinated with the bowmen and how those who rode fought differently than those who walked. These were all mysteries to the boy. They could have been creatures other than men and would have been just as alien to him.

He sat in the abandoned camp and listened to the stream and the slight sound of leaves. Another wordless morning after an entirely wordless two days and nights unnerved him. It was also a revelation. He did not feel that he had to talk but sensed that he would soon want to. Solitude was better than his sisters' criticisms and his mother's coldness, but it would not be appealing forever.

As he tried to understand these things, the boy discovered something in the air around him, something his ears felt not as sound but as a relief from pressure, like the feeling of a storm's passing. It was a feeling familiar only by analogy, and he did not know how to describe it clearly. *Like I've been underwater.* He did not say this out loud, but he heard himself think it. *I'm not underwater anymore.* That was the best he could do. Recognizing how he felt was itself a miracle.

He wondered if the rest of the freed goats would be found and brought back to their pen, and in wondering, he knew that he at least would not be brought back. He looked in the direction the armed men had gone and considered their way.

He idled too long at the streamside. He was consumed with hunger when he finally stood and walked back to the hidden hollow, over the rise and up into the woodland, bringing the nanny her water.

He walked casually, no longer trying to hide in the landscape. As he approached the thicket clearing, he noticed the outline of a man's boot print in the soft ground but failed to consider it closely. He walked into the clearing and only then registered that something was wrong. There was no bleat of goats to welcome him. There were no goats at all. His pack was gone, as were his knife and his blanket. All that remained was the small clay bowl, upended and abandoned.

4

92 BCE

THE BOOT AND hoof prints led the boy deeper into the forest. The boy followed, though he had no idea where they would take him. He sensed that conflict awaited him, something akin to the armed men's brutality by the stream. He walked the path anyway, not knowing what else to do.

The boy followed the path uphill past wild thicket and brush until the sun's shine began to wane and the foliage finally opened to reveal a lone stone home that boasted an attached barn. Subtle bands of smoke drifted from a tall chimney in memory of forlorn flames. A large man sat on a large stone between the house and barn door, leaning against the stone wall behind him.

As the boy approached, he saw that the man's brow was broad and lined and bore a scar that ran down his nose and reappeared at his chin. The wound was old but still looked raw. The man held an axe with a long handle across his knees.

"Soon enough," the man said. He stood and turned and entered the house, his broad shoulders filling the entire doorway as he passed through. The door remained open behind him.

The boy approached and looked inside. The room was dim and smelled of cooking and fermented sweat and animals. There was another open doorway at the back of the room through which the boy could see the barn and, through a series of open arches, he could spot a pen beyond where a whole flock of goats circulated.

"You've had nought to eat," the man said.

"I have water," the boy said.

"Aye. And none shared with the nanny. A nanny in milk needs her water."

The boy said nothing in reply.

"She can't make milk from grass and leaves alone," the man continued.

As his eyes adjusted, the boy saw that the home's floor was hard-packed earth. A series of wooden planks lay on the ground as a table. He spotted his pack and the long knife beyond the table, set neatly together against the wall.

"You have my things."

The man moved to the fire and brought a squat stone pot back to the table, setting it in the middle and removing the lid. The remnants of some prior meal lurked in its depths. Beside the pot the man placed a small loaf. He considered the bread for a moment, and then tore it in half. He pushed one half to the boy's side of the table. "Leave the bowl outside," he said.

The boy looked at the bowl he was still clutching in his hand and turned then back to the man.

"It's clay," the man said.

"Yes?"

"You watered the nanny from it."

"Yes."

"It's unclean now. If it were stone or metal, you could clean it, but not clay. Leave it outside."

The boy set the bowl down and then entered the house. The scarred hulking man reclined at the low table, already swirling a wedge of bread about the communal pot before bringing it to his mouth where juices slopped into his beard as he chewed thoughtfully.

He gestured again at the bread and the boy settled himself at the table. His flat and anxious stomach growled, and the old man nodded and helped himself to more.

The boy broke off a small piece of bread and gingerly dipped it in the broth. His stomach clamoured for more as the flavours hit his tongue, but he forced himself to eat slowly, methodically, as if eating with caution would protect him from the man's watchful eyes.

Finally the man broke the silence once more.

"You're a skittish eater."

The boy did not know how to respond to that.

"Too fast. Too slow," the man rumbled. "Do something. Finish it." He tossed the last of his crust at the boy. The boy caught it, hesitated, and then scraped it about the pot, gathering the last of the juice and grease that remained.

The old man studied the boy with dull black eyes.

The goats in the barn made noises to one another. Outside, two birds started a conversation.

The boy looked at his pack and knife and then back at the big man across the table. "I should get my things and go," he said.

"How do we come to have things?" the man asked. "And how to come to think of things as *our* things?" He looked over at the pack and knife. "I've seen the old scribe down the way wear a waxed pack like that." He turned his gaze back to the boy. "How'd you come by an axe with no handle?"

"It's a hand-axe."

The man grunted at him. It was an extended grunt that tried to be something like laughter. "It's a hand-axe because the handle is missing. And that short sword. Too long for any use in your mother's house and too short for a real weapon. You've come to think of it as your own, yet you took it off the body of a dead man."

"I need to go," the boy said.

"I know who you are," the man said.

"I need to get my goats and go."

"*Your* goats?" Again came that deep wheezing, extended grunt. "Or the widow's goats? You know how far you'd get with those goats?"

The boy did not answer.

"You'd get as far as it took for someone to recognize you."

The boy still said nothing.

"It ain't just your mother that hates you, boy." The boy grew even more still. "This whole land is full of people that would kill you just for who you are. Who you came from. They hate her too. She might've been a victim in all that, but she was with him and she bore you and she kept you.

Some around here wanted to burn out that farm and take the widow and her daughters and sell them to the slavers at Joppa. If that scribe hadn't come along, you'd have been born on a slave ship. They might burn that farm yet with the scribe gone. His funeral was a disgrace. Was it you who had run off the goats? Or did you just take two for yourself?"

The boy looked down at the table.

"Was it?" The boy still did not answer, and the man slammed his fist on the table.

"Was it?" he yelled and the boy jumped and tremored and nodded quickly.

"And you still think they're your goats?" the man asked. "You made a disgrace of the scribe's last meal."

"The scribe liked me," the boy said.

"Did he? And you scattered all the goats to say your thanks."

"She was going to kill the nanny and the kid for the funeral meal."

The fury in the man's face froze and his apparent confusion cooled his voice. "The nanny is still in milk."

The boy nodded. After a brief pause, the man finally conceded.

"That's a damn fool choice."

A pause expanded while all within the house observed a strange silence, and after yet more waiting, the boy wondered if the huge man had fallen asleep. He could see only shadow where the man's eyes should be, shadow beneath the weight of dark hair in the dim room. The lower facial scar drew the boy's attention. After some peering, the boy realized that the man was awake and watching him stare. The boy looked away.

"It was good you brought the nanny to me. Mine died. Some kind of bleed. I've two kids here that your nanny will give suck to."

"They're my goats," the boy said.

"We covered ownership already," the man said. "And how keeping them will make everyone know you. Eager to be stoned, are you? Or nailed to a Greek tree? There are old wounds in this land. Many would happily put you through the pain your father put many others through."

"Can I have my pack?"

"It's the scribe's pack. He has no use for it now. I don't see why you can't keep it. Anything in the pack, and the sword for that matter, you can keep. I won't have anything in this house that belonged to the widow."

"The goats were hers."

The old man grunted. "And the dye maker's before your time. Where did you get the sword?"

The boy told him about the marauders. He described the healthy and the wounded and the horse riders and the riderless horses that followed and the wagons and the weapons. All he could remember—even the dog.

The man was silent after this report. Again, he seemed to sleep. The boy concluded the man was studying the tabletop and what the patterns in the grain and stains might tell. Finally, the man spoke again.

"Violence looks different from different sides," he said. "Like fire. Cooks your food. Lights the darkness. It looks different if you're the fuel. It's all the same to the fire. Marauders, you say? No, they're not marauders, boy." He got up with difficulty, crossed to the stone hearth, and then returned with his long axe, laying it down on the table between them. The wooden handle was old and worn. The head was dark but for the blade's bright edge. There was a chip in the metal that marred the perfect bevelled arc.

"Do you know what happened at the Fall Festival two years past?" the man asked.

"Do you mean the Feast of Tabernacles?" the boy said.

"Yes. Sukkot. Do you know what happened?"

"No."

"Have you ever been?"

"No. But I know about it."

"The scribe told you?"

"Yes."

"Did he ever take you?"

"No."

The man touched the worn oiled axe handle, the empty pot's black stone, and then the table. "Violence came to the temple two years ago. The weapons were just citrons. People threw fruit at the high priest who, under these damned Maccabees, is also the king. It was violence all the same."

"Why?"

The man waived at the air as though shooing flies. "Our king, Alexander Jannaeus, was brought to the throne to end wars. Instead, he is the author of five wars in just the last five years, all of which were failures. The treasury is drained and the mercenaries on the front lines suffer, as do the Jews at home. Then he made a mockery of the temple traditions, and the mob responded with violence and citrons." The man brooded in silence for a while before raising his head to look at the boy. "Do you understand?"

The boy nodded, though he did not.

"Jannaeus's first war was the one that killed your father,

and perhaps that is the only good thing Alexander Jannaeus has ever done." The man stared at the boy as though searching for signs of the Tyrant's blood.

"Last year, Jannaeus took the city of Amathus. He failed to take Amathus the first time. He lost ten thousand soldiers trying. But last year, he succeeded. Things looked better. Better for the king, not Amathus. The citrons were quiet at last year's festival. Then he lost Gadara. It took a ten-month siege to win that city seven years ago, and when the king lost it this year, he made sure it was truly good and lost. The Nabataeans ran him back to this side of the river with barely his life, and now he has ceded everything east of the Jordan to King Obodas. To the Nabataeans." The man said this last word as though it were a curse.

"You don't understand," the man said.

"I do."

"You don't. It's all about the Pharisees and the Sadducees. The Sadducees favour these wars—Jannaeus's wars of expansion—and the Pharisees are against them. The king spends his time winning and losing and recruiting more mercenaries, and all that costs money. He keeps pressing us for more taxes to pay for more wars and stealing from the temple treasury to fund his failed adventures and building fortresses that guard only Jerusalem. All this leaves the rest of us to suffer pillage and plunder and somehow grow our crops and provide his taxes. We have had nearly twelve years now of Jannaeus and his mad wars. A year longer than you've been alive. Jannaeus has become the king of stupid wars."

The man looked at the boy carefully. "You don't look nearly eleven years old. You're small."

The boy said nothing.

"Small and thin."

The boy looked down at the table and then at the earthen floor beside it.

The man grunted. "The Pharisees have had enough of Jannaeus and his nonsense. Now it's a civil war: the Pharisees against the Sadducees. The Pharisees have gone to war against the king, and the Sadducees are with the king. It's a war to end all the wars." The man grunted again, his laughing grunt.

"It's not just Pharisees versus Sadducees," the man continued. He frowned and studied the table. "It's also rural areas against the cities. Partly. Jericho is with the king. Most of the Galilean towns are not. What you saw on the road—they weren't marauders, boy. They were Galileans. Men who are with the Pharisees and against the king. You saw them going home."

The man stopped talking and stared at the boy, and when the boy expected him to speak again, he only continued to stare. The man ran his thick fingertips along the table grain without looking at it. Then he touched the stone pot. Then the handle of his axe. The man wrapped his fingers around the handle and held it there, on the table, gripping the weapon until his knuckles turned white, still staring at the boy.

"While all this is going on, you've decided to run away and leave a scribe unburied and steal your mother's goats!" he suddenly shouted.

The boy stayed where he was and did not move and did not make eye contact.

"The rape son of Zoilus! Carrying an Egyptian short

sword and an axe! An axe he claims is just a hand-axe, but any fool can see is a good battle axe that only needs its handle. Zoilus's own bastard is on the land amid this conflict and armed in both fists. Do you have a mind to reclaim your father's old dominion, boy? Do you?"

The man's fingers flexed around the axe handle.

"No. I just want my goats."

"Your goats!" The man roared a wordless and throat-tearing cry and lunged to his feet. He dragged the axe up with him and then swung it wide within the low room and drove it deep into the wooden table with a roar and a crash of pot and mugs. He crouched and leaned over the table, looming over the boy before him.

"What is your name, boy?"

The boy's heart galloped while the rest of his body froze rigid where he sat. When he tried to speak, only a slight sound came out that was strange even to his own ears. Dust now hung in the air. Thin beams of light from the door and window cut through the motes, illuminating the otherwise dark corners with fractured specks that drifted and swirled in languid and mesmerizing currents of light.

"Your name?" the man repeated.

The boy told him, and the old man stared down at him in disbelief. Then he worked the axe free from the table. He sat again with his legs folded beneath him and cradled the axe across his palms as though considering whether to present or redeploy it.

"Your mother hated you," the man said.

The boy nodded.

"You cannot go out into the land with that name. You need to take a new name. No goats. You're not getting the goats back. You need to get rid of your old name. Never use it again. When you leave this place, you will take nothing with you that will connect you to this coast. You will go inland, far from here and be someone new and never come back to this coast or people like me will hunt you down and kill you. I might kill you yet."

The boy nodded.

"What will your name be?"

"I don't know," the boy said.

5

92 BCE

THERE ARE TIMES when we are gifted with true clarity, when we see into the truth of things and understand how it all shall pass. It is the moment the warrior can see the battle's end, the moment lovers know if they are meant to be. The boy was too young for such insight, but he did know the facts. The goats were lost to him. His visit with the scarred man was over.

The boy stood in the yard outside the man's stone home. He stood there nameless and homeless, without his goats. The man had said he could take the pack and knife, yet he stood out in the yard with nothing but his water skin. A tumult filled his mind the way storm winds had churned the sea beyond the widow's house. He could not settle himself. He could not order his thoughts.

He heard a sound behind him, the big man coming into the doorway. The boy waited without turning around. He expected to be clubbed, to be killed by this stranger who hated him. The man knew who he was and what he was. The boy had no will to run and just stood there and waited.

A great deal of time passed. No blow came, nor did he hear the man move. Finally, the boy turned and saw the old man looking down the forest trail. He seemed to sense the boy's attention and turned to meet his gaze. When their eyes met, the big, scarred man gestured for the boy to come back inside the house and then left the doorway dark and empty.

The boy walked slowly back towards the house. His shoulders drooped, but his steps did not falter. At the doorway, he stepped inside without checking where the man was. When his eyes adjusted, he saw the man once again seated at the far side of the table.

"Bring me your pack," the man said.

The boy hesitated. When the old man gestured, he walked over to the wall and fetched the pack and long knife, setting them on the table.

The old man put his axe aside and emptied the pack. He sorted through the items of interest, shook out the blanket, and properly rerolled it. When he finished, he carefully placed everything back into the pack except for the boy's axe head, which he held for a while longer. Eventually, he set it down and picked up the long knife.

"Come," he said and lumbered to his feet. The man gestured with the long knife, indicating for the boy to go into the barn. The boy hesitated, and the big man gestured forcefully, swinging the blade with impatience.

The boy went into the barn with the man's presence behind him pressing against his back. Once inside, the man grabbed the boy's shoulder and forcibly stopped him in front of a skinned and gutted goat carcass that hung from a ceiling beam.

"My old nanny," the man said.

The goat hung exposed—its skinned pink flesh and white cartilage and strange sheets of pale connective tissue wrapping the body in symmetrical patterns all lay bare for the boy to see. The boy stood frozen as the man approached with the long knife. He chose one of the goat's legs, felt along the ankle, and then hacked at the muscle with the blade. Little changed with his effort. The man felt inside the gash, nodded to himself, then hacked again, felt again, cut again, and finally came away with a pair of white tendons. He tentatively pulled until he got a proper grip on them, then yanked and tore through muscle until the tendons hung from the back of the knee joint. He gripped the dangling white cords, cut them free, and handed them wet and limp to the boy. Then the man performed the same operation on the other leg. With this task finished, the man went back into the house. The boy followed him, still holding the limp, wet tendons in front of him.

The boy sat down again at the table while the man rummaged in a dark corner until he came out with a long handle, several small wedges of wood, and a square fist-sized rock. He sat at the table opposite the boy with the boy's axe head between them. The old man's gaze rested on the handle, then drifted to the axe head, then to the boy, and a cloud crossed his features. The old scar and the skin around the man's eyes turned red. The boy knew then that the man had changed his mind and would now kill him, but the boy held his ground. This was not an act of bravery but a learned habit. Running would only delay his destruction and heighten his fear.

After a few moments, the man's visible hate relented. He picked up the axe head and tested its fit to the handle. It was a good fit. He set the handle and head down and turned his attention to the tendons, tying them together in pairs to make two long cords. He tested the strength of his knots and then picked up the head and handle. The blade wobbled on the wood, and the old man shoved a wedge into either side, hammering them in with the square rock until the blade was firmly pinned in place. Satisfied, he set to work on the bindings, wrapping the tendons round and round the joint in a crossing pattern, first with one cord and then the other, tying them off in a neat knot.

"They're still wet," the man said, looking at his handiwork and not at the boy. "When the tendons are dry, they'll tighten and the joint will stay strong as stone for years to come. Treat it well." He passed the axe with the new handle across the table to the boy. "You touch a Pharisee or the son of a Pharisee with that blade, and my ghost will follow you wherever you flee and skin you like that goat. Do you understand?"

The boy nodded.

"I'll do it while you're still alive."

The boy nodded again.

"Haim," the man said. He stared at the boy. His eyes were black and his face hard. The scar grew a darker red.

The boy looked at him, not comprehending.

"Your name is Haim now. Do you know what that means?"

"Yes. The old scribe taught me."

"Taught you what?"

"To read."

"Scrolls?"

"Yes."

"The scrolls he carried in that pack?"

"Yes."

The old man snorted. There was no laughter in it—just contempt. "There is nothing you need to read in scrolls. They serve no one in any way. What needs reading is in the sky, on the land, in the wind. Life. That is your name now. Take it with you."

"Thank you," Haim said, looking at the axe.

"Now get out of here," the man growled. He stood stiffly, grimaced, and picked up his own much larger axe. "Get out of here and do not come back. If I ever see you again, I will drive this blade into whatever part of you I reach first, and I will keep driving it until you are nothing but food for the grass."

The boy stood. He shouldered his pack and stuck his knife once more between the crossed straps. He thought to ask the man about a sheath, but when he looked up at him, the red scar and bloodshot eyes changed his mind. The boy picked up the restored axe and made for the door.

From the doorway, he turned to the man one last time. "Please be good to my goats."

"They are not your goats!" the man roared. He rose and lunged with axe raised and the boy fled down the trail and whether the man gave chase or halted, the boy did not know, for all his focus was on running faster and faster until he tripped and fell, sprawling in the grass near the main road. When he lifted his head, gasping for air and looking back at the line of trees behind him, everything but his heart was still. There was no sign of pursuit.

The boy picked himself up and continued down the road. He passed the Galileans' old camp and crossed the stream. Some miles later, the road branched east and, with the old man's warning still ringing in his mind, he took the route inland. Towards evening, he realized that the knife was gone. Lost running. Lost falling. Lost somewhere on the road. He did not know when or where.

He walked on into darkness. Eventually, by moonlight, he found his way to a hollow at the base of an old tree. He was tired and lay down there and used the pack as a pillow. As he lay there, alone, he felt his hunger again. He missed the goats butting into him and making noises in the dark. He missed the milk, and then he remembered his bowl left on the ground at the man's doorway. The lost knife, the stolen goats, his hunger, and finally the abandoned bowl brought tears. Everything had unravelled in just one day. While Haim was creeping up on the Galileans' abandoned camp and contemplating loneliness, the old goat-stealer had taken everything from him.

Haim wiped his face in the dark and looked up at the moon and starlit silhouettes of trees overhead, and he heard the cacophony of forest noises anew. It all seemed to mock him. Long after the moon had disappeared from Haim's view, the creatures of the night finally grew quiet and only the trees disturbed the dark with their creaking.

6

92 BCE

WHAT CAME NEXT was hunger, hiding, furtive gleaning, and outright theft. With the goat-stealer's warnings haunting him, the boy was too afraid to ask anyone for help or directions. On his own, he sought what seemed like the best paths, walking away from the ocean, doing his best to avoid people. On the third day, he hoped he was far enough away that it was safe to begin asking for help. Then he looked up and saw a lightning-struck tree. It was distorted, dead, and brittle, a signature on the landscape that made his heart sink. He had rested below the tree once already. The boy remembered that over the next rise lay an isolated farmstead from which he had already stolen eggs two days before. He had cracked and swallowed those eggs raw along with old figs and wild onions. There had been nothing to eat since.

The road ran close to the house. The farm was a busy

place with many children and workers. It was hours until dark, and Haim was at risk of being seen. His legs trembled. He crept off the road once more. He lodged himself in bushes with another fistful of wild onion bulbs and ate and slept as he waited out the day. When darkness came, hunger woke him. He crept past the dim glow of the farmstead, keeping his distance, not daring another egg run.

Late in the night, he saw two moving lanterns ahead. The boy crept off the road to hide behind a screen of low branches until two men went by.

Over the next few days, he walked a circuitous route that generally drifted eastwards until he came to a place where the land was uninhabited. He walked the better part of another day and then came upon a village where he was confident that no one would know him.

He first viewed this new settlement and its thin spires of welcoming cookfire smoke from across a small valley, the buildings topping the far slope. A copse of willow and myrtle and a rise of beige-bronze stone blocked Haim's view of the village as he descended into the small valley. The irregular stones scattered across the valley floor were shaped like giant misplaced loaves towering above Haim's head. Across the low basin, he continued barefoot down the path and then began to climb again. Though he had been on the road less than a week, his once well-fitting clothes now hung loosely on him and the pack seemed larger than before. His arms stuck at his sides like sticks of inert driftwood, and his head dipped as he climbed. He followed the path's unhurried adherence to the contours of the land until he came to a cut through a tall stone loaf that led to the village entrance. His posture made no threat. His frame bore the shape of supplication.

The buildings were composed of the same bronze-brown stones of the land that had been cut, fit, and mortared into uniform homes. Yet each door bore unique frames of various broad stones and strangely shaped woods that boasted the virtue of variation to their neighbours. Those discordant frames may have been beautiful once but now stood charred and scarred and barren. Each entrance hung gaping, their mouths still smoking, filled with teeth of rubble and ash. A great fire had consumed this place.

Past the first burned-out houses, the boy found the bodies of women who were unburned and barely marked except below the waist. The boy turned away with a start, fear and shame bringing heat to his face.

The boy soon found more of the villagers; some had been half-consumed by fire and others butchered in passageways or streets—men, women, and children. The boy came across the corpse of a young man who still clutched the shaft of a harvester's scythe from which hung a patch of bloody hair. As the boy approached, giant dark birds rose on funereal wings. After the boy passed, the birds returned with a click of claws on the stone street and a settling of wings and the low bird murmurs of business among them.

In a small courtyard, the boy found a mule. Its brown, nearly black hide glistened as it stood silently, head lowered, a golden mane shining. The white hair at its hocks and around its eyes, ears, and nose beautifully contrasted with an otherwise dark appearance. The boy set his pack down and removed the axe. The mule stood listless, a javelin protruding from between two ribs and the broken shaft of an arrow at one hip. The boy approached the animal slowly. He talked to it quietly, and though it shied away, it did not try to run.

After some time, the boy came alongside the mule. The beast's eyes were dry and flies bothered it, yet the creature seemed no longer willing or able to protest. The boy lifted his axe slowly and then brought it down on the mule's neck with as much power as he could muster. The axe carved a mere finger's width into the thick neck before being deflected by bone, and the beast brayed and clattered away and slipped on the street's smooth stonework and fell. The boy found himself still holding the axe, and in desperation, he raised it again before setting its weight back down on the stone courtyard.

"You killed yourself," the boy said.

The javelin protruding from its ribs had caught in a gap between stones and been thrust through the animal when it fell. The mule kicked frantically for a moment, and then its legs settled and it grew still.

The boy dragged out charred wood from the smouldering rubble and used flat stones to carry hot embers to the pile until flames took. He then gathered fresh fuel from the thickets surrounding the village and added them to the smoking mound until the fire was steady and strong. With the fire started, he then used the axe to hack at the mule's haunch. Though it took more effort than he imagined, by late afternoon his face shone with grease and flecks of blackened meat, and his stomach groaned and was satisfied. The old scribe would not have approved of him eating the mule, but the boy had not had meat or bread since the goat-stealer's stew. He gave little thought to his crime.

The boy slept then in the courtyard's heated shade before the fire and the dead mule and his pack, and when he awoke, it was evening. He was thirsty. His water skin was empty.

"Where is the well?" the boy asked the mule. When the mule did not answer, the boy left with his pack and his water skin and axe.

He found the well on the western edge of the village. What he found in the well changed everything.

❧

"Are you daft?" the boy asked. Then louder he shouted, "What are you doing down there?" He lay on his stomach on the hot, hard ground, his head extended over an abyss.

"I'm not daft," a girl's voice called up from the dark.

"What are you doing down there?" he asked.

"Who are you?"

He did not answer.

"Are you one of them?"

"I'm just a boy," he said.

"Who is with you?"

"No one."

"Is everyone still up there?"

Haim did not know how to answer that either.

"Are they all dead?" the girl asked.

"Yes," he said finally. "Everyone is dead."

There was a cry in the darkness below and some splashing and then a gasp before she spoke again. "Can you get me out of here?"

"How did you get down there?"

"The stones at the top have gaps. I climbed inside. The men were coming and I hurried. The lower stones were slippery and I fell."

"Are you hurt?"

"No, I landed in the water. There's also a cave down

here where the water comes through. They tried to drop things on me, but I hid in the cave. I screamed so they'd stop dropping things. They thought they got me, and I stayed quiet after that."

The boy looked at the fading sky and judged that there was little daylight left. "You must be cold."

"Yes. There's a little ledge in the cave I can sit on, but now I'm in the water and getting cold again. Can you get me out?"

"Is there a rope?"

"I have it. They threw it down."

"I'm thirsty," Haim said.

"Some of the houses have ropes in them."

"They're all burned."

"If you can get me out, I'll bring the rope with me."

The boy could not see the girl, but she must have been able to see him or at least his silhouette, for each time he moved away from the opening she called up to him. His head hung uncomfortably over the lip of the well.

"How old are you?" he asked.

"Nine. What difference does it make how old I am?"

"I want to know how big you are if I have to pull you up."

"I'm small for my age. You have no rope. How old are you?"

"I'll be twelve next year."

"What's your name?"

The boy was silent. He was careful to keep his head over the opening and trusted she could not read his expression.

"What is your name?"

"Haim," he said.

"That's not a name."

"It's mine."

"Our names mean the same thing then. I'm Chaya."

After a short silence, Chaya spoke again. "I need a ladder. If you can get me far enough up, I can throw you the rope. With the better handholds higher up, it should be easy to climb from there."

"Do you know where I can find a big ladder up here?"

"No. Just little ones."

A jackal came then from an opening between two houses. It stopped, sniffed the air, finally sighted Haim lying by the well, and darted back the way it had come.

"What is it?"

"A dog. A jackal."

"Can you drop down something to eat?"

"I'll go find something," Haim said.

He left his pack beside the well, took the axe, crossed the open ground, and entered a side street. He found several ransacked cellars left empty and gaping, but he eventually came to one trap door that was still closed. He pulled it open and entered the tunnel shaft. In the faint light, he found a small supply of dried grain and some hard figs. Upon moving the food into a discarded sack, he discovered a small folded packet. When he opened it, he saw that it was papyrus with writing in an amateur hand. The words spoke of something holy, something important to its writer, but Haim remembered what the old man had said and decided that it was useless. He put the packet back and turned his attention to a clay jar. The liquid inside smelled sweet but not fermented. He drank it down and then climbed out to continue his search.

In the trees beside the village, Haim found another collection of bodies. Some wore bloodied clothing while others were stripped of every dignity. Among the bodies, he found two woollen mantles. He picked up the two cloaks, checked them for signs of blood, and finding them clean, he took them.

By the time he made it back to the well, it was growing dark. As he stuck his head over the rim, he was fearful she would not be there.

"You're back," Chaya said.

"Yes."

"Did you find a ladder?"

"No, and it is getting dark. But I found food. And two blankets for you."

"You're still thirsty."

"I found something to drink. Can you see me?"

"A little."

"I'm going to drop the first blanket to you. It's tied up in a bundle."

"Okay."

He did so, and she caught it. "Wait a minute," she said. He heard splashing below and then she returned from the cave. "Can you put the food in the other blanket?"

"Yes. It's a cloak. Wool. The sack I've put in it is full of wheat and barley and figs. Don't drop it when you open the bundle."

"Okay," she said.

He released the second bundle. There was some splashing, a brief silence, more splashing, and she returned to the darkness below him. "I got it," she said. "Where will you go?"

"I'll stay here."

"How will I get out?"

"I don't know. Tomorrow. We'll think of something tomorrow."

"I want to get out of here today."

"I know. I need to think of something."

"What if they come back?"

"They won't come back. And if they do, I have an axe. I'll use it if I have to."

"You have an axe?"

"Yes."

"Have you ever killed anything with it?"

Haim thought about the mule. "Yes. Not a person, though. Eat something. I need to think."

He lay down beside the well and looked up and saw the first early stars. It was a long while before sleep approached. He was afraid that he would roll into the well. He was also conscious of leaving her alone in its depths, prisoner of her long fall and the darkness that lived inside the earth. When he did sleep, he slept poorly. He dreamed that the underground stream was a maze. Again and again, it forked deep, deep in the rock, supplying water to every well in the land. Chaya's pleas for help were carried along in watery echoes and rose in columns of starlight at every vertical shaft. Still, no one gave heed to her—none except for evil creatures who searched along the wet tunnels of perpetual night.

7
92 BCE

IN A DARK forest, Haim heard a girl's voice that echoed among the trees as though through tunnels of stone. He heard longing and fear in her small voice. No one had ever called to him in need before. Then he awoke.

Above him rolled the stars over Samaria. Around him lay the ruined and silent village. The sun had not yet risen, but the sky was no longer black and the buildings now stood as dark silhouettes against the grey sky. He heard the girl's voice again.

Haim felt his way to the well's edge and stuck his head out over the opening. "What?"

"What have you thought of?" she asked.

The boy remembered his dreams about the underground maze and the dark, echoing forest. "Nothing. I was sleeping. What have you thought of?"

"Our cousins were cutting poles north of the village. Look there for something you can use as a ladder."

"I'll go look," he said.

Haim found his way to where the buildings ended and then waited until it was light enough to see into the forest. After searching for some time, he found a stack of long, delimbed tree trunks along the edge of the woods. Most were no wider than his leg.

He pulled somewhat aimlessly at the pile, scattering its neat order while he tried to imagine how to build a ladder out of this material. Near the bottom of the pile, he came across a promising pole. This trunk was thicker and its delimbing process had been less precise. Stumps of former branches jutted from the dark trunk every which way, with split, sawn, and even torn wounds attesting to the rough trimming. It was a ladder of sorts.

Finding the butchered tree was one thing. Dragging it back into the village proved to be another matter entirely. The stumps dug into the ground, and however he tried to turn the trunk, there was always another series of anchors seeking purchase in the cracks between stones or digging into softer earth. He wrestled and pulled for a long while getting the thing into the village, and then he still had to move it through the village to get to the well.

As he finished his task of hauling the tree to the well, he heard Chaya shouting up to him.

"Did you find something?"

He looked over the edge. He was tired and just wanted to lie down. In the morning light, he could roughly make out her shape now. "I brought the biggest pole. It has cut-off branches. It's kind of like a ladder."

"Will it reach?"

"I don't know. I can't see the bottom of the well. It's too dark down there."

Her voice came up to him, excited. "Well, just put it down! Let's see if it works!"

"I can't lift it. It's too heavy. I need to rest."

Haim lay down at the edge of the well, and he imagined that the old scribe was here and that he could ask the man how to solve this problem of a girl in a well. It seemed like the perfect start for one of the old man's parables. The boy felt pressure in his chest, and tears came unexpectedly.

"Are you rested yet?" the girl asked. Her voice was quiet and thin as though transmitted through many passageways and not just this one tall shaft.

"Yes, I think I am."

He stood up and dragged the ragged beam to the well's edge and then gave it a final shove so it overhung the opening.

"I see it!" came the voice from down below.

"I'm going to send it down now," Haim said. "So get out of the way. Get in the cave."

He went to the far end of the beam and hoisted it up, first to one knee where he let it rest for a moment, then up onto his shoulder. Once steady, he used both hands to get the beam above his head. The tree barely angled into the well, and Haim saw the flaw in his plan. He walked sideways with the trunk, trying to fix his problem, but it made no difference. The well was too narrow. He would have to get the beam vertical before it would go down. He tried walking forwards, pushing the trunk's angle higher and higher, but then it slid forwards and wedged itself against the far side of the well. He released the beam, and it stayed stuck at that awkward angle. He walked to the edge of the well and looked in. The beam was only a few feet down.

"Is it stuck?" Chaya asked.

"It's resting," Haim said. "I have to get some kind of lever. I'll be back soon."

He walked around the village until he found a large, unburned cart with tall sides. It took some doing for him to get the cart moving without a donkey, but once it was going, he was able to get it beside the well. The weight of the beam kept it jammed in place, and he needed to pull it back to release it, but to do that, he needed to be taller. It was not what he had brought the cart for, but he wound up standing on the cart to get the right angle. Then with a great deal of effort and noise, he freed it and the beam tilted, its weight pulling him off balance as the upper end crashed to the ground behind him. He was left holding up the end that was supposed to be down in the well.

"That's not working," she said.

He tried lifting the beam into the well again, but this time, instead of positioning the lower end in the well first, he left it on the flat ground as he raised the log up. He braced the lower end against the cart, also not what he had brought the cart for, and then continued lifting the beam as he walked towards its base until it stood tall above him. In this position, it looked much more impressive than it had lying down. He pivoted the base back and forth ever so gently, careful not to let the trunk's momentum throw him off balance, creeping the butt end towards the smooth lip of the well.

"Get in the cave," he reminded her, breathing hard,

feeling the beating in his chest, the edge of the beam's base creeping over empty air. He heard splashing; then all was quiet below.

He started pivoting again. The beam hung on the well's lip by the narrowest strip of wood. His feet trembled at the well's edge, and he gripped the tree with weak hands. A ragged stump came at his face, and he had to twist his head around and under to avoid it. Then it occurred to him that if he let the beam drop into the well like this, the stump would tear his head off as the tree plummeted downwards. He twisted himself into a better position. He cast a glance upwards to see what else might come down at him.

Once ready, he wanted to shout down to her that he was about to drop the beam but was afraid that she would come out of the cave to answer him. He hesitated but then realized that if he waited too much longer, she would come out anyway and tell him to hurry and with that thought, he gave the beam one more small pivot. It shot out of his grasp like a dart fired at the centre of the earth. A branch caught on the edge of the well and the beam tilted, but there was at the same moment a dramatic breaking sound, and in a second, the beam was gone. It had vanished past the lip of the well and crashed to the bottom with spinning flakes of wood dust and torn bark floating slowly down and out of sight after it.

He heard splashing and screaming, which turned to laughing and more splashing and finally words as she shouted and praised his find and work.

The top of the beam-ladder was at least ten feet below ground level. She was already climbing.

"Are you bringing the rope?" he asked.

"Yes."

"Okay. You're going to need it. The ladder doesn't reach to the top."

She climbed, and then he could hear her pause, hear her fussing with the rope, detaching it from some snag, and then she began to climb again until he could see her more clearly. She looked up at him. "Some of the branches aren't very good for holding on to," she said. "They're too short. And there are sticky bits. I've got sap on my hands."

"How about you keep climbing?"

"Okay." She continued to climb until she came to the top of the beam and then stopped, looking up at him. "I'm afraid," she said.

"Of what?"

She did not answer. Her hands gripped the end of the beam, and only one foot was standing on a branch-stump. She was frozen. Seeing her now at the top of the beam but still so far below him gave Haim a better sense of the well's scale. It made him feel queasy.

"It's not long enough," she said.

"Climb the gaps in the rock. Like how you climbed down."

"I was able to go down, go down fast. I didn't think about it. The men were coming. I can't go up. Going up is harder."

"Just don't look down."

"I can't move."

"You moved going down."

"They were chasing me! They killed my family." She began to cry.

"Chaya—"

"I can't let go. The walls are slippery. I'm wet. I've been wet for days. I'm cold. I can't move. You didn't bring me enough to eat. I can't do it."

Haim lay with his face over the well's edge. He felt sick and his palms were sweating and, even lying down, his legs felt jittery. His head hurt.

"Just hang on," he said. "I'll think of something. I'll be right back."

He left, not knowing where he was going, knowing he could not climb down the well to get her and there was nothing around the well that could help. He walked towards the poles, then once there, an idea came to him. He grabbed the thinnest pole he could find. It was light and whippy in his hands. Back at the well, he looked down at her, confirmed she had not fallen, and then with the axe, he cut a very narrow, steeply angled wedge near one end.

"I've got a pole with a hook at the end," he said. "You have to wedge the rope into the hook thing I've cut. A groove. Wedge the rope in there so I can get it up here. Okay?"

"I can't."

"Just do what I tell you to. Just do that. Wedge the rope into the groove. Okay?"

"Okay."

He lowered the pole down to her.

"I see it," she said.

"Do you see the groove?"

"I see it."

"Put the rope in the groove. Wedge it in, so it's jammed in there tight. Don't let it fall out."

"I can't move."

"I can hear the bandits coming back, and if you don't move fast, they're going to come, and I'm going to run away, and they'll find you down there, and then you're dead for sure."

"Haim!"

"I can hear them! Do it now, Chaya!"

She freed one shaking hand and released the rope from around her shoulder. She stuffed the loop into the groove and gave it a hard pull to wedge it, which he had not expected, and nearly pulled the pole from his hands. Then she returned her hand to its death grip on the beam. He pulled the pole up and then tossed it away and gathered the rest of the rope. He found the soft-sided well bucket tied to the end of the rope and within it were the two woollen mantles from yesterday. He formed a loop at one end of the rope and lowered it back down to her.

"Put that around your shoulders, under your arms."

She looked at the rope and then up at him.

"I can't."

"Then just do your right arm, okay? You already took that arm off the ladder once. Do it again, just once more. To get the rope under your arm."

"Haim."

"Chaya, you already did it once. Do it again. Just the one arm."

She did it.

"Now the other one."

"I ca—"

"Chaya! The men are going to enter the village soon! I need you to get that other arm in there now, and I don't want to hear another 'I can't' or I'll leave you down there for the bandits!"

"Haim!"

"Left arm, Chaya! Left arm! Left arm! Do it! Now! Left arm!"

She started to move.

"That's it! Now!" Then he tightened up the slack and the loop tightened up under her arms. "I'm going to put this rope over my shoulder, and I'm going to start running, and you're going to come off that ladder and start climbing, and I'm going to run, and you're going to climb, and you're going to come out of the well and then run as fast as you can when you get here! Run from the bandits! Do you understand me?"

"Haim!"

"Can you run, Chaya!"

"Yes, I can run."

"Say it! I'm going to run!"

"I'm going to run."

"Louder! I'm going to run for my life when I get out of this well! Say it!"

"I'm going to run! I'm going to run!"

"Okay. Now go! Climb and run!" And he cinched up the rope and he started to pull and she screamed and he felt her weight and then he began to walk fast, ignoring the friction of the rope sliding against the rim of the well, ignoring the bite into his shoulder, the crushing of the rope around his hands. He walked and she thrashed in open air below him and she screamed again and then suddenly she hit the wall of the well and kicked off. He took another step and she began to climb and he walked faster and she climbed quicker and then she came out of the top of the well in terror and wild-eyed and fell sprawling on the ground beside the well.

Haim lay down in exhaustion and exhilaration. He lay there as she freed herself from the rope and started to run, and then she stopped and started again and stopped and looked at him on the ground.

He slowly unwound his end of the rope from his hands. When he looked at her again, he saw that her fearful expression was changing.

"There are no bandits coming," she said.

"No. No one is coming."

Chaya shouted then and ran at him and pounced on him and he had his own terror, his memory of his sisters, but she was smaller than them, smaller than him, and he shook her off and stood up and was about to get angry and then saw that she was still kneeling where he had lain, kneeling and curled up and crying hard. He had no experience with such a thing. Haim thought of his goats and knelt beside her. Holding her felt natural while her crying felt foreign, and soon he found himself crying with her. They stayed like that for some time before she pulled back. Her dark hair clung to her neck and cheeks, and streaks of dirt ran down her face.

"You scared me to make me climb," she said.

"Yes."

"Don't do it again. I don't like it."

He nodded. "Your family is gone," he said.

"I know."

"Mine is too."

"The marauders?"

He nodded, and a sudden ache in his throat surprised him. "I'm getting thirsty from too much crying," he said. Haim wiped his face and looked around at the destroyed village. "It's not safe here," he said. "There's a war going on." He turned back to her. "Did you know? The marauders were probably the king's men."

Chaya looked at him with large red-rimmed eyes. She pointed around them at the burned village but did not say anything.

"Sadducees against the Pharisees," Haim said. "Jerusalem and the king's men against the Galileans. It's a civil war."

"But we're not Galileans," Chaya said. "We're Samaritans."

Haim thought of the old scribe's stories and the few things the man said about Samaritans.

"Being a Samaritan is worse," he finally said. "If the king's men don't kill you, they'll sell you overseas as a slave. That's how they pay for their wars."

8

92 BCE

IN THE MONTH of Av, the heat in Samaria's valleys was like fire. Without the ocean breezes Haim had welcomed at the widow's house, Samaria's still night-time air brought little relief. The daytime heat lingered through the night, and the two children were sticky with sweat by morning.

Chaya shuffled forwards on her elbows below a screen of low bushes. She came up beside Haim, one shoulder touching his. "Who are they?" she whispered. Many thousands of well-armed men were passing. Most were on foot.

"Probably from Jerusalem," Haim said. "They are with the Sadducees and the king."

He felt her nod beside him in response. The company passing them was not like the small Galilean band he had witnessed on his second day from the widow's house. This looked like a proper army.

"Are they the ones who destroyed my village?" she whispered, peering through parted leaves at the passing force.

"I don't know. Best to just stay away from everyone until we're across the Jordan River," he said.

They had been moving very slowly through the region, staying to the outskirts of villages, foraging for food and avoiding notice. "We could ask for help," Chaya had suggested several times, but Haim would not listen to her and she was too afraid to act on her own.

Another month passed. As the hot season faded, the pair finished creeping in circles around and through Samaria and made their way down a canyon trail, eventually traversing a plain and then making it to the Jordan River. Slow water bore the tribute of grey mud. They had come upon the river at a place where the bank was overgrown with long grass, tangled with broad-leafed plants, and punctured by the occasional white and gold trunks of trees and short palms.

"It doesn't look fit to drink," Chaya said.

Haim said nothing. The river looked deep and neither of them knew how to swim.

"You're bent on crossing," a sexless voice said.

Downriver there was a large stump, uprooted and burned. Its broken roots poked skywards like stiff, stark fingers shattered and remade into the shape of agony. There was no trunk left, just the upturned stump. The rest of the tree had previously been cut off and cleared away. Vegetation overgrew all. The stump was black amid greenery and beyond it flowed grey water.

The voice seemed to have come from the uprooted stump, but then Haim spotted two people sitting beyond on a dull patch of rock and dirt. Their clothes bore the same tones of upturned earth. Skin lay over them like garments fit for other forms. Creases held dirt in their faces and their clothes held more. Haim could not tell if they were a man and a woman, two men, or both women. Neither wore a head covering. Their skulls displayed memories of hair in long strings. Wisps of beard were present, beards too thin for a man and of the same pokey irregularity that decorated some rare women. Haim decided they were women. Chaya said later that they were men, and they agreed finally that the pair had been a couple, older than Eretz-Israel itself, grown from the soil above the riverbank, overwatered and melted back into the ground. Certainly mouldy.

One of the pair was heavy and the other thin, and it was the large one that spoke again. "Going over?"

"Is there a way?" Haim asked.

The pair turned slowly and gazed at one another as though consulting on this question silently. Perhaps this was an old question, and it was the shared repetitive experience that caused them to confer.

"Once you cross," the heavy one finally said to Haim, "there is no way back."

Haim looked across the river. The Jordan River. If it were solid, he could cross it in ten or fifteen long steps. He was unsure how far he would get swimming. Chaya would drown in the first five feet and pull him under while doing so.

"There's a creature over there that consumes full-grown men in one sitting," the heavy one said.

Haim looked across the river again. The other side had the same tangle of grasses and broad-leafed plants and dwarf palms and trees with patchy white and golden bark. He saw nothing that suggested anything more dangerous than what already existed on this side of the water.

"Na-ba-ta-ea," the sexless voice said. Cheeks trembled through each syllable and created a strange resonance.

"What is that?" Chaya asked. Her voice was small in the air.

"It's the name of the people over there," Haim said. "They're making things up."

"No more Judeans," the river sitter said. "No Samaritans. There are just Nabataeans there now. Whatever presence your god might have once held there is gone. Nabataean gods rule that land now." Eyes sought Haim's from beneath heavy clay-like folds. "New gods. New rules." The large shape leaned in towards them and spoke again with the same forced resonance. "They offer new ways to be hungry and evil solutions for satisfaction."

"Is there a way over?"

"Why would you want to go? They will eat you."

"We need to find work," Haim said. "Homes. Food."

"And get away from this war," Chaya said. "They killed my family. My whole village."

"There's no way back," the sexless voice said. "If you go, you are lost. The devil will find you."

"Show us how to cross," Haim said.

The reclining pair shifted laboriously as though their bodies were part of the solid ground itself. They contemplated one another silently and then gave each other silent nods. One arm pointed down the riverbank.

Haim searched where directed and found a stake driven into the ground. Tied to the stake was a rope that stretched downriver. He pulled the rope and from beneath a mop of vegetation emerged a small boat. He pulled it up the river until he could grasp its wooden rim. There were no paddles. The rope was long enough to stretch across the river, but no rope was visible on the opposite bank.

"Is there a pole or a paddle?" he asked.

The pair on the bank did not confer with one another. They just watched him in silence.

"I guess you've made your warning," Haim said quietly so only he could hear.

Chaya came behind him. He was just started to form a plan when she pushed past and clambered aboard. "Let's go," she said.

"How do we make it go over?"

"Push it."

Haim looked across the river. It was not far, and the current did not seem to move at all.

"Just push it and jump in. We'll float over."

"What if we don't make it? If we stop in the middle?"

"We'll pull ourselves back and try again. Come on, go." She turned away from him. "Let's go."

"They seem to think there's trouble over there."

"Haim."

He pulled the boat around so that its nose pointed at the opposite shore. With the boat in position, he estimated the far bank to be five or six boat lengths across. She was not looking when he pushed and jumped and fell into the back of the boat, nearly upending it. He sat up, frustrated by their lack of movement forwards, the danger his jump had caused, the effort he had expended, and her general lack of concern. He sat up to complain and found her looking back at him, bright-eyed and happy. She was holding on to a fistful of woody shoreline branches.

"We did it!" she said.

Chaya used the plants to pull herself up from the river and through the bushes to the flat ground above.

"Come on," she said.

He threw his pack up to Chaya, climbed out, and then kicked the boat. It drifted lazily back across the little river, softly rustled against the bank's overhanging grasses, and came to rest in the same place he had found it. The rope was taut. It waited for the next crosser.

Haim looked up at the couple on the western bank. They seemed to have faded. They were still there but appeared to be farther away than their small boat ride could explain. Crossing the river seemed as momentous as leaving the widow's house and as religiously significant as losing the old scribe. It had happened without time to absorb it. They were over. Behind them was Eretz-Israel. Ahead lay something else—something the river sitters called man-eaters.

9

92 BCE

A DAY AFTER CROSSING the Jordan River, Haim and Chaya found a small rundown orchard. Together, they searched the ground beneath one of the trees, inspecting sparse vegetation and loose rock.

"Found one," Chaya said, standing up and holding a small oval shell for him to see. She bent down again and continued her slow search. "Another one."

They kept looking together and came up with several handfuls of the dry, papery shells easily broken open for the almond inside.

"My mother made cakes with these. With honey." She looked at Haim. "Did yours?"

Haim did not answer. The shells came off easily and the almond flesh was sweet. Adding honey was a fantasy from some other existence.

They sat in the dappled shade of the tree, sharing the

almonds mounded in Chaya's lap and drinking from their shared water skin. They did not hear the footsteps approach from behind them.

"We can't do this much longer," Chaya said.

Haim nodded and did not reply.

"It will get cold," she continued. "The rains will come. And there will be times in the winter when there is nothing to harvest."

"There is always something," Haim said.

"Not something good," she said.

"But I'm sure you're finding the almonds to be very good," a new voice said.

Both Haim and Chaya jumped at the sound of the stranger's voice. Haim first spotted the man's thick sandals and thin ankles. Then he looked up and took in a haggard man around thirty years old, his hair and beard sprinkled with white and his face long and gaunt.

"Did you see the river back there?" the man asked, pointing westwards. He was looking at Chaya.

Chaya looked back at him, an almond frozen halfway to her mouth. She did not say anything in reply.

The man turned his gaze on Haim. "How about you? Did you notice the river? Might have gotten a bit wet crossing, I would imagine."

"The Jordan River?" Haim asked, nodding as though to confirm his guess.

"Good fellow. The Jordan River." The man smiled, but there did not seem to be any humour in it. His eyes remained hard and flat. "What's on the other side of the Jordan River?"

"Eretz-Israel," Haim said.

"Right again. And now that you're on the east side of the Jordan, where are you now?"

Haim thought about the river sitters who had warned them about this place. "Nabataea."

"You're a good student," the man said. He turned his attention back to Chaya, who was still staring at him, mouth open, her almond still held away from her lips. The man studied Chaya for a minute, his eyes moving about her and taking her in. Finally, he turned his attention back to Haim. "She's a bit young," the man said. "Your sister?"

Haim nodded.

The man turned back to Chaya. "You Jews allow beggars to glean at the edges of fields during a harvest, don't you?"

Haim nodded, and the man seemed to pick up on his response without turning his attention away from Chaya.

"Do your customs apply here?" the man asked. "In Nabataea?"

Haim opened his mouth and then realized he had nothing to say.

"Well?" the man asked, still looking at Chaya.

"No," Haim said. "Nabataea probably has its own customs."

"Probably," the man snorted. He turned his eyes back to Haim. "Probably? Do you Jews think that in other countries we don't have our own customs? No laws of our own? No manner of conducting ourselves?" He crouched down, still staring at Haim. "Are we just animals to you Jews?"

"No," Haim said. "We were just trying to escape the war in Eretz-Israel."

The man frowned, and then his smile reappeared. "The

Jews can't fight Nabataeans and win, so now they're fighting themselves."

He stood up and motioned for Haim and Chaya to stand with him. "These are the boss's almonds. Come with me. You can explain yourself to him."

Haim's experience with people in charge was limited. His mother had been late winter weather: sunshine and rain, bright and cold, a continuously changeable and uncomfortable state that begged the relief of spring. And the old scribe had been that spring sunshine: not too hot, always offering the gentle familiarity of knowledge, parchments, circuitous questions, and an ear willing to listen to a boy's rambling ideas. The goat-stealer had been thunder in the month of Av, like his mother's storms with none of the rain: brutal heat transmitted with mistless clarity.

Standing before the landowner whose almonds they had eaten, Haim quickly realized that this man was nothing like his mother or the old scribe or the goat-stealer. He had a long head, the front and top of which were bald. A fringe of hair circled the base of his skull at the back of his head and his beard turned patchy as it approached his ears. The effect was an appearance not of natural balding but rather disease.

The landowner's strange appearance did not alarm Haim as much as the coldness of his manner. The man sat on a stump. He wore a disinterested expression as he listened to what his foreman had to say. When the landowner asked a question, he spoke with neither anger nor kindness in his voice. He asked merely for the facts of their case, looking at the foreman. He barely cast a glance at either Haim or Chaya.

On one level, his calm was reassuring. He asked his questions calmly. He clarified petty details calmly, including the approximate number of almonds consumed on this and previous days. No one asked Haim or Chaya for these details, and the foreman supplied his own assumptions. The landowner calmly asked for the names of his two trespassers, asking the foreman, not his visitors. When Haim called out the answer, the landowner waited for the foreman to relay this information as though he had not heard the boy's response. The landowner was just as calm when he suggested that perhaps the pair should be executed as either spies or common criminals.

"How about labour?" the foreman countered. "No pay. They need to work off a debt. They can eat for each day they work. They're used to sleeping on the land, so no need for special accommodations."

The landowner frowned at that, bunched his lips together, and turned his attention towards Haim for the first time.

"He has a good axe," the foreman said.

"Can you chop wood?" the landowner asked.

Haim nodded.

The landowner looked then at Chaya. "She's a bit young."

"She can work with the kitchen women," the foreman said.

"Can you tend a fire?" the landowner asked her.

Chaya nodded.

"One chops, the other feeds the fire," the foreman said. "The bakers and cooks stay focused on what matters."

"Several things matter," the landowner said, smiling for the first time. It was a twisted smile that raised only one side of his mouth and did not touch his eyes at all.

10

92 BCE

HAIM PUT HIS axe down, picked up his water skin, and drank deeply. Rain fell on his face and ran through his hair and clothes. The barley harvest was two months away, and it was cold and wet, but men still needed to eat and fires still needed to be stoked. He was the operation's sole axeman. He supplied and hauled the fuel that Chaya burned. She was also responsible for hauling water and cleaning out the ashes each morning before restoking the fires, and Haim did not know which of them had the more demanding job.

Late one morning, Haim noticed a few of the more senior farmworkers gathered around the well. Haim looked at his water skin and decided to join them, a refill as his excuse. He approached the men with his eyes down, the water skin conspicuous.

"What about the girl?" one of the men asked, appearing

to direct his comments at the foreman who had first caught Haim and Chaya. The man who spoke was the shortest of the group, powerfully built and completely bald. There was laughter among the men at his question.

"Which girl?" the foreman asked.

"The new one," the short burly man replied.

"That's her brother," a third man said, nodding in Haim's direction as he approached. The conversation suddenly lagged and then fell silent as he refilled his water skin from the well. He had hoped to join the men's conversation even though he was still just a boy, but the silence was not welcoming. He walked back to his collection of logs, passing out of earshot once more. He began to work again with the axe. When he looked up sometime later, he saw the men disperse.

After dark, Haim and Chaya sat outside the spare goat pens they called home at night. There were two pens side by side. The flock of goats stayed in the larger of the two, its stone walls topped with thorn branches to discourage nocturnal predators. The smaller pen had a thin, straw roof and only had half-walls that left the space exposed to wind and rain. The shepherds used the pens for sickly goats, of which there were none at present. The cooks had given Chaya a screen of woven reeds, and together they had affixed it to the windward side of the smaller pen. It blocked off the open space so that water ran down the screen when it rained but did not run into the pen. This was their home now and it was as good as sleeping under a large old pine, except when the wind changed direction.

Chaya sat beside Haim this night, pressed up against him. She sat with her knees drawn up to her chest, looking out at the farm and the distant stars but without her usual chatter.

Haim wanted to speak to her, but he had no words. He was not even sure what the problem was. He merely had a strong feeling that something was wrong and that it was on him to expose and solve it. He stayed silent, feeling her shoulder against his upper arm. Her breath caught for a moment before she regained control, but that single lapse into a cry further fuelled Haim's need to speak.

"Chaya," he eventually said.

"Hmm?"

He still did not know what to say. He frowned into the night and wished he could speak to the old scribe or to one of the cooks or bakers, the women who might be able to give him wisdom.

"What is it?" she whispered.

Her whisper was strange in this place. They were far away from the main house and the men and women's separate barracks. Some workers even had their own homes that they returned to each evening. When alone together in their pen, Haim and Chaya spoke quietly but plainly to one another. They did not need to whisper.

"What's wrong?" Haim asked.

Chaya grew even more still beside him. Even her shoulder's pressure against his arm lessened. It was not as though she had pulled away from him, but rather as if she had shrunk and grown lighter. He was about to ask again when he heard her breathe in deeply, and he waited.

"One of the men came for Osnat today," Chaya whispered. "An hour before the evening meal."

"The Egyptian woman?" Haim asked. "The baker?"

He felt Chaya nod.

"She told him that it wasn't nighttime yet." Chaya's voice hitched, and she stopped talking.

"I don't understand," Haim said.

"He came for her. Among the ovens," Chaya said. "He just walked in and said, 'Today it's your turn.' And she said, 'It's not nighttime yet.' And he said, 'It's your turn, and I'll decide what time it starts.' It was just like that."

"I don't understand," Haim said. He turned to look at Chaya, and he saw in the moon's glow that her cheeks were wet. "Did someone hurt you?" he asked.

"No," she whispered. "They come for the women at night. The women have to take turns letting the men hurt them somehow. The women are not just here to cook and bake; they are also here for the men."

Haim thought about the interrupted conversation at the well. "What did the man look like?" Haim asked. "The one who came for Osnat."

"He's the shortest one. Very strong. No hair. His eyes are mean."

Haim nodded and did not reply. He felt a constriction in his throat as though he had swallowed something wrong and it had lodged there, stuck halfway down.

"They brought her back early," Chaya said.

"They?"

"And when they saw me they said something."

"Said what?"

"They said that it wouldn't be long for me, and I could learn how to cook and bake just like the other women." Chaya's voice hitched again, and she leaned into Haim. "They laughed when they said it, like what they said wasn't everything that they meant."

There was silence for a long time outside the small goat pen. Haim remembered the scribe telling him about such things, accounts from the Torah and more recent history, which the old man had dispassionately explained. There were parallels between what the old scribe had said and the rumours about his mother and his own conception.

Haim felt a strange tension come over him as the darkness descended on the farm. He understood now the interrupted conversation at the well. He wanted to protect Chaya, but sitting beside her, he felt a darker thought enter his mind. He wondered if he was destined and doomed to grow into a man that would take pleasure in such power, claiming violence as his birthright. Working day after day for months with the axe, he had grown taller and stronger, and in recent months he had felt a new passion and anger start to burn within. Sitting beside Chaya, he had the thought that if such violence was his genesis, then maybe it was native to who he was, and he should toughen himself to its implications, embrace the passion, and learn from anger.

He closed his eyes and thought about the old scribe. Then he thought about his real father—the Tyrant of Dora—and wondered what counsel that man might give.

"The men will come for you eventually," he said. "I've heard them talking. You're too young now but won't be for long."

He stayed still, listening for her held breath. He could not decide if this was the cruellest thing he had ever spoken or the wisest. He wondered which he wished it to be. Did he want to retract it? He could not decide. She breathed out and then in and held her breath again, and he could feel heat radiate from her. He maintained his silence, determined to see what might be on the other side.

"You wouldn't let them," she said.

He did not answer. He had no way of knowing when her first bleed would be, the time he knew from the old scribe's stories that girls became women in the eyes of men and began to shoulder the risks that came with it. For Chaya, perhaps it was a year or two away. But whether he would let them or not was just numbers. He was one and they were many. When the time came, there would be nothing for him to decide. They would overpower both her and him. The issue that pressed on his mind now, in the dark, was whether he was one of them or something different. His father's blood said that he was one of them. His heart shrank within him at the thought. He wanted to be the dye maker and feared that he was the Tyrant.

"They could come as early as the end of the barley harvest," he said. That was a lie. Why was he scaring her? Why was he sabotaging their situation on this farm? The barley harvest was a short time away and the threat still a long way off. He wanted to believe it was a long way off. He did not know, had no one to ask, hoped that she had not heard him.

"Then we have to go now," she said.

"We can wait until after the harvest," he said. "The weather will be drier and warmer."

"It could be too late then."

He felt trapped. He had a lie now to live up to. As he felt panic rise within at this new direction, he heard himself say, "What do we need to take?" He wondered again at his mouth. It betrayed him at every turn, firming up action he had not had time yet to properly think through.

She prepared a list, whispering it to him in the dark. She made him repeat the parts that he would find for them. He thought of his own items and volunteered to also steal a sling.

"Can you use one?"

"The old scribe taught me," he said.

The next morning, he arose and hoped that it had all been a dream, but Chaya made him repeat his list to her before they parted. When Haim finished chopping wood that day, he took extra care sharpening his axe. He was tempted to steal the sharpening stone, but it was too large for them to carry far, wherever they might go.

Two slings hung on a fence near the well. As dusk settled over the land after the evening meal, Haim took one of the slings, returned to their shelter, and packed it in his original bag with their mantles, blanket, water skin, cups, and bowls. Chaya had a bag of her own, stuffed with stolen food.

"We should leave now," she said.

"If we leave, they'll chase us down." He spoke as though they should stay despite packing the stolen sling into his bag while she watched. His intention was clear. He had no choice but to leave and wondered as he waited for her response what his words said about him. They were heading in a new direction of his own making, but he would not own the final decision.

She said nothing but shouldered her pack. They set off without another word, going silently into the dying light.

11
92-91 BCE

THEY WALKED THROUGH the night, never stopping to rest. Though exhausted, they kept on, fearful of the landowner's wrath. They tried to keep moving eastwards, tracking their route by the stars. In the morning, the sun rose over a barren desert beyond which lay forbidding, treeless mountains. The sun rose in a gap between two distant cliffs, illuminating their path in a narrow tunnel of light as though the two were trapped once more in a well's wet shaft. This time both of them were trapped, squinting up at their salvation.

Chaya took Haim's hand and pointed northwards, towards green fields and distant, manageable hills.

"If we knew how to live in the desert or those mountains, we'd go there," Haim said, nodding towards the sun.

Chaya gave no reply but began to stumble north, still holding Haim's hand.

After a while, they came upon a line of bushes well off the road.

"Here," Haim said.

He led Chaya behind the natural cover. The ground there turned out to be hard and uneven. He looked at her apologetically.

"I don't care," Chaya said and sat down.

Haim pulled their blankets and mantles from their packs. He layered the blankets as best he could to insulate them from the cold and even out the ground, and then she lay down on the makeshift bed. He lay beside her, wrapping them both up in their mantles. Despite the hard cold ground below and the brightening cold air above, it did not take either of them long to fall asleep.

Riders passed around midday. The pair behind the bushes did not know whether the riders were common travellers or the landowner's men. Once the danger had passed, they adjusted their positions and again slept for many hours. They set out again after dark, their way lit only by the moon and stars.

Through the rest of that winter and spring, they travelled in a vast northerly arc from the harsh Plains of Moab to a rough crossing of the Jabbok River, then from the city of Gerasa beyond and to the dense forests north. They found and worked small jobs and collected their pay at the end of each day. They never stayed more than a week in any one place, even when there was more work available.

"The women are the same here," Chaya said. "They are trapped the same way."

Other places had no women, but the men were cruel to the animals and to one another. Chaya and Haim worked for a few days on a small family farm. The man was kind enough to Chaya and Haim and paid them at the end of each day without fuss, but he beat his family for inexplicable reasons. Chaya could not bear the farmer's outbursts and violence against his family and so they passed on from that place quickly, not working again for more than a week. They ate through their packed supplies and had to buy food in small villages, gradually losing what little money they had saved.

"We'll need to find work again soon," Haim said.

They came to the Yarmuk River as summer came on, and the heat and fertility in that place created an abundant wheat harvest. They walked slowly into a land of tall grain stalks and fruit trees.

Haim looked at himself, at his legs and arms, and then at Chaya. They were both thin. Threadbare clothes hung loosely, bound at their waists to keep from billowing when the wind blew.

"What about cities?" Haim asked. "Have you ever lived in a city?"

Chaya shook her head. Her face was dirty and her hair, although bound up, had escaped on one side and puffed out as though she had just awoken.

"I've heard of Bet Yerah," she said. "My father used to talk about it. It's on this side of the Jordan River but at the border of Eretz-Israel. It's probably still Jewish."

⁓

In Bet Yerah, Chaya clung to Haim's arm as the crowd around them surged forwards. There were shouts in front of and behind them. The crowd's momentum pulled the pair along as the soldiers herded them all into the town square.

Galilean men had come across the river from Eretz-Israel earlier in the day. They were fleeing for their lives carrying bloody scythes and hooks with women and children running with them. Behind them had come another mob of men only, carrying spears, swords, and bows. These civil war predators had followed their prey across the river.

Haim and Chaya, having fled the Jewish war, now found themselves surrounded by it.

"They have no business on this side of the Jordan," a shopkeeper had growled as he crouched behind his stall with Haim and Chaya earlier in the afternoon. The man had hired the two to help purge the shop's backroom of the summer's accumulated mounds of garlic skins, fruit pits, mouldy rinds, and nutshells.

The Sadducean mercenary army had continued its pursuit past the shopkeeper's stall and through Bet Yerah. They clubbed locals who stood in their way and cut down Jews who resisted capture. By midday, they had rounded up more than two dozen of the fleeing Galileans for being Pharisee sympathizers and opposing the Jewish king.

"I don't want to go," Chaya said as she, Haim, and the shopkeeper were rounded up that afternoon with other locals and herded through the town's streets.

They moved as directed, stood where ordered, waited as commanded through a long and terrible afternoon. The square was full of locals, Jews and non-Jews, the crowd a polyglot of Jewish, Greek, Nabataean, Egyptian, and other tongues. The local Nabataean authorities were so overwhelmed that they stood silent on the stage beside the leaders of the raid while great vertical posts of Greek and Persian legend were erected around the square. Egyptian and Thracian mercenaries moved through the courtyard barking orders. When the time was right, the pounding of hammers and strangled screams filled the square as both men and women were slowly crucified on soil that was no longer even Jewish. For this one day, the ground was Eretz-Israel once more just so that Jews could see to the execution of their own people.

The hours-long cries speared through Chaya, and she clung to Haim through the long afternoon. He held her head against him and covered her ears with his hands and would have hid her entirely inside himself if he were able. Neither dared to leave or draw any attention to themselves. When the crowd cheered, Haim cheered. They were strangers here, and he sought to keep them both invisible.

The square was also filled with old signs covered in inscriptions that imparted history and lessons and deeds worth remembering to the literate. Haim did not tell Chaya what the signs said. She could not read and did not ask. Bet Yerah, it seemed, was like any other city: a settlement built on accumulated horrors.

That night, in the half-cleaned backroom of the shopkeeper's stall, Chaya wept and declared that to have been raped by the Nabataeans farther south would have been better than to have witnessed that day's horrors.

"That's not true," Haim said.

"We did nothing!" Chaya said. "We just watched."

Haim tried to remember the old scribe's words. Something about serving justice by bearing witness; something about good coming from evil, honey from a corpse; something about funerals. Haim tried to explain what he remembered from the old man, but he made a jumble of it.

"When you pretend to know things, you're like one of them," she said and turned away.

They made their bed in the middle of the floor and said nothing else that night. She lay down, as did he, but they kept a large space between them. The weather was warm now. They did not need each other's warmth.

He lay awake in the dark long after she had finally fallen asleep. His thoughts roared at him and around him. He relived the day's emotions, yet he was beyond mourning. He lay in the dark, recoiling from the idea that he had positioned himself on the side of evil. He wanted to grieve with her for what they had witnessed.

I feel what she feels, he thought. Her contempt diminished him in ways that he could not describe. He was like one of those signs he had read and not translated for her. His intentions were as unknown to her as the written pronouncements in Bet Yerah's square.

As he lay in the dark, Haim's thoughts lingered on the evils that clung to them like a mire they could not escape. He could not protect her from the vile men in the south—all they had done was flee—and now he had proved unable to provide any comfort at all. Even his words were useless. All he had was proof of his bad blood. He remembered the goat-stealer's words about him.

Haim looked up at the dark ceiling above. *I want to leave,* he thought. He could abandon Chaya here. She only knew part of his history, and he could not bear her learning the whole of it—finding out about the Tyrant and his conception. Thinking about the goat-stealer's words made Haim remember the goats again—the nanny and the kid. He remembered the kid trying to nibble his hair, nibble his clothes, and the nanny giving him her milk and cream. Then the tears came.

As he lay crying as silently as possible, a deeper shame came over him. *I can cry for goats, but not for what happened today.*

In the morning, Haim and Chaya gathered their few belongings.

"We haven't finished the job yet," Haim said, looking at the remaining refuse in the small shop. "If we don't finish, we won't get paid."

"I'm going," Chaya said. "You do what you want."

12

91-90 BCE

AFTER BET YERAH, Haim and Chaya found grudging gifts of work in small Nabataean villages and farms but stayed away from larger cities. They worked in exchange for food, sometimes for coins and less often for shelter, but they found no one who would take them in as children. They slept in barns, fields, and forests. Haim did not know how to conduct himself each day, how to talk to Chaya, how to make decisions, how to banish their constant hunger.

"Where do we go next?" she would ask.

"I don't know, Chaya" was all he could answer.

He wondered how it was that he had become responsible for them both. There was nothing in the old scribe's words to guide him. He looked at the sturdy homes of stone and wood that they passed and at the abundance of flocks that shepherds and day labourers cared for. He saw fields of grain with full heads, trees heavy with fruit, and grapes that hung on thick, healthy vines. He did not understand how anyone planned and paid for such fields. Their tending was a mystery. He simply fed off discarded scraps and barely managed to patch his thinning clothes. He did not know what lay over the next rise in the road. He did not understand how the world worked, how its innumerable parts fit together.

They came to Antioch of Hippos, the former Seleucid settlement, now part of the Nabataeans' new territory which the Jews still called Sussita. The city overlooked the eastern shore of the Sea of Galilee and they approached it carefully, at night, as the city burned.

The starless night sky hung overcast with both clouds and smoke, and deep red flames lit the darkness. The black shadows of smoke that drifted overhead passed before the backdrop of orange clouds which reflected the flame's angry glow back to the earth below. Haim and Chaya reached the city as its inhabitants filled the roads and the two were turned from their way and fled inland with the city's inhabitants.

"Pick up what you can," Haim ordered.

They spent several days gathering the supplies that the Sussita refugees had cast off in the frenzy. They stopped within sight of Gamla bearing extra rations of food, a jar of wine, and some new clothes. They took turns stripping off their ragged tunics behind a screen of brambles and then continued on in clothes that were new to them and clean. Chaya's face was soot streaked but happy. That night they drank the wine and became drunk for the first time and laughed in the dark hollow where they had taken refuge. Later, Haim remembered it as their only time together east of the Jordan when Chaya was happy. She had been happy when they successfully crossed the Jordan's shores and when they found the almonds but never since until their wine after Sussita. They shared no other laughter east of the Jordan.

They slept where they were, drunk under the stars. They no longer slept touching, not since Bet Yerah. Despite this, they always remained near one another. They only had each other.

A week later, in early-fall rain, they sat on one of three hills near the northern end of the Sea of Galilee with their mantles wrapped around them, sheltered in a grove of trees that still bore a few late-season figs. Their backs were against an exposed ancient root as they looked out at the other two rises. The rain picked up, and Chaya pulled the edge of her mantle over her head. Though figs bothered her stomach, eating them was better than hunger.

A bruise marred Chaya's face from a violent field manager a week past. Its harsh edges had faded, but its grey tones stained her complexion. The scar on Haim's leg from a driver's whip had been hot in the spring, a spreading redness in his flesh that he kept hidden even when it had burned in the night and made sweat pool. Now it was just another scar, indistinguishable from those he wore from the widow's house.

"We need to go back to Eretz-Israel," she said.

"That's where we're going," he said. "To Upper Galilee anyway."

"We need to be west of the river. Among Jewish people."

"There's still a war there," Haim said, handing her a few more figs.

"Maybe it's not come that far north."

He wanted to please her. He did not know why, but he needed her to be happy. Other than their journeys to Bet Yerah and the fringes of Sussita, they had kept to rural regions. They had not seen anyone else crucified, but these rural lands had their own ways of assaulting the mind and body. Here, war was not necessary to spread suffering. The people of these lands did not compact their cruelty into one dramatic execution. Instead, suffering came by hunger, the strike of a fist, or the sting of a whip. You would survive. Tomorrow there would be more. And always it came with the laughter of those who did not care. This suffering stretched across seasons and wore the soul down, for there was no escape. These lands nurtured slavery without chains—slavery induced by the need to eat.

Haim felt his words grow more clipped as he and Chaya talked about what to do next and where to go. He was angry that the figs hurt her stomach and angry that she did not eat more, for they were desperate for food. Yet he was also angry when she did eat the figs because they caused her pain. When he wanted her close to him, his awkward words of comfort drove her away. When his words were intentionally short, even harsh, she drew closer. He did not understand her. Her responses made harsh behaviour more appealing, behaviour that Haim would have been ashamed to confess to the old scribe. Being unkind to her might give him more of what he wanted, and that thought scared him. It was the path that would lead to becoming like the landowners and supervisors of this place: first you use cruelty to get what you want, and then cruelty itself becomes what you want.

He would not admit to himself what he wanted, what

a warm touch would do to both set his heart at ease and make it race, but suppressing how he felt made him stir uncomfortably in the rain. Desire and hunger and hurt morphed into ordinary anger.

Haim knew she would be sick soon from the figs, and he felt both compassion and hate. The water filling his eyes was the only outward sign of his inward conflict. He looked up and let the rain wash the tears away.

She put her hand on his arm. "When we find good people, we will be whatever they are. We must find a home again."

Haim looked back down and scowled. "We're not children anymore, Chaya."

"You're not. I still am."

"Soon not," he said.

"We have to find a home. Everyone belongs somewhere."

He did not answer her, and he did not adjust his mantle. The rain ran through his uncut hair. He saw the mist rise in the valley before them. The mist gradually climbed up the hills until the peaks faded into whiteness and disappeared.

"What makes you think the Jews will treat us any better?" he asked.

She did not answer.

"I'll be despised," he said, "and so will you. You're a Samaritan."

"They do not need to know who we are. We will be whoever we choose to be. We look the same as them."

He watched where the hills had been.

"We can be Jews from Nabataea returning to Eretz-Israel," she suggested.

He felt a hint of inspiration within and also fear and

a yearning sincerity and a deep need for something he did not know how to name. He did not trust himself to say anything good or know the right way to say it. He shuffled uncomfortably. He wanted to get up and walk away, and he wanted to hold her. Both.

The rest of the fog-enveloped afternoon passed in silence. When the figs did what they always did, he held Chaya while she moaned. When she was sick, he gave her wet leaves to wipe her mouth, and then he supported her as they moved down the hill. They came to the Upper Jordan near the Sea of Galilee, crossed the two branches of the river, and then continued to Kfar Nahum to see what might await them this time in Eretz-Israel.

"It will be good," Chaya said. "You'll see."

Or they'll kill us, Haim thought. But he said nothing out loud. Her hand on his arm was enough.

13

90 BCE

THEY APPROACHED KFAR Nahum as rags within rags, approaching houses on the outskirts of the small town.

"We have to pick one," Chaya said. She walked beside Haim and clutched a fistful of the mantle he wore. In his twelfth year, he had begun to grow at a rate that surprised him. He was much taller than she was now and she more convincingly his little sister. Though their features were different, living on the fringes masked their differences with wear and weariness.

Haim nodded and was trying to decide how to make such a decision when Chaya stopped them and pointed at one of the first houses. "By the door," she said.

Haim did not understand at first. She continued to point at the house, and he focused on the door as she insisted. A cylinder of baked clay hung from the home's door frame by braided woollen strings with dangling tassels. Then he recognized it. It was a mezuzah. Inside the cylinder would be a curled slip of paper with specific verses from the Torah written upon it—the words of the Shema, a Jewish prayer the old scribe used to pray every morning, noon, and night that Haim had known him.

"I see it," he said. He felt now like they were truly back in Eretz-Israel, and the thought made him unexpectedly happy.

They stood looking at the building and Haim felt the happiness build within him. A large arched window faced the street with its shutters hanging open, inviting visitors to look in. Cleanness emanated from the house, and the smell of bread coming from it was unlike anything east of the Jordan. More than the landscape had changed. This was something cultural, something religious, something familiar to Chaya and Haim as well. His mother and the old scribe had made their home more Jewish than he had realized.

The spirit of the house seemed to open Chaya wide. He felt it in her posture beside him, and when he looked at her, he saw pure joy on her face.

"We have those as well," Chaya said. "My father made ours."

She tugged on his hand, and so they walked forwards together. As they approached the house, the door opened. An old woman appeared with an infant bound and secured to her chest with a thick cloth. She held a shepherd's rod in both hands, and hair sprouted from her knuckles. Her grimace exposed rough and yellow teeth. One was broken.

"You will not pass here," the old woman said.

Chaya flinched and both her hands now clutched

Haim's cloak. Haim looked around and noticed an even older man approaching from around the side of the house. He was clearly no more the father of the infant than the old woman was the mother. He was a wrack of angled bones and thinned beard, and he too had an excess of troubled teeth. He came limping as though on hips that pained him, bearing a long spear. He advanced with a murderous expression. Haim put his hand on Chaya's shoulder to make sure she saw him too, and they quickly retreated down the street.

"I don't understand," Chaya said.

"Something has happened here," Haim replied.

They left that armed house and kept moving towards the town. They could spot glimpses of the lake between houses, and they stopped to look south down the length of the Sea of Galilee. They knew Bet Yerah lay across this long body of water, but the only thing they could see in the distance was the horizon. The water was still and dark and reflected light like a polished rock. Boats in the far distance looked like children's toys, incapable of containing men. The scene did not look real.

"We'll find somewhere," Haim said.

"What happened here?" she asked.

Haim did not answer. He had no answer.

They had no money for the fish market, but they tried to barter with the few items they had in exchange for something to eat. The marketgoers stared at them with faces distorted by contempt. Each time Haim tried to propose a trade, the vendors would only stare. Their eyes might squint just a little, but their mouths were silent. None would barter with them, and none would offer them discarded portions in mercy. When the pair left Kfar Nahum, silent tears tracked Chaya's cheeks, and the hollowness of hunger made them both light-headed and restless.

They continued westwards across the northern tip of the Sea of Galilee and approached the town of Gennesaret from the east. They came to a stand of willow trees that grew near the steep shoreline within sight of the town. Chaya removed most of her clothing in the trees' shelter, keeping only her thin undergarment on, and then together they bathed in the lake and scrubbed their hair.

A burn from the cruel use of an iron fire poker still streaked across the back of Chaya's neck and shoulder. It was the work of an ill-tempered cook from the week before. It no longer looked as red as it had previously. As she sank into the water, Haim carefully wiped it, patting and touching to release the dust dried in the damaged skin before guiding her down into the waters again to float away the grime. He did this several times until the wound showed pink and she complained that it was more tender for his attention. But it was clean now. She re-dressed and he wrung out his wet clothing and they stood in the shade under the willows and looked towards Gennesaret.

As they approached the town, they came upon a blind man waiting on passers-by and asking for alms. Oddly, he sat a considerable distance from both the town and the road. They made their way up to him, and he turned expectantly at the sound of their footsteps.

"We don't have any money," Chaya said.

At the sound of her voice, the blind man pulled back into himself. He said nothing in reply.

"Can you tell us if this is Gennesaret?" Haim asked, and the sun-baked man also shifted at the sound of Haim's voice but said nothing.

"Can you hear us?" Chaya asked.

"I hear you," the man said.

"Is this Gennesaret?" she asked.

"Yes, it's Kinnereth of old."

"Are things well in the town?"

The wizened man's cracked lips pursed and twisted. It was as though he held a cracked almond shell in his mouth and sought to extract the nut by his tongue and lips alone. Haim looked down at the man's hands to confirm they were there, and they appeared to be in good working order. When one lifted to comb through his beard, the action confirmed his ability. Still, the mouth twisted, and the blind man gave no reply.

Chaya sat then, her clothing still wet from the lake, and the man reacted to this with a sightless, distressed expression.

"You are a long way from the lake," Haim said. "You must need water. You have no shade."

"I would not take water from a gentile," the old man said.

"I'm not—" Haim began.

The old man waved his hand in the air before him, his lips suddenly open and empty. "I know by your accent," he said. When Chaya breathed in to speak, the man cast his off-target gaze in her direction as well. "Nor a Samaritan. You have their accent. You people will always be strangers in this land—corrupters, half-converts, Assyrian slaves, Babylonian refuse. I will not drink water that either of you have touched. You have no business in these parts."

The old man sat then in silence. Where his clothes had slipped, the man's exposed skin was inflamed, and thin whisps of hair stuck to his bare shoulders and nearly bald crown. His beard was also long and thin where it existed at all. The vacant eyes were glassy and white, though with health and care and sight, he might have at one time been handsome. He lifted and pointed a hand first at Haim, then Chaya. It was a hand that never would have been handsome. It sported the thick, knobby knuckles of a poorly pruned branch joined by protruding twigs of fleshless bone and skin.

"A Samaritan woman and a gentile man, together spying in Galilee and inquiring about the welfare of its cities. You don't even know the proper names. An unclean alliance on an unholy mission. Is there to be an invasion of Galilee then, not just from Jerusalem but other cursed lands as well? Are you allied with the Sadducees? Or are you just vultures circling a kill to steal a bit of flesh for yourselves like your kind has always done?"

"We're hungry!" Chaya protested in childlike tones. It startled Haim. She sounded like she had when he first found her, and he realized how much she had changed in the last year, even if her size had changed little.

"Hungry," the old man said. He tilted his head down to the ground. "The cursed King Jannaeus is hungry. He devoured the pagan lands, though they cost all that Galilee had, and now that Galilee can give no more, he devours Galilee as well. Judeans have spilled Galilean blood again and again. Is that not enough? Now your people also come for their share of the spoils?"

"I don't . . ." Chaya started, but her voice cracked. She tried again. "My family."

"Samaritans," the old man said.

"Yes."

"They are dead, I trust."

"Yes." Tears formed and she quickly wiped them away.

"Soon, you will be too," the blind man said, "travelling about Galilee with a gentile, in the service of an evil king."

"I'm not a gentile—" Haim began again, but the swing of the old man's arm was violent enough to startle him a second time into silence.

"Go to the town," the old man said. "If you leave with your lives, then there is not a man left in Kinnereth noble enough to defend it and they deserve their fate. But I'll not take your water. Go."

The old man put his head down, lips to one shoulder, refusing even to sightlessly regard their departure. Chaya was already down the path before Haim rose. He stood over the old man and looked at the curve of his back, at the ridge of spine visible through the cloth. Without moving his footing, Haim looked about the man for some sign of bread, but there was none.

He wanted to argue with the man. He felt the pull of boldness and even cruelty. Here, he could fight back against all the hatred that had ever lashed against his existence, do something other than run, protect in some way other than flight, and cause hurt instead of receive it. He was no longer a boy. He was no longer small. Her tears made him believe that action was necessary and that necessity was as much for himself as it was for her. He was here to act and inaction would be a violation, would bring a reckoning. He would be damned if he did nothing. He trembled above the old man, staring at the profile of the boney back. He considered what his axe would do against such a back, and his anger grew murderous. He focused his thoughts on the axe. It was a weapon made for war, not for mules or firewood or birds brought down by his sling. The axe was for killing men, and he would start here.

Her hand on his arm woke him. She tugged as she had at his mantle earlier and led him back down the path to the road. He followed behind her, reluctantly, and they had gone many steps before he finally came alongside her. Then they walked hand in hand.

Just as they approached the town proper, they came to a stream running from the hills to their right. Without words, they agreed and followed the stream up the hill. They stopped to drink and fill their water skin, and then they continued travelling westwards, waiting until the town was clear from their path before turning south once more. As they crossed the creek, Chaya slipped but Haim caught and carried her through the rest of the current.

In the fertile black grassland beyond the stream, they passed below a tract of vineyards and onto the formal Plain of Gennesaret. The plain extended south along the western shore of the lake.

A distant pillar of smoke billowed as though one of the southern towns were burning. They were too far away to tell for sure. Chaya continued walking confidently in that direction, and Haim followed. Her hand was not on his arm now, but the memory of lifting her across the stream sustained him. They might be going to a furnace or a battlefield or something worse. But she was determined—she was going there. So he followed.

14

90 BCE

AFTER THE BLIND man's rebuff, Haim and Chaya travelled slower and slower around the Sea of Galilee. Late one day, they came to a new town that one traveller called Taricheae but another said was Magdala. The town lay nestled on a stretch of flat land between Mount Arbel's sharp slopes and the sea's sombre waters. The city's trade pierced the sky above with pillars of oily smoke. The smell of pickling and smoking smothered the cleaner smells of stripped wood and drying barrels from the cooper's trade.

As the two travellers stood on the edge of the lakeside food market, the smells of cured and fresh fish mingled in their lungs. Their hollowness inside pumped madness into their limbs and together, crouching in the shade of another willow, they devised anxious plans. They considered whether Chaya should cause a distraction, giving Haim a chance to steal unnoticed, or whether they should just madly rush and consume all they could swallow before the beatings began. Chaya was more inconspicuous while Haim was the faster runner, but they could not decide who would be the better thief. They were too hungry to properly plot.

A boat pulled up in the shallows nearby, the men aboard dragging their nets up from inside the hull. They began to sort their catch, pulling each fish from the mesh and tossing most of them into some receptacle out of sight. Haim was trying to explain another idea to Chaya when she suddenly squealed and fled from the willow's shade towards the boat. She ran with no regard for her bare feet on the rocks at the water's edge. Her legs hit the lake and she kept walking, fully clothed, before dropping into the water and thrashed madly, half submerged, seemingly trying to swim in the shallow shoreline. She emerged, soaked head to toe with a huge and ugly fish in her small hands. Haim picked up their packs and came to the water's edge while the watching men in the boat said something to one another before going back to sorting fish.

The soaked girl practically glowed and held the great fish up for Haim to see. It was still alive but lethargically so, having weathered the net and the boat's hold before being tossed back into the lake.

"What is it?" Haim asked.

"I don't know," Chaya said. "But I've seen the traders eat it. They like it. The Jews won't eat it. Samaritans don't eat it either, but right now, I don't care. It lives a long time out of water, I know that. You have to make a fire."

They backtracked up the lakeshore, settling in a spot with the large willow between them and the market. They gathered driftwood from the shore and thrust a long stick through the great flat-headed fish's gills, pinning it to the sand. It stared up at the sun with one bulging, lidless, golden-brown eye and gasped, though Haim found it hard to believe that the creature still lived. He set Chaya to collecting what twigs and dried leaves she could. He found a flat piece of bark about the size of a serving tray, scooped sand into it, and then carefully carried it towards the nearest column of smoke.

At the first fire, the men there pretended to have trouble with his coastal accent, and they mocked him both in Aramaic and in awkward phrases from old Hebrew. At the second fire, the men were younger and even more scornful and drove him away. He was searching out a third fire, still holding his sand-filled tray before him, anxious of leaving Chaya on her own and afraid of not finding fire, when a mere boy, younger even than himself, found him. The boy dumped a few coals from a clay pot onto Haim's tray of sand. The boy followed Haim back to the lakeshore, saw the place where he was going, and then departed without a word.

Back at the shoreline, Chaya had already butchered the great fish. The guts floated out on the lake, and the fish itself lay cleaned and splayed open on two sticks that were threaded through its flesh. Chaya kept her makeshift frame upright, leaning it against a small log to keep the whole fish out of the sand. The smile on her face at seeing him and his little pile of coals was the most beautiful thing Haim had ever inspired. In that moment, he did not feel hunger but rather a different, unsettled feeling in his stomach. Something he did not understand. Something to do with her.

He knelt and tipped the coals into the place she had prepared. Their hands were identically darkened and cracked and worn, and as they knelt with the coals between them, their four hands worked together in a practised rhythm, each piling leaves and twigs atop the coals. Then they both crouched down to bring their mouths level with the shrouded ember and blew. Chaya's sour breath passed through the leaves and twigs and washed over Haim before pushing the developing smoke against his cheek. He blew from the opposite side, trying to tease the smoke back in her direction, and the laughter that emerged at the first sudden flame was the purest joy that the Magdala shoreline had witnessed in seasons upon seasons.

He left her to finish adding the larger sticks, for she knew what she was doing with fire. He turned to the fish to inspect her crude axe butchery, and he once again mourned the loss of the long Galilean knife, although something even smaller would have been more practical for this task. For all the flaws of her tool, the fish was well prepared and the sticks were green. He was impressed by the amount of effort it must have taken to force the sticks through the fish as she weaved the two-stick frame through the tough skin and thick meat.

He walked up the shore and found a large rock, almost more than he could carry, and took it back to her. When he got to the fire, he was staggering under the weight, and Chaya helped him lower it until the straight, flat edge nestled up to the fire.

"I should have made the fire by the rock," she said.

"Carry all the wood there or the rock here." He shrugged to show her his indifference and felt the relief in his shoulders when he did so. He shrugged again without thinking and then noticed her watching him.

"I'll go get water," she said and left with the water skin to fill it in a small nearby creek that ran into the lake.

She was at the creek when Haim heard a sound behind him, and he whirled around in the late-afternoon light, feeling about him for the axe but knowing it lay by the fish and his heart raced as he tried to focus on what was before him. There was dizziness in his head from the sudden movement and hunger and effort, and it took him a second to realize that it was the young Jewish boy again. The boy held a basket, and from it he removed a small loaf of bread and a clutch of olives and figs in a string bag. He looked around until he found Haim's bark tray. He brushed away the remaining sand and arranged the loaf and the figs and the olives on the tray. The olives threatened to roll away, but the boy shaped the figs into a barrier, and they held the olives in place.

Haim stood staring at the tray of food on the ground, the richness it contained, the miracle of its arrival. Blood returned to his head and steadied him, and yet he still struggled to believe what he saw.

"Where are your parents?" the boy asked.

Haim thought about how to answer. He thought about the Tyrant of Dora and the old scribe and his mother. "The Egyptians killed them," Haim said, "in the war after Dora fell."

This left a lot unexplained since the war predated his birth, but the Jewish boy gave no response at first. "They killed my father too," the boy finally said. "Before I was born. The same war. And my two sisters died as well. My mother survived. She's a musician. My uncle looks after us now."

Haim's throat constricted and he could not speak. The boy was smaller than him, but not much smaller.

"It's good that you still have your sister," the Jewish boy said. Both boys stood then for a while. Silence hung between them, as though they were waiting for some tension to pass. They did not look directly at each other, and after a few minutes, the Jewish boy turned and went back up the beach to his community fire.

When Chaya returned, her face shone from having washed at the stream, and she looked beautiful. Haim reached out to take the heavy water skin from her and then stepped aside and pointed at the tray.

She let out a whimper and ran to the tray and knelt beside it and tore the loaf apart, and he knelt with her, and together they consumed a third of the loaf in a rush of tearing and chewing and tearing some more.

He gave her an olive, and her face brightened with happiness.

"We have to save some of this for tomorrow," Haim said. "We'll eat the fish tonight. The figs and olives will keep longer."

She nodded and tore off two more pieces of bread, giving one to Haim before taking a rag from his pack and wrapping up the rest, stuffing the olives and figs into the soft interior of the loaf.

"Where did this come from?"

Haim gestured with one hand towards the smokers while adjusting the larger pieces of wood on the fire. "A boy."

The driftwood burned fast, and soon he was able to

prop the skewered fish over the embers with one side resting on the rock they had placed by the fire and the other on a small log Chaya had found. The sticks were long, and they could sit on the small log as well, the stick-ends between them, carefully managing the fire as the fish started to sizzle. There was no salt to find in the Sea of Galilee and they had no spices, but when they finally began to tear into the smoky, charred flesh, it lacked nothing. Their hunger yearned for the oils and the fatty flesh and made no report whatsoever regarding flavour.

The sun was beginning to set when Chaya started to shiver in her wet clothes. Back under the willow, the veil of trailing leaves and the misshapen trunk provided some privacy. Haim held up a blanket, adding some more cover so she could change. They hung her wet clothes to dry as the light faded. A glut of fires sprung up throughout the town as every house lit its hearth. The two arranged their mantles and blanket under the willow's dark solitary shelter, settling under a roof of wordless whispering leaves to sleep.

The noise of the fishermen woke them close to dawn, the men moving their boats back into the light waves and rowing away from the town.

They stayed in Magdala for three days, and in addition to the discarded fish that the Jews considered unclean, the townsfolk occasionally gave them gifts of bread. Despite this, none would welcome or talk with them. They were given no kind words beyond the few from the Jewish boy on the first day.

On the fourth day, five men from the town came down to the willow. They looked related—older men, heavy browed, thickly bearded, all five equally silent. One carried a basket tied up in a large cloth. He set the basket on the ground. Finally, the one who seemed to be the oldest spoke.

"You need to be out of town by evening," he said. "Which direction you go is entirely up to you."

Haim shifted from one foot to the other. He gestured as though about to make a statement but said nothing. The men ignored Chaya and stared at Haim with hard eyes as though daring him to contradict their order.

Chaya unwrapped the cloth from the basket and transferred its contents to their two packs.

Haim made a gesture again as though to say something but one of the men distracted him by retrieving the now-empty basket and discarded cloth.

"Gone by evening," the eldest said again, and then the delegation turned away and left Haim and Chaya alone again under the willow.

15

90 BCE

Mount Nitai and Mount Arbel towered above Magdala, their heights encroaching on the town's borders. Slopes of loose stone and sheer cliffs loomed large near the waterline, and the town filled in the space between the mountains and the shore. Magdala, with its great stone backdrop, had held Chaya and Haim longer than any Galilean town had before, but now they were on the move again.

"We can pass for Jews somewhere else," Chaya said to Haim as they packed up their few things under the willow tree.

Haim stood to one side and watched. "Our accents are giving us away." He noticed his sling had somehow dropped near the base of the tree.

"We need to go somewhere where we can explain them away."

"Farther south is either Nabataea or Judea," he said,

picking up the sling. He was unsure where to store it, so he just held it in his hands. With the food in their packs, he would not need to hunt for a few days. He tucked it into his belt. "And the crucifixions were south of here."

Chaya looked up at him. "I'm not going back to Nabataea."

"There was a stream that flowed down between the two mountains," Haim said. "It might provide a way inland."

Peeking under the willow's curtain, Haim could see the green mountain base covered with patches of open grass and small stands of trees separated by sections of exposed rock the same white and orange shades as the higher cliffs.

"Let's go that way," Chaya said. "Along the stream, through the mountains. We'll see who's there. Maybe they won't know our accents so well."

As they made their way out of Magdala, a boy separated himself from a line of wagons and ran towards them. He stopped before Haim. He was the Jewish boy from the first night, and he offered a gift wrapped in rough cloth. Haim accepted the gift, and the boy turned and fled.

As they resumed walking, Haim unwrapped the cloth and discovered a small blade made of one smooth piece of flattened iron, its edges crisp and clean. Haim instinctually wrapped the unfinished handle with the small cloth until it fit comfortably in his hand. The blade itself was fine and sharp, perfect for preparing meat. He looked at Chaya, at the knife, then at Chaya again, but she said nothing. She smiled at him and adjusted her pack and continued walking. Haim rewrapped the cloth around the blade and slipped it into the pouch he wore at his waist for sling stones. They looked ahead to the mountains before them.

Haim's mother had been an unknowable draw and terror. The days when her sun shone had filled him with eagerness, but those days had never lasted. When things turned dark, his mind had always raced to find some source of blame. What mistake had he made? What grave error had he committed? It was never clear. She would sometimes drive him away in a flash of anger, but the cold weight of simple scorn had been more common. He had been unable to bear either state, the anger or the scorn, and could never figure out which punishment he preferred. Not that he ever had a choice. She would never explain why she punished him so, just would retell the story of his abominated birth.

Though she had hated him, Haim's need for his mother had never left. His ignorant hunger had validated the contempt crowning all her expressions, yet he was ever eager for her company. All she had to show was the barest hint of warmth, and he was hers. At least, so it had been.

Over time, he had finally begun to judge his senses as treacherous—they served only to pull him towards unhappiness. His fear of her and his yearning for her were one, and there was no cure. Such an inclination towards self-destruction was yet further proof that he was irredeemably flawed and her scorn justified.

As Haim and Chaya approached the gorge leading from the lake into the mountains, the landscape had the same brooding spirit as the widow. The opening lay in shadow, the rim of the hill nearest the lake cut by a recent slide. The people of Magdala called this place the Valley of Doves and others called it the Valley of Wind, and in that dual name, Haim knew he heard a lie, for doves were welcoming and wind was not. Mountains loomed above, and he expected to find a gorge with a narrow trail along its rim that they might traverse at the risk of their lives. He had planned to view the opening fully to confirm his suspicions. When they arrived, however, they found the valley much wider than expected. The well-travelled path before them led up Mount Nitai's steep slope on the right side of the gorge. This mountain looked like good goat country—at least for the goats. The jagged crags and unstable ground of loose stones would make a shepherd's day difficult.

Partway up the steep ascent, the path levelled out before rising once more into a near-vertical climb. Taking that path would be a terrible chore, though there were no better options for scaling Mount Nitai's heights. Haim could climb it in perhaps half a day of hard work, but all thought of that treacherous path left him as he turned to assess the other options.

Mount Arbel on the valley's left flank commanded more serious attention. The way up Mount Arbel's summit had small stretches like Nitai's bushy and passable but intimidating slopes. There were even patches of stunted and bent trees, but the rest was a fortress of bare limestone that struck upwards in defiance of the sky. Caves punctured the cliffs and great gashes ran from the sky to valley floor. Massive boulders sat precariously on steep slopes as if they were a giant's trap waiting to crush an army with a mighty crash.

But it was the valley itself that held all promise of safe passage. The valley floor was flat and wide and populated by myrtle and oak, and the stream that ran through it was small and unthreatening. The valley welcomed them, and yet Haim sensed danger on the path ahead. To him, it was not the Valley of Doves or the Valley of Wind but the Valley of Her. Not to be trusted. He said nothing to Chaya about these premonitions. The day was sunshine, and nothing could be seen or heard to warrant his fear.

Last of all, Haim turned to study Chaya's face. Her eyes were set on the valley before them filled with an expression he interpreted as happiness and expectation. "I'm ready," she said.

He had no idea why she was ready or what she was apparently happy about. "You look tired," he said, without offering to take her pack.

"When we run out of food, it will be lighter," she said. "I can carry it."

They put the lake, the Sea of Galilee, behind them and set out up the valley trail. There was enough heat still left in the day to make them sweat. Haim guessed that they would stop and make camp in a few hours. With the stream at hand, both drinking and bathing would be easy. There was nothing to worry about, yet he walked with a frown and responded to Chaya's chatter as succinctly as possible to avoid dampening her mood. She spoke of the need for a family and her time of womanhood, which would come soon. She needed an older woman to teach her. As they walked, it seemed to Haim that she was telling him another year of their strange pairing would not be. She needed to find a family who would take her in. She would accept the role of adopted orphan or servant—either would suit her. She described many possibilities but never mentioned what his part in any of it might be.

As she talked, Haim felt a new weight begin to wear him down. The day was warm, but he felt increasingly cooled and dull. His mind turned away from her speech and considered the trees, the stony grey and brown of exposed rock, the rare tufts of green. There would be bandits here. It was not a possibility but a certainty.

Chaya walked lightly, as though her pack weighed less than it did, and she continued to speak with energy about imagined things. Haim felt the coldness within him grow. He recognized the familiar seeds of despair arising within. This valley was another place like the lost lands east of the Jordan, and he felt darker the longer they walked within it.

There were sounds ahead, those of animals in distress and a human voice. They came from beyond a turn in the path. Chaya kept talking, unaware. Haim's feelings continued to churn inside, but something lay ahead, and his mind divided as he fought to push down the growing darkness within and focus on the new threat ahead while distracted by Chaya's lack of awareness.

Chaya grew more excited as she shared a new idea with hopeful energy, and then the sound came again, confirming Haim's fears. He was ten paces ahead of her, almost in a full sprint, before he was fully aware that he had chosen to move, and when he rounded the turn in the path, he had the sling out and fitted with a stone the size of a hen's egg. The sling was already arcing overhead when he cleared the corner. The first thing he saw was an old man in the distance, down on the ground, his shepherd's rod having been thrown towards a small collection of goats some fifty feet in front of him. His toss had covered less than half the intended distance, perhaps intended to distract the jackal that had the goats trapped in a natural hollow between two sprawling hawthorns at the base of the cliff. The injured shepherd was shouting and the jackal was growling and advancing on the goats and the bleat of the animals was the sound Haim had heard down the trail. He let the sling make one more circuit to adjust his aim and then let loose. The stone released on a fast, flat arc and hit the jackal on a rearward rib with the sound of cracking followed by a loud, nearly human screech as the animal spun sideways and went down. Its skinny rear quarters twisted wildly and when it scrambled back to its feet, the old shepherd yelled louder and Haim still ran and then the jackal was running as well, mad with shock and pain, but away from the frothing old man and blindly towards Haim, only at the last second seeing the slinger. The jackal swerved around Haim. It fled with a wild and limping gait as a wheezing squeak came from its mouth. Then it was past Haim and careening down the path as Chaya turned the corner.

Chaya froze and stared at the jackal racing towards her. Haim lifted another stone from his pouch and the sling only took one circuit this time and he let it fly with a hint of panic in his throw but his aim was nearly true. Had the creature not turned, the stone would have just grazed its cheek. But the jackal did turn. It was almost upon Chaya when it cast a quick eye back at Haim, its head cocked at such an angle that the errant stone connected, broke the bone below the creature's left eye, and sent it into a tangled roll, its legs and tail trailing in a strange spasm through the air. It landed just past Chaya, twitching and trying to right itself. More than stunned, the beast was a flurry of self-circling spasms, unable to control its limbs, fighting for coordination, and then Haim was upon the creature. He wrapped the sling about the animal's throat and tightened the bind and tightened it further. The creature's violent spasms finally coordinated and the animal heaved and tried to snap and stand and then its movements became erratic again. Then irregular. Then, after a long while, it stilled.

When he was sure the creature was dead, Haim looked up and ahead and saw the way they had come from Migdal. His back was to Chaya and the goats and the shepherd. He unwound the sling from the jackal's neck and stood. He nudged the creature's head with his foot, and it flopped on a loose neck. There was no blood but for the little that had filled the animal's glassy eye. Neither stone had penetrated skin, though both had broken bones. The old scribe had told him tales of the fear that slings caused on battlefields, the weapon that killed at a distance without drawing blood, that could bring death straight across the field or arcing in from above, whose projectiles the land provided in plenty. This was the first time he had ever killed anything with it larger than a bird.

Standing over the creature and still breathing hard, Haim looked down at the empty form on the ground. The animal did not move. He stepped over it, moving away from everyone and the beast. He walked back towards Migdal in silence and alone, and none followed. He heard only the sound of his heavy breathing. He walked until he came to his pack, which he did not remember dropping. He shouldered it, turned, and retraced his steps to the dead jackal. He imagined that Chaya and the shepherd were both watching him. He felt that he had just won a new place in a new community. He anticipated the shepherd's praise. Chaya would proclaim that he had saved her, and he would accept her childish excitement. He expected that the shepherd's gratitude would buy them entrance into whatever society the man belonged to, and in this way, he would give Chaya what she had talked about on the trail. He had won her a home.

All of these ideas coursed through Haim, but when he came to the jackal, he waited. He did not look up right away to receive his praise. Instead, he crouched over the lifeless fur, the violent killing already fading from his mind as though he had played no part in the struggle. He studied the creature's light gold and rich brown colouring and, for the first time, noticed how enormous the beast was. This observation made the animal seem even more remote from any action he had taken part in.

When Haim finally looked up, the path ahead of him was empty. The jackal's final tumble had taken it to the edge of the trail where dense foliage blocked the view of the clearing and the little hollow with the goats. Chaya had gone on into the clearing and Haim could hear voices in the distance, but he could not see anyone. Neither Chaya nor the shepherd acknowledged him or the dead animal.

Haim tried to shoulder the jackal, but it was too big and would not fit alongside the pack. He considered dropping the pack to carry the jackal, but he needed two hands to hold the jackal's forelegs over each shoulder and would not be able to carry his pack in his hands. He tried carrying the jackal in his arms, but he only made it a few steps before needing to set the creature down. Finally, he reset the pack to his front, the weight of it bowing out before him. Then, with his hands and back both free, he slung the jackal over his shoulders like a second pack. In this way, he could finally walk with the carcass and came into the clearing.

Chaya was kneeling beside the shepherd with the goats gathered about them.

"Put that thing down, you fool!" the old shepherd shouted at Haim. "The smell of it. The goats will run off again, and we'll spend the rest of the day trying to find them."

"He's hurt his leg," Chaya called over to Haim.

"My ankle, child. Just my ankle." The voice was kind and quiet when he spoke to Chaya.

"Should I leave the jackal here?" Haim asked.

"Jackal?" The old man snorted. "Jackal. That's a wolf, boy. You killed a wolf. You had better be sure it's dead."

"It's dead."

"Well, be sure of it. And leave it there. Leave yourself there too. You'll stink like wolf, now. Bring it with you, and Noach will cure the hide."

Haim did not know how to both bring it and stay where he was, and he did not see anyone else in the clearing who might be Noach. He lowered the drooping animal back to the ground and then dropped his pack as well. The goats eyed him suspiciously and bleated a few questions at the old shepherd. He and Chaya spoke too quietly for Haim to overhear.

After a few minutes, the old man rose to his feet, and Chaya supported him on one side. The man held his recovered shepherd's rod in his other hand.

"He lives up on the mountain," Chaya said. "There's a village there. These goats were lost. Came down the mountain."

Haim barely registered the ending of her declaration. Word that the man lived up the mountain stopped him from hearing clearly. He looked up at Arbel, at the imposing cliffs. He noticed again the shadows of caves and for the first time saw footpaths between them. The idea of bringing goats up or down those heights, of climbing it for any reason, made his legs weak.

Chaya and the shepherd started to walk. The old man limped. Chaya supported.

"Come behind, boy!" the shepherd shouted over his shoulder. "Keep your distance. The goats have your scent."

The man took to steep paths that were barely paths at all. They climbed narrow ledges in the cliff face and it often seemed that the shepherd was the one supporting Chaya, keeping her from falling out into open space. The goats held tightly behind the girl and the shepherd, moving ahead as soon as the passage was clear.

Haim struggled to follow. As he climbed, his legs burned and his back ached. Bearing both the pack and the wolf, Haim could not use his hands for support. He followed the old shepherd and Chaya, climbing on legs that shook more and more the higher they climbed. He looked down and was immediately dizzy. He looked ahead. Falling was a real danger.

When he finally reached the top of the mountain, Haim was barely able to breathe. His legs wobbled from exhaustion now. The climb, the load, the day's late heat, but most of all the wolf's still-warm body pressed against Haim's thin frame all made Haim's body burn with a sickly heat. His face and neck and torso ran with sweat. He could smell himself and the wolf and was unclear which odour was strongest.

The wolf's head lolled to one side, and its hind legs trailed, occasionally swinging into Haim's own.

Haim looked around. He was alone. He had lagged as directed, but they did not wait for him at the top. The trail faded into rock. He set the wolf down beside a clump of dead trees surrounded by a tall tangle of dense bushes and waited for calm to come again to his legs and arms. When he picked up his load again, he realized that in resting, he had also been waiting, but no one had come for him. He would have to go looking.

He staggered back to his feet and followed what seemed to be a trail between the mass of bushes and dead trees and then he saw the village. The top of the mountain was sharp edged on its northern valley side, providing a broad view of the Sea of Galilee below and distant mountains beyond. Away from that edge, however, the mountain was only a slightly sloping plateau crowded with boulders, patches of greenery and scattered homes. It was only beyond the village, to the south, that the mountain's slope began to steepen again.

Haim trudged on, heading towards the sound of voices. He saw Chaya from a distance. A crowd had gathered around her and the old shepherd and everyone in the village it seemed was talking at once. Haim stopped well short of the crowd and tried to piece together what tale Chaya was still telling. Her face was bright as though she were a long-lost daughter found again by her relatives. She seemed to be telling the crowd that she had saved the old shepherd, somehow driving the wolf away herself so she could attend to the old man's injury. Haim could not catch everything she said, but that was the gist of what he heard.

Chaya did not seem to notice him. She was distracted by the many gathered around her. A few of the villagers looked up at him briefly, but most ignored him as well.

A man finally approached and introduced himself as

Noach. He was the one who knew hides. He inspected the wolf, noting the lack of blood. "A lucky blow," the man said.

Another man helped Noach tie the animal's feet around a pole, and together they hefted the animal between them. It took some effort. Noach looked at Haim, and Haim met his gaze. Whether the skinner was about to comment on Haim's killing such a beast or carrying it and the pack up the cliff by himself made no difference. He just yearned for some kind of acknowledgement.

"A pole," Noach said, indicating the animal hanging between himself and his helper. "It keeps the stink off. No need to wrap it all over yourself." The skinner winked at Haim. "For next time."

The skinner and his companion moved away from the buildings and disappeared down a trail. Another man then walked up. He looked at Haim in a way that made Haim feel uncomfortable, then the man suddenly tossed a bundle at him. Haim instinctually started to dodge, but then he caught on to the man's intent and caught the package before it fell.

"A robe," the man said. "Some soap. Go back down and get clean in the stream. You can't bathe up here. Get yourself and your clothes clean. You look like you were dirty before. With the stink of wolf, you're worse. I've a shed you can sleep in tonight."

Haim felt the weave of the robe in his hands. Something coarse. A gesture of hospitality that Haim registered as rejection.

Haim traced his way back to the cliff's edge. Anger churned within him as he climbed back down. When he reached the valley floor, he drifted towards exhaustion and the despair from earlier in the day grew dark again within him. He scrubbed himself and his clothes. Gloom followed his ablutions and laundry. He put on the coarse robe and had no desire to do anything more. The sky was clear. It was not yet dark, but in such a deep place, the light would fade quickly. If he did not start climbing soon, the coming dusk would hang slippery shadows across the valley and he would be unable to navigate back to the village.

Standing beside the stream, Haim considered staying where he was. He could sleep alone in the woods as he had in the days before Chaya. He had not been alone for over a year. Something about it here, on the valley floor, attracted him. The sound of early evening and the leaves and stream soothed the tumultuous feelings inside. It promised peace undisturbed by human voices. It was the first night in over a year when he did not feel responsible for someone else.

In the end, he climbed back up to the mountaintop village. Chaya had their food and he was hungry. His legs were more tired now on this, his second ascent, but the air was cooler and his hands were free, so this climb felt easier. As he neared the top again, he became aware of a hardness within his chest that was different than the damp heaviness he had experienced on the valley floor. It made him wonder if anger could callus over like a work-hardened hand, becoming a permanent barrier to protect a man against the world's bitter winds.

At the top of the trail, the man who had provided the robe and soap was waiting for him. "You can stay with us," the man said. "I am Yechiel."

Yechiel led Haim through the darkening village to a small house where he lived with his wife and four young children. There was a shed near the home. A bed was there for Haim. The family had already eaten, but Yechiel's wife provided Haim with a small plate. He ate slowly while the wide-eyed children watched and then he retreated to his solo shelter. Chaya had told their story already, and he had to infer what Chaya's version was from the comments Yechiel and his wife made while he ate.

Later, as he lay in the dark, Haim pieced together the comments into a cohesive narrative, the tale that Chaya must have told the villagers. Chaya was of a Jewish family who had settled in lands bordering Samaria, which would explain her accent. From what he understood, Haim was her stepbrother born from their father's first wife, a woman from Gaza, and Haim had lived most of his life with relatives in Gaza after his mother's death. Only recently had he returned to his father's household, which would explain their differing accents. Shortly after his arrival, their village had been massacred and only Haim and Chaya had escaped. There were gaps in this narrative, but it was all he could piece together that first night. She had invented a new past for them. He had the duty to catch up and not betray her inventions while he did so.

As he lay in the dark alone, he felt new things he could not name, but he could identify their cause. Killing the wolf caused one feeling, and the injured goat herder's contempt caused another. Chaya's apparent welcome into the village set against the skinner's mockery caused the third. His banishment, the climb down and bath and journey back up, his eating leftovers and being left to this dark shed all combined to cause the fourth. Under the willow tree, in Magdala's open air, he had been amid the town even if that town did not want him. He and Chaya had been there together. Not alone. Alone was now the fifth thing he felt. That she had created their story without consulting him caused the sixth. From the wolf kill in the late afternoon to these solitary ruminations in the night, he saw that he had become superfluous to his own story. That realization caused the seventh.

He found cause for more grievances, and it was late into the moon's arc when he realized that anger was keeping him from sleep and this was another thing that he could be angry about but otherwise could not name. He added up the causes for his grief, and it occurred to him, looking at the dark ceiling above, that he could not even follow the moon because of the roof. He had seen the moon or the stars or the rain every night for a year now. But this night, there was only dark. He added this to his grievances, the count of which he could no longer track.

16

90 BCE

THE VILLAGE OF Arbel was a collection of low stone structures with burnable roofs overlooking the Sea of Galilee. For the first few days, Haim did not see Chaya at all. He eventually found ways to catch sight of her between buildings or amid villagers who seemed keen to bring her into the routines of their lives. She did not grind wheat as many of the other girls her age did. She did not carry water. One specific family had finally taken charge of her and were teaching her to work with textiles. He sometimes saw her moving raw materials between buildings but mostly she seemed to sit with two other women and work clumps of wool with various hand tools. It took Haim some time to work out the order of things, but as far as he could tell, without daring to ask anyone, it seemed that she was learning to comb the wool and then brush it. For what purpose he did not know. She seemed to be making fluffy balls of wool that were undoubtedly cleaner, but he had no idea how this might turn, eventually, into thread or yarn.

Haim once saw her standing near a loom while one of the women patiently explained its workings. In the low light of evening, he watched her practise as the woman provided instructions out of Haim's earshot. She was stiff and awkward at this task. It did not seem to Haim that Chaya was comfortable with the loom, but the women gathered around did not seem to notice.

⤶

On Haim's first full day in the village, Noach took him aside in the afternoon and inspected his knife's blade. He shaped a leather handle for it without explaining what he was doing. When he was done, he sat Haim down on a stump in the tanner's yard.

"You sharpen it this way," Noach said, drawing a picture in the dirt to show Haim the shape he should be sharpening the blade into.

"I get thinner and sharper blades my way," Haim said.

"That don't last to their second cut. Always give them a bevelled shape. That way, you have strength, durability, and sharpness. Your way is only sharp."

Next, Noach inspected the axe blade, giving it the same critique. It was a full morning of labour before Haim had the axe's and knife's edges sharpened to the skinner's satisfaction. For the next two days, Haim used the knife to skin the wolf as Noach directed and scraped at the hide's wet interior, removing the excess flesh and thinning the membrane.

"Don't remove so much that you start seeing the hair

through the skin," Noach said, "but you need to make it thinner still."

Haim worked the skin.

"You've cut through it here," Noach said.

"The knife's too sharp," Haim said.

Noach shook his head. "You're just doing it wrong." He took the skin from Haim and sewed up the hole. "Now, do the rest, but don't cut through it. Make it thin, but not too thin. Hold the skin tighter. Stop letting it slack."

By the end of the second day of Noach's instruction, Haim's hands hurt as much as his shoulders.

The stench of the following days would become Haim's strongest memory of the process of preserving the hide: the smell of urine, the smell of the wolf's brain chopped and ground and beat in a stone pot until it was a pink froth, the smell of the brain slurry as it was heated and rubbed into the flesh side of the wolf's pelt, the smell of smoke transmuting the curing skin.

His second strongest memory of those nauseating tasks was tactile, flesh to flesh: the exhaustion in his hands and shoulders as he worked the skin, stretching it, drying it, flexing it for long hours to resist nature's hardening and, in doing so, creating something beautiful and supple.

On the days Noach did not need him, Haim worked for Yechiel. He chopped a great deal of wood for the family since his axe was good and Yechiel did not have one like it. Haim cleared stones and weeds and hunted rodents with the sling to protect the family's stores. When he killed one of the small animals, he buried it in Yechiel's field to fertilize the ground. He thought of the old scribe's mixture of kitchen scraps and seashells and wondered how both sea scraps and dead rodents both managed to enrich the soil, but Yechiel offered no wisdom on these or any other matters. Yechiel would explain what to do but not how it worked. He did not have the old scribe's instinct to teach.

The bindings on Haim's axe head tore loose one afternoon, and Yechiel's young boy, Ira, was there to see it happen.

"What are you going to do now?" Ira asked.

Haim thought of the old goat-stealer. "I'll show you," he said. Haim gathered up the loose wooden wedges and put them into his sling pouch for safekeeping. He left the axe head and handle where they lay. The two went walking.

They found a reasonably sized target quickly. Ira pointed it out. It took a moment for Haim to name it.

"A hyrax," Haim finally said. "Its legs are too short."

It was the better part of an hour before they found a hare. The creature made two large bounds to put some distance between itself and its watchers. It settled itself then, as though intending to ignore them.

"Just stay quiet," Haim whispered. He unwound his sling as Yechiel's boy watched. He loaded the swing and moved smoothly into his windup, letting the sling circle one extra time to impress the boy, and then released the stone as hard as he could. The hare flew into the air and somersaulted before landing with its head crushed and legs kicking frantically. Ira shouted in triumph and rushed across the field to the bundle of energetic fur. Haim put his sling away and took out the Magdala knife with its new handle. The boy came back some moments later, dragging the dead hare by a hind leg.

Ira stopped then and looked at the hare, the fur backcombed and matted with debris. He turned back to Haim. "I messed up the fur."

"I don't care about the fur." Haim took the animal from the boy and hoisted it up by one leg. He sliced the hare's leg as the goat-stealer had sliced the goat, searching for the creature's tendon. He was not as efficient as the goat-stealer. The hare's tendon was shaped differently and was smaller than the goat's. Eventually, Haim had one dangling white cord free, though his work was far bloodier than the goat-stealer's. It occurred to Haim that the nanny had been bled and left to hang and that any remaining blood would have been cold. That was the difference, but he said nothing to the boy about this realization. Ira watched him work with fascination glowing in his eyes, and he held the loose ends of the tendons while Haim finished pulling the cords from the carcass. The boy pressed his fingers one by one to the hard and slick cords as though each finger experienced the strange sensation differently.

"Should we bring the rest to your mom for the pot?" Haim asked.

"We don't eat hares," Ira said, looking up at Haim in confusion.

Haim recovered with a grin and the boy grinned back. They left the hare in the field, its head crushed and its legs butchered.

Haim reset the axe head on its handle, tapping the wedges back into place, then wound the tendons around the joint as the goat-stealer had done and tied the cords tight to finish the job. The boy was in awe as Haim explained how soaking and drying the shaft would set the joint and keep the bind strong. When Haim resumed chopping wood, Ira watched to see if the binds would hold and then left to tell his father what he had learned.

⁂

Haim often saw Pharisees among the people of Arbel.

"Why are they here?" Haim asked Noach one day.

Noach looked at him closely as though the question was strange.

"The war," Haim said in realization.

Noach nodded and said nothing.

The Pharisees lived in the cliffs below the village, finding shelter in the caves there and setting themselves apart from the village. One of the Pharisees stopped Haim early one afternoon. He did not touch Haim—the Pharisees would not touch any of the villagers. He spoke instead. "Come with me. Bring your axe."

Haim followed behind the man as they left the village. The man wore the clothing of Pharisees, a severe black robe with a wide belt and long tassels. Though Pharisees often had such ropes hanging from their robes, Haim had ever seen ones as long as those that this man wore. A leather band wrapped around the Pharisee's left wrist, circling up his arm before coming back to loop around two fingers and tying off at the wrist. A tiny box hung from this band. Haim wanted to ask the man about it. The old scribe had never worn or described such a strange adornment, but the Pharisee did not seem interested in conversation, so Haim stayed silent.

They made their way to the cliff's edge and took a narrow path down that Haim had never spotted before. They passed several caves before the Pharisee stopped and entered one. He began dragging a pole out from its depths. He lifted one end of the pole above his head and pushed it into a natural notch by the cave entrance. Haim guessed what the man was doing and looked to the other side. As he expected, there was another similar notch there chiselled into the stone. Haim figured out what the problem was just as the Pharisee spoke.

"I need the pole to be shorter," the Pharisee said.

"How much shorter?" Haim asked.

"So it fits."

Haim looked hard at the length of the pole and the distance between the two holes.

"Don't make it too short. I want a snug fit."

Haim nodded and estimated where to chop by sight alone. When he finished, the two tried to fit the pole in the notches again, but it was still a bit too big.

"I'll cut off a little more," Haim said.

"No. It's enough." The Pharisee pulled on the pole until it began to bend under the weight. Then he took Haim's axe and pounded its blunt side against the errant end of the pole. Wood dust smeared into the wall's dark stone as the pole began to budge, and with a few more hard swings, it slammed into the notch. The pole settled into a slightly angled horizontal line just above head height.

"There. Now all I need is a curtain," the Pharisee said.

Haim looked at him in confusion.

"Not from you. Your sister is making me one."

"Oh."

"Spinning and weaving are valuable skills for a wife to have. She has yet to learn everything she needs to know."

Haim looked at him in surprise.

"It's good that the people here can teach her," the man said.

Haim said nothing. The Pharisee looked to be nearly fifty years of age. Perhaps older.

"You two have been living like animals in the wilderness. The women here will teach her what she needs to know."

Haim waited.

"And you need to learn how to read," the man said.

"I can read," Haim said.

"Aramaic?"

"And old Hebrew. The old script. And some Greek. The scribe taught me."

"What scribe? A Galilean scribe? Or a proper Jerusalem teacher?"

"He was from Joppa," Haim said.

The Pharisee considered this but said no more.

That night Yechiel left the family dinner table early, taking both of the children with him and making it clear to Haim that he should stay behind. Yechiel's wife was pregnant, and she settled her hands on her rotund belly as she looked gravely at Haim.

"They will consult you," the woman said. "You are her oldest kin now that your father and the rest of your family are dead. As her brother, they will consult you. As a courtesy. Because it is right."

"The Pharisee is too old for her," Haim said.

The woman did not look directly at Haim. "He can give a child as good as any man, I would imagine. He has six already."

"Six? He's already had a wife?"

"Yes, she's currently in Jerusalem," Yechiel's wife said. "They've lost a few children but still have six. She and the children are safe enough there. The Sadducees are not hunting Pharisees' wives, but she cannot be with him. Since she cannot give him any more children, he can take another wife."

Haim's chest tightened. *I found her. I saved her from the well.*

He opened his mouth to say something, but the woman had turned away. She did not see him try to speak and therefore did nothing to draw any words from him. He thought about the supervisors and abusers across the Jordan River, about the times of illness and furtive meals and nights in the rain and days in the sun and sleeping under the willow tree at Magdala. All with Chaya. He wanted to scream but nothing came out.

The family returned and Haim left the house and returned to his solitary shed. There was no moon this night. No stars. He lay down but could not sleep.

"I found her," he said to the darkness, but he did not cry. He was too old now for crying.

17
90 BCE

THE MONTH OF Elul extended the heat of Av. The scorching sun was penetrating and merciless. But Elul was also a time of transition. By its end, fall would be in the air and the land would begin to cool. The rains would soon follow.

The Village of Arbel was a hive of activity at the beginning of Elul, the busiest that Haim had seen in his few months on the mountain. Messengers came from surrounding villages. Villagers hauled and stacked wood near the square, erected poles, and made sure the canopy over each stall was secure.

"What's going on?" Haim asked Noach.

Noach looked at the preparations and then at Haim. "Sukkot," Noach said. "What kind of Jew doesn't know about Sukkot?"

"I know it. But it happens in Jerusalem." Haim spoke

boldly, hoping that this was not yet another custom that the widow and the scribe had failed to practice at home.

Noach's expression softened. "It's the war," he explained. "The men can't go to Jerusalem with the king in his current state. He's the high priest as well. You know that, right?"

Haim nodded.

"We'll hold Sukkot here for now."

Haim watched the preparing villagers try to recreate a festival he had never seen before. An air of excitement infected everyone in the village as scattered voices frantically planned. Should they set up a ceremonial hut by each house in the village or should all the huts be gathered together in the town square? Where should the additional temporary shelters for visitors be situated? What trees were okay to cut down or prune for the festival and which should be preserved? The village talked more about this one event than anything Haim had ever seen.

The days passed, all was prepared, and the first day of the festival finally arrived. The Pharisees came up from their cliff-face caves, and the roadways swelled as distant neighbours from the surrounding villages joined in the festivities. Haim had not seen a crowd this large since the crucifixions at Bet Yerah.

The day passed and the evening came and Haim moved from one place to another in the newly crowded square as he tried to find somewhere to belong. As it grew dark and lamps and fires lit up the square, an elderly couple from another village stopped to talk to a boy in front of him. "This is Ira, Yechiel's boy," the old man proclaimed. The boy had his back to Haim, and Haim had not realized he was standing so close to someone he knew.

The woman praised the boy for growing as he had. Ira beamed and stretched up tall. Haim felt himself lean forwards to take a step, but his feet did not move. He wanted to speak, to tell them of his role in Yechiel's household and show that he too belonged to this village, but then the boy ran off and the couple went on their way. They did not seem to notice Haim.

Haim then noticed Noach standing across the way and talking about important matters with a group of fellow men, discussing Jerusalem's politics and the shift and flow of the war. No youths were part of the discussion, and when he passed by, the group did not open up to invite Haim in. He was too young.

The Pharisee he had helped, the one who had laid claim to Chaya, sat with the other Pharisees. He did not acknowledge Haim even when Haim passed in front of him. The Pharisee seemed unable to see Haim. His gaze passed over and through Haim as if through a shadow.

Haim found Chaya among the unmarried girls. He could not enter that circle to sit with her, for the unmarried boys did not sit with the unmarried girls in this village. From what he had gleaned, this custom was held throughout Galilee, but he did not know for sure. There was no one he could safely ask.

He did not associate with the boys his age. He was the skinner's assistant and jokes had been made early on about how he smelled because of that trade. Only the much younger Ira had time for Haim.

As the sun disappeared, he moved about by the light of fires and lamps. He stood under a canopy that had protected the festivalgoers earlier when the sun had been hot. Today was a Sabbath, a day of rest, so the poles had been erected before the festival. Despite the Torah's law, Haim wished he had a task to do, to carry something, chop something, do something. He decided a festival on the Sabbath was the worst sort of festival. He did not know where to stand or what to do. He was at odds with himself and everything in this event.

The goat herder brushed past before turning and meeting Haim's gaze. The man's eyes were dark and flat like Yechiel's wife's had been when she spoke of Chaya's future.

Haim's next interaction was with a stranger from another village, a mother swarmed by a dozen children, who offered Haim a miniature loaf of bread that had been cooked the day before and preserved for this Sabbath celebration. He accepted it and wanted to talk with her, but there was no place for him. Her brood claimed her attention.

Haim wondered if he still smelled like the wolf. He considered that perhaps his age—no longer a child but not yet a man—created this awkwardness. He felt unable to join this community's otherwise universal spirit of mirth and merriment. This day of rest and celebration was more taxing than any work Yechiel or Noach had given him.

The festival became a place for Haim to observe the strange expressions on the faces of those enjoying the night. There had been nothing in his mother's dark and isolated household like the untethered joy he witnessed here. The old scribe had never taken him to Jerusalem. Perhaps the joy Haim saw here was what he would have seen on that untaken pilgrimage.

The mood in the village was alien to him, but it seemed familiar to everyone else. Residents and visitors alike were swept up in the evening's joy. Haim was the strange one. After the absence of this or any other celebration in the widow's house, he did not have what he needed to participate. He brought no gift. He carried no skill or art to share, and he had nothing to say. No one put a hand on his shoulder or introduced him to others.

Haim looked around as he considered how different he was from these people, and then he remembered what he had started to forget: he was more different than any of them knew. He was only a half-Jew. He was Zoilus's son, the Tyrant's spawn. Haim thought of the old goat-stealer's words about his lineage and worth. He wondered what the people of this place would say if they knew. He wondered how hard the hammer would fall, how it could shatter the night's celebration if they recognized the monster that he was, moving in their midst. Chaya was wrong. He could not pretend to be one of them. One Sabbath festival and he was undone.

Haim closed his eyes, and in the darkness, his state as a perpetual stranger seemed further proof that he was unfit for this kind of people—for good people. He did not need the widow or the goat-stealer to tell him now. He could see it for himself.

Haim looked around and understood that the only thing he could expect from this night was to further plumb the depth of his strangeness, and he needed no further revelations on that subject.

It occurred to him that a second thing might happen here: he might be exposed.

He moved away from the busy mother to preserve her kindness and protect her from his presence. As he circulated through the festival, he found the effort to hide as tiring as the many night flights and dangers he and Chaya had endured fleeing from one work camp to another over the past year.

He looked for Chaya again. When he found her in the crowd, he saw that she belonged. Her conversion to Jewry was an easy transition from whatever her way had been in Samaria. Watching her, he realized that her trauma in the well and their journey through the new Nabataea had shrunken her. In those days, she had lived with him in grief and isolation and deprivation. Together they had been outcasts from society, but she had known another life. This village was now home to her, a place Haim had never been.

When the night's darkness had finished settling in, there came a time of dancing. There was not much musical talent within the village, but they spoke glowingly of other Galilean communities' gifts for song. Still, there were a few on Arbel who could play the timbrel or improvise percussive curiosities, and many others clapped along with inconsistent beats. Sticks clacked together and cheers sounded as the first village men took to dancing, and the Pharisees and unmarried boys followed soon after. Haim did not take part in the dance. He shrank back into the crowd's recesses. He noticed that everyone seemed to know the steps. Even the small children dancing on the periphery knew the rhythms and movements of Arbel's dances, and the oldest in the village had not forgotten—everyone danced.

When the unmarried girls took to the centre of the dance floor, Chaya was among her peers. Haim ached to see that whatever the Samaritan dances were, they must have been similar to these Galilean steps—that was why she blended in so well.

Except, for Haim, she did not blend. Not anymore. She had changed. She had grown in their short time here, or at least he now noticed these changes more. She was taller, but it was not just her height—her face was different, and her eyes and form were becoming those of a woman. Though there were girls older than her, there were none like her. The thin and small bones that had huddled against him the previous winter were gone. The girl he now saw was not yet fully grown, but for the first time Haim saw the woman Chaya would become.

Haim watched her dance. He saw only her among the other girls. Her feet were fast, striking quick kicks below her skirts while her hips moved at half the speed, less than half, and in a languid, rolling movement, as though they were part of some other body altogether. Her arms and torso moved in yet a third rhythm. The complexity of it all integrated together as each part of her body fluidly answered the different yet complementary rhythms of the timbrels, the sticks, the improvised drums, the wooden blocks and bells and calloused, clapping hands. Haim felt a knot in his throat. He was her brother in this place. The girl from the bottom of the Samaritan well had become beautiful without him.

Haim moved away from the light of the fires, away from the glistening of her face and throat and arms, away from the people and the tuneless rhythms and the voices and the collective mirth that seemed to flow from person to person but not through him.

He walked in near darkness by the light of only the moon and stars. He went back to the shed on Yechiel's property. Though he moved mindlessly, he was not surprised to find himself reloading his pack and feeling about for the axe, his blanket, the knife, and the two mantles—the few belongings that were his own. Then he left Yechiel's home and slipped down the path towards Noach's place. The path led away from the cliff-face, away from the festival. The south side of Arbel's heights did not crumble into a cliff but descended into a long, steep slope with a wide path. Haim knew the trail led through more mountains, oscillating up and down over many valleys and peaks before opening up onto the Great Plain of Esdraelon. Beyond that plain lay Samaria and the remains of Chaya's village, and beyond that lay many more hills and valleys that eventually led to Judea and Jerusalem.

As Haim walked alone out of Arbel, his eyes fully adjusted to the moonlight and his ears remained alert. He knew of a turnoff near Noach's place where he might find the goat herder's flock. He considered raiding the pen and taking a few goats with him on his journey but decided against it. He would not steal from the village. The goats might not follow him. The villagers might blame Chaya, and through him, she could lose her place.

He left Noach's home and the wolfskin untouched and continued south down the mountain until he came to a crossroad in unfamiliar territory. After consulting the stars for direction, he chose the most southerly branch and so began a new journey.

18
90 BCE

HAIM HAD WALKED a long ways from Arbel into the moonlit night and his legs were tired when he heard light steps in the dark behind him. He slipped into the shadow of a pine tree to wait. The smell and texture of needles in the dark identified the tree for him. The night was quiet and sound carried well. It took longer than he expected for his follower to arrive.

When she crossed the moonlight in front of him, he was so surprised that he almost said nothing. She was almost past him before he finally called out. "Chaya!"

She stopped, turned, and squinted into the trees. Though it seemed that she had not seen him yet, her body relaxed. "I knew it," she said.

Haim stepped out from under the tree. "How did you know to follow me?"

"It was obvious. I've seen that restless look on your

face hundreds of times now." Her small pack bulged and sagged against her back. She finally caught Haim's gaze and pointed towards his tree. "I'm tired. Can we sleep there? Like before?"

Once they were under the pine together, Chaya leaned against Haim, and her warmth made him happier than he had been in a long time.

"Why are you here?" he asked.

She pulled away and turned to gaze properly into his eyes, a habit she often used to claim Haim's attention. Though he could see none of her features in the dark, he knew she had a smirk on her face as she looked at him—just a smirk, nothing unkind in it. It was her form of affection and humour.

Haim pressed on. "It seemed like the village was everything you wanted."

"They would have found me out eventually," Chaya said. "A Samaritan in a Galilean village. Second wife to a Pharisee no less." She laughed then, quietly, and there was something deeper in her voice that reminded him of her changing appearance.

They slept that night wrapped in their old mantles with Haim's blanket over them both. In the morning, Haim found out she had fewer reservations about theft than he did. She pulled from her pack bread and nuts and dried berries and some salted lamb. They ate frugally in the early light and repacked their supplies carefully.

"You didn't take anything from the village?" she asked.

"I didn't want them to blame you."

Chaya exhaled through pursed lips, a brief, dismissive expression. It made Haim feel as though he were the younger and less experienced of the two. She put a hand on his arm and left it there for a moment. She was more confident than she had been in Nabataea. He felt a new kind of uncertainty about her.

"It's good to have food to put away for later," he said.

She smiled. "You carry it then."

She unloaded the rest of her pack, and Haim was surprised at the weight. She had prioritized heavier foods: more cured meat, dried fruits, and preserved cakes.

They divided the load between them with the heavier portion in his pack. "We could use a donkey," he said.

"You'll have to do." She said it kindly and with a slight smile, and it made him feel happy and strange.

They set out southwards with no clear destination. By the time they reached Esdraelon's flatland, it had begun to rain and they took shelter beneath a bridge.

"This would be a bad place to be resting in during a flood," he said.

She said nothing in reply. They slept pressed against one another, the sound of water on the stone and wood insulating them from the night's usual chorus.

After another day of travel, they left the great fertile plain and climbed back into hills. As they approached Samaria, they came to a land covered in limestone and sidra trees. As the day was turning to dusk and the two were considering where to rest, they turned at a bend in the trail and encountered a rough company of two men and three women.

Haim put up a hand to hold Chaya back, but the group had already seen them. The men looked like the sort they had encountered across the Jordan—the same darkness was in their eyes and their hands and arms bore similar scars. The shorter man's nose had a horrific scar as well, though long healed, while the bigger man's ribs bore a more recent injury. One of the women was rebandaging the man's bare, injured torso.

The women were disconcerting as well. All three moved with the bitter confidence of those familiar with violence. They wore their hair uncovered. Their clothing was not longer or shorter or more open than was common, but its fit was tighter, its fabric thinner. They looked like they had endured violence but did not passively accept it like the women across the Jordan. These were not cowering victims. Their gaze was bold and direct—a brazen quality that immediately unsettled Haim.

The five were resting at the side of the road under the shade of the largest sidra Haim had ever seen. Its ancient and erosion-exposed roots tangled and rose into two tortured trunks. The figures assessed Haim and Chaya and seemed to silently agree on something among themselves. Before Haim could decide what to do, one of the women came forward beaming warmth. The woman seemed to have sized Chaya up in a single glance, recognizing the girl's deepest needs and desires and drew the girl to her with barely three sentences. There was something about a welcome and something about Chaya's beauty and something about the day and how its pleasant qualities related to Chaya's eyes—later, Haim could not remember the specific details. The words, in the end, were not important. Haim would later discover that in its various forms, this intuitive and warm approach was the woman's gift. She could see into people and seduced men and women alike for her purposes, and this power made her a leader within the small group. Her name was Klotho.

Klotho drew Chaya into the community of five, and she gestured for Haim to join them as well. Haim found himself helping to rebandage the silent wounded man. Both of the rough men watched while the women managed the smooth entry of the young couple into their midst. Haim was dimly aware that the men were scrutinizing him while the women pulled him in with soft words and familiar gestures. The woman managing the bandages touched Haim's arm twice as she directed his actions, putting pressure on his hand to hold the bandage steady, then touching his wrist to get him to ease off that pressure—she touched Haim more times in those brief moments than any had touched him during his entire stay at Arbel.

Chaya seemed captivated. She told a new version of their story with a brightness in her voice that was once again childlike.

When they finished bandaging the man, Chaya made room for Haim in the centre thicket of women while the rough men stayed seated at the border of the tree's shade. The community below the sidra belonged to the women, and the two men simply observed and said little.

After a while, Haim realized that they were preparing to share a meal in this place of rock, coarse grass, and sparse trees. Haim's discomfort grew as the women pulled his and Chaya's entire store of provisions out onto the ground while the women offered only small portions of their own food for the meal. Chaya continued to be talkative, and the women drew out her stories with a steady stream of warm smiles and soft words and eyes that followed her every expression. Haim said little during the meal and the men less.

Finally, the woman across from Haim, the one who had worked the bandages, caught Haim's eye. "I'm Decuma," the woman said. Her smile was direct and warm. She was beautiful, yet it appeared that she had not bathed in days. None of them had. The entire group wore quality clothing streaked with creases, dirt, and dust. Decuma's sleeve was torn and stained with a suspicious dark spot, but she wore no other sign of a wound.

"This is Klotho," Decuma continued, pointing to the tall, black-haired woman next to her whose angular face was still focused on Chaya. Haim could not imagine these women working in Nabataean kitchens. They seemed like warriors' brides from some northern Galatian tribe, the sort of women who might claim a man before being claimed herself and who would have no qualms about killing her mate should the need arise.

"We're happy you've joined us, Haim," Klotho said. Evidently Chaya had already made introductions and the women only deemed it necessary to catch Haim up halfway through consuming the food that he had carried for two days.

"Morta," the third woman said. The single word was her entire introduction. Lids as weathered as the old scribe's shaded Morta's eyes, but her hands seemed stronger than the old man's had ever been.

"We're bandits," Decuma said simply. She said it smiling, still holding Haim's attention. The shape of her eyes made him wonder if she was Egyptian or of some other nation that he was unfamiliar with, although everything about the group's clothing and accents indicated that they were Judean.

"You're not part of the king's war?" Haim asked.

Decuma and Klotho both laughed, and when they looked at the men, Haim saw wry smiles on their faces, though they remained silent.

"The king's war has dried up traffic between the north and Jerusalem," Decuma said. "We've had the worst season in years. Fewer travellers mean fewer rewards for our efforts."

"During the festivals, we raid," Klotho continued. "In the heat of Av and in the wettest winter months, we have a place in the south where we stay."

"We had a place," Decuma said.

Klotho nodded. "Had a place. We're not so welcome there anymore."

"These two make extra money in the off season," the short man with the broken nose said, finally speaking for the first time and nodding at Decuma and Klotho. "Whatever they make, we share."

"That's enough," Morta said.

"There were seven of us and two donkeys," Decuma said. "Just a week ago."

"We were at a vineyard north of Cana," said Klotho. "A winemaker's place littered with the stumps of an old orchard."

"A beautiful estate," Decuma said. "I don't understand why someone would chop down so many trees."

"There was a fat bald old man in charge of it," Klotho continued.

"With a dovecote on his land," the shorter man said, re-entering the conversation with a growl and spitting to one side. Haim wondered why the dovecote offended the man so.

The story came out slowly. The company had decided to assault the farm rather than search for travellers on the roads. At first, the farmworkers and residents had responded to their attack by running into a stone tunnel and retreating into the cliff-face dove tower that it led to. The imposing stone dovecot jutted out of a natural ledge in the cliff. The doves flying in and out of the windows had hidden the human movements inside. Arrows fired from those openings had already killed two donkeys and one of their men before the raiders had realized the threat.

"We moved away from the tower then," said Decuma. "The farm had no money. We don't traffic in slaves. We should have left it altogether."

"They came out of the tower that night when we were sleeping. He was wounded." Klotho indicated the larger of the two men. "Another friend of ours was killed. Then the farmworkers went back into their stronghold. We left that night. We got some wine. Some food. Nothing to justify our trouble or losses."

After the failed raid, the five survivors had crossed the Great Plain of Esdraelon and converged on Haim and Chaya's route. There seemed to be nothing left of the wine they claimed to have looted.

"Where will you go?" Klotho asked. She spoke as though there was nothing odd about candidly confessing their crimes. She seemed to assume that Haim and Chaya were on a similar path. It took a moment for Haim to recall that Chaya had chattered a whole new history for them, and he was back to playing catch-up.

"We don't know," said Chaya. "What do you suggest?"

She said this in a tone Haim had not heard from her before. She was mimicking Klotho's smooth delivery. If Klotho noticed the change, she gave no indication.

"You could join us," said Klotho. She looked at Haim with eyes that held his attention in uncomfortable ways. "We need a new man."

"And you are a treasure," Decuma said to Chaya. "You would be a wonderful addition to our shared purse."

At this, the two women glanced at Morta, who nodded her approval. Chaya was delighted, as though banditry were a child's game. Haim watched as their new path was settled quickly and casually. He had said hardly anything. The two men had said even less.

Haim sat beside Chaya and watched the fire as the three women occasionally fed the flames new fuel, and neither he nor the men did anything to help. He wanted to say something, but he did not know what to say. He wanted to ask what this meant. What did joining a bandit company entail? Would they have to kill and steal? How had he been roped into this agreement without uttering a single word? What was this other profession that the women worked in the off season? When was banditry's off season? How had he managed once again to become a peripheral figure in his own story?

19

90 BCE

THE NEXT MORNING, Haim arose to discover that the bandits were already awake. He and Chaya joined the five in a quick meal and then set out on a new course. The group walked in a generally westwards direction, towards the sea, but Haim had misplaced the mountains in his memory and was disoriented as he studied the hills around them and so could not confidently identify their location. They consumed what remained of Haim and Chaya's store at midday, and it turned out that the five had little of their own left to share.

Decuma rebandaged the big man at the end of the day with Haim helping once again. Afterwards, he sat near the big, reeking man while the women parcelled out what little they had left. They divided the portions fairly, though each was small.

"You've not done this before," the big man said.

"This?" Haim asked.

"Killing."

"I killed a wolf once."

"But not a man for his money."

"No," Haim admitted.

"You used that sling on the wolf?"

"Yes."

"Have you killed anything else with it? Or were you just lucky once?"

"I've killed birds. Hares. A mule once."

"You killed a mule with a sling?"

Haim touched the handle beside him. "With my axe."

"It's a good axe," the big man said. "I don't know why you'd kill a mule with it, but that's quite the axe. But you've never killed a man?"

"No."

The big man grunted. He seemed unsurprised but also displeased.

"You don't lie with the girl. Her name?"

That first comment seemed to be a statement, but Haim was unsure whether it was an observation or command. He chose just to answer the clear question. "Chaya."

"Yes. You don't lie with her. Have you yet?"

"No. She's just a child."

The big man grunted. "Hardly. You haven't been watching. But you don't lie with her. Not within the tribe. None. Not her. Not the women—though Decuma and Klotho will lie with any man outside the tribe who shows a coin and is foolish or drunk enough to risk his years with one of them. But nothing within the tribe. That's Morta's rule. Do you understand?"

Haim nodded.

"The women will teach Chaya whatever she needs to know. We share the profits. That includes what the women make. You break our agreements within the tribe, and you'll have a sword run through you. Morta might be the first to do it. She'll do it while you sleep. That woman is a witch. She doesn't ever sleep."

"What do you mean, 'what Chaya needs to know?'" Haim asked. "What are the agreements?"

"You'll discover them as we go. They change, but once they're in place, they're as sacred as Zeus's mountain."

Haim did not know how to respond to that. He felt like he should protest, but he did not know what he would be protesting. He imagined that banditry came with its own code, but as he was still struggling to understand how he had become a part of this company to begin with, the code itself seemed to be a peripheral concern.

The big man reminded him of the goat-stealer. His head was large and lumpen on one side and scarred in various places. His thin black hair was always in disarray. Walking along the road, the man occasionally tried to smooth it flat, but it quickly defied him and rose in irregular directions. In contrast, his beard was orderly and thick and black except for three uneven streaks of grey that dripped down his chin like sloppy brush strokes.

The other man was smaller, bald, the line of his crushed and redirected nose alarming. It had been brutally damaged in some violent accident or fight that seemed to make breathing from it impossible. One nostril was crudely notched, whether as part of the original damage or a secondary insult to the man's face, he never did tell. His head was turbaned in wool far too thick for the season. His shoulders sloped with an excess of muscle about the base of his neck, and his oddly narrow torso made his arms look exaggeratedly large.

Haim wondered if Morta's rules for purity served to maintain social order among the thieves or merely to cover for the unattractiveness of the men. The two recently dead could not have been as equally misshapen as the two survivors, and with four, the men would have outnumbered the women. The arrangement must serve some utilitarian function or be the product of an ancient thieves' creed, or perhaps it was just Morta exerting her matriarchal power over her clan. What that power was, he could not divine from listening to the clan's discussions, for she said little.

That night, they slept curled up in their separate blankets off the road. They did not light a fire because they had nothing to burn. The next morning there was nothing to eat.

Finishing their food stores meant to the band what the end of spring rain meant to a farmer. Hunger was the tribe's signal to commence new work.

The fall air was cool and rain threatened. The big man turned to Haim and said, "You'll take a share when you take a share."

Haim did not understand. He looked around and saw Morta watching him, and she nodded but said nothing.

They set out from their camp and began the search. The post-festival roads were starting to become busy again.

"But not many will go through Samaria," Klotho said.

"And those that do will have empty pockets and empty packs," Decuma added. "Everything will have been given to the temple or spent in the city."

The big man walked in front now. He tilted to one side as he walked, favouring his injury, and pointed with his other hand over the countryside, away from the roads. "Fewer people," he said cryptically. "Let's go that way. We just need someone with a proper larder."

They walked across bare rock and along sheep trails for much of the morning. As they walked, Haim wanted to pull Chaya aside and talk with her. In their two days alone together after Arbel, conversation between them had been easy. It was as though their separation in Arbel had made them hungry for one another. Among this company, however, conversation between them had once again dried up. Chaya talked a great deal with Klotho and Decuma, and when Chaya lay down near Haim at night, she did not want to talk.

"There," the big man said.

Haim looked to where the man pointed and saw a thin column of smoke. They picked their way across rough country towards the smoke and found their way to a farm surrounded by a narrow circle of grass. They kept on an oblique path through sedge until they came near the homestead.

"Here," Morta said. They paused while Decuma and Klotho changed into clothing that looked more like the region's modest and practical wear. Both women tied scarves over their hair, helping each other tuck stray strands away as though they were respectfully married women. Morta took a rag, wet it from their water skin, and with Chaya's help, wiped down the women's arms, hands, and faces.

When they were ready, the big man spoke. "You stay here," he said, indicating Haim, Chaya, and Morta. The broken-nosed man and two women continued towards the isolated house while the big man stayed hidden in the thickets as he flanked the other side. He carried a bow and five arrows in addition to his sword. Haim stayed as directed with Chaya and Morta and watched the scene unfold.

Klotho, Decuma, and the broken-nosed man approached the house. A matronly woman stood before the dwelling, and it was Klotho who called out the first greeting to her. They discussed something then that Haim could not hear. The broken-nosed man rubbed his right shoulder and repeated the gesture three more times. Then he did it once more with his left. It was subtle, but the woman of the house noticed and said something. She seemed concerned, and the man laughed quietly and bowed sheepishly. A boy just a few years younger than Haim came from the animal pens, stopped when he saw the visitors, and returned to the enclosure. When he reappeared, he brought with him an older man. The broken-nosed man made his odd shoulder-rub gesture once more.

The family stood talking with their three visitors, and then the broken-nosed man made another exaggerated gesture with both shoulders, shrugging as though to ease some deep tension. The farmer was focused on the broken-nosed man and speaking when an arrow struck his side and slid through him, exiting in a spray, sliding along the stony ground, bouncing back into the air, and then falling with the arrow point up, blood shining in sunlight.

The man grunted and staggered, and the band immediately erupted. Decuma and Klotho grabbed the wife's arms, and the broken-nosed man caught the startled boy's shirt sleeve and swung the butt of his large knife into the child's skull, knocking him to the ground. The farmer's wife turned towards her husband's cry and struggled against her captors, but she could only watch as he sank to the ground and blood bubbled weakly from his mouth. The woman inhaled as though to scream, but Klotho rushed to relieve her of that effort with a quick dagger stroke, opening a new and silent hole in the woman's throat.

Decuma stepped past the collapsing wife and took control of the unconscious clubbed boy on the ground, straddling him indecently in case he awoke, the rest of her attention on the actions of the others. The broken-nosed man walked past the wife and into the house. The husband looked to his son, their assailants, and then the house, issuing sounds that Haim could not discern across the distance.

The broken-nosed man came out of the house sometime later, and when he did, he carried the bloodied body of a baby and dragged the still twitching corpse of a girl about half Chaya's age. He dumped them beside the now bled-out mother. The father still lived, but he sat on the ground in horror, only able to watch, panting as blood pooled around him.

The big man emerged from his place of ambush, and the three in wait left the cover of tall grass and bushes and approached their companions. Chaya was twitchy and pale. She did not run and she did not cry. She did not avoid Haim's eyes, but she did not seem to see him either, her gaze glazed and hollow.

In that scene of blood and new death, the seven stood in silence until the big man said, "Five. You indicated four."

"She didn't mention the girl," the broken-nosed man said.

"What do we have?" the big man asked.

The broken-nosed man looked around. "Crops. One donkey. Some sheep in the pen."

Klotho started towards the house, but Morta stopped her. She looked at the big man and pointed at the unconscious boy, Decuma still on top of him, and then at Haim.

"Time for your share," the big man said to Haim.

Haim instinctually took a step back, but if anyone noticed, none acknowledged it. The big man relieved Decuma of her perch, roughly pulled the boy to his feet, and shook him. He pinched the boy's cheek and twisted, and then the boy roused. He saw his assailants and at first was confused. Then he saw his family and inhaled to shout and the big man smashed in his lips and drove a fist into the boy's belly and the boy stopped and gasped and knelt. The big man stood behind the boy. He took a fistful of the boy's hair and pointed his head at the ground. The boy fought for air and tried to raise his head, but the big man's grip would not let him.

The big man took out a long knife like the one Haim had previously lost and tossed it at Haim's feet.

"Your share," the big man said. "Pick it up."

Haim picked up the knife with a trembling hand.

"Come," the big man said. "You've slit a goat's throat, right?"

Haim shook his head. "No."

"The wolf then."

"I didn't cut it," Haim said. "I strangled it. With the sling."

"Strangling. He starts at the top, with strangling. A wolf." The big man laughed out loud, looking at the broken-nosed man and the boy still kneeling before him. Then he fixed his gaze back on Haim. "Have you ever killed with a knife?"

"Birds."

"Birds. Fine. Now this boy. He's your share. Cut him now."

Haim did not move. He could not move. He looked at Chaya, but her eyes were fixed on the boy. She stared at the farmer's boy with a look that Haim could not read, and she did not blink.

"Don't make it harder by thinking it through. Here, I need to say something to you." He dragged the boy by his hair over to Haim, and then the big man bent down. He spoke very quietly, so only Haim could hear. "This is your share. You become one of us here and now, or you are not one of us. If you are not one of us, you do not leave here alive. Your sister's fate also rests on your choice. You've done a bird. A man is harder. A boy is harder. But it's the same."

He stepped back again, still holding the boy's head down and steady but at arm's length.

"Do his throat," the big man said. "Like she did the mother."

Haim stood with the knife shaking in front of him. He felt something rise in his throat though their dinner had been light and there had been no breakfast. The farmer's boy looked up then, and though he had not yet met Haim's eye, Haim could see that he was about to. Later, he told himself that it was the boy's fault. If the boy had not looked up, if he had given Haim more time to think, he might have done something different. But the boy looked up. It spurred Haim's hand. His stroke was steady and swift and without thought. It pierced the boy's throat from the side as directed. He drove the blade hard through flesh and cartilage, and when he pulled back, he twisted his wrist in a final slice and the blood that came made a shocking stream. Haim stepped out of its wet heat in surprise. The big man laughed loudly and thrust the boy forwards, hard, and the boy thudded against the ground. The broken-nosed man shouted in triumph, and then Klotho and Decuma each whistled their victory sound and ran towards the house. The boy grasped fistfuls of his father's stony earth and tried to rise and then tried to hold closed the gash in his throat and in doing so filled the gash with dust where it quickly washed out and soon there was no boy left to think at all and where he had gone was a mystery. Only his body remained with that of his mother and younger brother and sister.

Haim looked at Chaya, but she only stared at the boy. He looked at Morta, who regarded only Chaya, and then he looked at the big man, who was looking elsewhere, smiling. Haim followed his gaze and saw that the father still lived. The farmer was reclining on one side, his eyes on his son, his mouth moving in some rhythm of prayer or maybe just trying to breathe or to say something to his son, but no sound came.

The big man started walking then, going to retrieve his fallen arrow.

"You had to do it," Chaya said later, but she did not look at Haim when she said it.

She ate well alongside the others in the house as they emptied the farmer's cupboards. She seemed like some other creature than the small girl he had rescued from the well, the scared girl across the Jordan, the dancing girl at Arbel.

He did not know this Chaya who ate noisily from Death's table among Morta's brood. They talked and she talked. Haim had nothing to say. He did not know himself. He did not eat with the others—he ate nothing at all. He drank only a little.

Inside, the farmer's home was tomb-like with its raw stone walls. Murderous living souls ate within the house while the dead lay unburied in the yard.

They stayed one night in the farmer's house and then set out again across pastureland and into low hills, driving the farmer's few sheep before them and letting the donkey carry their wealth. They came to an abandoned farmhouse, for there were many empty homes in Samaria after years of Jannaeus's purges. Entire cities had been razed and their citizens sent to Joppa where they were loaded onto ships and taken to slave markets in Egypt and Rome. All that remained of those ghosts and distant slaves were the shells of their long-abandoned homes.

Near midday, Haim looked up from the ground passing under his feet and saw the broken-nosed man watching him as they walked. The man's gaze was predatory at first and did not falter when Haim met it. Then the man smiled. It reminded Haim of that first landowner's smile, the one with the almond trees east of the Jordan. It was a smile that promised cruelty, and Haim faced a decision: which side of this man's cruelty would he stand on? Would he be one of the man's crew and learn well the role of banditry—or would he be one of the victims? In the landowner's words, was Haim to be a cook or a foreman?

20

90-89 BCE

THE FIRST ABANDONED farm they found did not suit Morta. The seven moved on until they found one on higher land, commanding a wider view of the surrounding countryside. Nearby, there was a sheep pasture, a creek, a pen with tall stone walls, and a house large enough to comfortably fit the seven.

The two men and Haim separated three of the younger sheep from the flock and let the others into the pasture. They slaughtered, skinned, and prepared the three sheep while the women tended to some smokers that had been left in disrepair, preparing the racks and building up fires beneath. Within a few hours, the women were tired and dusty, the men sweat covered and bloody. They draped the drying racks with long bands of butchered meat that covered the fires like tents. They scattered what salt and spices they had looted over the outside of the meat, for none had thought to spice the inside beforehand nor had the energy to turn the meat now, and so it was prepared with only one side salted.

Haim and the men bathed in the stream, and when they walked nearly naked into the house afterwards, they found new clothing and burned their old clothes in the fire. Their old clothing's sweat and blood turned to smoke and coated the interior of their tents of drying meat. This, Haim understood, was to be their winter residence. Whatever city held their usual winter home was forbidden to them this year, something to do with an obligation their dead companions had been committed to and that the remaining members chose to disavow.

The following week was a time of debauchery. Though the decorum of Klotho and Decuma's dress deteriorated in those following days, neither of the men violated Morta's rule, and so the women were untouched. This tribe's moral boundaries transfixed Haim, how such a group could be both murderous and measured, heartless and controlled.

The store of wine they had brought from the slaughtered farmer's home had been over half the donkey's load. The house they had claimed for the winter likewise had an ample store of wine and some beer.

In those days, the entire company consumed food and drink in copious amounts. They slept where they ate and desecrated the land about the house and pens with their waste. By the end of the week, Haim had witnessed Chaya drunk, Chaya half dressed, Chaya vomiting in the yard— Chaya becoming one of the women of this corrupt brood. This descent was eclipsed by his own slide into illness, laughter, overconsumption, and exhaustion. The solace of a new wine from yet another clay amphora eased the ache in Haim's head and sickness in his stomach. That an excess of wine caused illness and could also be a cure for that illness was a new discovery.

Wine spilled over and over again into whatever cup might be at hand, and days of dissolution wove together conversation, laughter, shouted threats, and fond remembrances while Morta sneered and drank but said little as she oversaw her brood.

Haim roused himself from this madness at the end of the week. He shifted onto shaky legs and made his way out of the musty house. He came to the fire and the drying racks, and he saw that only a small portion of the meat had been eaten, though he had little memory of having eaten any. The meat that remained, the majority of what they had butchered, had been left on the racks, the fire untended. The meat had cooled and been wet by rain and accumulated flies and now swam with maggots. The stench drove Haim away from the yard and out into the pasture where it occurred to him that the rest of the sheep were gone. He investigated the stone pen to see if they were there, but all that greeted him was the donkey. They had securely tied it there with a thick rope and left it without water. Some beast had eaten through one of the donkey's haunches and pulled its innards about the pen. The entire area swarmed with flies.

After Morta awoke and roused the rest of the crew, they packed up what little they had and left with their clothing and minds in disarray. As they walked through the hills searching for a new home, Haim felt anger boil within him, compounding the ache in his head and the weak sourness in his stomach and the burning in his throat. He felt hatred towards Jerusalem and Jannaeus, the king whose policies forced them to live in this desperate manner, though as he walked, he could not clearly remember why their chosen path was Jannaeus's fault. There had been something in their days of drunkenness and arguments and conversation and laughter that assured him of Jerusalem's complicity in their behaviour, and this was enough to console Haim as a cold wind began and winter threatened.

It was nearly a full day before they found another suitable home. They broke the door in rather than simply open it and found little left in the stores that had not already been eaten by mice. The house was clean except for dust and leaves and dried excrement. The women set Chaya to sweeping, and the men grumbled as they walked about the perimeter looking for the underground cellar. When they found it, it gave up a little wine, some vegetables, and a hanging leg of meat, properly salted and cured. The group ate modestly, watered down the wine they drank, and slept in the common room until late the next day.

The winter was not a good time for raiding Samaria's roads, but they found sufficient victims to keep up their supplies through the winter. One afternoon the sun came out, warmer than usual, and Haim wrapped himself in an extra blanket and went to sit in the yard. Chaya was there already, similarly wrapped up. He did not sit beside her but nearby. Close enough so that they could talk.

Twice Haim opened his mouth to speak, but each time he was unsure what to say. She was becoming a younger version of Klotho. Her voice was sweet when needed, cruel when called for, and her eyes strangely un-haunted. Her manner did not match how Haim felt. He needed to speak to her and hear in her voice how she felt about this company they had become a part of, seemingly by accident.

Haim opened his mouth yet again to start, and then he noticed that Chaya's attention was elsewhere. A man was approaching from the south.

Haim closed his mouth and squinted and studied the man. He was a medium-sized man with a barrel-shaped chest, big and soft-looking arms, and bowed legs. He was as ugly as the other two men, and Haim found himself not at all surprised when the broken-nosed man left the house at a fast walk, raising a hand in greeting. The two embraced and their voices carried back to the house, though Haim could not make out any particulars of what they said.

The broken-nosed man brought his friend up to the house. "This is Gershom," the broken-nosed man said.

It seemed that the others in the company knew this Gershom already. They welcomed him back into their fellowship, and when Chaya got up to join the others inside, Haim stood and followed her.

"You're recruiting children now?" Gershom asked as Chaya and Haim seated themselves.

"He's a dead shot with a sling," the broken-nosed man said, pointing at Haim. "Six you've killed?" he asked. "We don't even have to get our swords wet."

The new man's beard looked insect infested, its mismatched hairs jumbled together like a mutated mixture of curly sheep's wool, thick bear fur, and spiky dog whiskers that crowded to cover a square and bulging jaw. Haim wondered if there were some rule that required all male bandits to eventually become disfigured. His own appearance would forever be that of a child's until his face and hands gained scars to match his back and legs.

Gershom stayed with Morta's brood as a returned member, and through the rest of the winter, the company conducted desultory raids on isolated farmsteads and against travellers on the road. When they came upon shepherds' caches, they left the loot untouched, for the testy outdoor breed had been known to track thieves through any weather. Every man feared the shepherd's sling.

Throughout that winter, the rain came in long and purposeful slants, scrubbing one side of buildings' stone walls while creating an angle of dry air on the other side for the band to take shelter in. But when the rain caught them on the roads, it swirled, not content to merely pressure them from one direction but intent on washing them from every angle as though the wind and water knew that the band needed to be cleansed.

During those months, Klotho and Decuma picked through their dead victims' belongings while the men abused survivors spared for that purpose and only spared until that purpose was satisfied. Afterwards, the women finished off these victims as though to expunge some offence from their midst. Haim was horrified and refused to participate in either the abuse or its conclusion. He killed in the assault, but at the first opportunity, he refused an invitation to take a woman, and the men mocked him and offered him a young boy instead. His even stronger refusal made the men make sport of him. But not for long—Haim was as good as any shepherd with his sling, and that maintained the men's respect for him.

Morta patrolled her brood's activities with a supervisory

eye and otherwise saved her energy for the long walks these raids entailed. They had yet to replace the donkey, for none of the travellers they had encountered on the road had borne such a luxury. Anything they looted, they carried. They drank little wine the rest of that winter, and a foul mood built through the cold months. The mood of the entire band became worse when the winds blew hard and it rained for days at a time.

Winter turned to spring and they continued moving, and then summer came on with its unrelenting dryness and heat. Through all seasons, the band fluctuated between long periods of scarcity and occasional weeks of drunkenness. There were times when the malevolent spirit of boredom lingered among them and times when their exhaustion met the blood-heat of violent assaults and left them sated and their pockets filled.

On one raid, in the heat of summer, Morta did not join them in their search for victims. She stayed at the last stone house, and the six went on without her. It was on this venture that they first strayed from their regular habits.

21
89 BCE

MORTA WAS INJURED. It seemed that she had injured her hip in a fall, or perhaps it had been some foolishness climbing over a wall or an unexpected conflict as she dispatched a victim. None dared to suggest that the injury was merely the product of age. She snarled at anyone who suggested she was old, like an animal defending her status in the pack.

They had lost track of the months and timing for Jerusalem's festivals and hungered for better fare than any of them could prepare. None were cooks. They left Morta at the house and went out into the heat to reap the road's harvest, but they encountered little to tempt their violence. What met them instead was the discovery that they could only talk about one intense shared desire: they all wanted better food.

They craved meats properly cooked, the fat not burned

away, spices wisely selected. They wanted freshly baked bread. They wanted creams and sweet fruits and sauces, and they talked about vegetables that were not withered but still carried spring rain within. They described every kind of drink, not merely the dregs of looted wine, and they told stories of decadent feasts of pure sensual delight from past memories or present fantasies.

At the end of that day of fruitless searching and talking, they did not go directly back to Morta and her stone house and cold hearth and stale fare. The six continued westwards towards the coast, and so they came to Dora.

Haim said nothing of his history with Dora or his mother's house south of here. Three years had passed since he had last been in these parts, and he had never been to Dora itself before, the former home of his father. The Tyrant. The Jews or the Egyptians—Haim was never sure which—had decimated Dora in the year of his birth. Though the scars of that destruction were still evident, the restored port city was once again prosperous. The smell of the sea carried across the wind and Decuma spoke about the shellfish they could have here. It had been, after all, the Philistine coast populated by a people who cared nothing for Jewish food laws.

They rented rooms above a tavern that gave them access to gorgeous Greek baths. In the hot water, the company removed layers of filth and stench from their bodies like snakes shedding their skins. Even Gershom's beard seemed less like a demented bird's nest. The women showed Chaya how to apply the paints of their other trade, and she glowed with enthusiasm for the new look they gave her.

The owner of the tavern supplied them all with new

clothes. He seemed exceptionally pleased to take their coin and suggested other treats they might wish to acquire. He could not have known that the money he accepted came from pilgrims' temple offerings and that the lives of its original bearers had passed beyond knowledge in the empty byways of Samaria. The Jewish civil war and the conflict with the Samaritans were of no concern to Dora's people. The world had done its worst in Dora a decade and a half ago. The tavern keeper's job now was to seek the day's commerce and not worry about other matters. This was his season to sell what travellers would buy.

Haim waited for the worst, expecting that someone would recognize the Tyrant of Dora in him, but none looked at him in an unusual way. He did not even know whether he bore any resemblance to the city's former master. He wanted to ask after the boy who had stolen the old scribe's funeral goats three years ago, but he knew it was unlikely that any would know or remember the tale. It was no tale here—such a story would have been a forgettable trifle in this city.

The company ate richly, starting early in the evening in their private upstairs room. The tavern owner and his family brought plates as they were ready, and the company dubbed it the Great Feast of Dora while it was still in progress. A dish of scallions, small green onions named after the Philistinian city of Ashkelon, came in a dripping dark wine sauce with a thick bread that gave off heat as it was torn open. Next came wild dog meat that had cooked in a small stew the entire day. Following that came half a small boar surrounded by mounds of shelled pink seafood. The company consumed every sort of flesh, spice, and juice with no regard for the religious prohibitions against nearly everything offered. The bandit company haunted Eretz-Israel, but those who had been were no longer Jews.

Haim looked at Chaya as she consumed new delicacies. Three different forbidden foods greased her face. He said simply, "Imagine the Pharisees of Arbel," and she laughed. The others ignored the youths and their private joke. The company talked loudly and took more wine and celebrated like kings and queens, demanding more sweet foods. The tavern keeper gave orders for fruits in sauces and creams and for honeyed nuts and dates. He stood among his wife and daughters as they worked and seemed like a king in his domain.

There were other sorts of establishments in Dora, ones the women had frequented in leaner years to earn money. Gershom knew of one such place. The men took Haim with them. There, with a woman the others had selected, Haim discovered what he had rejected when it had been paired with violence over the previous year.

He had needed his mother's touch for as long as he could remember. The day of the seeds and the touch of her wrist those many years ago still lingered in his memory. It was the most vivid of all his memories from that house.

Haim remembered Chaya when she had straddled him after he had rescued her from the well. He remembered her attack and his fear and disengagement, but then afterwards, he remembered the force of her body against him. They had both just been children then. The memory of that moment had haunted him during their nights and days across the Jordan. He wanted her against him again the way he wanted the old scribe not to keep him at arm's length, wanted his sisters not to be cruel, wanted his family to embrace him. He had not minded the cold nights when he and Chaya had been alone together. The cold had drawn her near him. The warmth of her forehead against his shoulder focused all his sensations of the world on that one place. Her touch made his heart beat differently.

He wondered how serious this flaw within him was. He had seen the Pharisees of Arbel live without touch. The men of this violent company touched only with violence, and Morta's rule prevented any other kind of physical contact among her crew. He alone craved connection like the others craved drink. Haim imagined a world where no one needed to eat and all were blissfully unaware of hunger, except for one person who did need such sustenance. That person, in that situation, would be the weakest one alive because of their constant hunger. Haim was like that person. Haim was the weakest one in Morta's company because of his need. No one hungered for touch as he did, and it made him feel ashamed.

The whore in Dora proved to him that he was beyond repair. The other men caroused and left soon after. Haim stayed with the woman all night. She let him sleep against her until daybreak. He discovered an unfamiliar kind of breathing, a new source of sustenance, as her warmth flowed through him and her breathing synchronized with his. The experience was like a strong drink that did not just intoxicate but nourished as well. From all he had seen, Haim understood it was unnatural for a man to need this. Haim said nothing about it afterwards to anyone.

They left Dora the following day to return to Morta and the stone house. He said to himself that he would never enter another brothel again. It was a place where he would lose his way. From that point on, he studied the men to learn how to be like them. He killed more often in the days that followed, less with the sling and more with the knife. He improved himself. He was growing up now in the way that he should. Soon he would be less of his previous self. Soon the pain would subside and he would not yearn for that which he could not have.

22
87 BCE

ONE NIGHT, A year and a half after Dora, a three-quarter moon crossed a dark sky that bloomed with faint stars. The band had just finished two days of feasting, for they had raided well. They had stolen an amphora of very strong wine, and by the time the fire was burning low, the household was dull and sleep claimed each of them one by one.

While the bandits slept, a company of one hundred men, six horses, and two mules pulling small wagons moved through a fertile valley in the east and passed the quiet city of Shechem. The company's captains gleaned what intelligence they could from Samaria's scarce inhabitants and continued in their search. They investigated caves and remote homesteads. They left the central valley behind, passed the ruins of the city of Samaria and continued into the night.

❦

In the morning, Gershom woke first and Haim second. Morta rose shortly after and eventually the others followed suit. The day passed in lethargy. None touched the strong new drink, but all drank the watered wine and doused their heads in the stream and sat about in the heat and picked at what remained of the previous day's meal. They were tired, their heads sore, and the effort to wave flies away from the remaining crusting meat was nearly beyond them.

❦

Once the afternoon had peaked, the company of a hundred soldiers roused from the shade. They ate from the wagons, watered their horses and mules, and then set out once more. Four of the riders detoured to interrogate distant farms, and each time they returned to correct the company's course.

❦

As evening approached, Gershom again uncorked the new amphora. He poured for all and then sat before the clean-picked bone and waited for the others. When all were present, he cast the bone and stone dice on the ground, but Morta gathered them up again with a clicking of her tongue, for only she was permitted to start the game.

"Why is it that she sets the rules?" Gershom complained. The heavy-lidded and sullen creatures who drank from the cups he had poured ignored him.

Morta motioned for Gershom to pour her another

drink. Only after he had done so did he seem to realize how the motion symbolized submission. The darkness in his eyes spread.

"Why do we live by her rules?" He looked into his cup as he said it, asking like a madman consulting a medium in the black liquid. "Who made her queen among us?"

The big man stood then and moved away from the others and out of the circle of light. It seemed to Haim that he had left the house, but Haim was too tired to track the big man's movements.

"She's old," Gershom said. He looked up at the other players. "She does not raid. She does not kill. She gives orders and we obey and she shares in the spoils and she cannot even cook and she lays with no man and earns nothing to add to our spoils." His words hung in the air. The picked bone gleamed in the firelight. There was nothing left to consume but drink.

Night flies attracted to the light settled on those seated, and even Klotho and Decuma made little effort to wave them away. A familiar hungry drunken state was upon them. Only Gershom seemed to have any fight left within. Haim looked around and he saw that Morta was watching Gershom closely, though she remained silent and motionless.

"She consumes what we kill and gives nothing back," Gershom said. "Why do we allow it?" He met Morta's gaze and sneered at the old woman. Her expression did not change.

Watching this unfold, Haim could see that the man misread what he saw, misread why Haim and the others in the circle started leaning back. Gershom grinned in triumph and reached for his blade. As he did so, the big man stepped back into the circle of light behind Gershom. Haim shuffled back quickly.

Gershom rose on one knee, and just as he thrust his body upwards to stand, the big man's spear struck him hard in the back and punctured his flesh with a wet cracking sound, driving him back down. The barest tip of the spear emerged from Gershom's chest. The only sound Gershom made was an expulsion of air that became a gasp and then a groan as his eyes bulged and he dropped his knife. The big man wrapped both hands around the spear and gave a sudden downwards thrust and the rest of the point burst through with a wet tearing sound and a great gout of blood that spilled over the picked-clean bone below him. Gershom fell to his knees and the big man pulled back hard and the spear point disappeared into the chest again, but then it got stuck on some complication of flesh or bone. The big man pulled harder but only managed to drag Gershom with him. The big man kicked Gershom flat against the ground and adjusted his stance, making short tugs on the spear as he turned the shaft this way and that until it began to move freely again. But now the shaft was wet. His hands slipped. Gershom thrashed below him and made guttural sounds into the earth. The big man tried to dry the shaft with his hands, but still they slipped. Klotho finally tossed him a rag and he used it to secure his grip and pulled the spear free. The gaping wound welled with blood that was black in the shadows and scarlet in the firelight and abundant everywhere.

The broken-nosed man roused himself and indicated Haim. The two of them grasped Gershom's feet and dragged him from the house into the yard.

"You vouched for him," the big man said once they were settled in their circle again about the meatless bone.

"And I dragged him into the yard," the broken-nosed man replied. The dark blood trail between them reflected the light in dull witness.

No one else spoke or had the energy to feed the fire or refill their drinks. The flies settled back upon them, and night stole over and claimed them each one by one. Only a few had the wits about them to leave the fading circle to find darker corners to sleep where they would succumb to what visions awaited. In this way, only a few of that group decided where to lay their heads, but none chose how they would awake.

The company of one hundred Jerusalem soldiers came into the yard as the moon drew near the end of its nightly tour. When they sighted Gershom's body, they knew they had found those they sought.

23
87 BCE

Haim dreamed that night of a subterranean system similar to what he had first dreamed of the night Chaya was in the well. Those long underground corridors echoed with the voice of someone calling. It was his voice. He haunted the underground maze, but he was unsure if he was the lost soul or the mad animal that stalked its sightless tunnels.

When Haim awoke, he was not underground, nor was he curled up on the floor against a wall lit only by the remaining coals' meagre light. Instead, when he awoke, he was in the air, being thrown from his resting place into the middle of the room. The room was now blazing with torches and packed with far too many men for the small house. Hands grappled and lifted and tossed Haim again between the rows of men and towards the door where he fell hard on the dirt floor, his face down in Gershom's bloody trail.

Disoriented and still waking up, Haim tried to stand and was kicked through the doorway and back onto the ground. There were loud sounds and words spoken about him, but his mind was still sleeping in the corner and his head was drunk and his legs shook though he was not even standing. He heard laughter. He found himself vomiting. Someone wrenched his head back and tore his hair at the roots and his burning scalp focused his attention. They dragged him by his hair farther into the firelit yard where Gershom lay in a pitch-black blood pool. The big man lay beside him in an even larger pool. Some fight had occurred while Haim had been dreaming of tunnels.

The men outside pulled Haim up, and it was then that he saw his broken-nosed companion. The man's face was freshly swollen. His wrists were bound together and then tied to a rear bar of a wagon. The rope continued to trail down from the man's wrists with enough length to bind Haim's wrists so that he could easily walk behind the broken-nosed man. But the captors did not give their binds any slack. They bound Haim's wrists directly to the broken-nosed man's so that they stood there facing one another. They would not be able to walk sideways for long, yet they also could not walk facing forwards without their shoulders constantly colliding together.

The group of soldiers moved out shortly after. Haim looked around, but there was no sign of the women or Chaya. It was a stumbling effort to follow the wagon and not get tangled up with the broken-nosed man or trip over stones in the road.

They stopped later in the night at an enclosure connected to the black shapes of two buildings. It soon became clear that this was where they were to rest. The soldiers retired and silence settled over the camp. The broken-nosed man sat down, dragging Haim with him. With no other choice, they lay on the road behind the wagon facing one another, wrists still bound together.

"Best sleep while you can," the man said. "There is no knowing what tomorrow will bring."

The broken-nosed man tried to use his own hands as a pillow some hours later, dragging Haim's hands with them, and Haim pulled back. The man snarled and tried to roll over, but there was no use in that either. They both slept poorly.

In the morning, the soldiers moved out early. They emptied provisions from the cart Haim was tied to and shared the food with all but the two captives. A Jewish soldier approached them with water, and both Haim and the broken-nosed man drank their fill. Their captors gave them nothing else.

After yesterday's ample wine and meagre meals, both Haim and the broken-nosed man were light-headed. The wagon started forwards again, and they walked as dead men. At midday, Haim stumbled and fell and pulled down with him the broken-nosed man who shouted and gripped Haim's shirt with his fists and refused to rise. He rode the Haim's sliding body as the road tore through Haim's clothing until a soldier called a halt and clubbed the older man and pulled Haim to his feet. Haim's shirt was nearly torn off his back, and his skin was abraded but not bleeding. The soldier splashed water across his back, which burned, and then he gave water to both captives and the company set out again. A trickle of blood dripped from the ends of the broken-nosed man's uncut hair. Haim said nothing about it.

The soldiers seemed to speak many languages, but often they spoke the common Aramaic. When they did they spoke of the war, of Jerusalem or Jericho's politics, or of similar things that men like to discuss to pass the time, things which are not things at all but merely a means to measure the tone of a man's voice and the alignment between that tone and his posture. Sometimes, though, they spoke about their current mission. Israel's civil war was approaching a climax. Alexander Jannaeus was planning a great demonstration to put an end to the years of rebellion.

"The Bandits of Samaria," the broken-nosed man croaked out. "That's what they're calling us."

It had not occurred to Haim that Morta's brood would have come to the attention of Jerusalem, earned a name, and inspired the formation of a company such as this to arrest their crimes.

"We're to be part of the king's prize," the broken-nosed man continued. "Some kind of spectacle. It's meant to show order. Establish that the king's in charge."

Haim said nothing. He could still see how the man's black eyes had glowered down on him during their struggle on the road. They had not been the eyes of a companion. There was no bond among Morta's brood without Morta.

On the second night, they struggled with the same wrist-bound barrier to comfort, and Haim felt his anger grow to match the broken-nosed man's. The next morning came with no water or warning from the soldiers. The cart's lurch gave the captives a rude awakening, and they struggled but managed to get on their feet just in time to avoid being dragged behind as the soldiers set off again.

Late in the day, Jerusalem appeared in the distance. As they approached the city, Haim saw that the surrounding open fields were littered with evenly spaced and neatly dug holes in the ground. Up ahead, men laboured in a crowd, and then Haim saw beyond the men a forest of poles, limbless tree trunks awaiting human decoration.

"Zeus in Hades," the broken-nosed man said.

Haim felt himself grow cold. This scene was Bet Yerah again, but there were not just a dozen or two crosses here. Hundreds of poles stood erect, arranged in double rows on either side of the road. And there were many more holes yet to be filled.

A pavilion stood on a hill overlooking the scene. The wagon stopped, and the captain of the company came back to see to his captives. He looked down from his horse at his dust-covered prizes and then followed their gaze from the forest of poles to the pavilion.

"The king will watch your crucifixions from there," he said. "Every rebel in this nation will know that there is no law but the king's law. You will scream with your kind in this place, and when you do, you will send the king's message for him."

"I'm no rebel of the king," Haim said quickly. His heart raced, and his legs were weak and jumpy and terror gripped him. He remembered the hours at Bet Yerah and the unending suffering of those hanging Galileans.

The captain laughed. "The Bandit of Samaria says he's not a rebel."

"I'm just a boy," Haim said. "They captured me against

my will and made me stay. If I hadn't worked with them, they would—"

The broken-nosed man roared and tried to swing at Haim, but their bindings made it easy for Haim to resist, and the two twisted around each other, wrists tied to wrists. When Haim fell, the broken-nosed man was quickly on him, roaring profanities and lifting his fists again to bludgeon the boy until a soldier stepped in and clubbed him a second time. They dragged the stunned man off Haim and finally cut the bond that joined them.

Once he was back on his feet, Haim turned again to the captain. "I swear it," he said. "My mother is of the tribe of Benjamin. My father taught me the Torah. These bandits killed them, and my sister and I have been their prisoners since."

"The young girl in the band is your sister?"

"Yes."

"We have eight hundred crosses prepared, but I don't yet have eight hundred prisoners. Barely six hundred. The festival is in five days, and we have wasted our time crossing Samaria looking for the bandits that were terrorizing that land. All we found were four. One already dead. One we had to kill since he wouldn't be captured. Your sister and the women ran off, and we let them go. And now I am to give you up too? I will have only one man on a cross for my week of searching?"

The captain adjusted the reins of his horse to turn away.

"I know where Pharisees are hiding," Haim said.

The captain stopped. He turned back towards Haim, tilted his head, and nodded for him to continue.

"They're two days of travel from here," Haim continued.

"They're not armed. A village protects them, but it's a quiet village. There are five, maybe ten Pharisees. Probably more by now. They live in caves outside the village—they do not respect the villagers. But the villagers honour and hide them. They do not go to the Jerusalem festivals any longer but have made their own customs that no longer require the temple."

"How many in this village?" the captain asked.

"Fifty. Maybe more."

"Fifty in the entire village?"

"Fifty men. There are women too. Altogether maybe a hundred."

"Women. Have you ever seen a woman crucified?"

"No."

"Neither have I, but they can scream the king's message as clearly as any man. How did you come to know of this village?"

"We passed through there."

The captain dismounted and approached the broken-nosed man where he knelt on the road. The captain lifted the man's chin and looked into his broken face. "Would you take us there?"

It was unclear if the bandit had followed the conversation at all. He frowned as he struggled to focus and finally spoke in a groggy voice. "I would take you to Hades." He tried feebly to spit at the captain, but his dry mouth had nothing to spit with. The captain dropped the bandit's head in disgust.

"Where is this village?" he asked Haim.

"In Galilee. Near Magdala."

"And you would do this? Take us there?"

"My father was loyal to the king before the bandits came and killed him." Haim's voice cracked. He thought of

Chaya and how he would have to explain their new back-story to her, but Chaya was not here. Her absence confused him. He was not used to being the author of their stories. He was thirsty and dizzy from hunger and the heat. "The people of Arbel gave the bandits shelter because the bandits were against the king. I am for the king, as were my family. They're all dead now except for me and my sister."

The captain stared at him, silent and unblinking.

"The bandits assaulted my mother before they killed her," Haim said. "I am no friend of them or the villagers of Arbel."

"After you did this for us, what would you do?"

"Search for my sister."

The captain nodded. "Cut him loose," he said to one of the soldiers. "Keep him with you. Give him food. Clean him up. We'll leave in the morning."

When Haim remembered Noach's face as he travelled on the road, he focused on where the man's home was relative to the road and the village. When he thought of Yechiel, he did the same. When he thought of Yechiel's wife and their children, he yanked his mind away from the family altogether and thought of the cliff path to the Pharisees' caves. When he thought of the old shepherd, he felt a narrow kind of hate that sharpened his memory as he mentally traced the cliff path to the canyon floor in case they had to search there as well.

Haim looked around him. There were twenty men on horses and two hundred on foot. They were travelling deep into Galilee for this assault, and so they had come with great numbers and caution.

Haim's hips and legs still ached from his rough journey tied to the broken-nosed man, who now sat in Jerusalem's prison while Haim rode to Arbel, paired with a different unhappy soldier during each leg of the journey. The soldiers passed Haim from man to man, always keeping him close to the captain. No one else in the company had ever ventured this far north. To this Judean force, Galilee was another country.

Haim rode unbound and carried no weapon. There was no escaping this mission. The soldiers were men from Egypt, Cypress, and other distant lands. It seemed that all the surrounding nations were happy to supply mercenaries for the Jewish king's army, though the king himself was not. While the soldiers fought for Judea, none were Jews themselves save for the captain and a few of his senior aides.

Scouts kept the road ahead clear, and by the time they were near Arbel's peak, they had already collected seven men, who were now bound and tied behind the supply cart the way Haim had been two days before. Five of the captives were Galileans, and where their loyalties lay none inquired.

"We need eight hundred," the captain said. "If they sound like northerners and they breathe, they'll do."

The captives stumbled along behind the carts in the same unbalanced posture Haim had known. Jerusalem's mercenaries explained nothing to them. Haim turned his mind away from the captives' voices and faces. He tried to focus on Chaya and wondered what had become of her and the women. Without the men, they could no longer rely on banditry. That left them little else to sustain themselves. He told himself that he was trading the people of Arbel for Chaya.

24

87 BCE

A CURSE PULSED PAIN through Haim's head and reached beyond his skull, sliding through bone and muscle and into his throat and his chest. A stone spider had fastened itself to the back of his head. It gripped the base of his skull and sank in its fangs, and poison seeped into him and twisted his mouth. It gave his eyes a fevered look and his countenance a deathly cast. While he walked, the sun glared down on him, cooking the stone at the back of his head, heating his skull, burning him within. He felt the hate of the unspeaking universe. He liked it, the hate, and did not try to escape, for he deserved it. Unlike the hate his mother had bestowed upon him in years so long ago, this hate he deserved. He embraced it.

Haim came to a place in Samaria where the bandit company had once camped. He could still spot traces of their passage here along with evidence of other travellers since.

In the days that followed, Haim walked back and forth throughout Samaria. He grew thin and his cheekbones became prominent. His hands clutched at the sword the captain had given him, which had been looted from Arbel, and he plucked at the sling he carried but did not use.

When he found the final home they had shared, he discovered that Gershom's and the big man's blood were still black stains on the stony ground, but the bodies were gone. The large picked-clean bone was still in the house where they had left it. The women and Chaya were not there.

Haim wandered across Samaria, sometimes travelling west, at other times north. He climbed to places the women would never have gone. He sat near roads and did not talk to travellers. A company of three came upon him once, rough men who could have been a new bandit fellowship. They approached Haim, but then they smelled him and looked in his eyes and muttered among themselves and went on their way. They never said a word to Haim.

Noach's face came to him again as he approached a dry streambed. A rock and patches of powdery sand floating on the dry ground's surface marked his passage. The tanner's face that came before him was swollen and beaten on one side from the fight at Arbel, but then later agonies distorted it further.

Haim stopped. The smell of powdery dust comingled with that of blood.

⁓

The tanner had been just one of eight hundred Haim passed on his way out of Jerusalem. The captain had released Haim only after all the king's victims were nailed and hung and beginning to cry out the king's message as foretold. The broken-nosed man was somewhere in that throng, though Haim did not see him or seek him out.

He saw Yechiel on his cross and the Pharisee who would have wed Chaya. The Pharisees of Arbel hung as naked as the villagers, as naked and pain wracked as the hundreds of others brought for the king's sport and to tell the king's message. They hung with their feet a hand's breadth from the ground, and every villager saw Haim make his escape, for their faces hung near eye level. The old goat herder spoke to him as he passed.

"Boy," the old man croaked. "Boy."

Haim stopped.

"Don't let them know you stayed with us, or they'll hang you too."

The old man did not know Haim's role in Arbel's betrayal. It had clearly been torture to say those few words, and the old man shuddered as he sank and hung and twisted against his nails. His face distorted and a barely audible cry rose from his parched throat. Haim gave him water from his water skin and then hurried away for fear that the soldiers would take offence. There was laughter then. It came from the hillside pavilion and he looked up to see the king, Alexander Jannaeus. The king had risen from his couch and come out from the shade of the pavilion. He stood overlooking the grisly scene of eight hundred souls in agony, and he laughed again. He gestured and two women came to him, neither one the queen and neither fully clothed. They handed him a cup and he drank and laughed a third time and pointed at the youth. One of the women said something, and Haim hurried away.

ॐ

Haim came back to himself at the streambed. He knew not how long he had stood in that place in the Samaritan desert. Dust had settled on his skin. The air was quiet and calm, as though nature itself waited for him to rediscover his place within it. He took a step forwards, and the dust rose in response. He climbed up onto the far bank of the dry stream and a bird came chittering and a light breeze picked up and he pressed on. There was no one there to question his passage through those empty places.

He killed a rodent with his sling, one he had never seen before and could not name. He had no way to cook it, and though his stomach hung empty and shrunken within, he could not bring himself to eat it raw. So he discarded it. He found a few remains of berries, dried on the vines, some so brittle they crumbled in his hands. He ate what he could recover and devoured the stems too and found a small spring of water that refilled his water skin and quenched his thirst. The clear cool drink ballasted his frail frame. Then he pressed on. He was intent on making it to some sure destination, though his feet had yet to discover what that place might be.

Haim looked at his unscathed wrists. He remembered the screams of the villagers. So many souls who had hung in his place. He moved suddenly with high steps, like the earth itself was hot and thrust his feet upwards. His upper body trembled strangely. He walked faster and found himself making a strange sound, a different form of the king's message. This variant he spread for the trees and rocks of that place to take heed. Madness came upon him, and that madness was the price of his freedom.

A spectre of the broken-nosed man came to Haim then in that place of hot stone and renewed thirst. The apparition said nothing but leaned over with an evil visage, wearing the wool of a haggard sheep over its shoulders, its skin grey and crawling, its face wearing Gershom's matted and infested beard. Signs of recent crucifixion were upon it. Insects crawled in its open wounds, and when the spectre opened its lips, nothing came forth but a foul wind.

Haim fell in a narrow channel between large stones and a hard scrape swelled up one side of his ribs but did not bleed. In other dry places, the faces of all the people of Arbel assaulted him and his tongue cleaved to the roof of his mouth and he staggered with his hands out before him, fingers splayed, bumbling like a blind man, for he could not see through the walls of spirits that clamoured for his recompense. Then the faces of banditry victims came as well, faces that had never before haunted him, ghosts that had been previously swamped by drink, by the companionship of like-minded people, and by his self-consuming hunger. Those ghosts came, and he had nothing to drown them with—not even the refreshment of water, for his water skin was again dry. His mind created scenes of greenery where there were none. He fell with his face pressing into a false waterhole and scooped the powdery sand into his mouth and knew then with a final sliver of clarity that he would die here. This drinking of dust would be his last act. Birds would pick him apart, or his skin would dry as his insides shrank. He would become a tent of sun-leathered skin, a hollow shell. If the birds did not tear him apart, then the seasons would disassemble his sun-dried body with sliding rocks or rolling winds. He imagined his mind to be a shallow, fragile lamp in the night, the wick guttering as it sucked in the final drops of oil and began consuming itself, preparing to waver and flash one last time in the dark.

Some time later, bony arms lifted him. They moved him and then a cart rattled and Haim's skull rhythmically tapped against its wood like some persistent emissary that relentlessly sought entry until hands lifted his head and set it back down on a roll of cloth. He knew nothing but the taste of water on his lips. He discovered that his throat could swallow without his consciously choosing to. After this drink, he knew nothing and went out of that place with no memory of its passage. He dreamed no dreams.

When Haim awoke, he was in a different place. There were trees and shade, and the earth beneath him was dense with many seasons' worth of pine needles. He sat up and his head swam, but this was no dream. He was on a hill overlooking a city. By the sun's position, he gauged it was late afternoon or early evening. His water skin was at hand and refilled. He drank long and rested and then drank more. There was a bundle of cloth that, when unwound, revealed a heel of bread, a small dried fish, and some figs and nuts he had never seen before. Haim ate carefully and tried to remember his rescuers, his passage to this place, and what circumstances led them to take him this far and no farther. He could remember voices but not their accents. Some men. A woman. He did not know if the hand that had steadied his head in the cart had been a man's or the woman's. He could not remember anything else of the journey. The city before him was beside a sea. Beyond the city, the late-day sun was out over the water, so he knew it was the Great Sea, the one he had grown up beside and not the Sea of Galilee or some other inland body of water. He looked again at the city, studied its walls and its buildings, and finally concluded that it was Dora. He had come back to Dora.

Haim rose to begin walking, but one leg cramped. He buckled on the hillside and fell back to the ground and gripped the rebellious muscle and drove his knuckles into it. He writhed there on the ground until the tension released, and then he lay there, matted with needles, as his sweat dried and his breath calmed.

After a while, he rose again. This time he moved slowly and his leg did not rebel. He went to a nearby creek and drank long and refilled the skin and bathed. He held his head underwater longer than he ever had before, and when he raised it again, he gasped and felt alive. Weak, but alive. A slick of stained water swirled and shifted downstream.

He thought then of a wild donkey he had once seen, high in some pass of rock and sun. It had been dead, unattended to by scavengers. Hard skin stretched across the creature's frame outlining its jagged ribs. He knew this image had inspired what he had believed to be his final thoughts. He had envisioned his thin frame would share the donkey's fate as he lay in that stream of powdered sand, waiting to die. After drinking more cold water from this stream, Haim stood in the evening light and felt reborn.

There was a small purse by the water skin that was filled with a few coins, enough for a week of room and board in Dora. He looked about the forest, and there was no one in that place that he could thank. He sat beside the water skin and ate from the cloth package and felt as though he should cry or rejoice but instead just felt empty and tired.

Before the sun set, he was asleep once more, and he did not stir again until late the next morning. When he arose, he had only one thought on his mind.

I have to find Chaya.

25

87 BCE

Entering Dora for the second time, Haim expected to see the big man and the broken-nosed man and Gershom and Klotho, Decuma, Morta, and Chaya. He went to the inn they had stayed at before, but the keeper did not recognize him. The man sized Haim up in a single glance and seemed disappointed with what he saw. He led the thin wraith to a room that was little more than a closet. The slave that brought Haim's bath was more attentive. He seemed to recognize his guest but said nothing and departed in silence.

Haim ate simply and alone as the sounds of the inn around him reminded him of normal conversation among ordinary people. He left his small room and went out to a drinking place attached to the inn where he ordered water and wine, and he mixed the two, for he did not want to get drunk. He wanted only to be alive among this intermingling of humanity. He spoke with a few there, offering only simple statements and smiles as though he were a creature unused to the company of others. When he grew tired once more, he returned to his room alone and slept to the muffled sounds of people in rooms around him.

Haim found Chaya a few days later. She was in the brothel where Gershom had taken the men nearly two years ago. Klotho and Decuma had returned to their old trade. Morta still ruled them. He feared that the women's ancient profession had claimed Chaya as well, but he could not ask her and she did not say that first day, though based on her manner and suggestions, he believed it had.

"Come with me," he said.

"You have nowhere to go," Chaya said. She wore a tattoo now. The head of a snake lay etched in the flesh between her thumb and forefinger, its body curling up her wrist and arm.

"Anything but this," Haim said.

"Anything?" Her expression held both contempt and indifference. "I've had anything. It did not serve me well. Take me back to Arbel."

He refused and they fought. He could not tell her that the village was no more. She clearly misinterpreted his refusal, but he dared not explain.

"Stubborn and stupid," she said. "Nothing can be done with you."

"You would never pass for a Jew now," Haim said, pointing at her tattoo, a mark forbidden to Jews. "The people of Arbel would know you to be a dirty Samaritan in an instant."

He just said it. He had chased the conversation away from

Arbel but in doing so had chased her away from him as well. He did not know if he would ever see her again after that. Two days passed with no contact. They met again on the third day, but a new stillness and coldness came from her. They said nothing of earlier insults. She had covered up her hand with a cloth.

"We're going north," she finally said.

"North? To Acco?"

"Farther."

"Tyre?"

She shook her head. "Near Antioch."

"Antioch? To the Seleucids?"

She nodded. "There is a place there. A garden. A temple."

Haim looked at her, puzzled.

"A grove," she said, as though that explained it better.

He still did not understand.

"I could become a priestess," she said.

"A priestess? Of what? Baal?"

"Yes."

"Chaya!" Haim was alarmed. This was more than Gershom's house of rented women. This was more than a snake tattoo. "Chaya!"

She flinched at his response but not as much as she should have. She did not square her shoulders nor did she retreat. She met his gaze firmly. "I am young, and I look different than the Seleucids or Africans. I look like a Jew."

"I don't understand."

"Morta says I would bring a good price."

"A good price. For who?"

"Sometimes, the priestesses marry. Men from Antioch take them home. They pay the temple for the right, and they cannot divorce a priestess of Baal if they marry one."

"Chaya!"

"I would not live as I have lived here, and I would not live like we did when we robbed and killed in Samaria, and I would not be hungry and hunted like we were across the Jordan. I will be my own woman. I will be rich in that garden, and if I ever leave it, I will be provided for as long as I live. The law says so."

"Chaya."

"It's an honour for a Seleucid to marry a priestess of Baal. They usually go to rich homes."

"From a common whore to an uncommon whore."

It was the last thing he ever said to her. She left immediately and would not see him the next day nor the day after. Haim wandered about Dora alone, taking in his late father's city with dull eyes, sitting in shaded places and eating frugally on a stomach that was still unused to large meals. Late on the fourth day, the innkeeper met him as he entered the courtyard.

"You had visitors today," he said. "Your companions from before." The man looked at Haim closely, then grunted. "Yes, it is you. I did not recognize you alone, but the women, yes. They left you this." He held out a package wrapped in a large blanket. Haim recognized it.

"Did they leave a message for me?" Haim asked.

"They were leaving town," the innkeeper said. "I did not see the men from before with them. They left on a temple wagon."

"Did they leave me a message?"

"The beautiful one. The older one. Not the hag. The Egyptian. She said some things, though not for you."

"Was there a girl with them?" Haim asked.

"The girl from before? Yes, she was with them."

"Did she say anything?"

"Yes. She said, 'It's more than he deserves.' I guess you and her don't get along."

Haim took the package back to his room and unwrapped it. Inside was the old scribe's cloth pack, flattened and empty, alongside a pouch of money, a short sword he did not recognize, the knife the Galilean boy had given him at Magdala, and another water skin, so now he had two. There was also a shirt that was not his and not new, but it fit. That was it. There was no note. He did not even know if any of the women could write.

Haim put out the lamp. The innkeeper charged for oil. He sat in the dark and tried to focus. Neither Chaya nor the women had said anything about the big man or Gershom. None had asked about the broken-nosed man or the road to Jerusalem or how Haim had escaped and found his way to Dora.

Haim felt hollow like an empty cistern and remembered the skin-stretched donkey carcass again, the one he had found on Samaria's hot slopes. He wondered how birds or insects or weather had not punctured that tight dried skin and how long he could go on before the cage that housed his own chest would fail him.

It had been years since he had left the widow's house. He turned his head and could see nothing in his lightless closet. He felt more alone now than he had leaving the widow's house. He lay down and what he felt made it hurt to breathe, but it brought no tears. His life had cost an entire village. More than fifty souls had hung on crosses because of him. His life had also cost the lives of travellers on Samaria's roads for the better part of two years, the count of which he did not know. He thought about the boy, his first killing, Chaya watching. He thought of Chaya and their last words and tried to remember her childish chatter in the days after the well before they had crossed the Jordan, in the Valley of Doves before the wolf, during the few days between Arbel and meeting Marta's brood. Everything good he could recall had occurred just before something bad.

Haim pulled his old blanket over himself even though he was not cold. He felt tired in a way that went deeper than a need for sleep. He examined phantoms and the unsupportable weight in his chest. He did not toss and turn but lay as though chained in that position, staring sightlessly, unsleeping. He knew that his mind would go dark eventually and that he would awake more tired than when he had lain down.

He left the inn the next day and walked south from Dora. The road took him past the widow's house. He felt no fear of that place, only dim curiosity, and when he looked in on it, he found the house abandoned. Mice had taken up residence inside. The old goat pen was gateless and overgrown with weeds up to his shoulders. He was unable to find the garden he had carefully prepared at the old scribe's direction.

He went on from there to Strato's Tower and encountered a welcoming family.

26
87 BCE

SOUTH OF DORA and the widow's abandoned home lay the town of Strato's Tower. There, a Jewish family who held to the old ways welcomed Haim. Warm light bathed the common room. The man of the house settled himself around the low table with his wife and five children and indicated for Haim to join them.

Haim sat, and they served a barley porridge with onions, leeks, and ground olives. It was simple and plain and reminded Haim of the widow's house and the old scribe's frugal diet. There was no leg of stolen lamb dominating the centre of this family circle. This was an honest household. After the meal, they sipped barley water flavoured with dill and salt.

"We've put some wine vinegar in this drink as well," the man said.

"With a bit of honey," his wife added.

"Honey." The man shook his head and looked at Haim.

"You don't need the honey. Better for your stomach without it. She puts honey in it for the children. Now, tell me your story."

Haim had not thought through the cost of hospitality when he had entered the house. He would have to give them a story in return.

"I'm from Arbel," he said without thinking. Haim wondered if his tongue would forever betray him. He went on to claim to be a refugee from the village, a survivor of the king's raid, and created a story to explain his escape.

"Do you know what happened after the raid?" the man asked.

Haim shook his head.

The man nodded gravely and gestured for his wife to take the children away.

"Do you have a wife?" he asked. "Children?"

"No. Neither."

The man frowned. "The men were all crucified," he finally said. "The king had a number to meet." He caught Haim's eye, and for a moment, Haim thought the man knew his lie, but then it seemed that he was just angry and wanted Haim to know it. "Crucifixion wasn't all. They took the women and children as well."

Haim nodded.

"They brought the families before their crucified husbands and fathers and stood them right there so they could see each other. They matched up each man with his family." The man stared at a section of the floor as he spoke. "Jannaeus made the families watch their men as they suffered. Made them speak to one another. Then after a while, the soldiers cut the women's throats."

The man trembled, and his voice shook with barely controlled rage. "They held the women up by their hair while they bled. Then they did the same to the children. All this, right in front of the men on their crosses, because having them hang there in physical agony was not enough. They had to hurt *deeper*. That's what the Sadducees did to the Pharisees. That's how Jerusalem repaid Galilee for years of service."

The man described the horrors further as though he had witnessed them himself and continued telling his angry tale without a single glance up to see how Haim was taking the news.

These were the events that had occurred after Haim had left Jerusalem. Sitting at that table at Strato's Tower, hearing what he had failed to witness or even imagine, Haim twisted and turned as though trying to escape his host's report. The man pressed on and told of Jannaeus celebrating on a hill overlooking the scene.

"He became drunk with his whores like some filthy Seleucid. Eight hundred crosses entertained him and thousands more bled on the ground in front of those Greek trees." The man suddenly snatched the clay bowl before him and pulled back his arm to throw it, but he restrained himself in time. The bowl clattered back onto the table still intact. "Jannaeus's mercenaries spent two days afterwards just hauling away the bodies. This is what Eretz-Israel has come to."

By the next day, Haim had become famous in Strato's Tower for having escaped the crucifixions. His shock and pain were cause for sympathy as the city understood him to be mourning family and friends. The people of that city had little love for the king, and they wanted to do something to honour Haim and his village.

Haim, consumed by grief that was clearly written on his every feature, fled before evening. Shame tore at him, and he ran until his breath carved a raw path down his throat and burned in his chest.

He kept moving south. He kept to the coastal road, sleeping behind bushes along the way, until he came to Joppa. Autumn's cool air had arrived, and he did not want to sleep outside. He found another house and another family who still held to the traditions of hospitality and welcomed him to sit by their hearth. In this house, he was careful with his stories, avoiding any lies that would bring him pain or risk challenging his hosts' unknown loyalties. Instead, he told tales that were true of others. He talked about being attacked on the road by Samaritan bandits, and his story was authentic, even if his role in it was reversed.

From Joppa, he walked farther south for two more days, stopping only to sleep. He lay hidden away from the road at night. Close to the sea there were fewer trees and the air held a salty scent he remembered from his childhood. He listened to the pounding of the waves and watched the stars pass as they spied on him in that open place.

Late on the second day, he came to Ashkelon, the place of the small onions from the Feast of Dora. He remembered it from the old scribe's stories of Samson, and he remembered that the blood of his mother's husband, the dye maker, may have traced back to Ashkelon. Through that blood, Haim could be connected to the Philistines, and he wanted that connection to mean something, to be a sign of his salvation, though he was no actual son of the dye maker.

The city gates were closed. He had no desire to talk to the guards on the other side and try to convince them to open the bars for him. He sat on a long slab of raised stone near the road and watched the sun as it fell into the sea. Dusk gave way to darkness.

An old man approached carrying a lamp. He settled near Haim and set his light between them. The small flame was now the brightest thing around.

"It'll be a long night if you're waiting for the gates to open," the old man said.

Doomed encounters rarely come with a warning— danger wraps itself in mystery and evil unfolds so slowly and with such charm that by the time a victim understands what is occurring, it is too late. Haim had walked two days without anyone to talk to except his own haunted soul. He needed to commune with another. He was open to a new voice and new ideas, and so his thoughts were dull. He should have run away.

As much as Haim welcomed the company, as soon as the old man started speaking, Haim's attention strayed. His mind fixed on trying to remember the name of the city south of here and weighing whether he should continue travelling towards it. If he had paused to consider the old man carefully at the beginning, he might have noticed his similarity to the old scribe. The old Ashkelonite was not a Jew, but he had the same deeply grooved expressions, the same measured and calm voice, and he was a comfort to Haim, though Haim was not consciously aware of it. He remained fixated on cities' names and where he should go next, so he did not see what advanced upon him in plain view.

When the old man did not receive a response, he spoke

to Haim in a different language, which Haim did not know. Haim noticed the old man switch to a third and then a fourth tongue, so Haim finally spoke.

"I've got nowhere in particular to go," he said. "I can wait here or somewhere else. It doesn't matter. I can't walk in the dark. I can wait here."

"You are lost," the old Ashkelonite said.

"It's Ashkelon," Haim said with a gesture.

"Many who come to Ashkelon are lost. You are not the first."

"I'm not lost."

"The last Jew to come through here was also lost."

"I'm not a Jew," Haim said, "and I'm not lost."

"You are a Jew." The old man nodded at this, his movement barely more than a shadow in the light of the small lamp. "The other Jew died as soon as he entered the city."

"How did he die?" Haim asked.

"The way all Jews die. He stopped breathing."

"Other people die some other way?"

"You should ask what caused him to die."

"How did he die?" Haim asked again.

"The cessation of breath," the old man said. He made an elaborate gesture as he said this, his hands fluttering about his ribs with his cheeks puffed out as though to demonstrate some particular sort of not-breathing that was dramatic and uncommon but well known to wise men.

"I don't need this," Haim said.

"What do you need?"

As much as the old man's words irritated Haim, there was something in his manner that brought back strong memories of the old scribe. They were good memories.

"What do you need?" the man asked again. It was not the words that pierced Haim but how the old man said them. The tone of the man's voice made the question sink deep within. Haim opened his mouth to speak, but no sound came. His throat tightened so that only air escaped. Haim closed his mouth, and then he understood that his mind had waited to hear what his mouth would say. Unable to speak, he was left not knowing his answer. The realization that he was not always the author of his mouth's words and that he waited to hear his answer like any other listener alarmed him. It were as though his outer self was a slave to whatever unknown inner part controlled his tongue.

Something arose within like heat, and it spread from his chest to his shoulders and up into his face.

"That last Jew wanted the same thing as you," the old man said.

Haim felt something he only partially understood, and the word that best described it was pain, though that word was not complete and did not fully express the thing beneath the heat, a thing like anger. He needed to not be mocked by this old man, and he turned to look at him, and what he saw in those watery, lamplit eyes was not mockery. The old man's eyes held the same expression that the old scribe's had when he would ignore the household's female voices and carefully instruct Haim on some matter of history or the Torah or geography. The old scribe's unwaveringly calm voice had made him seem ageless. He had shared wisdom untroubled by the noise around as though he had already been removed from all of life's turmoil.

The man on the stone seat at Ashkelon, if he noticed Haim's tension, ignored it like the old scribe had ignored the widow and the girls. It occurred to Haim that this Ashkelonite man was speaking to the secret part of him, the part that had tried and failed to operate his voice. The old man was not speaking to the outer Haim. He was not speaking to the surface part that listened like any other stranger on the road. The Ashkelonite spoke to the inner Haim that knew what needed to be said, the part that lay below his conscious mind and gave the mouth its words.

The old man spoke then of living as though in darkness. It was a long and rambling discourse by the low light of the small lamp. When it seemed that Haim's attention was fading, the Ashkelonite changed his tack and began to describe a blind man's journey through a building.

"The building had many passages," the old man said. "Its corridors curled around one another. There were no dead ends. No doors to the outside. Only a ladder hidden above on a high ledge that needed to be pulled down for anyone to escape, for the building was carved into a great rock in the ground and the only way out was up.

"In fact, it wasn't a building at all," the man continued. "It was a maze, open to the air above."

The old Ashkelonite described the way the blind man lived within this maze. He described the violence that was done to the blind man by five other blind men travelling in a group, for the five were all desperate to escape, were all blind and could not see the ladder above them, none knowing they lived within a maze.

"The five blind men believed that the first man blocked their way, so they killed him." The Ashkelonite adjusted the lamp's wick then set it back on the stone ledge between them. He looked up and met Haim's gaze then looked out into the night. "In time, the group of blind men re-en-countered the body of their victim, for they had circled and crossed the maze aimlessly for years. They passed the body without much thought, and eventually they came back to stumble over it again and again.

"The first of the five made no connection between the body and their victim, for their victim had been upright and struggling and the dead body was only a stumbling block. Do you see how a blind man might not recognize a struggling man and a dead body as the same being?"

Haim nodded.

"The second of the five blind men thought that the obstacle might have some greater significance. It was different than the level floor and vertical walls and sharp corners that had become their universe, but he could not figure out the object's significance. It was just something to step over. He dismissed the insight that had stirred, and it died in his darkened mind."

"What about the others?" Haim asked.

"The third blind man perceived that the obstacle was the body of their previous victim, but he did not think on it further. He could have discovered more, but he did not know what to do with his insight, so he too put it all out of thought.

"The fourth man understood what the third man understood: this was their prior victim. He took this reasoning a step further and realized that the body could be used as a marker, differentiating one place from another. He could map every lane and corner now by where it stood in relation to the body. He named the feet's direction rearwards and the head's direction forwards. He now had his cardinal directions and could map the entire maze by counting steps forwards and rearwards. But it was the fifth man who understood the most."

Haim waited, but the old man seemed to have stopped his story. He followed the man's gaze to the dark walls of Ashkelon. "What about the fifth man?"

"The fifth man understood that the maze was too complicated to map with only one waypoint body, and so he killed each of his companions in turn. Once they were dead, he dragged them about, scattering them throughout the maze as markers. Finally, he could run from body to body, confident in where he was going. In doing so, he learned the maze's every twist and turn. He became the master of his domain. But he remained alone. He never discovered the ladder overhead, and so he never escaped. He eventually died there. After the fifth man, there was no one left to use him as one more marker. The world of that maze became silent, and only birds passing over saw what remained of the drama.

"Do you understand?" the old man asked.

Haim knew that the Ashkelonite did not expect him to respond immediately. He recognized the story form from the old scribe's lessons.

The old man turned his attention to the lamp and adjusted the wick once again before carefully measuring more oil and refilling the bowl in the awkward light. After this, he sat in a state of contemplation. In telling his story and asking his question, it seemed that the man had completed his night's work.

Haim looked up at the sky and the wheel of bright stars that were now visible. He knew they were turning but turning so slowly that his eye could only see it if he looked away for a time and then looked back. Their movement was steady and slow and beyond direct perception. The sky was the most patient of all predators. In the stars, he could practically see the seed of his own story, a vision of the person he could one day become, but he was like the second man in the maze: aware that there was something there but unable to draw any insight from it.

"The men could not see," Haim said. "They needed someone outside the maze to tell them about the ladder, or someone within the maze with eyes who could look up and see."

The old man smiled in the dim light. "If there were no eyes at all in the world of that maze, what then?"

Haim knew there must be a way for the blind men to escape. The story was a lesson in a riddle, and such riddles always had answers.

"Hands," he said finally. "They saw with their hands in front of them. Hands held up could feel the ladder. But they could not walk with their hands out in front. They would have to walk with their hands raised to find the ladder on the high ledge."

"How would they avoid injury while walking in this way?" the Ashkelonite asked.

"With a map based on the dead man—then they would have the confidence to walk with their hands raised high and not fear running into a wall, for they would know how many steps there were until the next turn."

"Good."

"Or there is another way where no one needs to die. One blind man could lead with his hands in front of him, wandering aimlessly like they were before, and another could follow with one hand on his guide's shoulder and the other in the air. If they had left the first man unharmed and added him to their number, they would have six men and could divide into three pairs, each wandering around separately. When one pair found the ladder, they could shout to their companions, and soon all would find the ladder and climb out together."

The old man agreed. "There are many solutions. But first, you have to see. First, you have to know that you are not looking for a door before you or a window beside you. First, you have to imagine that out is up and that there might be a ladder on a ledge above you. Having explored all the walls, the fifth man, left alone, might have spent his final years searching the floor for a trapdoor. He may never have considered a ladder somewhere above."

The Ashkelonite sat in silence then. The lamp flickered, but not from a breeze. There was some impurity in the oil that made the flame waver.

"So, what do you want?" the Ashkelonite asked again.

"I want to see," Haim said. "I don't know how things work. How things fit together. I don't know where to go. I don't know what to do."

The old Ashkelonite smiled. Haim could not see him well in the failing light, but he could hear the smile in his voice. "Now, I know you," the old man said, "and I can take you to what you need."

27
87-85 BCE

THE COOL OF the late-harvest air became the cold wet winds of winter. Then spring came, summer progressed, and yet another year cycled through the seasons before Haim finally made his escape from Ashkelon.

The light of a merciless sun found him south-east of the city. He fled across a field of rubble and stone and carried on towards the treeline where he hid in terror, startled by the slightest hints of sounds. But he recovered and rushed on. His feet were bare and left traces of blood to mark his passage. He was naked above the waist. His ribs and the round ridges of his spine moved visibly below thin skin. His exposed legs and knees were not those of a healthy eighteen-year-old but the misshapen knobs and sticks of an ancient wreckage. His eyes stared from darkened pits and his tongue was an unnatural colour, a product of the Ashkelon temple's ministrations. His mind flashed with recurring visions of the priestesses and the eunuch-priests of that place. They had kept feeding him their potions months after the euphoria had faded, and the stunning visuals and the substitution of colour for sound had morphed into anxiety and then paranoia and finally this terror.

The sight of a potentially innocent mushroom in the forest, yellow capped and fragile, filled him with fresh waves of fear. He began to run again, and he was as mindless of his bare feet as the frenzied celebrants at Ashkelon's temple festivals were mindless of their cut skin.

At the last festival, young men in madness, amid the flutes and drums and horns, had seized the temple's sacred swords, and on the steps of the great temple, they had castrated themselves to the triumphant roar of the crowd. They had held up their severed organs and run into the streets of Ashkelon, where women had served them with screams of adoration. He ran like those unmanned and soon-dead worshippers. He was as blind to his pain and hunger and near-nakedness as they. Still, where they had run for madness and towards ecstasy and insanity and death, he ran in terror and towards freedom. He prayed out loud, with tears, to the old scribe's Jewish god to save him, and he ran, though he did not know where to run to.

That night he slept in a hollow under a great and spreading tree's raised roots. He slept nearly naked and was cold and awoke in the morning in a continual shiver. He crawled out of his hole, and his mind was still awash with a confusion of colour and sound. He had unhealed sores on his body that sacred temple dogs had previously licked clean, but now, fleeing through the wilderness, he had no way to clean himself. He began to walk again, and there was a humming sound within that only he could hear.

As he walked, memories of the previous seasons came in irregular flashes. The memories came like a drug's delayed hallucinations, but he knew some of the memories were real and some nearly real, with mild distortions, and they came to him out of order, for his mind was out of order.

He walked, as best as he could judge by the sun, heading east, and he tried not to stop.

He remembered the youths of Ashkelon coming to Ashtaroth's temple and shaving their heads in homage to the Queen of Heaven. Those memories mixed in his mind with the licking dogs.

He remembered the young women who had refused to shave and chose instead to stand within the temple for one day, available for the pleasure of any foreigner who would take them, and this was their alternative sacrifice to the goddess, all for the sake of saving their hair.

These memories washed over him and then mixed with his jagged last memories of Chaya and then he found himself on the ground, on his elbows and knees, sobbing. He did not weep with natural grief. He sobbed as though he could force some form of evil out of his mind and body through his cries and trembling and tears. He did not know whether it was a demon he needed release from or simply a bleeding of his mind's visions. It could have been death, signalling the end not with an external murderous advance as most men feared but as a spirit violently vacating him from within. He did not know. He could not tell. He could only prostrate himself on the ground, nearly naked, and weep.

After a while, he stood again on shaky legs and continued walking. Sheep freshly sheared came into memory. They had bleated their distress as they had been taken from the temple to a pyre of a dozen pines trees that had been felled and dragged and then stacked together, the logs not lying flat but leaning on one another and rising high with chains binding their middles and peaks, seeming to form into one new, giant pyramidal tree. The priestesses had then bound the strangely naked sheep and hoisted them up into this new tree formed of many trunks. So they had hung in the air and bleated to the crowds. After the libations of the god and the goddess had been poured and their images paraded about the spectacle, the priestesses set the entire creation on fire.

As Haim's mind was lost in these unrelenting visions, his body came upon a small, lone house in the desert east of Ashkelon near slopes that had started to become green again. As he looked at the house and imagined its inhabitants, he remembered surveying such homes in northern Samaria with evil intent and with evil friends. The feeling that followed was more than he could bear. He stared, overcome by memory. Then a new vision filled his mind, one of offerings at Ashkelon. There had been one family in particular, a family of five who had brought their sixth, a small child only a few weeks old. The priestesses had prayed and blessed the family. Eunuchs had poured strong wine. The father had spoken his part to Ashtaroth, the Queen of Heaven, and the priestesses then said the liturgy. The baby was then bound within a sack and taken to a place atop the temple's wall overlooking a rocky pit where the priestess hurled it, and the rotating, kicking bundle fell into the sacrificial pit where it burst on the rocks below.

Haim forced his mind away from the scene. He thought

instead of the animals in that place. Unlike the baby, the animals brought to the goddess were taken home alive after the ceremonies. The animals were unharmed in the temple. Later they were ritually dispatched at home and consumed as part of the household larder.

The pigeons of that place were considered sacred. None harmed them within or without the temple. The same protection applied to the healing dogs who cleaned the sores of supplicants. At the end of their lives, the dogs were buried in a grove outside the temple with great care and ceremony.

All this came to Haim as he looked at the isolated house near temporarily green slopes and he remembered the infant again and imagined the children in this house. Though he was hungry and needed clothing and shelter and aid for his wounds, he walked away. He found the road beyond and turned north and continued to walk on blistered feet long into the night.

28

85 BCE

"I TOLD YOU HE wasn't dead," said a man's voice.

As far as Haim could remember, it was late on the fourth morning after Ashkelon. He opened his eyes and saw stonework in front of him.

Haim rolled stiffly to his back and looked up the wall to where its broken top ended in the open sky. A few broad beams traced where a roof had once been. The beams were deeply pitted and grooved by the mining efforts of generations of insects.

His body ached and his head ached. His mouth was parched. His tongue lay thick against his teeth. His throat was nearly closed, letting through only a whisper of breath.

Haim turned towards the voices. Three men sat around a bed of brightly glowing coals near the open doorway at the far end of the room. Two were busy eating and looked only briefly at Haim as he sat up. The third regarded him with a stern stare as though eyeing some specimen or deception or something else of particular interest.

Haim's head swam. Its floating pain shifted from behind his forehead to above one temple and then settled at the rear of his skull. He closed his eyes and stayed where he was for some time just holding his head.

It was finally the closing dryness in his throat that made him rise. He could hear a creek nearby. He remembered hearing it in the night but had been unable to find it in the dark.

Haim stepped across the room on stump-like feet. The sharp pain from many cuts registered as high, shrill shrieks in his head that verberated against the deep tones of soreness in his legs and hips and back. He walked carefully around the men. They stopped eating and watched his progress in silence.

Out the main door, he made his way through bright sunlight and past a wagon and a grazing donkey to the bush-concealed creek. At the water's edge, he stripped off his waist covering, walked carefully into the water, and sat down within its cold, quiet flow. Life came back to his limbs in the stream and soon he was able to summon the strength to dip his mouth into the creek and let the water run in. He lifted his head and swallowed and discovered no damage to his throat, just dryness. He drank repeatedly and then lay back and let his head slide under the current and felt his hair and beard float free and clean.

After a while, Haim sat up again, dripping and cold, and he laughed. By himself in the water, he laughed and then wept and then laughed again and started to cry once more and lay back in the water to stop the cycle. When he sat up again, he was calm. He could no longer endure frenzy. He no longer trusted any food or drink prepared by unknown hands. The creek he trusted, and he drank again from the cold water.

Haim scrubbed his open sores and cleaned his feet and had no regard for pain in that cold water, and when he stood, he was naked and thin and scarred and bore recent wounds that were still red, but he felt like himself for the first time in seasons. He believed it was four days since his escape, and he had not eaten anything but a few late-season berries and the raw roots of some wild plants the old scribe had once shown him.

He left the loincloth, his only possession, where it lay and walked naked from the creek back towards the ruined house.

A bird at the house was harassing the three men. It had a crow's loud call but it was the same size as the pigeons of Ashkelon's temple, and it dived at the men above their coals and was trying to chase them from a cake of seed bread. The men waved the bird away, and it landed on the donkey's haunch and pecked sharply at the beast, which brayed and bucked and pulled at the rope that held it. One of the men cursed and began to stand, but the others stilled him and pointed at Haim, who stood scrawny and naked on the edge of the clearing.

The bird swept back into the house and past the men's heads and up through the roofless ceiling. It crowed at them again from the top of the wall. The men were disoriented. They looked at Haim, at the bread near the coals, at the bird. The bird came through the men's circle again, veering between outflung arms and then flying across the yard. It made for the donkey's head, startled and upset the beast again, and then sat on the bare limb of a nearby oak and squawked.

Haim stepped into the clearing on tattered feet and made for the rear of the wagon, where he picked up a sling that hung there. Before the men realized what he was doing, he slipped a stone into its pouch. As he wound up the sling, the three stood in alarm, but he turned his face away from the men, adjusted his swing, and then released the toggle. The pouch opened and the stone flew straight and the bird became a flurry of feathers and fell from its perch. Haim continued walking away from the wagon and the house and the men. When he got to the critically injured but not yet dead bird, he wrung its neck. Once the life was gone from the little creature, Haim dug his thumb into the base of its neck, forcing his nail through feathers to pierce the skin. Then, having penetrated the bird's flesh, he jerked his wrist in a fluid motion that broke the bird's head from its spine and started peeling the skin down the body. He twisted and broke off the wing bones and kept peeling the skin down until the carcass of the bird emerged. He held it in one hand, his thumb pressing firmly into the neck hole, and with a final pull, he ripped the feathered skin and tail from the body. Only the feet remained with a few small feathers still clinging there.

Haim let the bird finish bleeding out onto the ground below the oak and then dug his nail into the white and blue belly and stripped the organs away as well, leaving only meat and bone in his hand. Only then did he turn and look at the men watching him. He bent and picked up the sling in his one unbloodied hand, returned it to the wagon, and then advanced naked towards the doorway and the fire, holding the cleaned bird before him.

"I need a corner of your coals," he said.

The three men resettled themselves to make room for Haim. They were all Jews. One of the men handed Haim a stick, and he impaled the bird carcass on it and sat and held the stick over the coals.

The men retrieved their bread, and one offered Haim a corner. Though his stomach leaped at the offer, he declined. "Haven't had meat in a long time," Haim said simply.

"Shouldn't be a problem with a sling hand like that," one man said.

"I'll get another sling soon," Haim said.

"You've fallen on some hard times," another man said. He had a rectangular head, a heavy jaw, and a friendly smile countered by oddly prominent veins at both temples like great blue worms just below the skin, imprisoned in jagged wriggles. "You could use some bread too."

"Perhaps instead of hard times, you've just had some hard companions," the last man said.

"No good ones," Haim said. He turned the roasting bird and did not look at the men. "Beware the priestesses of Ashkelon."

At that, the three men sat back, and the heavy-jawed man exhaled slowly. "What do you know of the priestesses of Ashkelon?"

"I am just four days from the temple there," Haim said.

"They didn't let you go willingly," he said.

"No."

"You have nothing."

Haim nodded.

"You had things when you entered that temple," the man said. It was an accusation.

"I entered the temple at night," Haim said. "At the invitation of an old man. I did not know where I was going. What month is it?"

The men told him. Haim counted. Nodded. "Nearly two years I was there."

"You should not have lived to return," the heavy-jawed man said.

Haim nodded. "That was their intention."

"The sling." It was the second man talking now. "Where did you learn to handle a sling?"

"I was a goat herder along Samaria's border," Haim said. "I hunted birds and drove off jackals with my sling. Even killed a wolf once."

"You did not," the heavy-jawed man said.

"I did. The skin now hangs in the temple I fled. I won't be returning to reclaim it."

"Have you ever killed a man?" Tension suddenly spread around the fire, and Haim did not know if the civil war had ended or what part these men might have played in it.

"Once. Bandits attacked us on the road. In Samaria."

The men nodded. "Those bandits were caught and crucified along with the other rebels against the king." The men seemed satisfied by Haim's answer.

"Where will you go?" the heavy-jawed man asked.

Haim had begun eating the bird. The grease and meat were intoxicating, and he had to force himself not to become frantic in front of this group. "I have nowhere to go." He waved his hand vaguely. "The bandits." The flesh was a consuming distraction, and it made him want to scream and weep, and he felt it like the madness of the temple was coming again. He restrained himself and told himself he would cast the bird away if his rebellious body did not submit. It did submit, but an edge crept into his voice.

"They took your family."

Haim nodded. His gratitude at being misunderstood made his eyes water, and he stuck the undercooked side of the bird back over the fire and waited.

"What about your clothes?" the heavy-jawed man asked.

"They were from the temple."

"You buried them?"

"Yes," Haim said. "In the bushes."

"Good enough. You did well to bathe. You cannot take that filth into Jerusalem. We'll get you something else to wear."

Haim went back to eating the bird, picking through what little remained. The men spoke of the war with the Pharisees that was now past. They talked about the siege of Tyre, which Alexander Jannaeus had launched shortly after the crucifixions. They spoke about the comet that could still be seen in the distant sky as it departed. According to some, the comet had initiated a new era—that of Dionysus, the fifth son of Grypus. He was now the ruler of the southern portion of the Seleucid empire with his throne at Damascus. Because of the comet, people now called Dionysus the King of Kings.

"He'll go after the Nabataeans," the heavy-jawed man said with a bass voice that projected authority. "He won't bother Eretz-Israel at all. Do you have goats to go back to?" he then asked Haim, changing topics.

"No," Haim said.

"Family?"

"No."

"We'll take him to the captain," one of the other men said.

"What if I don't want to go with you?" Haim asked.

"You've got no clothes," the heavy-jawed man said.

"Well, there is that."

The three were ready to depart for Jerusalem. Haim finished his bird and then climbed up into the back of the wagon, naked. As they approached a village, the men found a blanket in the wagon's supplies, and he wrapped himself within it. They moved among stone houses, and in the centre of the small village, they found a woman alone with a cart. The men bartered with the woman and purchased some stew, but Haim would not eat it. Instead, he asked for some of the woman's fruit and roasted grains of barley measured into his cupped palms. The woman looked at him closely during the exchange. She appeared to be studying him to determine if he was a captive or a simpleton. He said little and retreated to the wagon and was grateful when they set out once more.

The men talked on the road, sitting three abreast at the front. Listening, Haim learned that the Jewish siege of Tyre had been going on for some time now. This trio planned to be part of its conclusion.

"Alexander Jannaeus is going to join the siege himself," the heavy-jawed man said. "That way, he takes the city in his own name. A proper Jewish conquest."

They passed stands of pine and oak groves that bore none of Ashkelon's ominous signs of blood and decay among the fresh fruit. Instead of drumming and human chants, these groves were alive with scattered birdsong. They passed outcroppings of limestone and reefs of chalk and marl and occasional swathes of sand mixed with grass, but the land here was mostly dry, and the pines were the most consistently green things in that place.

They came to a temporary encampment that was full of Jewish men and had no women. They threaded the donkey and wagon between stacks of provisions and small thickets of spears and javelins bundled together like thick sheaves of grain.

To Haim's relief, this camp's captain was not the same one who had led the Arbel raid. In fact, Haim had not seen him in Jerusalem at all. This captain sat outside his tent on a rug wearing a frown.

The men told Haim's tale while Haim stood behind them, still wrapped in the borrowed blanket while they introduced their strange guest.

"You're a Jew?" the captain asked.

"Yes. Of the tribe of Benjamin, though my mother married a man from near the Samaritan border. That is where I am from."

"So you're half Jewish," the captain said.

"He was a Benjamite as well. My father. Jannaeus made land available in Samaria after his father's conquests."

The captain nodded. "How did you come to be naked in the south?"

Haim was unsure how to reply. The men had already told the captain what they knew of his story. The captain saw his hesitancy and waved it away. "Ashkelon. Yes, I know. But surely you were not held there naked."

"I had clothes."

"And you come to have none now—how?"

"I left them when I met your men," Haim said. The captain looked at the three, and they nodded. "I could carry the stain of Ashtaroth's temple no further. I cleaned myself in the stream, and your men saw fit to take me with them. Even without their assistance, I still would have gone on naked as I was. I could not bear to wear the filth of Ashkelon any further."

The captain pondered this information.

"You're a slinger."

"Yes."

"What do you think of the king's war against Tyre, so soon after our war with the Galileans?"

"I have only just learned of it yesterday. From your men."

"What do you think of it?"

Haim shrugged.

The captain leaned back, looked at the three men who had delivered Haim, and then turned to the other men witnessing this exchange. None spoke. The captain leaned in again and regarded Haim before finally breaking the silence.

"Gentiles surround us," he said. "Now that the Jewish war is over, the king will go back to the conquests that made his father's name great. Jews fighting Jews is shameful, and these men and I took no part in that war. The king's mercenaries killed our Jewish brothers. We did not."

The captain looked around at his men, who beamed back at him, proud of what they had not done.

"War with gentiles is another matter. You see, this company did not fight in the king's civil war, but we have now hired ourselves out for the king's new wars. Plenty of Jews are joining up now. Eventually, we'll replace all the gentile recruits. These new wars are good. It's time that all the gentiles learned to fear us the way they feared our ancestors when Joshua led our armies. David. Hezekiah. Hyrcanus too, in his early days at least. You weren't allied with the Galileans, were you?"

"Galileans? No."

"Have you any sympathy for Galileans?"

"Sympathy?"

"I don't know if they are even proper Jews," the captain mused. "The Galileans. Too many of them sided with the Pharisees."

"No. No sympathies. Our family was from Benjamin."

"Where was it?"

"Benjamin?"

"The temple. Ashkelon. Where was it?"

Haim stared at him.

"In relation to Ashkelon."

"Beside the city. Adjacent. To the south."

"Hmm." The captain pondered this. "Filth like this needs to be eradicated even beyond Eretz-Israel's borders." He looked around at the other men. "Perhaps we can influence the king's agenda and turn his attention to eradicating Ashkelon. Make it like in the days of Samson again. What do you say?"

This last question he directed at Haim.

"I can use a sling," Haim said.

"So I hear. So, you'll join us then?"

Haim nodded.

"Then get him some clothes," the captain said. "And sandals. And a doctor. And a sling. I want to see this young man hit something."

29

85-84 BCE

EIGHT DAYS LATER, after joining the king's company of soldiers, the madness of Ashkelon came over Haim again. He awoke as if from a dream, standing in one of the great tents, surrounded by men he barely recognized, a long knife in his hand. He knew that the monstrous distortions on their faces could not be real, yet the horror of this reality felt stronger and truer than anything he had ever felt before. The images before him rivalled the worst of Ashkelon.

Haim's mind divided as he circled an opponent. He could not remember why he was fighting the man. The part of him that could speak before he knew what he would say saw a secret it would later tell to his ears only. For now, it just whispered *fight*. That secret part of him saw images of rampant horror that made him want to run. Other than the voice telling him to fight, he could not hear anything.

Ashkelon was alive and fresh before him again. Undiluted feeling burst into the disused chambers of his mind and spread deaf declarations of prophetic urgency that overwhelmed him and made him want to scream even as he tried to focus on his opponent.

Haim slashed with his knife and cut the big-headed man in front of him. In his mind, fog comingled with the sun's great clarity. His arm had the speed of a viper, and madness and faith coursed through him. He had power as he had never had before, even as a bandit in Samaria.

A corrective thread asserted itself in his mind as he circled within the tent. It was like burning oil sliding along the surface of a watered pan, but in the end, it fixed nothing. It spilled, the burning oil leaping into the world beyond to spread fire all around. Now he was the fire here. All instincts that were not Ashkelon survival slid away, discarded, like a shed skin. Even Samaritan banditry was not foul enough or violent enough for what he needed to do here. His grin was rigid, his blade unhesitating and fast. He could hear nothing.

Together, two of the newer recruits hit Haim. They struck him like men shunting a heavy load, their shoulders down, and Haim flew but retained his grip on the blade. As he came up, he saw one of the two assailants was already dead, a great throat hole blooming. The other staggered away, and then it was the big-headed man again. Blood ran from the man's left arm and side. He bore a rope in the bloody hand and the contentious bowl of stew in the other. The big-headed man flicked his rope out like a makeshift whip and then flung the stew at Haim and charged. Haim did not flinch but charged too, and just before impact, the big-headed man pulled away and around and shoved Haim past.

They continued to circle around each other inside the great tent. The rope came again like a soundless whip and wrapped around Haim's knife arm. The big-headed man pulled hard, but instead of the knife falling away, all of Haim's body rushed forwards and the rope went slack, freeing up Haim's blade hand. He slashed through ribs, his blow deflected only by bone.

Two more men came at Haim and the butt of his blade connected with an ear and the man fell with a scream and so the combat continued and a human wreckage accumulated.

Haim felt numb as the soldiers continued to come at him. He saw signs in the air. Above the splattered, poisonous stew, colours hovered that he knew could not be there. The stew's poison had turned into an ingestible evil, desperate to find any passage into Haim's body, be it through breath or blood or merely contact with his skin. He heard the music of Ashkelon, here among these tents, among these men, outside Jerusalem. He could not hear the room, but he heard Ashkelon. He saw the spirits of Arbel, those hung on Jerusalem's crosses, and the priestesses with lewd smiles, and he lost his smile and charged at the men before him like a caged and frantic beast.

He could have fled the tents, but he did not. He knew not to run. His mother had taught him that. The burning and flung oil in this place called, *Stay and finish. Here it all ends.* He could kill a demon or die in this slaughter, and he did not care which as long as the fire inside died and he was free.

Haim lost feeling in one arm. He stepped through a real fire and did not register the burning. He lost sight in one eye as it filled with either his blood or the blood of another. He heard a bone crack that was not his. He felt hands on him, and his thumb slid into some socket, wet and rolling, and screams mingled with his own and those of ancient beings. He saw his half-sisters morph into a new species of priestess and his thumb convulsed in its wet cavity and something crashed against his skull and then he was on the ground.

He lay still then in mud created by blood and an unremarkable stew. A man sat on each wrist and ankle, but he could hear now—not Ashkelon, but this room, this tent, this place. He listened with eyes closed to a report he could only make out in dim fragments.

"I said, 'A skinny sack should take what fill it's given.' He was in a mood before any of this started." The speaker's wormy temples continued to flex even though he paused his story to let the surrounding men finish bandaging his ribs.

The captain was the primary audience for this debrief. Around them were other survivors. One man had lost an eye and was in the corner making terrible noises while the surgeon tried to attend to him. The man addressing the captain bled from multiple wounds on his chest and one arm. The surrounding men were bandaging a deep gash in his ribs, tightening and padding as they went. Blood soaked through. He bobbed his head before he started again. Red from his beard flicked outwards.

"That man just isn't normal," he continued. "This whole mess started with a bowl of stew. Stew! I just said he should eat—these guys heard me. I said he should eat and pushed a bowl at him—he hasn't even earned a share yet. I offered him some free stew, and he attacked me! These guys saw."

"A skinny sack?" the captain said. "That skinny sack took you and the rest of these men apart."

Haim lay where they held him. He did not fight but lay still. He closed his eyes but stayed aware. He did not outwardly acknowledge the captain's presence.

"I figured he was just ashamed to beg," the big-headed man continued. "He said no to the stew, but I didn't believe him. He's so skinny. I told him 'a man's got to eat,' just like his mother would. I said so. I invoked the maternal." He grinned at the captain, who did not smile back. "I pushed the stew at him again. He stared at it like it was the devil— those eyes. Then he started stripping off his clothes like that was the normal thing to do. I said some stuff, I don't know what, then he came at me."

"Like a lion attack," one of the other injured men said.

"I don't know where he conjured that knife from," said another.

❧

"Some of the men want you dead," the captain said.

Haim nodded. His chains gave him little room to move more than that.

"Others want you for the catapult at Tyre. The siege. They want to fling you over the wall and set you upon the people there." The captain smiled at that and waited for a reaction. When none came, he frowned. "They want to see what kind of damage you can do on the other side of the wall. Like some kind of deranged Samson."

Haim nodded again. He kept his eyes open. He honoured the captain by trying to stay focused.

"Ashkelon should have killed you," the man said. "Then

you go and take this beating. You should be celebrating a second chance at life instead of trying to kill one of the men who saved you. Why won't you eat anything?"

"I'll eat some grains," Haim croaked. "Plain. Roasted or raw, but with nothing else on them or done to them. Unpeeled fruit. Roasted meat, but nothing else added to it."

"You think we're going to slip you some more of Ashkelon's poisons with your food?"

Haim just looked at him and gave no response.

"Okay." The captain got up to leave. "All this over a perfectly fine stew."

✿

Haim had another episode a week later. He was alone this time. He arched against the chains which would not release him, and as he strained, he felt himself slide towards wildness again. Chained, he knew he would only tear himself apart. He pulled away from the precipice. He worked to manufacture stillness. Visions raged and danced, but they were in his eyes now, not his mind. He wondered how long Ashkelon's potions would maintain their delayed effects. Would they keep coming back forever?

He felt the fire in his burned leg and focused on the difference between the pain there and his phantom visions of the dark liquids of Ashkelon's temple ceremony. He struggled to keep the pain in his leg and the pain in his mind separate. In desperation, he licked the ground, and the grit against tongue and teeth was like the burning in his leg. The taste transferred to the back of his throat was real in a way his visions were not. The nightmare receded. He grew calm. Sweat covered his body in silent testimony to what no one else had witnessed on that dark and moonless night.

～

"Demons," the scholar said. It was just he and the captain crouching over their prisoner. Haim had just given his third report about these attacks to the pair and now waited.

"How will we know when he is safe again?" the captain asked.

"He won't ever be safe again," the scholar said. "Ashkelon cannot be purged."

"There must be some herb," the captain said. "A counter for Ashkelon's poisons."

The scholar shook his head.

"They picked it in the forest areas," Haim said. "A mushroom. They mixed it—" He did not finish the explanation. It made no sense. Even a drunk would not do what he had done.

"There is no cure," said the scholar.

"Well, can't take him to Tyre then."

"No. He should not be allowed near any of the king's men. Another vision while he's unchained, and he will go wild again. He's a danger to everyone."

～

The captain came to see Haim again.

"There are madmen in the mountains of Galilee," the captain said. "Some have suggested that we take you there and release you to patrol the north country and roar at the sky. We could drop you off on the way to Tyre." The captain smiled down at Haim. "They say that the Galileans deserve you."

"I have no desire to live among Galileans," Haim said. "Nor to roar at the sky." He said the latter with a half-smile, and the captain smiled back.

"You have sympathizers," the captain said. "We don't get many men with families signing up to be mercenaries, so the dead have no one wanting revenge. As for the others, their cuts are healing."

Haim had heard the men talking outside the tent where he was chained. Ashkelon was a legend. The city was a two-day walk away, but its temple was an unpassable place from which came stories to terrify children. The soldiers whispered other tales that no one would tell a child. This company feared Haim and was in awe of him. The survivors took some pride in their scars. They had fought one of Ashkelon's demons and won. None of them had witnessed the following hallucinations and ravings, though they had heard about them later. The stories grew with each retelling.

The Seleucids awoke in the north and returned to Eretz-Israel's borders. They disrupted Jannaeus's siege of Tyre. Dionysus, the comet-watchers' King of Kings, drove the Jew's mercenaries away from the coast and then let them be. Eretz-Israel's forces were now en route back to Jerusalem. These events provided time for a more protracted deliberation regarding Haim's fate in the camp outside Jerusalem.

Following Tyre's liberation, the Seleucids advanced eastwards across northern Galilee and through Iturea. They would soon enter Nabataean territory somewhere near the three hills where Haim and Chaya had eaten figs in the rain many years before.

"At least the Seleucids are leaving Judea alone," the captain said.

"Jerusalem schemes and Galilee burns," Haim croaked. It was a quote from the old scribe.

The captain looked at him sharply. "Is this the return of your Ashkelon insanity?" he asked. He did not wait for a reply but left the room, motioning for his aide to leave the food where Haim could reach it.

❦

Deliberations within the company took months, but eventually, the captain returned.

"You can go to the gentiles," the man said. He dropped a small pack on the ground between them. "The men have agreed to this. There is no gossip between Jewish and gentile companies."

"Where?" Haim asked.

"Outside Jericho."

"What will I do?"

"The Seleucids are east of the Jordan now, in the north. Jannaeus left half his force around Jericho in case the Seleucid war with the Nabataeans spills back south into Judea. If the conflict stays east of the Jordan, you'll have little to do. If they do cross the river, there will be lots of work for a capable slinger."

"You just want me to leave Judea," Haim said.

"That's about it. It's far away from Ashkelon, so it's a good place for you to go. If you think you're going to go mad again, just cross the river. No one cares what happens over there to the Nabataeans and Seleucids. Do as you please on the eastern side of the river."

The clicks of the lock sounded to Haim's ears like bones rebreaking. A strange victory sound. They were not his bones breaking. He was to be let loose like a wild man among gentile mercenaries, and if that failed, he would be banished across the river. He was free.

Haim rubbed his wrists and immediately knew the lie. He was not free. His hands were free, but he could still feel the pressure in his head. His mind was not free. He smiled at the captain—a smile that looked properly grateful. As he walked away from the soldiers' camp, he wondered if perhaps there had been a bit of the broken-nosed man in that smile. A bit of the almond farmer. A bit of his father.

30

84 BCE

HAIM TOOK THE road to Jericho wearing the sandals of one of his victims. The captain's pack of supplies hung on his back. He walked in bright sunlight past lines of filled-in stump holes. There had been a forest of crosses here not long ago. He could have hung on any one of them. Then. Now.

For three hours, there was only emptiness. The scrape of his feet on the hard road and the wind in the canyon were the only sounds to accompany him. Occasionally, he was aware of his breathing. Twice he saw a bird. Only twice. After a long while there came voices.

The sound of people jarred him. He assumed that he was hearing other travellers approaching and stopped to wait. Even after a long time had passed, the voices did not grow closer. Yet they continued, muffled and ever distant. The exact words were hard to hear. He wondered if this was a new form of madness, but he had never heard of or experienced such a thing before, so he doubted it.

He continued on the road to Jericho. The voices did not abate but grew closer as he walked. The blending tones became distinguishable as individual men's voices. Yet he still could not make out their words.

Haim came to a sharp turn in the narrow path. As he crossed around the canyon's bend, the way opened and the voices were suddenly clear. Some distance ahead, the road widened, and in that place sat a group of five men. There were two donkeys nearby. The men sat about the remains of a frugal fire sipping something hot from small cups. As Haim approached, one held up a spare cup, already full, as though they had been expecting him.

"Heard your steps," a white-bearded man said. "A slow walker, you."

Haim sat without saying anything, unsure of the man's accent. He nodded his thanks and added a smile. He nearly sipped from the cup, then remembered himself. He smiled again and made an expression of great satisfaction, eyes closed in the afternoon sun. When he opened them again, the men were inspecting a small pot.

"Digging into the river," a bald man said, "is a lot of work."

Haim closed his eyes and just listened to the men's voices.

"How far out do you have to go to get the good clay?"

"Two feet. The water there is only half that deep."

"It must be getting deeper the more clay you pull out."

"There is that, but there's only a layer of the good stuff. Maybe a foot deep. Then it's just the usual clay. Or something else. Greenish. Not like this."

"Is it worth it?"

"It fires better."

"But is it worth it for you?"

"Can I get a better price? No. No one can see the difference just from looking at the finished product. Only if you break it would you know."

"It's harder to break?"

"Yes. And it takes heat better. Then cold—say you drop it in water, then put it back on the fire—it handles the changing temperatures better and doesn't crack as easily."

"Hard to prove, though, to a buyer."

"Without ruining it, you mean?"

"Yes."

"Which is why it's not worth it. But it's interesting."

"If a man discovers a better clay for making pots, he ought to be able to make money from it. Otherwise, clay is just clay, and there's no benefit in really knowing your craft."

Haim opened his eyes and saw that it was the white-bearded man who had made this last comment.

"I need a way of measuring things so I can prove how much more it takes," said a man to Haim's right. "So I can prove it's stronger."

"Then you could charge more for it," the white-bearded man said.

"And people would pay your price," said a man to Haim's left.

The white-bearded man held the pot. He offered it to Haim, who looked at it quickly and then passed it on to the next man, who turned out to be the owner of the pot. The man put the object away.

There was another man with a narrow face. He dug

into his bag and brought forth a red pan. He presented it to the group.

"Why not just make it out of metal?" the bald man asked.

"It would cost too much," the narrow-faced man said. "And it would tend to warp in the fire."

"What is this bit?" asked another mostly bald man. He wore the barest fringe of grey hair near his neckline. He was fingering a depression on one side of the pan's edge.

"It's for pouring," said the narrow-faced man. "Also for holding a large stirring spoon."

"Is there anything else about it that we should know?" the white-bearded man asked.

The narrow-faced man shook his head. "There's no fancy clay. It's just a straight glaze. I kept it simple."

He passed the pan to the white-bearded man.

"Heavy," the white-bearded man said. "It's about right for the size, though maybe a bit big."

"It's for big households," the narrow-faced man said.

The pan made its rounds as the men discussed its design. Some commented on its form while others focused on the materials and crafting methods. The men bickered about different types of kilns and firewood. Each comment seemed to glancingly reference old arguments. Haim grasped only the edges of their discussion. It had never occurred to him that a pot's manufacture could be subject to such a critique.

Other pieces were revealed and passed around and discussed, and in the end, a small lamp, which had first circulated before Haim had arrived, was named the winner of the review.

There were only two paths from this wide place in the road: the route to Jericho and the road back to Jerusalem. The five men had not journeyed together but had come from disparate locations and met here, at this strange middle ground in the canyon trail. Haim wanted to know how they chose it, why this place, whether this was a chance occurrence or a regular affair, and how many had come from Jerusalem or Jericho or another home town altogether. Yet he said nothing. He asked no questions. He just listened and avoided drinking the tea.

When the reviews were over, the men continued talking among themselves. They did not include or exclude Haim. He was just there. After they exhausted the particulars of pottery, the conversation turned to other aspects of their craft. They discussed a knee that was sore from always leaning on a large amphora at the same angle. They discussed the fussiness of a particular patron, the necessary chore of hauling away shards and ashes, and their difficulties sourcing and transporting raw materials. There were observations about dye recipes and which recipe maintained its colour best once fired in the kiln.

The talk of dye reminded Haim of the widow's dead husband and his seashells. The purple dye that came from the shells was for fabric, not pottery, but this was his first opportunity to connect with these craftsmen on the Jericho road, and he almost said something.

He stayed quiet, for the widow's husband was not his father. His father had been a killer. He thought about Morta, about Gershom, Arbel, and the wolf, about the havoc outside Jerusalem, and he felt a sinking feeling. He shared no heritage with the dye maker, even though his mother had been the dye maker's wife.

Chaya swam into view, and her image shocked him. He

understood then that by saving Chaya, he had killed her as well. He had introduced her to Morta and the rest. He had taken her from Arbel and destroyed Arbel so she could never return. He was as deeply enmeshed in the art of ruin as these men were in the particulars of making pots. Their tools were clay and kiln. His tools were sling, knife, fist, and somehow finding and befriending poisonous people. The betrayal of innocents. A forest of crosses. Those were his tools, and his harvest was always rich.

Haim stood up abruptly. The men stopped talking and watched him. He saw himself clearly, even if they did not. He was a demon in their midst. His tea was untasted, left on the ground. The men said nothing and waited for him to speak, but he did not. He did not want any part of his presence to lay a curse on their fellowship.

The Jewish captain had directed him well—Jannaeus's encampment of gentile mercenaries was the right company for him. Haim turned and walked away, down the path to Jericho. He would go where the captain had sent him. If Ashkelon's demons came upon him again, he would cross the river and take out his rage on the Nabataeans there.

The road in front of him became empty again. The same emptiness blossomed inside him, and he knew that this was good. He had a purpose now. He understood where he fit. He understood now why he could never grasp how things were made, how systems worked, how parts combined to make a whole. To make was not his art. His gift was to kill. The goat-stealer had known all along.

31

84-83 BCE

"Y ou've been in some scraps," the recruiter at Jericho said.

"I'm better with this," Haim said, holding up his sling and pouch of stones.

"Show me."

Haim chose a stone the size of a small egg. "How good are your eyes?" he asked, indicating potential targets across an empty field.

"Aim for that man over there," the recruiter said. "The one with the striped cape."

"I'll kill him," Haim said.

The recruiter looked at Haim with a grim expression. "That was a joke. My eyes are good. Impress me."

"The bell on that wagon there then."

"But it's moving," the recruiter said.

Haim swung his sling once, twice, three times.

"It's got a driver," the man said.

Haim released the stone with a forward lunge and grunt, and the bell's ringing a sudden note across the field startled the cart's driver. The man looked around in alarm, spoke to his donkeys, and picked up their pace across the plain.

"Son of Zeus," the recruiter said.

"Just David," Haim said. "The Jewish god's first slinger."

The recruiter looked at him with an unhappy expression.

"That was a joke," Haim said.

"You sure you want to sit near me?" The man reminded Haim of Gershom with his powerful, misshapen body. His question was reasonable. The Egyptian mercenary wore a leather belt about his waist with a chain hanging from it. When he walked, the chain dragged behind him the empty skull of a pig and a sack loaded with its bones.

"I'm not much of a Jew," Haim said.

"It doesn't stink no more."

"How many more days do you have to pull it?"

"Two."

"I guess that keeps you out of Jericho."

"That's the general idea."

Haim set a rack of head-pinched locusts over the fire while the man watched.

"I'd eat that maybe if I was starving," the man said. "Then again, probably not even then."

Haim gave no answer. He was learning not to explain his diet.

There was a gasp of breath all around the circle of men. Three men were fighting in the circle's centre, two men against one—no weapons. The crowd that had gathered to watch breathed in along with the fighters.

Blood streamed from one of the pair.

"I thought he was just a slinger," said someone in the crowd.

"I would have bet on two spearmen against one slinger," said another.

"You did."

The fight went on, but it was clear who was going to win. Individuals in the crowd noted to themselves not to challenge the Jew, the solitude seeker, the strange eater. People already told wild stories about his ability with a sling. These reports came not from professional exaggerators but from taciturn slingers with reputations and experience. In the year spent idly waiting around Jericho, this moment with the spearmen capped the Jewish slinger's growing reputation.

"And he doesn't drink," someone said to no one in particular.

Later, another man tried to tell an imaginative rumour about Haim, but his listeners silenced him. Even among the violent and often drunk mercenaries, there were limits to what they would risk mentioning in open conversation. They did not entertain rumours about Ashkelon.

⁊

The Seleucid Greek army grazed through the eastern side of the Jordan River, travelling from north to south, taking one Nabataean city at a time while the Jewish army sat across the river and waited. A year passed in this waiting. The Nabataeans were proving to be a poor match for the relentless Seleucid phalanx.

When the Seleucids had passed across northern Israel on their way to Nabataea, Iturea had suffered damage and losses. This was not the first Seleucid incursion provoked by Jerusalem's actions. The Itureans expressed their pain and anger by halting tax payments to Jerusalem. In response, Jerusalem sent a contingent of the army north to Iturea to suppress the rebellion. Haim's group stayed outside Jericho.

For a year, Haim stayed with Jericho's idle crew while the Seleucids fought their slow war southwards on the eastern side of the Jordan and other Jewish companies fought a slow war northwards on the western side of the river. The Jewish forces marched past Galilee and into Iturea. Seleucids killed Nabataeans east of the river, and Jerusalem's mercenaries killed newly converted Jews on the western side. Both east and west fought to reinvigorate their treasuries.

"None of these wars have elephants," one of the oldest of the slingers in Jericho said one evening. As always, Haim listened to the other soldiers in silence.

"You've seen elephants?" another asked.

"Elephants will scare a man out of this business," the old-timer said. "Slingers are no good against elephants. Spearmen no good. Phalanx. Nothing."

In those quiet days, some of the slingers began to talk about their eventual retirement. The older the slinger, the more intense his interest was in this topic.

"The Romans have a pension system," one man said. "Land conquered becomes land to settle on."

"That won't work here," another man said. "Jews don't want you around once they're done with you."

"Not on their land, anyway," the first man responded.

"And they're not doing much to add more land," the oldest of the lot added. "When they do add more land, they turn the locals into Jews too, so there's still no room for us."

"Certainly not when you're old and useless," one of the younger slingers said with a laugh. "Talk about retirement, and you'll wind up dead before then."

"What's your plan then?" the senior slinger asked.

"Stay alive. Sample everything Jericho has to offer. Then move on to the next city."

"That's not a plan."

"It's working," said the young man.

The older slingers said nothing in reply.

Haim was the same age as the young slingers, but he sat with the older ones.

"At least you can settle in Eretz-Israel in the end," one man said to him.

Haim gave no reply.

Haim often went off alone hunting. The company was used to his strange ways. When he returned one night, it was already dark, and the company of slingers sat about a fire in a discussion. Haim stayed back in the shadows. He was still hungry, having caught nothing and not being in the mood for greens or roots. He chewed a leftover rind and did not make his return known. He found a place to sit in the dark where no one would notice him but he could still hear their conversation. He could not always make out who was talking, but he could hear everyone. As he listened, he eventually realized they were talking about him.

"—not the only one," one slinger was saying. "Most of the Jews are like him."

"That can't be."

"The Jews are famous in the north country," a gravelly voice said. "Them and Cypriots. They were both the premium fighters in the early Seleucid armies before the Jews threw off the Seleucids."

"Are they all as mad with their diet as he is?" said someone from the left side of the fire.

"Worse. Jews are the worst for food."

"Egypt too," added a new voice.

"What do you mean 'Egypt'?" asked the man from the left. "There are Jews in Egypt?"

"They practically run the army down there," the gravelly voice said. "Did, anyway."

"I can see them running it. Fighting in it, though? Most of the Jews I saw around Jerusalem were city types."

"No, they're dead shots," repeated the gravelly voice. "As unstoppable as our Jew is up close. Especially the Galileans. Jews don't organize their forces into squares like the Greeks do, and they make middling horsemen, but as individuals, they are unstoppable. Great for rush companies. Relentless. They don't ever quit."

"I hear they show no mercy," said the lone voice from the left side of the fire. "The strictly Jewish companies, I mean."

"If you're not a Jew, you're dead," said the gravelly voice. "They'll kill you for free."

"He's with us. Why's that then?"

"Even the Jews don't want him."

"He's still a Jew."

"Maybe he's a spy among us."

"If he is, he's contaminated himself by sharing our fires and camps," the gravelly voice said. "They have laws about mixing with the likes of us that are pretty strict."

"You said they're relentless," a new voice said. "Maybe sharing our space is just part of the act then. He's relentless enough as a spy to make himself unclean among us. You said they'd do whatever it takes."

"He won't go so far as to eat our food," the voice on the left said.

"There's that."

"You've seen the way he fights," the gravelly voice said.

"I've seen it up close."

That drew a laugh from the men, and Haim tried to remember ever fighting one of the slingers.

"He can sling at a sparrow's eye," said the gravelly voice.

"I don't care what he is," said the voice on the left. "I'm just glad he's on our side. I wouldn't want him deciding on my skull from across a field."

The circle about the fire grew quiet. One of the men fed fresh branches into the fire, and as the light started to flare up, Haim slipped back into deeper shadows and away from the men.

The next day came the news that the Iturean campaign had been a success. Jannaeus's force was now marching back to Jerusalem with a down payment on back taxes loaded onto five donkeys. The Iturean revolt was no more.

§

Haim went out from the camp one evening, heading in the direction of Jericho. He did not go into the city but walked around it. On the far side, outside the walls, in a land of weeds and rock he found a vast clearing of soft grass. He needed company this night and did not care for the suspicions and ribaldry of the soldier's camp. He had heard enough speculation about wars and armies and campaigns past and future. He wanted something that had always been alien to his experience, something he had glimpsed at Arbel, a thing he did not understand yet longed to know.

Fires burned in this clearing, forming a large circle, the work of families who had gathered here in community. He found a group that looked safe and sat near them on the periphery of their shared space. He watched the centre of the ring where there were dancers. He was close enough to see and hear well but just far enough away to not draw attention.

Like in Arbel, everyone here seemed to know the rituals and the movements of their shared celebration. Old men performed along with the young. Children mimicked the men, and the older women joined them. A group of young mothers danced with their babies, and there was joy and quickness in their feet as they moved in the firelight.

Haim wondered who had prepared and served the food. Among all the shifting shapes around the several fires, there was no end to eating. He had packed nuts and cured meat for himself and ate quietly and alone.

Sitting in the semi-dark, Haim studied this people as though they were from somewhere across the sea. They were foreign to him. He shared no relation with these people, whatever his mother's bloodline. Their difference from him was not their blood, for they were simply Jews and his mother had been Jewish. A community, however, was not formed by blood alone. They were foreign to him because they had genuine bonds among them. They were like the people of Arbel. No amount of blood would make up for the isolation and emptiness that lived within him. He was the foreign one.

A stooped man silhouetted against the far-side flames suddenly straightened in surprise at encountering an old friend. Others, people it seemed that should be too old to matter to anyone anymore, also embraced the man. There was energy in the reunion that showed that these people had once been young and still cared for one another now. Haim saw a little girl come up to the oldest of the men, throw her arms around his waist, and then peel off and bury herself in the folds of a woman's garments. He saw a sour woman grumble to any that would hear, and then he saw her face transform and laugh when those around would not countenance her performance. There was a nakedness in her change, a humility that frightened him.

He became aware of musicians. The dancers did not dance just to a percussive beat as at Arbel. Though the music makers were across the way and partially hidden from Haim's sight, he could still hear the difference between this and Arbel's music. This group was profoundly melodic, and male and female voices intermingled from all around the circle so that the music seemed to emanate from everywhere.

The congenial atmosphere warmed him. It pressed around like something physical. When Haim focused and tried to understand how a young girl and an old man were related, something shifted within. When he tried to guess the reason a young boy seemed safe standing within folds of an old woman's dress, to piece families together, to discover the social order that determined who distributed the delicacies and who simply ate, or who cared for the young or fed the fires, the atmosphere he was experiencing lifted away. By studying what he was seeing, he stopped being a part of it. By trying to understand, something essential left the clearing, and the bonds he so desperately yearned for were obscured from both his eyes and heart. The gathering became a scentless forest, a stream with no sound, a starless sky. Haim lost his bearings.

He wanted to move freely among these people. He wanted to stop being strange.

He wanted someone in this crowd, or one like it, to know him. He wanted to have a small child dart from the safety of others and embrace his knees, to see something of himself in the old men, to have a woman gladly serve him from her family's supply and to know that he did not take what was not freely given. He wanted a *her* to be *his* and *him* to be *hers*. He wanted to be like all the others. He wondered what it would be like to have a woman with whom he could share things unspoken. He tried to understand and was losing the feeling by trying.

A fire over, a ladle was lifted and a bowl filled. The image jarred him, and he remembered the priestesses of Ashkelon filling such a bowl. He remembered the thinness of what appeared in the bowl of his mother's house and the hate that went with it, and the bowl left with the goat-stealer, and the mother in Arbel offering him something from her family's supply. He remembered that he had murdered the people of Arbel, and the scene before him shrank. Though nothing in the scene before him had changed, he imagined that all here knew who he was and what he was. He could not create. He did not understand how the parts of anything fit together. He could only destroy. He saw the goat-stealer's glare and the captain's leer at Arbel. He saw the old goat herder on his cross press his wounded feet against the torturous nail for the sake of breathing deep enough to warn him. Who would warn him now? Who would warn them?

He stood and moved away, away from the fires, into the night, towards Jericho, blind and chilled and hungry. He did not remember if he had passed through Jericho to get back to the slingers' camp or had walked around it again. He only registered entering his tent, sitting there without a light, and hearing the hollow sound of the night. He had not spoken to anyone. The night watchman must have said something, but Haim had no memory of it.

32

83 BCE

THE SELEUCIDS AND Nabataeans fought their grinding war on the Jordan River's eastern side for the better part of two years. Battles were won and battles were lost while Jerusalem's mercenaries played dice in daylight and told stories around late-night fires. When a break in the war came, it came with an unexpected twist.

"What's going on?" Haim asked.

"The Seleucid king, Dionysus, is dead," the senior slinger said. "A Nabataean with an arm like you got him. The Seleucids have run."

It was a turn of events that could scarcely be believed. The Nabataeans, until then, had only lost ground to the Seleucids. Now the Nabataeans were suddenly ascending.

Mercenaries stationed at Jericho raised victory flags as though Nabataeans, instead of Judeans, paid Jannaeus's army. Everyone hated the Seleucids. Cookfires roared and extra meat was laid out such that Haim was even able to eat in camp. He selected from untreated, roasted options and did not have to hunt rodents or insects to sustain himself.

"I found you," the recruiter said to Haim that night. They stood near a side of half-burned beef surrounded by a crowd of celebrating mercenaries—slingers and bowmen and spearmen and even non-combat auxiliary soldiers all mingled together.

"I have a job for you," the recruiter said. "I want you to go and find out all you can about how the war over there is going." He pointed across the river.

"Me?" Haim asked.

"It'll pay double if you come back with good information," the recruiter said. "If I find you camped out in a swill house in Jericho, you won't get paid anything."

"Why me?"

"You can forage. You're Jewish and lots of Judeans travel through Nabataea. You're believable. You don't drink. One of these will look like what they are and no one will tell them anything. They'll wind up drunk in a ditch. You can read, can't you?"

"Yes."

"There you go," the recruiter said.

"The Nabataeans are going to write things down and leave them out for me?" Haim asked.

"See? You can stitch things together." The recruiter smiled with his mouth but not his eyes. "Find out if the Seleucids are really gone. Our king needs to know."

⥋

Two days later, Haim awoke well across the Jordan River, deep into the territory he had first travelled years before with Chaya. He considered finding his way back to the farms they had worked at years before. He was older now and could safely carry himself among those men. He tried to remember the foremen's names and where the farms were in relation to mountains or streams. He could remember little of landmarks and no names at all. He did not know where he and Chaya had even crossed the river. He could work his way through their old route if he found one familiar place, but he did not have a starting point. He did not have a map.

Haim walked the land and discovered travellers on the road surprisingly keen for conversation, and he feigned a personability he did not feel. After Dionysus's death, the Nabataeans had kept the Seleucids from escaping north. All agreed on that.

"East," one trader said, slowing his cart for a short conversation with Haim. "We chased the Greeks into the desert."

"Is the army still chasing them?" Haim asked.

"No. They left the Greeks to the desert after enough days. The Seleucids won't be coming back."

He met a Jewish family, still working a farmstead that had once been part of Eretz-Israel before Nabataea. The Seleucids had briefly taken this territory, but now it had presumably reverted back to Nabataea again.

"The Nabataeans are desert people," the old Jewish farmer said. "They've got caravan routes stretching a thousand miles through that desert. Secret watering places. All hidden. The Nabataeans know their desert. They chased those Seleucids to where they'll be good and lost and then probably took their own routes back to where they keep their secret water caches. The Greeks won't find Nabataean water. The Seleucids are not coming back. They're dead or will be soon."

Over the following days, others told similar stories. The Nabataeans living in the land were the proudest tellers of their people's victory.

"The desert swallows all," one lined face reported.

"Only the people of al-Qaum can come through that land alive," said another, referring to the god of war and caravans.

Haim met a Nabataean standing before a house built of both stone and oiled fabrics stretched over wood. The man looked strange, with a pointed chin, lips that pulled in when silent, and unnaturally large eyes, their whites diluted with yellow. The man pointed east, away from the setting sun and towards the wind that was picking up distant sand and blurring the horizon as night fell. He spoke in ominous tones.

"Like the Egyptian mummified dead, wrapped, skeletal, the Greeks will wander, cursed for eternity. They will forever be ghost-rags in that desert." The speaker looked closely at Haim. "In that miasma of dust, they are lost and will stay lost for eternity. Their bodies will dry, and their unburied spirits will be tethered to bones." He stared at Haim for an uncomfortably long time and then cracked a smile. "You're a Jew. Do you need a place to stay tonight?"

"I have a way to go yet," Haim said.

"It's night. Stay with me."

"No, thank you. I cannot."

"I have a stew," the man offered.

"I'm sure you do."

The old man looked at Haim quizzically. "I can cook. The woman is dead, but I can cook."

"I have to go on."

"You won't stay in with me?"

"No. Thank you."

"You think I'm unclean," the man said, "because I'm not a Jew."

"No."

"Jews." He twisted his face and turned away, walking back to his little house.

It took another two days for Haim to reach the Jordan again, recross it, and find his way back south to Jericho and the mercenary camp. The recruiter took his report with a studied frown.

"How many did you talk to?" he asked.

"Dozens," Haim said. "Jews and Nabataeans. Travellers and homesteaders."

"You've done a lot of talking for a loner."

"I'm finished now for a while."

The recruiter counted out coins, and then Haim sought out his old company. They accepted him around the fire without any comment on his absence.

Haim sat among the slingers and said nothing but felt more comfortable than he had in the weeks and months prior. Eventually, he began to talk and told the others what he knew about the Nabataean victory. Days later, he heard his own stories come back to him with strange embellishments and outright lies. As the mercenaries talked, they began to omit his role as the source of these accounts. When next he saw the recruiter, the man did not seem to recognize him. Two weeks had passed, and his status in the camp had returned to what it had been before.

News continued to trickle in from the desert months

after Haim's journey. There were rumours of a skeletal army sighted here and there by one nomadic group and then another. As winter arrived, the scarce reports disappeared. It was assumed that sun and wind and sand had consumed the Seleucids. Still, Antioch sent stubborn expeditions to search for the lost army. They found only rumours. The desert swallowed all. Some said that the gods had eaten the army of Dionysus. Others said that the Seleucid soldiers had continued east into farther deserts where they might yet be found, a leathery and skeletal throng wading in rags through a sea of sand.

Over time, reports from the far north, beyond Eretz-Israel, trickled down and through the camp outside Jericho. Seleucid prophets had begun to report that a fog of dust hovered at the eastern end of the world, and once free of this cloak, the army would return and seek its vengeance on the Nabataeans.

As dusk rode up the sky, trailing its black cloak, rumours circulated of the Greeks making sacrifices for the missing. Greek search parties ventured ever deeper into the desert until they too were lost. Eventually, the northern empire stopped sending and searching, and their oracles ceased to prophesy.

Jewish scribes recorded their own speculations and conclusions. As they distributed their ideas, they sought a consensus where evidence was lacking. Each with his pen created new accounts, but the truth was known only to the dead.

One afternoon, as the slingers discussed these things, Haim imagined rags of clothing flapping over the dried shells of soldiers stretched out on the sand, their hard skins baking in the sun like that donkey in Samaria—tented skin stretched over bone. He wondered if they had all fallen together, in orderly Seleucid rows, or if they had scattered, the stronger men stubbornly going on long after all hope was gone.

Haim remembered trying to drink powdery sand in Samaria. He shook the memory off by dipping a hand into his bowl of soaked barley grains. He consumed the last of it and then drank the milky water without any dill or vinegar or honey. Still holding his empty bowl, he continued to just sit below the shade of a leaning wall and listen to the slingers' gossip. He could afford to sweat here and feel the dripping track down his skin. He thought about what might come after Jannaeus had no more use for his slinger's arm and what he would do, but then he put those thoughts out of his mind.

The night dreams and Ashkelon visions still came to him, but they no longer drove him mad. He was able to control them. He was happy in the daytime when he could just enjoy soaked barley grains in water and the shade of an ancient wall surrounded by the smell of bloodless sweat.

The days of rumours and memories and idle eating did not last much longer. Once it was confirmed that the Seleucids were truly vanquished, Jannaeus decided to reclaim the formerly Jewish lands east of the Jordan River. Jericho's idle army packed up for the first time in years and began to march.

33

83-77 BCE

WHEN JANNAEUS AND his mercenary army crossed the Jordan once again, the Nabataeans had two choices: fight the well-rested and fully supplied Jewish forces to defend landlocked farmland or abandon it. When all there had been to fight over was this fertile valley, they had fought, though the Nabataeans were largely traders and caravan managers. Had the Seleucid army returned home instead of getting lost in the desert, the Nabataeans might have defended their holdings along Eretz-Israel's eastern border, but with the Seleucid army defeated, the northern lands were available. And those lands had trading cities, like Damascus and Antioch, and access to the sea. The Nabataeans lost interest in Eretz-Israel's border territories and left its inhabitants to defend themselves.

While Jannaeus's army marched, Haim listened to the slingers trade theories on Nabataea's other motives as he kept an eye on the changing vegetation around them. His diet made meal gathering a full-time occupation.

Jannaeus's history east of the Jordan had been a record of expensive failures, but he met with only success this time. They marched south to north. Most of the cities they encountered surrendered to Jannaeus relatively easily, taking their time with negotiations but rarely showing any actual military resistance. More than half of this region's inhabitants were originally Jewish and amenable to a new Jewish king. Negotiations were more about one-time tributes and annual tax rates than any measure that would truly humble the conquered. Fighting was rare. The residents of these cities had other priorities.

"The king must be happy," one slinger said to Haim. "All he has to do is march us around, and he adds territory to his kingdom and revenues to his treasury."

Haim wondered, was Eretz-Israel's economy really that simple? If it was, why did the Nabataeans surrender it without a fight? He eventually voiced the question out loud.

"The Nabataeans cannot do everything," one slinger said. "They can defend these lands for the taxes, or they can claim available Seleucid territory. Seleucid ports are worth more than Jordan Valley farmland." Much of what Haim learned from his fellow slingers was like this—fourth- and fifth-hand opinions regurgitated with authority.

As they marched from city to city, Haim wondered about his route with Chaya through this country so many years ago. It seemed to him that they had not encountered half of these places on their journey, yet they were all ancient locations.

The next day they stopped and set up camp outside a

new city whose name Haim could not remember. Though they only met success, their progress was inefficient and slow. The army marched. It camped. Negotiations began. Weeks might pass before an agreement was reached, another few days would be spent gathering the initial tribute, and then the gold was boxed up and sent back to Jerusalem along with the paperwork setting future taxes. They could spend up to three days just organizing the caravan and its paperwork for the Jerusalem run, leaving the conquered city puzzled as to why the invaders were so slow to depart. Once Jannaeus settled affairs with one city, they marched on to the next. Sometimes they marched for only an hour or two and then would start the process all over again. Scribes tried to prepare agreements ahead of time to speed up the process, but local compromises and sensitivities changed the language at nearly every town and city. Papyrus rolls were wasted with too many alterations and eventually the scribes abandoned their attempts to expedite negotiations.

"This is going to take years," one of the slingers said as the fire burned low. He was one of the youngest in the company, barely more than a boy.

"Still, it's faster than fighting every place one at a time," a white-haired slinger offered. "And we get paid the same."

Haim tried to understand how the operation they were part of worked by comparing it to his own experiences.

"It's like bandits," Haim said. The men around the fire turned and gave him their attention. "Without the killing. Like sophisticated bandits."

The leader of this group of slingers made a gesture with his knife, circling the tip in the air as though encouraging Haim to explain himself.

"Well, imagine bandits that attack a house on its own," Haim said. "They show up with five men and attack. Maybe one or two dies. The household is all killed. You take what's there and move on."

"Are you planning a career change?" the youngest slinger asked.

"Hear him out," the white-haired man said.

"Instead, imagine a force of one hundred bandits," Haim said. "They don't fight. They just show up in force, camp out, display their weapons, and so on."

"And then send in a negotiator," the young slinger said.

"Right," said Haim. "Nobody dies. And the deal is a one-time payment—a tribute—and an ongoing annual payment."

"Taxes," the leader of the group said.

"Right," said Haim said.

"So, we're the one-hundred bandits?" the young slinger said.

"Just a show of force," the white-haired man said. "Suits me. I get paid the same, and my arm is getting a long, long rest."

The leader of the group laughed. It was a scornful laugh, but his scorn was not echoed among his men. He looked around, lost his smile, and then scowled at Haim. "Don't you have roots to dig up somewhere?" he said. "Leave kingly work to kings."

One year turned into another, and then more. Each new year passed in much the same way as the one before. The men marched. They camped. They stood in lines throughout the day, showing their discipline. Sometimes they trained. Very rarely did they fight. A day, a week, at most a month would pass, and then victory would be for-malized and the gold and paperwork sent on. The army's hardest-working members were the messengers and guards that went back and forth between Jerusalem and the Jordan Valley to file paperwork and store wealth with the queen. Everyone knew that Salome Alexander now ran things in Jerusalem while Jannaeus played the victorious army general in the field. The king was collecting trophy cities like his brothers and fathers before him, though doing so in the most tedious way possible.

One day they came near Sussita, the city that Haim had seen burn in his days with Chaya. They waited at Sussita while Jewish negotiators began their usual process. The army awaited a resupply shipment for the cooks. Meals had become thin and repetitive. Complaints about cuisine had become the army's most serious concern, and so a new larder was in order.

While everyone waited, Haim left the camp on one of his foraging trips. He set out east across the country until he came to a hamlet many hours from the army's fringe. It was near sunset when he arrived. He stayed hidden on a hill near the edge of the village. He watched for signs of music and celebration and dancing, but there was nothing like that to be seen in this country braced for invasion and negotiated pillage. He watched a man walk across an open field. He saw children poke sticks into what seemed to be a small hole near the house, playing a game whose aim he could not discern. A cookfire sent smoke up through a stone chimney, and he knew by the smoke's thin and white whisps that it was hardwood they were burning.

The man went into his house, and the children continued their play. Another child, one much younger, ran from the house to the other children and crouched among them and studied the hole. Haim could hear the boy's chatter but could not pick out any of his words. The little boy stood up straight again and ran over to a stone fence where he peed against it. Then he returned in a rolling hurry and crouched again with the others.

There was a long low animal shed attached to the house, and before the sun fully set behind him, Haim saw the head of a goat stick its white face out of the open door and bleat at the farm. Haim pulled his attention away from the one house and viewed similar chimneys and scenes throughout the little village. When he looked back at the playing children, they were gone.

Haim slunk back into the forest and found a soft place between two fallen trees with a decade's worth of leaves mounded between the softened trunks. He lay there through the long night, wrapped in his blanket. He did not try to decode the village scenes but thought on them the way some people meditated on the rhythm of verses. Eventually, he slept and did so quietly with the sounds of forest oaks creaking above him through the long night.

When they were finished with Sussita, Haim walked with the other slingers and just listened to their gossip. He compared the atmosphere of the village he had spied on with the air that moved through the army's ranks. Some slingers decried negotiations and boldly wished a stout fortress would resist so the men could prove their worth. These same men would complain bitterly when they encountered such a stubborn foe and had to sling until their arms were weak and then, though their arms were spent, were forced to help move the siege works. There were also the usual arguments about the ideal stone size, whether woollen or linen slings worked better, and how to angle a shot just right without compromising accuracy or power. They grumbled about the food, the rough makeshift beds, the dull duties. In every discussion, Haim felt out of place and alien.

After Haim had tried to discuss his theories on the economic motivations for war, the slingers' leader had begun to shun him. The others, who had taken little interest in him before, now refused to even make eye contact with him. They had learned years ago not to fight him. They respected his prowess with a sling. But they were not inclined to converse with the lone Jew.

As Haim walked in silent solitude among hundreds of soldiers, he wondered if those in his former bandit crew would be the only real companions allocated to him in this life. The ribald arguments, the drunk punches, and the intimacy of searching and killing and feasting in Samaria were his only experiences of friendship. That and his time with Chaya.

The years with the army progressed through their seasonal changes, one city blurring into another, dry heat turning to wet cold and back to heat again. During this whole time, Haim drank with no one, confided in no one, and shared familiar laughs with no one. When the slingers had their moments of laughter and shared reflection, Haim found himself increasingly on the outside. The company was becoming like Arbel. No one remembered him as the spy who had first brought details of the Seleucid defeat. He was just the strange Jew in a company of gentiles.

He remembered how he used to long for touch. He

knew as he watched the dancers embrace outside Jericho and the children crouch close together in the village near Sussita that there was still a vein of this yearning deep inside him. That pulse, however, was weaker than before. It was a memory of what was no longer needed. Not as much. Not anymore. Not since Ashkelon.

They were in the sixth year of this conquering tour when the queen left Jerusalem and joined the army in the field.

"Jannaeus is ill," the lead slinger reported. "He's got a quartan fever."

The army continued to move, but rather than ride his horse, the king was now either carried on a litter or rode reclining in a wagon. Their travel continued in this way until they came to the fortress Ragaba, and there they set up a full siege.

"Are we going to get into a proper fight?" the youngest slinger asked.

"They might make a show of it," the white-haired man said, "as a way to bring down the tribute or the taxes or both. But when it comes down to it, I doubt they'll actually fight."

The lead slinger went back and forth to the various meetings he was required to attend. They were always held in the king's tent. Each time he returned, his face reflected a sour expression. Finally, after a few mugs of a particularly strong wine, he began to talk one night around the fire.

"It seems that the queen is in charge now," the lead slinger said. "The king stays in bed. He never leaves his tent. The queen does most of the talking."

"Will she replace Jannaeus when he dies?" the youngest slinger asked.

"Two queens before this one tried for the throne and died for it," said the white-haired man.

"Before Salome?" the young one asked.

"The king's grandmother was killed on the walls of Dagon, not far from here," the white-haired man said. "Jannaeus's brother killed their mother—they starved her to death, which is pretty harsh treatment, even for a Maccabee. Salina was supposed to be queen after Aristobulus, but she wisely sprung Jannaeus from prison, put him on the throne, and promptly retired. Two generations of queens tried for power and died, and the third declined to go the same way. Salome is crazy if she thinks she can do it. The Jews don't like queens."

"Who will kill this one?" the youngest slinger said.

"Does Jannaeus have another brother who can do the job?" someone asked with a laugh.

"If she takes the throne," the lead slinger said, "the Jews will have another civil war."

A few of the slingers looked over at Haim, the only Jew in their midst. Haim said nothing.

Haim had intended to stay where he was through the rest of that night, listening to the men, with them but apart, a slinger who rarely threw a stone. He had not meant to leave. He simply got up at one point to stretch his legs. The moon had not yet risen, and the city was quiet. The men about the siege fires were as content as they were ever likely to be—warm, drinking, talking.

Haim stood and gathered his things as he often did and walked from the camp. This time he walked farther than he had intended. He paused some two miles into the night in a narrow defile and considered returning, but with that thought, he felt burdened with some new feeling he could not name. He did understand one thing clearly: there was nothing to go back for and no one who would miss him. He did not really decide so much as simply follow a tilt in the night's path. He let his feet guide him, and he walked away from the army.

34

77 BCE

HAIM TRAVELLED SOUTH from Ragaba, and a quarter moon rose to light his way. He picked a star and followed it. If that star drifted through the sky and caused his course to drift in turn, the star still would not lead him astray, for his course had no aim. It was near morning when he stopped, legs sore and heart tired. He lay down between two large rocks, wrapped himself in his cloak, and slept.

It was midday when Haim awoke. He stood slowly, and it took time for his limbs to loosen again. When he was ready, he set out once more to no place in particular.

He spent two days walking this way and did not see another soul. The land carried him as the wind carried a fallen leaf. He was no longer eleven years old, but his feet followed the same kind of path that they had before finding Chaya: a direction without a destination.

He told himself that he had left the king's army because the queen was ascendant and he would serve in no new civil war, but how he had served Jannaeus's purposes before the queen's rise, he could not say. It was akin to his actions as a member of Morta's brood. He had just fallen into it through other people's choices, and he refused to consider himself the director of any of these events.

As he walked beneath the sun, Haim contemplated his life and who he had become. He was not a gentile—in Jannaeus's army, the gentiles considered him a Jew. The only real Jews he had ever known were the people of Arbel—and he was not one of them either. He wished that he could become a Pharisee, for the Pharisees were above all pure, the antithesis of the Ashkelon temple, and they openly opposed King Jannaeus. Haim could imagine himself as a Pharisee. But he could not seek out the Pharisees. His betrayal of Arbel had sealed that path, and besides, the Pharisees would not accept a half-Jew among them.

Haim realized that, in belonging to no one, he was no one at all. Neither Jew nor gentile. A stranger to everyone. He wished that he could form his own tribe, make his own choices, and set out firmly on his own decided future, but he did not know how. He wondered if every soul was merely a driven leaf without will. Did others predetermine everything? Did anyone truly stand outside the affairs of other people? Could anyone govern the outcome of their own life? Or was every soul a mere victim of other people's choices, whether good or bad? Haim could not accept himself as a tribe of one, and he could not imagine himself a member of any tribe he knew.

He stopped walking, his steps stumbling to a halt in a

patch of coarse sand and loose stone, and he found himself looking at the ground, thinking on this last idea. If he could not imagine himself anywhere, as anyone, why did he tire himself out walking? He had left his boyhood home to flee and save his goats. It was the first good choice he ever remembered making, and as he brooded on that thought, he could not remember making any other. Chaya had found the fish. Killing the wolf had been instinctual. He thought about the old goat-stealer and how, through that angry old man, Haim had discovered the immensity of the hatred stacked against him in that region between Dora and Strato's Tower. Continuing to walk these inland roads would not make him into a new Haim, yet he did not know how to choose anything else. Regardless of what road he chose, he would always be the same Haim, blown wherever the wind blew, part of no fellowship.

To be finished with life seemed the only path left to him, but he was not yet ready to die. He was twenty-six years old and wanted to know why he was alive.

Haim began to walk again, and late in the afternoon, he made camp below a trio of date palms. The palm trunks guided him to where water might be lying below the sand. Two dead tamarisk trees stood nearby. Beyond the palms a stand of sedge grass squatted stout and dense and hardy, and beyond the grass a cluster of cattails stood tall and resolute. Strands of headless barley stalks, their seeds having been taken by insects or birds in the months prior, were scattered across the rocky ground between the sedge grass and cattails like intermediaries in a conflict.

Haim dug at the base of the barley stalks and, with much effort, successfully pulled up the corms. Once he freed and peeled them, he chewed on the tough bulbs. The nearly tasteless liquid etched paths of pleasure through his mouth. There were locusts in this miniature oasis. They were not a cloud-forming swarm as he had witnessed in the north two years before, but they were present. As he moved about the camp, he flicked his sling cords at the creatures and stunned them and caught them and crushed their heads with his fingers and dropped them in the same spot. The pile slowly grew. He pulled up a few cattails and cut off the roots and put them beside the locust heap. It was late in the fruit's season, but he could see some old dates up in the palms, not claimed by birds, insects, or weather. Some unknown force had damaged their stems, starving the fruit of fluid and causing them to wither and inadvertently preserving them.

He began to climb the trunk that seemed to offer the most easily collectable fruit. His progress was slow. He climbed up the trunk carefully, the bark-like stubs providing easy footing, and he carefully filled his slinger's pouch with the old fruit. As he began to descend, he rushed and slipped and sliced open the side of one hand on the sharp edge of one stub. He cursed the tree and his carelessness and completed his descent. He had no spare cloth but his cloak and he did not wish to bloody it, so he stood for a while with his hand raised. The blood dripped into the sand where it soaked into the ground. Finally, he decided to use the sling and wrapped his hand in the linen pouch. It was a poor bandage with the cords trailing excessively, but it crudely served the purpose. He wrapped the excess of cords around his forearm and loosely tied it off. The makeshift bandage looked like a paler version of the adornments Pharisees wore on their forearms and wrists from which hung tiny boxes containing words from the Torah. Haim wanted to speak to someone then. It was the first time since leaving Jannaeus's camp that he felt the need, but there was no one to talk to here.

Using a small wooden trowel, the likes of which most soldiers carried in their packs, he found a place with the softest soil and began to dig. He was down only a foot when the soil became darker and cooler. He dug deeper yet, and just as the hole surpassed his elbow, water began to seep in. He widened and cleared the hole and then left it to fill and settle.

From the old cattails, he found fragile and tattered but still partially intact heads and gathered a mound of the fluffy seeds and the tufts at the ends of the grasses. He added dead and dried reeds to the mix, and so the different species of plants were finally cured of their disdain and unified in their place and purpose. From the dead tamarisk, he gathered twigs and small branches, and with the thick base of his sword, he hacked off some larger branches and kept them long so that he could feed them slowly into the fire once started. Now prepared, he used the flint as the slingers had taught him, and with only a few sparks struck into his mound of white and beige tinder, smoke soon appeared. He cupped his hands around the smoking ball, without actually holding it and blew on it, concentrating his breath, and orange flame leaped in response. He added the twigs which caught next, then the smaller branches took, and it was not long before he had formed a good fire, the sort that would produce coals. He had no pot. He did not know how he would cook the locusts and roots, but then a flat rock caught his eye. After manipulating his fire, he set the rock into the midst of the heat. He cut up the roots and placed them onto the stone. After a while, he turned the pieces and added the locusts, occasionally stirring them with a stick to roast them evenly. When everything was ready, he had to scatter the fire to retrieve his meal. While it cooled, he filled his water skin at the sink he had created and then sat down to eat the meal, mixing what he had cooked with the sun-dried dates. The dates were not fully dried and so had partially spoiled, making them more suitable for animals, but they added flavour to his simple meal. He ate carefully and considered his good fortune. He had eaten nothing the day before.

As he sat before the dying fire, the sky darkened and stars came out. The sedge grass swaying in the breeze caused the lower stars to disappear and reappear as though the sky near the horizon was winking at him. The silhouette of trees suggested that great creatures haunted or guarded this place. His satisfied stomach contrasted with the angry pulse of his injured hand.

Haim had that almost-forgotten desire to talk to someone again. As he sat before the fire that turned to coals and then to darkness, he once again brooded on his existence. He needed to redirect his ways with some new pattern of thought. There was no drink other than water here, and he had drunk nothing brewed since Ashkelon. There were none of the disreputable women who had followed the army and infiltrated the camps or who could be found in the larger cities they conquered. There were no village dances or rural farmsteads for him to observe secretly. There were no slingers he could sit among, pretending to be part of their fellowship and listening to the things men discussed. There was nowhere to walk to, for it was night and he was already at his camp. There was nothing here but his breathing and the invisible whisper of grass and the lightless shapes in the sky where the trees blocked out the stars.

Haim tried to turn his mind outwards, but there was nothing outward to hold him and his memories would not leave him alone, so he bent his remembrances towards the places he had travelled and tried to imagine places he had heard much about but never visited. He thought of Tyre and tried to remember everything he had heard about that city. He thought of central and northern and western Galilee, regions he had never stepped foot in and knew only from others. He thought about Jerusalem, which he had passed by and gone mad within its shadow but never entered. He had seen Jerusalem's temple on its mount from across a valley. He thought of each place he knew of but had never been to and imagined what purpose or deliverance each place might offer. Tyre was a gentile city, and he expected it would be another Ashkelon. Galilee's cities offered only guilt, for they were allied with the Pharisees, and his betrayal of Arbel would follow him for the rest of his days. Jerusalem offered the temple, which was the central place of Jewish worship, but Alexander Jannaeus was not merely king. He was also the high priest. Jannaeus's role corrupted the temple, and the Sadducees controlled it. It was a place central to the people of his mother's blood, but his mother was the one he fled from as a boy. Jerusalem was a tangle of conflicting emotions for Haim.

He remembered then another place, not far from here, to the south. To the immediate south was the Sea of Arabah, what some called the Salt Sea and others the Dead, for it was said that nothing lived in that sea, no fish or animal dwelled along its shoreline, not even plants within or alongside the water. Near the north-western shore, near the water, there was said to be a settlement built in the days of Jannaeus's father, Hyrcanus. It had been built on the ruins of a previous civilization. The settlement was called Secacah by his Jewish informers, and the Moabite and Egyptian slingers called it Qumran. All agreed that the people there called themselves Essenes.

Among the captains in Jannaeus's army, there had been only a few Jews, and they had only rarely mingled with slingers.

ട

"The Essenes are priests," one of the Jewish captains claimed. "Of the original line of Zadok. From the days of Solomon. They are proper priests. Aaron's sons." He was addressing a group of slingers seated around yet another fire. The captain lingered at the edge of the cluster, having been drawn into the discussion as he passed by.

"The temple is in Jerusalem," a slinger near Haim said. "What are they doing at Qumran?"

"The Essenes abandoned Jerusalem," the captain continued. "They've set themselves apart as proper holy men. They reject the corrupted temple and have started again in the desert."

"I heard they rejected the Maccabees," the white-haired slinger said.

"They reject the Maccabees for claiming both the throne and high priesthood," said the captain. He almost entered their circle and then stopped himself, remaining at its periphery. "That's what corrupted the temple. The Essenes honour the temple itself. They just reject its current corruption."

"They sound like an extreme group," the first slinger said. "Like Ashkelon."

"No, not like Ashkelon," the captain protested. "They are pure, completely pure. They are better priests than even the Pharisees. They don't allow any women among them. They take vows of poverty. They are devoted to the laws that Moses wrote. That is their only scripture. They study it, copy it, discuss it, and practise it. They are the opposite of Ashkelon. They are what Jerusalem is supposed to be."

"They are all this without the temple?" Haim asked, thinking about the old scribe and all he had taught Haim as a boy.

"They are better at observing Moses's laws than the priests who run the temple," the captain said.

"But they take no women," the white-haired slinger said.

"None," the captain said with an odd smile. "Those already married give up their wives to join. Perhaps a bit like you lot."

The slingers around the fire broke into laughter and exchanged a few ribald jokes commenting on the nature of the wives left behind.

"The priests of Qumran dress only in white robes," the captain finished. "They accumulate no wealth or possessions but their writings. They share everything in common."

After the captain had moved on, the slingers talked on into the evening. They spoke in tones of mixed respect and contempt. Heads shook in disbelief at the practices of the fabled Essenes.

❦

As Haim sat in darkness before the night-time silhouettes of palms and dead tamarisks, waiting for sleep to give him peace, he considered all he remembered of that one discussion.

The Essenes sounded as though they were as much the antithesis of Ashkelon's pagan temple as Jerusalem itself, but they were neither Sadducees nor Pharisees. They were a third party. Something altogether separate. The captain had claimed that their way was higher and purer than all the other Jewish sects.

Lying awake in the dark, Haim remembered how one of the slingers had talked about the hard trials that newcomers were required to submit to if they wanted admission into the Essene brotherhood. As the stars shone and the desert crouched soundlessly beyond his camp, these stories did not deter Haim. Such trials seemed part of the very nature of what he sought. Everything until now had been non-specific, the product of aimless drifting, and these paths had led him only ever downwards. In his desert camp, an ascetic vision drew him. Haim wanted the character of his pure and frugal diet to encompass everything, all of his existence. This desire was beyond money, beyond blood, beyond the passions that had consumed and gutted everyone he had ever travelled alongside.

Below the skin, every man was a leper in a wasteland, dying on the outside as they were eaten from within. As Haim lay in that grove of star-lined palms and reeds and cattails, he decided to seek out the city of white-robed Essenes. It was a choice he could make of his own volition and not arrive at by happenstance or others' decisions. It was something he could find on his own and, by trial, earn.

In the morning, he set the sun to his back and walked until he came to the Jordan River. He turned south at the river and walked along its eastern bank, looking for the easiest crossing. He refilled his water skin and continued to follow the stream south until he neared its entrance into the Salt Sea. Here the river fractured into smaller channels, and with the water levels low and the base rocky, he found some natural fords he could cross. The only difficulty was the chill he felt as he emerged from the last rill and climbed back up onto the Judean side. As he looked west, the sea was to his left, the Jordan behind him, Jericho perhaps an hour's walk to his right. He walked west, following the arc of the sea's northern shore as it turned south, and in a short time he too had turned entirely south while the sea remained on his left.

He continued walking, his head down and shoulders slumped until finally he looked up and Qumran appeared before him like a mirage. In the distance, lime-plastered walls shone in early light, their pale hues as pure as he imagined their legendary inhabitants would be in their white robes.

It turned out that Qumran was not so much a city as a complex. It had on the seaward side a camp of around fifty to a hundred tents, and nearby, closer to the salt water, there were groves of date palms. The collection of buildings that formed the solid stonework of Qumran was set on a marlstone ledge back some distance from the shore of the sea. Behind the buildings were dramatic cliffs, and behind those cliffs rose higher mountains yet. The late-morning sun came in on an angle that made the Salt Sea sparkle like glass, a translucent surface devoted to light. The stone complex was bright and clean with squared-off walls before the cliffs' irregular ruggedness and the jumbled mountains.

There was a road parallel to Haim's current course—a footpath, well worn. He presumed it came from Jericho and continued south beyond Qumran. He looked down this new road south to where the cliffs and mountains approached the sea. According to well-travelled slingers, the entire coastline was passable if travellers could keep themselves supplied with fresh water. The white-haired slinger had claimed that an oasis called Ein Gedi lay farther south on the Salt Sea's shore.

Haim slowly studied the settlement from a distance. He presumed that it was Qumran. No signs advertised its identity. The small and numerous tents looked like supplicants begging for entry before the compound's shining stone walls. Some of the complex's buildings rose two stories high. He could see windows below flat roofs and a tower that was even taller. The tower had no windows. Though it dominated the tents before it, the stone complex seemed small below the imposing backdrop of cliffs and mountains. The cliffs were jagged and unfinished—the mountains beyond a swelling of rough curves and slopes.

Haim catalogued what he observed and compared it to what the slingers had said. He sorted through imagination and memory and noted the unexpected. It seemed to Haim's eye that if this was Qumram, it projected simple purity below a looming mountain wildness. He felt his heart beat as he took it all in.

I am afraid, he said to himself, *because what I want is here.*

He was an unmet convert standing alone on the desert road, his being as frail as the tents below and his morality as ruined as the cliffs above. Qumran stood between the tents and the cliffs.

He could make new choices here.

35

77 BCE

Some distance still from Qumran, Haim noticed a giant boulder off the road that was broken into three pieces, each one considerably longer and wider than he was tall. He investigated the odd formation, and when he got there, he could not see over the broken boulder's highest point. All three pieces rested against one another like a loaf torn apart and then set back together. The trio of shapes made Haim want to look up to see where the great rock had fallen from, but clearly it had not fallen here, and he wondered what other forces would have caused the stone to fracture in this way.

Haim found a long, narrow gap between two of the stone shapes. One wedge stood straight while the other leaned in at a dramatic angle, creating an overhang that shielded the space beneath from bad weather. The nook was just the right size for his sheathed sword. Haim removed it from around his waist, slid it into the gap, and stuffed a few extra rocks in behind it to deflect both water and the eye.

With this task dealt with, Haim made his way back to the road and continued his walk to Qumran. He soon came upon a group of three men in white robes. They were struggling with what appeared to be a basalt millstone. The black stone proudly contrasted with the creams and browns of marl in the surrounding landscape. It was a northern stone, out of place along the Salt Sea.

Haim had noticed a broken wagon some distance back. The wagon's rear axle had been in two pieces, one wheel twisted, the entire contraption abandoned. The three men ahead carried the millstone together towards Qumran. Two poles bore the weight of the great stone. Two men held up the rear of this procession, each with his own pole to manage. The man in front carried a double weight with a pole on each shoulder. Clinging wet patches stained their upper garments, and all three seemed to strain equally as they hunched their way towards Qumran, the man in front being the strongest of the three. There was no sign of the donkey or mule that had pulled the wagon.

Haim walked up to the men and spoke a greeting. They grunted back but did not look behind.

"Give Elazar a shoulder," one of the rearward men said in a hoarse voice, his body slouching beneath the weight of the pole.

"Yes, I can do that," Haim said.

"Hurry up about it," the man said. He shifted his position in concert with his companion, each of them moving their poles to opposite shoulders.

Haim assumed Elazar was the muscular solo man in front, and he hurried past the other two. He reached out a hand to touch the rough black stone as he passed it, and at that moment, the scene came apart. The men behind cursed and stumbled and seemed of a mind to drop their end, and Elazar in front cursed as well in unseeing response and gripped at his poles and suddenly knelt, and so the men behind did the same, and in that startling moment, they lowered the millstone to the ground without dropping it. The men stood upright again, and the rearward men backed away from Haim. Elazar looked to his companions first, flashing irritation and only then surprise as he discovered Haim.

"Who are you, gentile?" the first man barked. His tone was hostile.

"Haim. I'm no gentile. I'm a Jew. Of Benjamin."

"You're not of the Unity."

Haim did not know how to answer that. He looked from man to man for an explanation. He came last again to Elazar, who stared at him with black eyes.

Elazar looked at his companions. "Did he touch the stone?"

"Yes," the first man said. He was a very tall man, though thin.

Haim looked at this man, and the expression he saw on his face was a mixture of anger and disgust. It was a look that Haim remembered most from his childhood and also from the goat-stealer's limited inventory of expressions. Though Haim had been one of the Terrors of Samaria and had survived Ashkelon and had lived to fight for more than half a decade in Jannaeus's army, he wilted before the tall man's glare. He understood that, in his introduction to Qumran, he had violated some custom of the place. He had no idea what he had done wrong.

"Now we have to deal with this as well," the third man said.

"Yes," Elazar said.

"Seven days," the tall thin man said.

"If uncleanness can travel up a stream," Elazar said, "it can travel up a pole. We are all unclean now."

"Because of this fool," the third man said.

"Aran," said Elazar.

"Seven days," Aran said, repeating what the tall thin man had already noted.

"Yes, but we can clean ourselves," Elazar said. Elazar motioned to Haim. "You follow us. Keep your distance."

With that, the three began walking again towards Qumran.

Haim looked at the stone which lay abandoned like the wagon before it. He looked towards the departing trio. He needed to decide, but he did not know what to do. Like speaking to know his mind, he needed to act to know what he thought. He followed the men.

Haim observed himself walking, not pausing to think any of this through, just immediately walking. Following. He was not naked and desperate as when Jannaeus's men had found him after Ashkelon. Soft words of welcome from a dangerous woman did not lead him here as when he and Chaya had entered into Morta's folds. He was not being baited and tricked into a trap as at Ashkelon. He had come here to join Qumran, but his first act had offended the Essenes, and now he was despised before he had even started. All signs told him to leave, but he followed. He did not choose to follow but simply noted that he was following and was surprised to find himself doing so. It occurred to him that again he had not been consulted. The part of his mind that spoke before he knew what to say, the part that decided to follow, that part was different than the part that watched and questioned itself and tried to understand. There was something in this walk towards Qumran that was of the old man at Ashkelon and something of Decuma and Morta and Klotho, but no one deceived him here or decided for him.

Haim felt disoriented as he followed the Qumran men. It was as though he were two people and one half of his self observed the other in puzzlement.

The three men did not go to the tents. They steered away from the dwellings and headed towards the north-west corner of the walled complex.

"Wait here," Elazar said as they neared a gate in the wall. "Do not enter the gate. Do not even approach the gate. Do you understand?"

"Yes," Haim said.

The three went on without him. By stepping off to one side, he could see past the gate and follow their progress into the complex without getting any closer.

The three men spoke to another man inside. The sentry looked out at Haim, shook his head, and then nodded to the three. They disappeared. Shortly after, they reappeared wearing loincloths only. They moved out of sight again, descending into a recess in the ground. There was the splash of water then, and when they emerged, they were wet from head to toe. Their hair and beards glistened in the afternoon sunlight. They moved out of sight again, and looking around, Haim could not see any other living soul in that place. All of Qumran seemed deserted.

36

77 BCE

THE THREE PRIESTS were inside Qumran's stone complex for perhaps as long as an evening meal. Only Elazar and Aran came out, exiting through a different gate and wearing new robes and turbans of the same white linen as their previous attire.

"You are not of the Unity," Elazar said again as he approached Haim. His eyes were still black.

Haim still did not know how to respond.

"You are not a trader," Elazar continued. "So, what are you?"

"I came to find the people called Essenes at Qumran. I wish to learn from them. To learn their ways."

"Qumran. Essenes. We do not use those names." By his expression and tone, the names were not unfamiliar.

"You call yourselves the Unity," Haim guessed from what they had previously said.

"The Brotherhood," Elazar said. "The Unity. Mostly we do not call ourselves anything but 'us,' for it is only us in this place. Secacah is not a place for idle travellers."

"I'm no idle traveller. I've come a long way to find you."

Elazar smiled, but it was not a friendly smile. "A long way. From Jericho, perhaps?"

"No. A long way. I've been through Tyre and Ashkelon and Gamla and Jerusalem. I've gone looking for meaning, and everywhere I've gone, I've not found it." Haim felt a strangeness in his voice. In these men, he saw the father he had never known—not the Tyrant of Dora but the dye maker who had never been his father and had not even been a Jew. These acolytes were the dye maker merged with the old scribe whose eyes would have understood these men even if he was not one of them. "Everywhere I've gone, I've found corruption, and I've taken corruption with me from place to place and added it to the corruption that was already there. I've come much farther than Jericho. I've travelled for twenty-six years on the road behind me. I want to know how to be clean of everything that is."

Elazar regarded Haim carefully. He looked at Aran, then back at Haim, and then again at Aran. "He might be different."

"Perhaps," Aran said. "But he's as ignorant as the others and his language just as crude."

"Like a child's." Elazar turned his attention back to Haim. "We have no children here—no women and so no children. As a result, we grow accustomed to our own company. It's easy to forget that there's a difference between corruption born of ignorance and corruption born of evil. Are you evil or are you ignorant?"

Haim again did not know how to respond, but the two men seemed willing to wait the rest of the day for an answer. "I have been evil," he finally said. "Previously, I was evil. What happened on the road was ignorance. Not evil. I don't even know the name of the offence I committed."

"We are different because our ways are righteous," Aran said.

Haim nodded. "Just tell me what to do."

Elazar turned to Aran. "Even if you think him irredeemably ignorant . . . "

Aran grunted. "Maybe." He made a gesture that Haim had never seen before but understood all the same. It communicated a non-committal disbelief. Aran still thought him irredeemable.

Elazar and Aran led Haim from the gate and towards the tents. It appeared that no one slept within the stone walls of Qumran. Haim expected to find campfires and cooking pots among the tents as there would have been among the slingers, but as they threaded between them, he saw that there was only empty space between the tents. There were no signs of hearths or cookware.

In an opening between a group of tents, his guides paused and signed for Haim to sit. Shortly after, a group gathered. Haim waited for his introduction.

A discussion started about tapping some of the older, spent date palms for sap, and Haim inferred that they made both wine and syrups from this sap. The men only talked to each other and said not a word to Haim. They discussed salt harvesting along the shoreline south of Qumran, but he could not figure out from what he overheard how far south this operation was. They did not introduce Haim and regarded him no more than they would an inanimate object, as if he had set only his pack down at the edge of their circle and not his whole self.

They spoke next about the wheat harvest that had recently passed. Haim could not imagine where on the narrow strip of land between the Salt Sea and the steep cliffs they might be growing any type of grain.

There was news from Jerusalem. It was old news about one of the decrees the queen had made before leaving to join her husband at Ragaba. But it was new information in Qumran. That he had come from Ragaba, Haim had no opportunity to mention. Listening to their tones, Haim could not discern whether the men despised Jerusalem or only its queen.

Finally, they spoke about Haim. The men glanced briefly at Haim as though he were a specimen of only illustrative interest, a representation of what Elazar was saying and not the actual object of his account. No one asked Haim any questions. The conversation shifted without reaching any kind of conclusion, and then Aran stood. He indicated for Haim to follow as he and Elazar set off without waiting.

They came to another similar clearing within the community filled with another group of men. Again, Haim sat apart from the rest. They discussed various matters and ignored him. Haim learned about a shepherd's flock of sheep or goats. As with the previous discussion about grain, Haim could not imagine where a flock could be pastured along the barren shore. Eventually, they introduced Haim, and despite the introduction, they again treated him as though he were not present. Then his guides stood and walked away, and Haim followed.

The trio passed through the last of the tents and walked south towards the shoreline. Their path led them down a marl terrace to a sloping flatland that bordered the water. A grove of date palms lay ahead.

After they had walked for a while and Qumran was well behind them, Haim finally spoke. "Does the place ahead have a name?"

"Ein Feshcha," Elazar said.

"No one lives here?"

"No. This land is for agriculture only." Elazar pointed to a cleft in the cliffs to their right. "There's a freshwater spring there. Just a trickle this time of year. It comes down from the upper lands above. Ein Feshcha is for agriculture."

The men working at Ein Feshcha seemed to devote as much time to discussing as doing. Their discussions served as a mixture of cooperative thought and resting. Haim had seen this type of chatter in his days with Jannaeus's army but had never seen it before then. It was the kind of labour that occurred when the labourers were many and the decisions were plentiful and portentous and yet strangely unpressured. It was the deliberation of artisans who took pleasure in vacillating between all the possible solutions.

Repairs were underway: the replastering of a stone pit, the repairing of mortar in a stone wall, the patching of a wind-damaged roof. Haim came to learn that it was here that they made the date wine in rare seasons when they had the sap for its manufacture. There were hundreds of the date palms in the adjacent grove. Rolls of coarse cloth lay below the harvested trees. Haim understood their use. Workers covered the clusters of dates with bags while the fruit still hung in the palms, protecting the crop as it ripened and keeping both birds and insects away. He had seen workers climb trees to secure coverings like these in his days with Chaya, before Morta, before Arbel. Unlike the isolated trees he had found in the desert, these trees had no fruit left. The pickers of Qumran were more thorough than the birds and insects of the desert.

The men were careful to keep Haim away from the wine house, and they kept themselves a cautious distance away from him as well. The introductions were the same as before, and when he passed from that place, he still had said nothing to the other residents of this community. None commented on his physical shape or what he might think or have to say. Surveying eyes lingered on the dagger at his waist and the sling, but otherwise, disinterest prevailed. It was as though they already knew him and whatever uniqueness he might think he brought to this place, they had seen it before.

Haim sensed that the things that burned within him were not things that concerned the citizens of Qumran. All of the outside world's distinctions and the flavours of passion in each person's diverse reality were all one and the same here. Any differences that the outside world might haggle over were like the differences found in varieties of dung. The camel's dung was large and round and black. A goat's was smaller and rounder, like a sheep's. That of cattle was a great pat. The refuse of birds was often white and poured out as a liquid. It was all dung. Any pride regarding the distinctiveness of one species' dung over another's was not something to be given any consideration whatsoever. It was all the same. The Essenes directed their attention to matters of another world entirely.

Haim walked in silence from Ein Feshcha back to Qumran. Both men could keep an eye on him as he walked off to the side, and it seemed to make them more comfortable to have him there rather than trailing behind unseen. The two men discussed private concerns on the way back to Qumran. Haim walked in silence.

As the two talked, Haim learned that there was ongoing work above the compound. Lime plasterwork was underway to repair water channels that captured the winter's flash floods. This work was proceeding on schedule. Seasonal floods filled cisterns and pools within the walls. The work needed to be completed before the winter rains came. It seemed like a trivial discussion to Haim, like the slow work of the men deliberating at Ein Feshcha. There was not enough rain in this country to damage the drying plaster, and the time of floods was a long way off yet.

One of the pools at Qumran remained uncovered. The old and now-dirty water from the prior year had been scooped out by hand, for the Qumran pools had no drains. Now that it was empty, others were cleaning and repairing this pool, and Haim gathered that there was some significance to this particular pool's being unavailable for a time. What that significance was, he did not know. He did not ask.

The rest of the afternoon was much like the morning. In the little discussion that Haim had with Elazar and Aran, Haim disclosed his unusual dietary habits. His ascetic practice was the only thing he said in their presence that met with their approval.

A call went out as evening approached, and the men of Ein Feshcha made their way towards Qumran. As they were walking, another call went out, and those closer to Qumran began their approach as well. The time for the communal evening meal had come.

Haim watched from the edge of the tents as the last man entered the walls. He remained outside. Initiate training would take one year. Though there were two other recent arrivals, they worked here as shepherds on pastures far away from Qumran and would rotate back to the complex in another week. Haim was alone outside the walls. It would be a year or more before he entered the holy gates to bathe and share in the communal meal, and that would only happen if he passed their examinations. They left him to the arid and barren landscape to find what he could for food.

Even the sea was dead here. He did not know what to eat. For the first time, he missed the slingers' inclusive pressure and their constant demands that he share the cook's pot.

Haim wandered north from Qumran in the direction from which he had come. He was hungry, and when he found a saltbush that still had a few of its triangular flowers, old and withered, he peeled them open for the seeds within. He ate the few he found and then walked on. He was within sight of the broken wagon when he came upon a broom bush. He dug out the roots and peeled back the tough outer skin. The interior was tough and called for roasting, but he had no fire. He had his flint but no tinder and no fuel except for the abandoned wagon. He walked to the wagon, chewing slowly, deciding to preserve the wagon's wood even as a dark mood came over him. He looked back the way he had come, and in the distance, he could see the shape of the millstone that the Essenes would return to in a week. Its banishment for seven days was the custom to cleanse it of Haim's touch. He was not of the Unity. He was not clean.

Haim sat with his back to the wagon, leaning against one slanting wheel, still hungry. He imagined the hundred men eating together within the walls and realized that his ascetic practice had not been what he had thought it to be. He had almost always eaten in the company of others. He had been separate from the slingers but had usually eaten near them. Or while observing a village or while watching a dance or in the corner of a tavern. His lonely fires in the desert had been transitory meals and not a committed pattern lacking an escape route. To stay here at Qumran would be to choose to be alone for a year. None would touch him. They would not even eat with him.

Haim contemplated the bleak land and realized that he had learned something new about isolation after spending only half a day in this place. He had thought that he had already experienced the full depth and breadth of solitude and that he had nothing left to discover about it. Yet now he had learned that it was one thing to choose separation. To want isolation, to escape a crowd, to be alone in one's thoughts, to mourn a loss—such solitude was one thing. It was another thing altogether to feel isolation within a crowd, a thing he had known most among the slingers. As he leaned against the broken wagon, he absorbed something alien to his previous experience. Here at Qumran was a new isolation. This was an isolation enforced by others as the collective response to his very self. This was beyond his lonely wandering before Chaya, different than his feelings in Arbel. There was no pull to the centre here that he was resisting. Here, the centre had a wall around it, which he was outside of and unwelcome within. He could not enter and accept the requisite abuse. He could not enter and be ignored. He could not attempt to enter and feel his difference and press on, choosing to join what was foreign to him. He could not enter at all. There was no choice to be made. Here he was truly alone.

His punishment was not for an act committed but a consequence of who he was. It was the result of his very being. He wondered if his infant self had immediately known this rejection when he had been born among the three females and immediately despised—despised even before birth. Leaning against the ruined wagon wheel, he decided that he would have been unaware as an infant. He must have only grown slowly into the knowledge of himself, and even that knowledge had been blunted by the scribe's limited form of acceptance.

At Qumran, he was freshly aware. There was nothing to blunt the force of that awareness. Not even a full stomach. There was no choice before him except to submit himself to their judgment and accept his cursed status at the periphery of this white-robed tribe.

Haim felt something he had not felt since the old scribe's death in his mother's house. In that moment, he had known that there would never again be a place for him in that house. Even if he were to have stayed—and he could have stayed—he would have been as alone as he had been at his birth. To stay here, outside Qumran's walls, was to choose the widow's house again.

As a boy, he would have been inside the walls but apart. As a mere boy, he had chosen not to endure that. He had fled to the isolation of his own choosing. Haim did not know if he could now choose Qumran's version of the widow's house. It would require enduring a suffocating solitude that did not seem bearable. The walls were too stark in this place. His hopes of how he might deflect and pretend, how he might lie to himself to endure the year, were defeated by the straightness and certainty of those walls and by the daily rituals that would leave him on the seaside while the others went inside. He would always be without, on the Dead Sea side of their fellowship—alone with his saltbush and broom bush. He might very well starve.

Haim thought about what came after leaving his mother's house. He thought about the old goat-stealer and the terrified creeping through Samaria until he had found Chaya. He thought about the lands east of the Jordan and Galilee, about Arbel, about the banditry and both tours of Dora. He thought of Chaya's last words to him, passed on by the innkeeper, and they hurt as much as the entire memory of his time with her. Based on what he knew from Jericho and Ashkelon and other places, she would be dead by now. If she was not dead, then the Chaya that he would find, were he to find her, would bear no relation to the Chaya he had pulled from the Samaritan well. He wondered if perhaps he were dead. Dead in Ashkelon. A ghost on the land, a ghost who had entered Jannaeus's mercenary army and killed for an evil king and only now, at Qumran, understood that his corrupted spirit and true holiness were incompatible and that his rejection by the Essenes was as it should be.

Haim tried to focus his cloudy eyes and could not. Unable to see, he followed his memory of the path that led to his stashed sword, and in his mind, he went there and removed the concealing stones and removed the sheath and from the sheath withdrew the blade. He remembered the old scribe's story about Eretz-Israel's first king, Saul, the failed king who ended his life in Samaria, in the shadow of Gilboa, by falling on his sword. Haim considered ending his ghostly life alongside the Salt Sea, perhaps in the very place where he had hidden the weapon so that his corpse would not be a further offence to this land and people.

Tired and unable to see clearly, he did not go looking for his sword and reflected later how much would have changed if he had. Instead, he climbed into the back of the wagon, which was tilted but provided a place to sleep above the rocky ground. He took off his pack and let himself and it slide with the wagon's slope until both were wedged against the wooden side. He rested there and closed his eyes. It was some time before darkness came, but sleep found him before the sun set, as it had when he had been rescued from the desert and carried to the hill overlooking Dora and left alone, found only by the darkness to come.

37

77 BCE

A DREAM CAME UPON Haim late in the night. It was an image of the Ashkelonite's maze below an unblinking spectral moon. The maze, however, had changed. It was no longer a square populated by many blind men, dead or otherwise, but rather it was a long narrow maze, endlessly falling into the horizon, inhabited by just one man who was utterly alone within his dark, stone universe. The ladder was also different. It lay, as before, across the top of the maze, unseen by the man. But unlike that of the Ashkelonite's tale, this ladder was not alone. There were many ladders, as many ladders as there were miles in this endless maze. Each ladder lay across the top of the labyrinth and was unseen by the man wandering below.

Haim viewed the scene from above as though he were a bird. He followed the blind man's progress and noted each time he passed beneath a new ladder. Sometimes only a small bit of one wooden end jutted out over the edge of the wall where a fortuitously upraised hand might encounter it. In other instances, the ladder extended well out into the space over the path or entirely bridged the maze channel, both ends resting on the tops of parallel stone walls. In his dream, he watched the man for days. There was no end to that blind journey, for the maze had no end and the man had no sighted companion or any other means to help him.

Haim tossed in his hard wedged bed and adjusted his pack as a pillow. He was sure that he was sleepless until morning came and the sound of a voice startled him awake and he realized that he had been dreaming a false insomnia. He opened his eyes and saw a man in a white robe standing outside the cart, watching him in the bright morning light. It was the tall thin man from yesterday's trio. He had cleansed himself yesterday but not re-emerged from Qumran to walk him about the community with the others.

Haim tried to sit up, but the wagon's tilt made it awkward, so he squirmed around and out and landed on surprised feet.

"I am Eli," the man said. He pointed at the wagon. "A strange bed."

"I supposed I've made it unclean now as well," Haim said, "by sleeping in it."

"Just touching it would do. Might as well have a good sleep while you're at it."

Eli held up a large shard of a former clay bowl that contained half of a prepared citron. He cocked his head at Haim. The offering violated Haim's principles, but the preparation was simple and his belly growled and he felt light-headed with hunger. He nodded.

Eli set the piece of clay on the ground between them. Haim picked up the shard and then took the fruit from it. The two men were careful to never touch the shard or the fruit at the same time. Eli stepped back, and Haim bit down into the rind. It was more sour than he expected but adequately caramelized, and he felt a rush of gratitude in response to the strong taste and the sweet. He unslung his skin and drank and then finished the citron.

"Thank you," he said.

"You were leaving," Eli said.

"I was thinking of it."

"Perhaps our cold welcome was to blame. You didn't get far."

"I didn't know where else to go. I came to Qumran for a reason."

"I heard."

There did not seem to be anything to say beyond this. Haim was not sure whether to give the shard back to the Essene. He lifted it and tilted his head. Eli tilted his and pursed his lips in response, and Haim tossed the shard off the road where it shattered, the dark clay scattering among the light stones. The sun would undo the work of fire, and the fragments would one day be the colour of the land again.

"No one is worth anything because of his belongings," Eli said.

Haim looked at his small pack, at the old water skin he held in his hand. "That's good."

"And no one's worth is found in their family heritage."

Haim looked at Eli directly. "That's good too. I come from a family of no consequence."

"You're only worth the lessons you're learning, your

adherence to the way, and the work that you produce. Do you know how we know this to be the truest measure of a man's worth?"

Haim shook his head.

"Adam. He had nothing of his own and was of no family at all, and yet he had worth in the eyes of God. He was made in the very image of God, made to learn God's ways and to learn the names of all the animals, for the naming of the animals required him to categorize, to learn, to begin the task that only Solomon could complete. And he was put in the garden to tend it. God created Adam to learn, to use his learning, and to work. Moses recorded all this. You know these things?"

Haim nodded.

"You know the stories?" Eli asked.

"Yes."

"But do you understand them?"

"I hadn't thought of Adam in the way you just described."

"What is Adam most known for?"

"He violated God's command."

"Yes. He took what was forbidden. The forbidden fruit bore no evil within it beyond the prohibition not to touch it, and by taking it, the only crime Adam committed was that of disobedience. The restriction was wholly arbitrary. Obedience is the sacred way. The first man could not adhere to that one law, and so a great curse was brought upon him, and though work and learning had always been present within his sphere, both became hard afterwards. Adherence was not banished. The requirement to adhere remained. It was simply that work and learning became hard as well. Trouble multiplied the burden of a simple law, and now we have many laws and many troubles, and still we must learn and we must work. The way of the Essene is to do both: to learn and to work and, while doing both, to adhere. These things have been with us since the beginning."

Eli studied Haim. Haim looked over at the Salt Sea's bright shine and the hills hazily visible on the far shore. He turned his attention back to Eli.

Eli was taller than Haim, perhaps thirty years of age, and had a triangular face, a lined brow, and curled hair at his forehead and temples. His chin was unusually large at the end of a narrow jaw. It was as though a knob had been installed there beneath the skin. His face looked as much like a contraption as a person, but the look was not off-putting. He was distinct.

"Can you read?" Eli asked.

"Yes."

"And write?"

"The old scribe taught me. My hand has had no practice since."

"Scribe?" Eli frowned. "Of what school?"

"I don't know."

"How can you not know?"

"We lived on the border of Samaria. Some would say within its borders. We were of the tribe of Benjamin. My father died before I was born. The scribe came to us when he was very old, and I suspect he pwas of a school of his own."

"So, you are not a Sadducee?"

Haim laughed. "I told you my family was of no consequence, even before my father died. We were poor."

"And not a Pharisee."

Haim thought of the Pharisees of Arbel. "Their ways

are remote and strict, and I cannot imagine that they would have taken me as a student had I had access to them. I have nothing against them. I fought in Jannaeus's army, but I have nothing against the Pharisees."

"So, you think they are strict?" Eli asked. "They do not go far enough. They are drunkards. They accept bribes, or did when they had power. They take wives and concubines and are as dissolute as the Sadducees. They conceal their ways better than others and demand more of their students than they do of themselves. They erect standards they don't try to meet. We erect higher standards yet, and we demonstrate the adherence that Adam could not. To prevent pride from overwhelming our efforts, we commit ourselves to live in poverty here and in our other communities. We do everything the Pharisees cannot, and then we do more. We claim nothing as our own; we share everything. We live in obedience, we work and learn, and any man can leave whenever he chooses. If a man does not adhere, we cast him out. It is easy to attempt to join us but hard to succeed. And we will not beg you to stay. Only those who are truly pure remain, and so we honour the Teacher of Righteousness and prepare for what is to come."

"What is to come?"

Eli smiled. "That is something you will learn in time if you stay. The first question for you to ask is, do you want to start?"

"I don't know if I can . . . adhere."

"You will only find out if you try," Eli said. "You will not be the judge of whether you can succeed or not. You do not decide that. We will decide for you and not until after one year. After one year, if we judge you sufficient, we will welcome you into Qumran's walls. You will share with us in the communal meals. Until then, you'll eat outside the walls. Given the current state of newcomers, that means you'll eat mostly alone. After one year, you will partake of our food with us, within the walls, but you will not yet partake of the wine. The communal drink only comes after the second year. If you pass, if you are found worthy after the second year, then you may join in the full Unity. Then you will take the vows of our order. They will be the last vows you will ever take in this life, and then you will become one of us for the remainder of your days."

"You do not marry."

"No. Adam's trouble came through Eve. There is nothing more to be said about that. Do you have a wife?"

"No." Haim looked at the tilted wagon, then Eli again. "Where would I live?"

"The wagon won't do. We have a tent we keep for travellers and acolytes such as yourself."

"How would I learn?"

"I will be your teacher."

"You are the one who directed me to help Elazar."

"Yes. And it led to your first trouble here in the community. The bakers are not pleased that their new millstone has been delayed now for another week. I spoke because I did not see you and did not recognize to whom I was speaking. Much bad teaching comes from the teacher not recognizing his student. I stayed behind yesterday after my purification for further confession and instruction, and the elders have determined my fate. I must now correct my error, and to do that, I will be your guide for your first two years. If you are successful, you will join our fellowship and I will remain your teacher for the rest of your life. You will sit below me in the seating order at our meals. You will follow my directions. I will always be responsible for recognizing who you are and saying what is appropriate for your needs. I must consider your status and your capabilities. You are my charge. Unless you leave."

"It would be better for you if I left."

Eli shrugged. "It would make no difference. The next novice to come along will be assigned to me then until I learn to recognize the face of a seeker and the spirit of an unclean soul in need of redemption."

"You could not have known who I was. I came up from behind."

Eli held Haim's gaze. He seemed about to say something, and Haim braced himself. The man's expression and posture suggested a rebuke, and the knob of his chin seemed to flex. Then Eli's face softened. Eli's shoulders relaxed. "To tempt me to defend myself is to awaken Adam's second sin within me. Do you remember Adam's second sin?"

Haim shook his head.

"He did not accept the guilt of his first sin. He blamed God for giving him Eve. He never acknowledged his weakness in accepting her as a gift from God to begin with, in listening to her without questions, in following her blindly. God supplied a test with the tree. God supplied a test with Eve. Adam failed both tests."

Haim felt conflicted as he absorbed Eli's manner and his doctrine. "How do I begin?" he asked.

"Begin what?"

"My first year."

"Acknowledging your error would have been a better

response." Eli studied Haim's expression. An uncomfortable amount of time passed before he spoke again. "I have much to learn about timing, for even this lesson is beyond you. To begin, then, we need to find you work. Soldiers are not needed here. And you cannot work within the walls. I have found you a place at the saltworks. You will begin there."

38

77-76 BCE

THE MORNING SUN breached the screen of Moab's mountains on the distant eastern shore, casting yellow and orange light across the Sea of Salt. Ein Feshcha's cold water made Haim's skull and chest brittle as he went down into it. He rose again to see the dawn-coloured mist over salt water roll like fire—it was the world seen through water-filled eyes.

Haim had bathed alone each morning for weeks. This, his first day with others, was a welcome change.

"The proper freshwater pools inside Qumran cannot be more bracing than the Salt Sea," Kalev said. Kalev and Manoach were the other two acolytes at Qumran. They had just rotated back to the shoreline compound after serving their time as shepherds.

"Up in the hills," Manoach said, pointing to the mountains above Qumran, "there are no pools. Just streams and eddies, but no deep pools for proper bathing."

The three men exited Ein Feshcha's waters, rinsed themselves in the freshwater stream, then re-dressed as the Essenes would within the walls and returned to the tent city, walking through it and up to Qumran's walls. Eli had left food out for them. They collected their gifts and went down to the shoreline where they conducted themselves as the Essenes prescribed.

"I'll start," Manoach said, and so their early morning time of reciting to one another began. They worked from memory as much as they could, starting with lines from the Torah and then moving on to the Manual of Discipline.

Some time later, the first of the day's Essenes began to file out of Qumran's gates. Manoach stood and brushed sand from his tunic. "See you at midday," he said.

Haim and Kalev nodded.

Manoach went back towards Ein Feshcha, trailing those of the Unity assigned to work there. Of the three petitioners to Qumran's community, Manoach was the most advanced. He had begun his initiation three months before Kalev arrived. Kalev was two months ahead of Haim.

"Well, let's go," Kalev said. As the two men started to stand, Kalev gave Haim a shove. Off balance, Haim staggered down the shoreline until he righted himself. He turned in surprise, but Kalev's face was a broad grin. "The first man to the saltworks wins," Kalev said casually, and then before Haim could register the challenge, Kalev was off and running. The saltworks was hardly a racing distance away. Before Haim had pointed himself in the right direction and got moving, Kalev was already there.

Haim shook his head as he walked past Kalev, joining the other Essenes assigned to the salt harvesting facility. He did not say anything, but he did smile.

At the saltworks, two of the broad, long-handled trowels were set aside for the two acolytes. The task here was to move the Salt Sea's heavy water through successive layers of vast drying pans, which stretched in both directions along the shoreline, each one wider than a man was tall. They were carved into the stone shoreline and would barely have registered to a casual eye as constructions were it not for the men working them. Trowels in hand, they would march side by side in the pans, pushing the slurry of thickening saltwater around and stirring up salt sediments in a bid to speed up evaporation. On days when the slurry was sufficiently thick, they would shovel the salt—and inevitably some water—into the next pan. In this way, they sped up the drying process. The pan farthest up the shoreline was a vast plain that was nearly dry after a few days of waiting and its load could soon be gathered and hauled to the final sorting and drying tables. After that, the salt would go to the bagging room.

Their work this morning was the artless task of trowelling, walking a long line north, and then turning around to trowel a long line south. It was not hard, but it was boring.

"The water level is lower today," Haim said.

Kalev said nothing in reply.

The grind of crystals against the bottom of Haim's feet was a strange dense feeling, different from sand, different from stone. Two hours later, exhausted men from the upper pans replaced him and Kalev. One such man nearly took Haim's trowel from him. Haim stepped away with a warning, and the man pulled back, alerted, his hand retrieved as though burned, wrist and hand held like a snake recoiling after a strike.

"Thank you," the man said and sought out a clean tool. Though they had worked together for the past four months, the man and Haim had never shared words before, and Haim never spoke to the man again after.

"Here goes," Kalev said as he lifted a shovel full of crystalline sludge from the deeper evaporation pan to the next-shallower level. Haim set to work alongside him, and twice their tools clicked edges. Kalev put some distance between them to avoid a confrontation.

Moving salt between pans took more energy than the mere churning of lower evaporation pools. As they worked, sweat ran in elongated streams down their bodies' own evaporation plains. Haim's shape was muscled with taut cords, whereas Kalev's was stockier and thicker. Of the two, Kalev could lift more and Haim could lift longer.

At lunch, Manoach did not appear. The Essenes at the saltworks left for the freshwater pools and refreshments behind Qumran's walls. Kalev and Haim sat together on a low row of dry-laid stone and ate together as an incrustation of salt formed over their lower limbs.

"Do you think he hurt himself?" Kalev asked.

Haim looked up. Tired. Did not answer.

In the afternoon, they stood before the sorting pans. Together, Haim and Kalev picked bitumen from the white expanse of salt. The Salt Sea was beset with the black substance. It floated up from some nether region and marred the salt's white purity, but on its own it could be sold to Nabataeans or other traders when they came through. Trade for bitumen ultimately ended up in Egypt or Rome where it was used to seal boat hulls and roofs.

"You're not much of a conversationalist," Kalev finally said.

Haim laughed. "Chaya used to say that."

"Chaya?"

"Someone I once knew."

"Relative?"

"Sister."

For their last task of the day, Haim and Kalev worked together to hold open a large sack. A big-eared Essene tilted a broad triangular scoop, and coarse white and grey grains filled the sack and poured over their hands and mounded in miniature white-peaked domes at the grooves in their wrists and then fell again to the salt pit below. Somehow, working together on this task did not corrupt the others, and the two newcomers tied the filled sacks closed and carried them on their shoulders to the salt house.

"This is practice for carrying scroll jars," Kalev said. "For when we get accepted into the full Unity."

Manoach reappeared in the evening. As the sun sunk below the cliffs behind them, the three sat together outside their tent and watched the salt water grow blue and then grey and finally black before them. Across the water, Haim saw a light wink from the mountains there, the reflected glint of something caught by the sun's last ray. A bright mineral. Some work of glass. A phantom in the air over the water.

❧

When the rain came in the fall, the water swelled in mountainous nooks and rushed down the dry rock canyon behind

Qumran in a torrent. A lion of water came roaring out of dark shadows. On a cliff ledge above and behind Qumran's walls, Haim watched its advance. The flow poured over an edge that Haim, Kalev, and Manoach had scaled some weeks before. The stream back then had been a faint trickle. Now the pool at the cliff's base boiled, but it drained through many small channels, calming the water as it faded away from the waterfall. Recently cleaned sediment pans downstream refilled with brown silt shaved from the mountain's thousand faces. As the flow travelled through successive pans, the water's surface became progressively clearer, and it was this purified surface that overflowed into the next channel and then into the cisterns and the bathing pools, each stage making the water purer yet. In the end, the wash was more than all the carved and plastered tanks could hold, and the final channels carried the excess clean water out of Qumran and into the Salt Sea.

"Above Qumran, the water is cleaned of sand and debris," Haim said.

"Makes it good for bathing, drinking, and cooking," Manoach said.

"Below Qumran, the water is the problem," Haim continued. "We have to remove it to get to the salt."

"Does that mean something to you?" Manoach asked.

Haim thought of the story of the maze, both the Ashkelonite's story and his dream. He thought there should be something else, a third maze, whether it be a real one, a story, or just a dream.

He thought of his confusion during his days with Chaya, not understanding the economy of crops and homes. This was one way. He thought of the same land covered with Jannaeus's army, the economy of which he also did not understand. That was a second way. Only the sparse economy of banditry had he been able to grasp: surplus and hunger, a dual economy composed of only two opposite states. Morta's gang had been the third way of living, an existence between the peasantry and the army. He had understood Morta's third way.

He thought then of the Sadducees and Pharisees' duality and how the Essenes closed that difference with another third way. The dualities in his life were only ever closed by a third way of a similar kind. But at Qumran, the water above was cleansed of impurity and the water below was removed in the saltworks, but there was no third thing to complete the trinity of waters. He decided that there must be a third form of water within Qumran, just like there must be a third maze as well. Something to knot the dualities that remained unbound.

"No. Nothing," Haim said.

"Stop thinking about your philosophies," Manoach said. He was further along in the Essene way than the other two and was more perceptive of Haim's introspections.

"I was only—"

"Just stop," Manoach said. "Focus on the writings."

The turmoil in the new pool above caused silt to overflow with the water, as it had not yet begun to settle out. This year of isolation at Qumran was likewise intended to settle out the three men. Qumran would accept only the pure. Of water. Of salt. Of men. A divided mind could not be an Essene.

"We'll go survey upper Ein Feshcha after the rain," Kalev said and suddenly offered Manoach the plaiting of broad leaves he had been using to shelter his head from the rain. It was an unexpected gesture, and Manoach was distracted from his scowl and reached for the offering. Just before Manoach grasped it, Kalev released it with a flicker of a smile towards Haim, and it slipped away and off the cliff edge.

Manoach put his hands back in his lap and grunted. "Now you're wet like the rest of us."

"But we're spared the lecture you were beginning. There's nothing in the Manual of Discipline about being a camel for company."

"There nothing about being stone silent either," Manoach said, indicating Haim.

"He was starting to talk when you interrupted him," said Kalev.

"He was going to talk about his philosophies again," Manoach said. "He's either questioning God's every manifestation or he's silent. He needs to focus more on what's holy. It's why he came here."

"Camel driver," Kalev said. He looked at Haim and repeated it, winking and nodding towards Manoach.

"I did follow the conversation," Haim said.

"He follows," Kalev said, but Manoach was no longer provocable.

Kalev and Manoach left the next morning to survey how the torrent had affected the land above Ein Feshcha. For the long day, Haim worked alone at the saltworks. Few of the Essenes talked with him during the day's labour, and none shared his afternoon meal. In the evening, Haim again ate alone. Through that day and into the evening, his thoughts had returned to puzzling through dualities. He was sure there was a third thing within Qumran that would fill the missing third part of both the waters and the maze.

It was dark when his friends returned. "There are uprooted trees piled up in the canyon," said Manoach. His face was dirty, and neither man bathed before they ate. They did not wash afterwards either, and so they slept in a manner abhorrent to the Essenes. In the morning, the three men left their tents after the others had all gone inside the walls so as to not expose their crime. The three walked to the now-heavy Ein Feshcha stream together, and there they bathed and then returned shivering to their tents and morning meal.

After eating, the trio idled until Qumran emptied. A group of more senior Essenes approached Manoach and Kalev. The eldest of the group indicated Manoach and then the canyon, without saying anything.

"There's plenty of wood washed down from the floods," Manoach said. "It's within an easy walk from Ein Feshcha. If we let the stream settle down, we can bring a donkey and axes up there and bring down a good haul. There is oak for sure. Other wood as well."

The men nodded and went away, again without speaking. Three days later, seven men returned early in the morning with a donkey and several axes. Eli was one of the seven. The leader of the seven indicated for all three of the acolytes to join them, and so Manoach, Kalev, and Haim set out on this new assignment.

"At least it's something different than churning salt all day," Kalev whispered to Haim as they made their way towards the Ein Feshcha stream.

Haim said nothing in reply. Eli did not care for chatty students.

As they walked, Haim thought about Eli's most recent lessons.

⚭

Haim and Eli had been studying the Essenes' Manual of Discipline, what others of the Unity called the Rule of Community. They were not far into the document, but Haim found himself unable to grasp the last two days' lesson. Previously, they had studied the division of humanity as laid out by the manual: some were followers of the Prince of Lights, held within the domain of what the priests called the Fountain of Light, and then some were of the Wellspring of Darkness, under the dominion of the Angel of Darkness. These basic ideas aligned with what Haim already understood from the old scribe in his childhood. The terms had changed, but the principles were the same.

Then came the teaching on how one became a follower of Light instead of Darkness.

"The enlightenment of the heart comes from his intimate connection with the Spirit of Truth," Eli said. The lesson went on to explain the benefits that flowed from this connection: long life, many children, eternal life, permanent joy in that life, a crown, a symbolic robe, and so on. Again, most of these ideas roughly paralleled what the old scribe had taught, though a few details seemed to be innovations. The bit about many children was a puzzle since the Essenes rejected wives or women of any kind, but otherwise, Haim was able to follow the teaching well enough.

"But hold on," Haim said. "I don't understand the first part. The 'intimate connection' part. What does that mean?"

"Communion," Eli said. "Communion with the divine."

"Yeah, so what does that mean? How do you do that or get that?"

"The blessings are one sign of that communion," Eli said. "But before those blessings come, what you get from that intimate connection—that communion—is a new way of living. A connection with God changes you. You develop a zeal for righteous government, an appreciation for the Divine Power, a fine purity that hates all filth, a love for others like yourself who follow the Truth, a—"

"Yeah," Haim interrupted. Interrupting the Essene teachers was not done, but he was frustrated. He was no longer a child studying with the old scribe. He was a man who had seen death and had dealt death and now wanted to know how to live. "I get all that. All that flows from the communion you're talking about. But how do you get that communion? You said that the enlightenment of the heart comes from . . . that thing. That connection, communion, whatever you call it. How do you get that?"

"Get what?" Eli asked.

"The connection. The communion."

"When you appreciate the Divine Power and love your fellow . . . "

The conversation had gone on in circles like that for two days. Eli told parables as well as stories, tales meant to help Haim find an answer but that just served to confuse him further. When he tried to talk to Kalev about it, his friend seemed less troubled by these details.

"Just study," Kalev said. "Manoach is right. You think too deeply about the wrong things. Memorize what you don't understand for the test and stop worrying about the details. Eventually, you'll understand it all."

❦

Haim shook his head as they hiked alongside the Ein Fesh-cha stream. He trailed at the back of the group as their path beside the still-flooded Ein Feshcha stream narrowed. They continued on their way towards their day's labour. The rain had cleansed the marlstone, and the stream bed remained swollen. They moved farther into the canyon and found a cluster of tree trunks and limbs and smaller brush in a congested tangle, as Manoach had reported. The waters were backed up behind this porous dam, flowing through the holes in hundreds of separate streams and miniature falls before recombining in an orderly flow below.

They worked the full day clearing the mess and then headed back to the tent community in near darkness. The black sky bore a rash of pinprick lights covered in a glowing smear that extended across the entire great dome above. It was like an overhead fog, the illuminated refuse of stars making a band across the heavens.

"It's an angel's road," Manoach said quietly in the dark.

They travelled well behind the seven Essenes so that there would be no danger of jostling in the dark, and they felt freer to talk this way. As they walked, Haim glanced at his companions and made a joke that caught Kalev's imagination, and he laughed on the trail. If the seven ahead heard, they gave no indication.

In the following days, they travelled back and forth to the blockage. The donkey helped drag the shattered trunks back to the shoreline, and it took a week's labour to harvest the wealth of Ein Feshcha's canyon blockages. The wood was for the bakers' ovens, the kilns, and other tasks.

After the week of salvage had passed, Haim and his friends returned to their regular routines along the sea. One evening, Eli came out from the walls early and found the three. They were sitting in the mild air alongside the sluggish sea, which glowed in the moonlight.

Eli settled himself a proper distance away and then began to talk.

"Ragaba has fallen," he said. "King Jannaeus is dead and has been for some weeks. The queen kept it a secret until Ragaba fell. She led the final assault on Ragaba and took it in her name."

There was an intake of air, and each of the men moved as though to speak, then settled back in silence.

Finally, Manoach spoke. "Is there going to be a civil war then?"

"I expect so," Eli said. "The queen has been a not-so-secret Pharisee all along. She knows where they have been hiding. Her brother is among them. She will call them out to her side, and they will reap their revenge on the Sadducees."

Haim thought of the eight hundred crucifixions outside Jerusalem.

"Blood will flow," Manoach said.

"Pharisee against Sadducee again," Kalev said. "Jews bleeding Jews. Again."

"What of Qumran?" Haim asked.

Eli shrugged. "The madness of monarchs makes our ways more attractive. When there is discomfort for the body that a soul cannot remedy, that heart seeks comfort instead for the mind. Worshippers are made more by hunger than by fat, which is why we fast."

Kalev nodded thoughtfully at this wisdom and then shot Haim a quick grimace that suggested he thought otherwise.

After Eli went back to his tent with the other Essenes, the three friends stayed together along the shoreline.

"If you think differently about something Eli teaches, you should say something," Haim said.

Kalev chuckled. "You're supposed to adhere to the Unity, not challenge it."

"You should still say something."

"Have you always been stubborn?"

"No," Haim said after a quiet pause. "No, just lately."

Kalev laughed, then quickly stifled the noise in the still darkness along the sea. "Eli's teaching is making you contrary then?"

Haim smiled but then realized no one could see his smile in the dark. "No, life is. Life is making me ask questions. I didn't use to before—and when I did, I didn't act on the answers."

39

76 BCE

Late in the spring, Haim and his two friends travelled back to Ein Feshcha. From a distance, the shoreline's most distinguishing feature was the long grove of date palms. Once at the palms, a walker's attention was drawn to the inshore water. The pools here seeped slowly into the Salt Sea. The water here was not fresh but brackish, almost drinkable, something in between salt water and fresh. All agreed that the Salt Sea was a cursed waterbody, beautiful to behold but deceptive and hostile to all life, whereas the canyon stream was full of energy and life. However, these brackish inshore pools were different, and upon closer inspection, they revealed a surprise: small fish lived in the strange water, along with insects and a few thin varieties of plants.

Haim had never noticed these pools or the life in them before.

"They can't live in the sea," Kalev told him. "And they don't move up to the fresh water. They seem to like the middle zone. So here they are."

Haim wondered if this was his third water, the final part that completed the duality of upper and lower flows. The Essenes neither harvested nor drained the water here. It was poor for drinking but gave life to a species of fish that chose it over both fresh and salt. He wondered what that meant for the unfinished duality of the maze, and his thoughts drifted inwards.

Up the valley from which the Ein Feshcha spring flowed grew an abundance of goosefoot plants. "Some of the priests make soap from it," Kalev said. "Opopanax also grows up there. The priests extract and dry the gum resin from the flower's roots. They can make a form of myrrh from it for ointments and other things."

"What kinds of ointments?" Haim asked.

"Medicines. Perfumes."

"Only the ovens are missing at Ein Feshcha," said Manoach. "To make myrrh, they need ovens. They do that part at Qumran."

The three set out to evaluate this season's goosefoot and opopanax crops, a task that needed only one person's attention, but the brotherhood's oversight on their three acolytes had slackened as surprising news continued to flow in from Jerusalem.

"Amnesty for the Sadducees," Kalev said, shaking his head in wonder. As expected, with the queen's coronation, the Pharisees had been drawn from their hiding places and were now ascendant.

"The Sadducees should now be the ones in hiding,"

Manoach said. "Instead, they live in Jerusalem like normal men."

When they found the goosefoot, it was nearly as tall as Manoach. The seed heads were immature and small. Manoach peeled off the leaves to eat as they hiked, and Haim did the same, found them adequate, and took note of the plant. They took broad measurements of the length and width of the natural crop and moved on.

"One of the priests will take our report and samples and calculate the potential for the soap works later in the year," Kalev said.

The opopanax still stood in its expected spot. Manoach made his notes, and then they returned down to the shore.

A few more months passed, and then Manoach sat before the Examiners to answer for his first year. He was judged a success and moved out of the shared tent that same day. He did not touch either Kalev or Haim in parting. His new tent was only a few steps away, but a great gulf had opened between him and his friends. He no longer ate outside the walls and said nothing that revealed the secrets inside.

"He's a friend that we'll recover," Kalev said to Haim. They waded out into the salt water in their loincloths, and when the water deepened, their feet lifted from the bottom, for the water here was more buoyant than a river or even what Haim remembered of the Great Sea in the west. There was no record of anyone drowning in this sea, for none could sink. It was a dead sea that would not harbour life nor would itself kill.

"You'll be alone soon," Kalev said. "My time is coming to go behind the walls. Will you be okay with no one to talk to but Eli in his lessons?"

"It's only for a few months," Haim said. "I'll join soon enough." He looked over at Kalev and realized somewhat belatedly that this was his first real friend. Neither man rescued, taught, or worked for the other. They were simply friends. The moon on the sea was bright this night, and Haim could see clearly. He relaxed and looked up at the stars. "I'm doing more memorizing, less worrying," he said, and both he and Kalev broke into smiles.

"Then the three of us will eat together within the walls," Kalev said.

Haim tried to nod as he floated, and the action called forth a languid wave in the water. When the water above Qumran came down, it did so with quickness and energy. The Salt Sea's water, however, was sluggish, heavier than a man. The separateness of the Essenes had transmitted itself into the very elements of the sea.

"It'll be a strange career for you to go from slinger to scribe," Kalev said.

Haim thought about nodding without making the action. Non-action took less effort. He said nothing. He thought again about dualities—his and Kalev's friend-ship was now among his catalogue of twos. Manoach was their third. Within the walls, the trio would reform. Haim decided that the duality of the water above Qumran and the water in the Salt Sea was truly closed by the third water at Ein Feshcha, where the brackish water housed life that would live nowhere else. Only the maze remained among his unclosed pairs.

That summer was hotter than any Haim had known before, and there were concerns among the Unity about water supplies. The uppermost pool within Qumran was said to have remained closed, though none would speak plainly to either Haim or Kalev about this.

Haim stopped working at the saltworks. Eli had transferred him to Ein Feshcha's facilities with a rotating series of assignments there, but one day Haim walked by the saltworks again. The Essenes were within Qumran's walls. The building was empty. He explored the silent space, and on an impulse, he picked up some of the salt there, the product of his first work at Qumran. He wore a small leather pouch on a string around his neck, within which was his copy of the Shema. All the Essenes carried the Shema. The initiates also had their own pouches and copies. It occurred to him, standing in the saltworks, that the salt related to the preservation theme in the first part of the Shema. He opened the pouch and let some salt stream from his hand and into the pouch with the curled-up papyrus. He pulled the drawstring closed and left the building.

Later that week, Haim considered the second part of the Shema, the part that mentioned grain. He spoke to Eli about the bakery. The next day Eli brought him a sampling of broken grains and flour and glossy shavings of chaff wrapped in a small cloth. Haim added these to the pouch about his neck. There was a third part of the Shema he felt compelled to recognize, but he did not do so right away. This incomplete duality created a new tension that was of his own making.

The end of the hot season came, and only a few weeks remained before Kalev's entrance exams into the brotherhood when Eli came with new orders for Kalev and Haim. The fuel for pottery and cooking ovens was again in short supply, and instead of going up Ein Feshcha's canyon to seek new supplies, they were going to climb the river's steep canyon behind Qumran itself.

This first trip was just a scouting trip, and they took with them a supply of ropes and left at dawn, climbing above the dry settling pans and modest aqueducts, looking back on the sea as they rested before committing to the nearly vertical ascent.

They came to a flat place around midday and settled themselves under an overhanging crag of rock to cool and water themselves in its shade.

"Ragaba is now a refuge city for the Sadducees," Eli stated. "That's the queen's doing. Salome Alexandra is a strange one. She's trying to make peace with her enemies and has now sent them to occupy the city that she conquered."

Haim drank from his skin and again made no mention of his knowledge of Ragaba. He noticed a patch of globe thistles in a gap between rocks and went to investigate. The spiny thorned plants formed a tight thicket. The stalks were bent, nearly prostrate, festooned with globular flowers, each petal a small outthrust narrow trumpet. He looked at the plant and he considered that the third part of the Shema spoke of blue. The flowers amid their thorns were blue. The flowers with their blue, their outward-facing protection that shielded its centre, the unexpected thorns, made him think of Salome Alexandra with her army, the nation's tensions, and the stone walls and spearmen of Jerusalem. He plucked a few of the blue flowers and placed them in his Shema pouch with the papyrus and salt and grain, with the flour and chaff.

"You have an interest in plants," Eli said.

Haim shrugged.

"The bakers can't burn that one. Let's climb."

They began to climb a section of steep cliff that was much taller than the height of a man. As they climbed, Haim felt his ankles weaken. He had never experienced such a weakening while on level ground. It spread, and he felt a dizzying lightness seep into his chest and arms that grew the higher they climbed. His breath sped up as they climbed. He felt like the Israelites in the desert who questioned their holy guide. Eli was his Moses, and floods of doubt and questioning coursed through him, spiked with fear.

It was Kalev who stopped the climb. He was above Haim, off to the right, while Eli was farther above, charting the way. Haim did not see what happened. He heard it. A scrape, then a double scrape, then a ragged release of breath. A strangled intake as Kalev slipped and the slap of Kalev's hand against the rock and another scrape, perhaps a foot, and then Haim saw Kalev pass soundlessly in the air, mouth open, nothing coming out, every cry contained in his eyes as he locked onto Haim, and then a scrambling of arms and legs in the air and then the sound of a great snapping and finally the scream. By the time Haim processed what was happening and focused, there was already a pool of spreading red below Kalev and a shock of white bone jutting from his thigh like a bright blade, shining and pale, gore pouring out.

Eli and Haim rushed down the wall while Kalev rocked on the ground, his leg and split bone a spectacle of gore, his hands red with blood and unable to act. Haim stripped off his shirt and quickly bound it above the opening in the thigh as Kalev keened and begged Haim away but did nothing to stop him. "Your staff," he said to Eli, who always carried a short one with him, had bound it to his waist for the climb.

Eli stepped back, staying out of the pool of blood.

"Your staff!" Haim shouted, but Eli made no move.

Haim released his knife, slipped its handle into a loop in the knot, and twisted it, twisting, tightening his makeshift tourniquet, trying to stem the flow from Kalev's leg. "Cloth. Cloth!" Haim shouted at Eli, who continued only to watch. Haim looked at Kalev in desperation, and Kalev understood and stripped off his shirt. Haim draped it over the exposed bone and looped it underneath.

"No, Haim," Kalev said.

Haim looked at his friend. He was pale and trembling.

"Hold the knife," Haim said.

"No, don't do it," Kalev said again.

"Okay, but just hold the knife," Haim said. "Help me stop the bleeding. I won't—" and then, with a savage lunge, he defied his words, threw his knee into Kalev's leg, and pulled hard on the cloth, slamming the bone back into its home of flesh.

Kalev screamed and twisted on the stony ground and tried to break from Haim's violence as the bone disappeared into flesh. Haim twisted the shirt bandage tighter to pin the bone where he hoped it belonged and to pull the skin closed. Kalev let loose an intermingled scream and groan that transformed into a whimper, a child's cry from a man's throat, and he stretched out long on the rock and arched his back, his hands clutching at the smooth surface below him. Then he stiffened and relaxed and was still.

Haim looked at Eli. "We need to get him down to Qumran."

"No," Eli said.

Haim started at him. "No?"

"I can't touch him."

Haim was uncomprehending. "We have to get him down to Qumran. He's going to die. We need to tend to this quickly. He's still losing blood."

"I can't touch him."

"Eli."

"He's unclean. He's still of the Wellspring of Darkness. He has not entered the Unity yet."

"He's Kalev!"

"He has not entered the Unity yet. I won't touch him."

40

76 BCE

THE SUN ROSE over the eastern lands of the Parthians and the Nabataeans and the Moabites. Bright rays cut across Moab's mountains and the Salt Sea and the settlement at Qumran and came to rest on the scene in the cliffs beyond the settlement. The moon was gone and told no tales of the night it had witnessed. It said nothing of the men from Qumran who had come up the pass late in the previous day—men who consulted, brought water and food, prayed, and left supplies of cloth and rope, but would not touch either of the two bloody men who lingered there. The moon did not repeat the words the two men spoke alone in the darkness, the unharmed man holding the other while tears tracked down his face and bare chest. It did not report how the red stream could be slowed but not stopped. It said nothing of the halting final words between friends, the dizzy fading of the held man, the shaking that Haim recognized and knew well, for he had seen many men die.

As the sun rose higher yet, it lit the way for Haim and exposed his friend's scarlet life spread on the rocks. Haim rose with the light and began to carry his friend down and down and down. Haim laid Kalev down in the first settling pan and cared not how this action would corrupt Qumran's water. He contemplated the bright sea. The Moabite mountains beyond were hazy in the early heat.

"A little farther yet," he said.

He picked Kalev up again, sorry for digging his shoulder into the man's stomach, but Kalev gave no complaint. "I had one other friend," Haim said. He knew not whether he said it aloud or thought it, and he intended it only for Kalev's spirit, wherever it might reside, heard in whatever way spirits perceived the thoughts of the living. "I could not help her either in the end."

He carried Kalev past the Qumran compound to the community's graveyard. Only Essenes were buried here. He violated one of the Essenes' tents, found the iron tools they used to dig into the soft marl, and took what he needed. He began to dig. The marl was soft and broken up in places, but it was still stone, and he dug the entire day. Some came near him, and he turned on them, standing over Kalev's body with the pick held like a weapon. The few who came near saw in him the revival of the mad slinger, and they shied away. Eli and Manoach stayed within the walls.

Haim dug all day, and when the hole was deep enough, he climbed out and lifted Kalev in his arms, carried him to his work and settled him on the grave's edge. He climbed back into the grave and pulled Kalev towards him, there being no one to help him even with this final labour. When Kalev finally tumbled over the edge, Haim caught him, laid him down on the hard ground, and arranged his limbs. Then Haim climbed back out. He was weary, but he did not stop.

Haim used the shovel now, scraping and lifting and gradually refilling the grave. By the sound, he soon knew that the bottom had filled and that Kalev could no longer be seen. He continued to fill the hole. He was no longer able to see clearly. He had been awake now for a day and a half. There was the sound of further shovelling then, and he became aware that others were now working alongside him. He was too tired to protest, to rage, to even weep. Eli was finally there. And Manoach. Haim said nothing to them. When they finished, others came, priests among them, and they began to speak words, prayers over and for the dead, but Haim did not stay to participate.

He walked to Ein Feshcha, letting the words drone and fade behind him. He sank into the stream there naked. He left his blood-encrusted clothes on dry ground, sank below the surface, and let his hair and skin float. His mind was empty and unconcerned, even with breathing, until he finally rose. Down again he went, and then he rose and walked naked back to the tents as he had once walked naked from Ashkelon. By the time he returned, the Essenes were again behind their walls.

Haim went through the Essenes' tents until he found a white robe. He took it, dressed, belted his knife to him, and then loaded his old pack with his few belongings. He was much too tired to leave this night, and he had not thought to refill his water skin at Ein Feshcha. He left anyway. It was darkening when he got to the place in the road where the millstone had lain. No sign of it remained. There was no indentation in the road, no place to mark its resting or passage. He walked on, continuing back the way he had first come to this place nearly a year before until he came to the spot he judged to be where the broken wagon had once lain. It, too, was gone, long since pulled into the compound walls and repaired by the carpenters there.

Haim turned off the road and searched for the hiding place he dimly remembered. When he found it, he pulled away the blockage, sighted the sword hilt, pulled the sheathed blade free, and found it to be dry and as polished as it had been the day he had put it away. He belted the sword to his waist, the dagger on the opposite side, and attached the empty water skin to his old pack. He looked back towards Qumran one last time, and then he set out north again on the road.

Going straight north from Qumran would lead him to Jericho, but Haim had no desire to go there. Its temptations held no draw, and he did not think he could endure the city's contrast with Qumran. He did not care to turn to the west and go into Judea. Despite the drying flowers within his Shema pouch, he was not ready for Jerusalem. He turned to the north-east and walked in that direction, into a land he thought of as Chaya's territory for the year he had spent there with her, though he had spent many more years east of the Jordan with Jannaeus's army.

Haim crossed the Jordan well south of Jericho and walked through a land of bare rock and coarse sand, a region filled with hills that bore the stubble of overgrazed grasslands, the remnants of grass now dry and hard, prickly and brown. Gashes of impenetrable rock cut this texture, and in those gashes lodged small patches of stubborn green that had found enough water and soil to provide fleeting indications of life. He travelled north-east, then west, and then north-east again, from the river to the desert and mountains and back again, criss-crossing the eastern lands. He slept in the open country at night and ate what he could find and travelled this way for many days as though trying to take a complete inventory of the territory.

Each day felt the same as the next. Eventually, he began to yearn again for conversation. He thought of every discussion and argument he had ever had with Kalev and Manoach.

He was nearly a week from Qumran before he wept again. It hit him late one afternoon, and he stopped travelling early that day. He found a hollow beneath an overhanging bush and crawled into it. He drew his knees up against his chest and there began to release the demons from within. This was not Ashkelon's madness reborn but was instead something like Eli's Angel of Darkness howling and howling. It poured out wrath and sorrow, and it seemed in his pain and his hate beneath the bush's shelter that Eli's Dark Angel was more of a friend to him than the priests of Qumran could ever be.

Darkness settled over the land, sleep came very late, and soon after sleep arrived came a dream. It was another dream of the maze, but this was not like the Ashkelonite's open-air puzzle. This labyrinth was like Chaya's well and the dream he had had that one night when he had left her down in the well.

In this dream, the labyrinth lay underground, deep in

the earth. It contained no blind men and no Chaya. It was he that was underground—Haim crawled along corridors of perpetual night, blinded by the everlasting darkness in its stone tunnels, searching in vain not for a ladder but for light.

There were thousands of branching paths in this underground prison, and none led him to the light. He awoke, sweating beneath the overhanging bush, wet from tears, but the damp on him felt like a waking-world remnant of the underground labyrinth's perpetual running water. The resonance between the dream and wet clothing upset him. He could no longer sleep, and so he crawled out of his hollow while it was still dark and began to walk again.

He turned more firmly north then and came to the Succoth Valley and could see the bright ribbon of the Jabbok River below him. The land on either side was bright green, and he knew from slinger marches through that valley that there were many villages and farms to be found here.

It was late in the day, the day after his dream. He had come far north. He had not immersed himself before every meal in the Essene way as he travelled, but now he wanted to go down to the river and swim there and wash his robe. It would be dark before he got to the river. Instead of making for the water, he contented himself with studying the valley and, in doing so, spotted a small house below him. It stood before fields marked with walls of stone and wood. He could probably get there by dark and make a bed in the barn. Perhaps there would be work at that house or somewhere else in the valley. The fig harvest approached. He knew about figs from his days with Chaya—he knew how to pick and press. He saw a narrow line of smoke rising from the house.

Even gentiles would provide at least some hospitality. This land had learned to accommodate a variety of people.

Haim climbed down the crest into a low haze of purple light that gradually changed as the sun sank into its rest. When the land levelled, he felt a spring of life again.

He walked across the last field with a good feeling in his bones, and then in the dusky light he heard a scream within the house and the tearing of cloth and without thinking he opened the door and the first thing he saw were several men, a woman, and the body of a man. A baby cried in a back room.

41

76 BCE

Dᴇᴀᴛʜ ʙʏ ᴀᴍʙᴜsʜ was something Haim knew well. It had characterized his time with Morta's brood, for they had not been the sort to engage in a fair fight.

Murder by madness had characterized his post-Ashkelon rages, and he believed that these rages had been remnants of some greater madness from his time within the temple itself. He remembered little of those seasons that he could clearly separate from the horrific visions that must have been false.

Killing as a soldier in Jannaeus's army had been a rare occurrence given the nature of the king's slow, largely negotiated conquest. When required, Haim had delivered on his duty with the sling. He had sent stones across a field or over a wall and had been devastatingly accurate, hunting men with the same precision he used for the birds of his meals.

Killing in this way, from such a distance, was impersonal, and Haim found he could eat afterwards with little disturbance to his mind or body.

During the first months outside Jericho, personal combat among the bored soldiers had been half-mad affairs. These contests had helped to bleed off Ashkelon's poisons and served to establish his reputation among Jannaeus's gentile mercenaries. By the time Ashkelon's spells had left him, his reputation had also reduced the number of idle soldiers willing to challenge him. His remaining years with the army had been relatively peaceful.

Only among Morta's brood had Haim been surprised. The big man, the broken-nosed man, or Gershom would come at him unexpectedly. Drunk or sober, they had attacked him often during his years in Samaria. Whether this had been their way to show affection or their method of toughening up their young recruit, Haim never fully understood. He had tried to talk to Chaya about it once, his lip and one eye swelling. Her response had at first been silence, then tender fingers on his lip and eye, and then a quick slap to his temple. "Grow up," she had said. "What's wrong with you?"

Haim did not know. That had always been the problem—he just did not know. Even with her response, he had not known if his stupidity had been thinking their assaults were a form of affection among men or if he was foolish for not recognizing training for what it was. Or perhaps simply asking the question had been stupid. He thought of Manoach then and his criticisms of Haim's naïveté and introspection.

It remained, however, that only among Morta's brood

had he been surprised. He had learned to react quickly in those days, countering an assault with force, agility, or sometimes even humour. He had never understood the situation, but he had learned to be fluid with his responses.

He had had no other real training for surprises since those days, but staring into the open door at the scene before him, Haim felt himself slip into Morta's folds again. It was as though his years in Samaria had been just yesterday.

The closest person to him was a living man, a wide-faced, red-faced man, and in the patches where it persisted, his hair thrust out in disarray as though possessed by all the violence it had been witness to for all of its years. This wild-haired man had been facing away from the door, and he turned only his upper body at Haim's entrance, half facing him in this contorted pose and wearing a strange grimace, hands balled into fists. On the floor to the right was the body of a much younger man, a cleanly trimmed man wearing the simple clothing of a poor Jew. His stomach and throat had been slashed open. Blood still weakly spread about him.

Across from the wild-haired man were two others who held between them the arms of a woman, young like the dead farmer, her clothing torn though not yet exposing her. One of the two was very big, bigger even than Manoach. He had long black hair and great arms like the pikers and sarissa soldiers in Jannaeus's army or the blacksmiths he had known in transient camps. The third man was smaller, his hair crudely shorn and patchy as though cut by his own hand with a butcher's knife and without skill. He bore a scar on one cheek and another two at his left ear and temple. He appeared to have been the victim of some frenzied self-mutilation or an attack by drunken sheepshearers. All three of the men bore cruel expressions, and the biggest of them, the long-haired man, was blood-soaked on one side, though the woman did not appear to be bleeding, so Haim took him for the killer.

On the floor were three blades: an Egyptian sword with a leather-wrapped grip, another of Seleucid design with an elaborately carved cross-guard and pommel, and a long, heavy knife with a forward-curving blade. It was what some of the Greek mercenaries in Jannaeus's army called a kopis. Cooks in the army had used knives like it for butchering meat, and only rarely had Haim seen it used as a battle weapon. It was this blade that was bloody. The closest, wild-haired man held an over-sized dagger called an akinakes, which Haim associated with Scythians. Its edge was clean and bright. There were too many weapons in the room.

Haim stood in the doorway without moving. His eyes took in the age of the sheep-shorn man's scars, the breadth of the long-haired man's shoulders, the tension in the woman like a bent bow, the ripple of movement in the wild-haired man's throat when he spoke.

Haim's ears blocked out the cries of the unseen infant and the crackle of the fire. There was no sound outside the house, and the lamps flickered in silence.

"Who in Hades are you?" the wild-haired man asked.

"Just a traveller," Haim said.

"You picked the wrong night to travel here," the wild-haired man replied.

Haim had seen Morta's gang toy with a final victim. He had seen violence done to a woman after witnessing her husband's death, but he had never participated in these after-affairs. And he had never seen this scene conducted indoors.

It came to him then that the men before him had not yet decided what to make of him. Surprise was as much on his side as theirs. His mind presented options as though from an inventory of Morta's tactics, and something shrank within him as he considered these things. But he did not act. Not yet.

Haim stayed in the doorway without moving. Against three of this size and type and hate, he stood little chance in a straight fight. His best option was to turn and run, for they had their victim and would not follow far. At this thought, any purity of Qumran that might have lived within him retreated like a candle carried away into the night. The cowardice of his first years with Chaya peered out and sounded an alarm. This was one way. He could run.

As these thoughts raced through his mind, a third Haim—the one he felt that he truly was—waited with a detached eye, watching to see how Haim would act. Qumran's light shrank but remained. It did not entirely go out. The third, observing Haim could not see how his lessons from Qumran could be of any use at this crossroads. He could see nothing in his memorized liturgies and nothing in his time of practical labour in that place that served any purpose here.

The frightened, childhood Haim had a workable solution. But he did not run.

The bandit-turned-soldier Haim calculated how he might proceed with comrades or stage an encounter more conducive to the slinger's advantage. He could not sling in this small room. He had no companions with which to stage an ambush. He did not attack.

All these thoughts came to him during a single intake of air, quickly, all of it, the air, the scene, the men, the body, the weapons, the woman, the mysteries of his own decision-making apparatus. He understood then that, despite its flaws, his time at Qumran stayed the runaway boy within him. It was the Qumran Haim and the bandit-soldier that were in a standoff with one another. Still, he did not have a solution, so the third Haim continued to observe and wait in suspense.

The biggest man, the long-haired man, was about to speak. Haim had only taken one breath in all this time.

Haim feared the big man's speaking the way he feared the weapons and the decisions, the way he had feared the boy's speaking, his first kill as a bandit, and so he spoke on his exhale, spoke without intending to, spoke such that his observational self listened even closer than those in the room to hear what he would say. He started with "You are." Just those two words. He spoke without any idea what would come next. Only "You are" followed by "doing this all wrong."

The woman's bowed body bent inwards at his strange words. All three men stared at him. In the gap he had created, Haim removed his dagger from his waist, and he was amazed to see his hand holding the weapon. He was aghast at what he was about to do, and without any ability to edit his actions, he flung the weapon, and it crossed the room, away from any person, and fell with only a faint and dull sound against the earthen floor in the left corner of the room. It lay there, away from him and the others in that place. He was relieved to see that he had not thrown it at one of the men. He had no skill with throwing knives. His sword remained concealed in the folds of his Qumran robe, and though he could not get to it quickly, they would not expect a simple traveller on the road to carry one. They watched his eyes. They did not search the rest of him. They were too surprised by his interruption to react to the dagger and equally surprised by his throwing it away.

Haim wanted to know what these actions entailed, but his words and actions both preceded understanding as he moved forwards.

"Does she have children?" he asked and was appalled to ask such a thing.

The men just stared at him.

"Does she have children?"

"A baby. In the back room."

He understood himself then and felt a sudden calm. "Then she'll cooperate." He did not allow himself to think about what that meant. He made his eyes and his voice speak in a manner that was cold and evil, and the candle within flickered like the strung body of a flogged captive, and then the light went out. Qumran was gone. He smelled the smoke from the woman's fire now.

"You're doing it all wrong," Haim repeated.

There was a quiet and high keening from the woman, suddenly silenced when Haim caught her eye. He held her gaze, and there was nothing but deep coldness in his eyes.

"What in Hades are you talking about?" the big man asked.

The wild-haired man had spoken first, but based on how the others looked to the big man when he spoke, Haim took the big man for their leader.

"You've just killed him," Haim gestured. "His blood still

flows." He looked around the room as though inspecting it for other witnesses. "You're still in the heat of bloodletting. Continue like this, and you will spend yourself in as few minutes as it took to kill this one, and you will have a satisfaction that is less than that of a common whore from Jericho. This does not look like a house rich with drink to entertain yourselves with after."

"What in Hades are you talking about?" the big man asked again.

The wild-haired man turned and walked over to where Haim had thrown his dagger, picked it up, and then moved closer to the other three.

"Do you have a better suggestion?" This came from the scarred and sheep-shorn man who still held the woman's other arm.

"When you go to the house on the blue street of Dora, do you leave in just a few minutes?"

There was silence from the big man and the wild-haired man, but the scarred and sheep-shorn man spoke. "I've been there."

"Did you leave as soon as you arrived?"

The sheep-shorn man still held one of the woman's arms. He continued to hold her. He studied Haim and took his time as though seeking to recognize an old acquaintance. "No."

The others looked at their companion, then back to Haim. The big man moved to speak again, but before he did so, Haim reached into his shirt and removed the small leather Shema pouch. He squeezed it before the eyes of his watchers to demonstrate that it held something. Something crushable. Haim felt everything of his days of banditry return, the shame of Arbel, the crudest of his nights with the slingers, all of it came back into him, warm like an old friend. It made him calm, and a strong taste like iron lingered in his mouth, along with the burned edges of fat and gristle, the raw roots of desperate forage. He took in everything with great speed, a speed that no longer alarmed him. It was as though his observations were being accelerated by the mushroom-enhanced colours of Ashkelon's priestesses, as though he knew what the men before him were thinking, as though this were a well-rehearsed scene and the stakes here only that of another dry run-through. He no longer waited to find out what came next but knew the words before he spoke them and knew what the men's reactions would be, each individually, and he knew what he would say next. Nothing slowed down. Everything moved fast but he was able to follow the speed, whereas the others in the room were still operating in normal time with ordinary minds. He had just as much the advantage of surprise here as he ever had as an ambush slinger. More. A stone could miss. There was no missing here.

He stepped into the room as he spoke again. "I have been to the temple of Ashkelon. I have tasted its pleasures and walked from it and returned and left again, for I am known there."

"You're a priest of Ashkelon?" the sheep-shorn man said. He said it with awe, and all three now took in his dirty white robe.

"I've travelled for some time," Haim said, "but I carry the potency of its secrets with me always." He lifted the pouch again, then let it drop. "Make the woman put on water. A large pot. Boil it, and I will add what's within here, and we will partake of the secrets of Ashkelon together, and you will last all night, and there will be no end to this night's pleasure."

The men stared at him in silence.

"We'll give some to her as well. I know the incantation. She will be like the women of Dora's blue street." He said the last part to the sheep-shorn man. "Better. And you will be better."

Still, there was no movement.

"Go!" Haim said, pointing at the woman. The men still held her, but he said it forcefully and pointed towards the fire, and he held her eyes fiercely, and when she moved, the two men released her.

"I am of Ashkelon," he said to the men as she wobbled away from her captors. "I have come to you that you might convert to the mysteries of Astarte, who degenerate Jews call Ashtaroth, the Queen of Heaven. If you do not convert, you will nevertheless be men who will tell of what the queen offers that others may find their way to her temple and discover for themselves what ecstasy is."

The wild-haired man laughed. "The priests of Ashkelon are eunuchs."

Haim smiled. "Not all. Not those she chooses." He lifted the pouch again. "There is more to Ashkelon's mysteries than the rumours that circulate on this side of the Jordan."

The wild-haired man sat then, stretched his legs, and reclined alongside the low Greek table. He toyed with Haim's dagger. The other two men stayed standing, dividing their attention between Haim and the woman. She was shaking as she lifted a large pot. Tears and fear shaped her every feature. She placed the pot on the stones amid the fire and began to fill it with water from a jug as Haim had directed her. He walked over to where she was, and she flinched away from his presence. His right side remained away from the men, the sword hidden in the folds of his robe. "There is wood outside," he said to the still-standing sheep-shorn man. "Bring some if you want to taste Astarte's heaven. The water must boil hard."

The sheep-shorn man departed eagerly. The big man started to approach Haim and the woman, but Haim caught his eye and smiled warmly. "Relax," he said and nodded to the man's reclining companion. "The Queen of Heaven will grace us tonight through this young woman. She won't go anywhere, for we have her child, and once it's finished here," he nodded to the pot, "she won't want to." The woman was openly weeping, and Haim kept his eyes away from her.

The scarred and sheep-shorn man returned from the darkness outside with wood. Haim stocked up the fire, and soon it roared brightly in the room. The sheep-shorn man reclined with his companions. The three were between Haim and the doorway. They watched him tend the fire, and they watched the woman. The wild-haired man continued to play with Haim's dagger. The big man seemed bemused, irritated, interested—all of it transparent in his eyes, his broad forehead, the movement of his mouth, the set of his oversized shoulders and chest. The sheep-shorn man seemed to be in the grip of some memory of an unslaked lust, and all three men exuded, in their various guises, silent malice that radiated like heat and produced a sharp odour. It was a thing that Haim remembered. The wild-haired man who toyed with the dagger looked up and caught Haim's eye and held it. Haim felt a chill and knew he risked facing his own blade, for the man was perhaps the cruellest and most skillful of the three, the big man the most powerful, all three familiar with Death's sport. Haim considered the sheep-shorn man's scars and decided that he might be the wildest.

Haim turned back to the woman and the pot of water. It was hot but not yet boiling. He opened the pouch and pulled from it the folded papyri. He slowly poured the remaining contents into the pot, the salt, the whole and broken grains and flour shavings, the crumbling blue flowers. The men watched closely. Haim muttered some nonsense syllables, and then he began to recite the words on the papyri.

"Hear, O Israel, the Lord is our God, the Lord is One." He said it very quietly, in the old scribe's old Hebrew, the language favoured by the Essenes, the language he had heard the Pharisees of Arbel speak but heard so rarely elsewhere. He knew the Shema's words well, and the woman reacted immediately to it, her eyes rising to his.

He spoke quietly so the men would not hear his mutterings distinctly from where they sat. They would have to contend with his low tone and the sound of the fire.

Haim closed his eyes and continued the Shema, trusting his ears to alert him to any sudden movements. He lifted his head in what he judged to be the manner of a wandering Ashkelonite priest, and when he finished the first part of the Shema with its reference to a house and its gates, he went on to the second part and finished the passage in a voice just above a murmur. He was quiet as he delivered the verse that promised to prolong days and the days of children on the land, as long as the days the heavens are over the earth.

As he finished the second part, the water finally began to boil. He dipped a long stick into the pot and lifted it and let the steaming water clinging to the stick travel down its length and pool in his palm where it burned, but he held his hand steady as a demonstration, and he had the men's attention. "The Lord spoke to Moses," he said, beginning the third part, still in the old Hebrew. At this distance, the words would be an incomprehensible, mumbling incantation to the watching men. He turned to the woman and held out his hand in which pooled the hot water. "Drink, child," he said in the common language. "Let the goddess Astarte, Queen of Heaven, fill you with her presence."

He had to turn away from the men to say this, but he spoke loudly enough for them to hear and he held her eyes when he spoke, and she seemed to understand, and she took his hand in hers like a cup and tilted his hand and drank the hot liquid from his rough fingers, a liquid that was merely water and little else, and then stood before him, both trembling and calmer.

When he turned back to the men, he found them entranced by the show. He used two rags from beside the fire to lift the pot, and then he stepped away from the fire and towards the low table. The big man with his long hair was on Haim's right at the far end of the table. The sheep-shorn man with his scars and lust was on Haim's left. The wild-haired man was across the table, also reclining, waiting, still thumbing the dagger.

"Bring five cups, woman," Haim said, facing the men, speaking loudly into the room. Then with a wink at the men, he said, "We will drink now and make her cook for us later."

They laughed at this and looked at one another, and Haim took another step, his face a mask of hospitality and joy. The sheep-shorn man to his left was salivating and eager. The wild-haired man before him tested the dagger's edge again, the least taken in. The big man looked as though he were about to rise. He had something perhaps to say. Haim turned, and before the man could get his legs fully beneath him, Haim dumped the boiling water into the man's horror-struck face and across his throat and chest, and there was the sound of a gasp halted, choked back, and the start of something like a strangled and windless scream. Haim pulled the pot around, and steaming water dripped, and whirling to his left, he slung the clay pot like an unwieldy club. The pot cracked against the scarred and sheep-shorn man's upraised arms, and there was a corresponding crack of bone and the sheep-shorn man screamed, not a windless whine like the big man's, but a loud cry, adding high notes to the big man's strangled, airy gasping. A bone appeared, thrust up against stretched skin, and there seemed to be more voices in the room than there were men. The wild-haired man in the centre, across the low table, leaped to his feet, his voice rising with the chorus, his expression torn by divergent alarms. He still held Haim's dagger in his hand, but he did not seem to register the sword that appeared until Haim was across the table. Haim slashed once, then twice, opening deep wounds on the man's right forearm. The wild-haired man dropped his dagger and Haim plunged his sword into the man's belly and turned it and shoved the man away from him.

The man staggered backwards and stumbled, holding his sliced arm against his stomach, churning his feet for balance, and in doing so, tilting and ramming himself into the far wall and bouncing off of it. There was a crack to Haim's right, and he turned quickly and identified the big man's skull as also having collided with the stone walls of the small house. Having stunned himself, the big man was barely conscious. Haim turned again to the left, to the now-standing sheep-shorn man whose lust had converted into a wild rage. The man's broken arm dangled uselessly, but the other had removed not a dagger but a long knife from his waistband, another kopis. He held the ritualistic knife not as a butcher but as a killer. Haim moved towards him, and the man's expression changed again as his lust-borne rage converted into something still and focused. The sheep-shorn man allowed Haim to steer him in a circle, backing him towards the big man, who was blind and still except for his frantic gasping as he sightlessly struggled to regain control. The flesh of the big man's face and neck visibly rose in savage blisters. His breaths were short and husky as he tried to master himself and his pain.

The sheep-shorn man adjusted his grip on the knife, and it appeared that Haim had not broken his most skilled arm, for he held the blade well—not like a priest or kitchen hand but rather like a man who understood its use for up-close murder. When, in this circling, Haim came to the big man writhing on the floor, he dropped his sword point, flicked it sideways, and opened a new mouth in the big man's neck. His victim held both hands to the opened throat, trying to close what could not be sealed. His long wet hair tangled in the bloody wound. Blisters forgotten, the big man thrashed against the table and the ground and lathered himself with the mud forming below.

The sheep-shorn man kept moving backwards, perhaps trying to make it to the front door, his long knife weaving this way and that. Though it was smaller than Haim's sword and the man was now one-handed, his manner, the large hilt on his weapon, the forward curve of the blade, the way he held it, all communicated to Haim that this was still an encounter he might not survive. He did not dare let the man escape into the night. He seemed to be the sort who would recover and return. Haim intercepted him before he got to the doorway. Haim kept the sheep-shorn man away from the door and the fire and the back room where the child lay.

"Who are you, priest?" the man asked. A vein pulsed on his forehead where the savage shearing had exposed skin.

Haim decided that he had been wrong. This man was not the insane one of the three, despite his appearance. He was not just a slovenly patron of Dora's house of shame. He looked nothing like either of those images now but looked—despite his one broken and useless arm—dangerous and focused and trained. Haim started to answer the question, and the man suddenly lunged. Haim's surprised sword barely parried the blow, and for a moment, their faces were intimately close, eyes locked, a wash of the man's bitter breath pouring into Haim. Had the man the use of both arms, Haim realized that he would have died then, struck down by a killing talent greater than his own. The man spat in Haim's face and retreated.

"Who are you, priest?" he asked again. "That was no Ashtaroth brew."

"No, I gave you salt water. Flowers. A reading of the Jewish Shema."

The scarred man spat onto the floor. "You're going to

die in this room," he said, but as he said it, he grunted and looked down at his leg in great surprise. A long shaft of wood had suddenly appeared there, a bizarre and straight and feathered branch that had sprouted in an instant. Haim looked behind him, and the woman stood at the fire with a bow, shaking so hard she could barely hold the weapon up.

"Hades be damned," the sheep-shorn man said, staring at the shaft that swung in front of him, just shy of his groin. The point stuck out from the back of his leg, the flow gushing out the back while leaving the front dry. "Hades be damned," the man said again, and he slowly sank down, not fainting, not rushing, easing himself down to avoid disrupting the arrow, his motions awkward with his damaged leg and dangling arm. His good hand did not let go of the knife. "Hades be damned."

Haim stepped back and looked at the other two men and the woman. Both men still lived, holding their wounds like that first Samaritan father who struggled near death while Morta's gang slew his family. Unlike the father, however, none of the three men showed any concern for the others. They all bled and laboured only for themselves. The woman put her bow down and stood slack for a moment before going to her husband's body and kneeling where he lay and then holding her shaking body against his lifeless form.

Haim believed that the sheep-shorn man remained the most dangerous, but the wild-haired man, who was holding his gut closed while his arm bled freely, was the closest to the woman. Haim walked over to him and thrust his sword into the man's neck. Haim looked over at the big man, curled up on the floor. He was not yet dead, but that darkness was mere moments away. The man stared in Haim's general direction with sightless orbs. Haim returned his attention to the sheep-shorn man.

"I knew you would be the death of us when you walked in," the sheep-shorn man said. "White-robed stranger. Then I took you for one of us. Lulled by your words. It seemed like you might multiply our prize." He said the last part while looking towards the woman. He said it without remorse. Only mild disappointment coloured his tone, like one who had discovered his map was out of scale and the journey would require an extra tiresome day. It was a tone of dull observation with no malice.

The man lifted his long, curved knife and tossed it towards the big man's body. "Like your move with the dagger," he said simply to explain himself. "But my move is without your art or planning." He held the base of the arrow where it entered his upper thigh, putting pressure there. "Where do you come from? You look familiar."

Haim did not answer. He walked over to the fire, picked up the woman's bow, set an arrow to the string, and then walked back to the sheep-shorn man.

"An arrow?" the man said.

Haim did not know what else the man had in his clothing. He had seen men among the slingers who had darts they could throw with deadly precision at close range. He did not owe the man an explanation.

"Wait," said the sheep-shorn man. "I know who you are." He smiled, a broad, crooked smile, and for the first time, Haim noticed the man's bad and missing teeth. "You're him."

Haim looked at the man, but did not recognize him,

did not know what this scarred and wounded man might be imagining.

"You're the Devil from Samaria. From that bandit crew. The Betrayer of Arbel. You're—"

Haim released the arrow, and it drove into its target, cracking through the man's rib cage and out his back, shunting him backwards and pinning him to the wall. The man struggled briefly against the shaft, gasping and convulsing and trying to hold the new arrow, his face swelling red and growing purple beneath his violent haircut and rough scars. Haim stared at him and waited to see if the man would try to speak again.

The man convulsed violently, the tremors oscillating between his waist and throat before his head finally nodded and he grew still.

Haim turned away. He went to the big man, who was now dead, and searched his clothing. The man's weapons he discarded. He found a small pouch of coins, which he tucked away into his pocket. He went then to the wild-haired man and repeated the search, finding another pouch of coins. He found a third pouch on the sheep-shorn man, which he left on the table near the fire. There were no secret darts in the man's clothes. Haim did not look in any of the pouches, nor did he count any of the coins therein.

He left the room and went into the back and saw the baby, now asleep by the light of a dim lamp. He inspected the room, then returned to the main room. The woman would not leave her husband's body, so he opened the door to the house and began to drag the body of the wild-haired man out into the yard. He did not know where to take it, and after a moment's consideration, he pulled it towards the field of grass he had crossed to come to the house. He returned to the house and began dragging the big man out next. The scalding had disfigured the man's face and upper body, and his features hung slack in death. He no longer radiated power but was an excessively heavy sack of ruined flesh offering premonitions of the stench to come. Haim grasped the man's heels and pulled him through the house and out the door. He gave no thought to the trail of blood left behind or the bumping of the man's skull on the threshold stone as he passed through to the outside. He dumped the body beside the wild-haired man and then returned for the last one. He had to break the arrow that pinned the man to the wall, for the point was deeply embedded in a gap between stones. Then this body too was dragged outside and left with its peers.

Haim returned to the house and did not see the woman in the room. Her husband's body lay alone. There were knee prints in the pool of blood.

The blood of four men stained and soaked into the earthen floor. The water from the pot had pooled with the big man's blood at the base of one wall, and the ground there was covered in dark mud. The humble home had become a place of slaughter.

The woman came then from the back room, holding the baby. She made her way past Haim, avoiding his eyes, saying nothing. She appeared now as afraid of him as she had been of her attackers. "I'm Haim," he said, but she did not answer. She slipped through the doorway and disappeared with her child into the dark.

Haim waited in the empty house for what would happen next, but no one came. He and the dead farmer were alone together, so he spoke to the room and then to the man. He crouched but did not sit, for there was nowhere to sit in that place. After a time, he went to the fire and found a loaf of bread beside it. He broke off a piece and put it in his pack. He poured water from the jug and quenched his thirst, and in the back room, he found some of the farmer's clothes. He stripped out of his bloody Qumran robe. He said a word to the farmer as he left, wearing the farmer's clothes, and then he followed the same trail that the woman had taken into the night.

He was deeply weary but no longer thought of sleep. Like on the night he had left the slingers' camp, he walked for a long time below the stars. He crossed the Jabbok River by the light of the moon, passed the shapes of farmhouses, and then climbed into the higher country and into forests. He walked by the moon's glow, and when that faded, he continued by the light of the stars. Eventually, he found a swath of high grass growing against a rock and made his bed there. He slept until the sun was high enough to overcome the shadows of the stone and high grass. Bright light found his place of hiding and called him into wakeful hunger. With wakefulness also came the loneliness that had driven him down to the woman's house the night before. Both hungers gnawed at him, and he did not know which was greater.

42

76-75 BCE

AMID AN AFTERNOON of thin rain suffused with a golden light that foreshadowed the evening to come, Haim rose naked out of the Yarmuk River with water streaming from his hair and beard. The cliff behind him and the steep slope ahead framed the river in shadow, the river itself a bright line in the middle. The Plain of Bashan was over the rise before him. He dressed and then climbed where the rock gave him leave and put the shadows and the bright water behind him. The light at the top was not yet as golden as below. Here the light shone blue and hard. A stubbly crop was unploughed and waited for heavier rains to soften the earth in the fields and attract a ploughman.

He entered Aphek in the morning. Inside the town gates, he put his hand to the mortared stone there, and it radiated cold. Someone was tuning a stringed instrument, and somewhere else, children were playing. He purchased supplies from a stall overseen by an aged woman who served him in silence. She looked to have Seleucid and Nabataean ancestry and was not like the others he observed in that small town. She was very old, and her eyes were tiny behind pouches of papery, veined skin. She said nothing, but she smiled at Haim with a warmth that surprised him—as though he were someone that she used to know, would have liked to have known, might have known in other times. Or maybe he just reminded her of one of her grandchildren.

Haim left the city and later that day bathed in the river north of Aphek in the Essenes' manner, wearing his loincloth. He washed the farmer's clothing in the river and hung them upon a thorn tree to dry. He then sat and waited for the better part of the afternoon.

Two days later, he sat on one of the three hills below what he judged to be the same fig tree he and Chaya had rested against more than a dozen years prior. Half of his life had passed since he last saw this view. He had purchased a mantle in Aphek like the ones he and Chaya had worn back then, and now he wrapped it around himself and rested his hand on what he thought was the same exposed ancient root that Chaya had touched. He looked out at the same two hills they had contemplated together in the rain.

The summer figs were gone, and the winter crop was not yet ready. Haim ate from his Aphek provisions and was better nourished than they had been in those years so long ago. He would have traded these provisions now for Chaya's company or Kalev's or Manoach's, taken the fear and the hunger of those years in trade for the people. He pulled the mantle tighter around himself until the fog lifted.

When he had no further excuse to linger, Haim rose

and crossed the Upper Jordan. He entered Kfar Nahum, this time with a full stomach and without worry. There, he purchased new shoes and then went on to Gennesaret and then Magdala. He did not sleep along the shoreline at Magdala but hired a room and had a hot meal brought to him. As he ate alone, he remembered Chaya's joyful laughter when she caught the fish here. The food in his room was well made, but he would have traded it for Chaya's saltless, burned fish on the shoreline if only he could hear her innocent laugh again. He went down by the water after eating and watched the fishermen clean their nets.

On his approach to Arbel, he killed a bird that he could not identify. It had run from him, one wing already injured when he came across it. He pulled out his sling on instinct, despite having sufficient supplies, and followed the bird and struck it down and cooked it alongside the stream as the clouds above pooled and prepared to sponsor a new flood season. He wondered, if he were to enter that same route from Magdala to Arbel a third time, whether he might again kill suddenly and without premeditation, as if death were a feature of the valley itself. The Valley of Doves. The Valley of Wind. The Valley of Sudden Death. He discarded the bird's feathers into the bushes. He could not remember what had become of the wolfskin.

He climbed the cliff path and passed through Arbel without lingering. He believed that there were none in the recovered town that he knew and none that knew him, for all witnesses had hung on their crosses outside Jerusalem or died before those crosses as they had bled in full view of their hanging men. The ghosts of those discarded souls hovered over graves outside of Zion, but they were mute. There was no one here to tell the tale of Haim's youth.

But the sheep-shorn man had known him. Haim could not place who that man had been.

Near Shechem, Haim sat in the shade in a row of lean, road-weary travellers—all stopped here simply for the sake of conversation. There were some here that Haim believed always sat at this crossroads. Others seemed to have come upon the place as Haim had, entering it as a mere way station between unstated destinations. Heavy rain had started a few days before, then had stopped, and a late heat had come again. The air was thick with moisture.

In a discussion about Jerusalem, one of the men at the crossroads referred to events at Ashkelon, and it roused Haim from his doze.

"What of Ashkelon?" Haim asked.

"The queen's brother dealt with the evil there once and for all," said a long-bearded man.

"Her brother?" Haim asked.

"Yes, Simon," said another man. "He's made quite a mark now that he's come out of hiding and his sister holds the throne."

The men continued describing the queen's brother, his survival as a Pharisee through the years of Jannaeus's persecutions, his revived boldness now that the Pharisees were again in royal favour.

"What did he do?" Haim asked. "At Ashkelon?"

"You don't know?" the long-bearded man asked.

"I've been travelling," Haim said. "What happened?"

"Huh." The man grunted and looked at the others as though asking where he should start. "You stay out of society too long under this queen, and you'll miss everything."

"She brought the country back together again," a thin man said.

"No civil war," said the long-bearded man. He both nodded his head and shook it as though trying to express both approval and surprise.

"Both of them did it," the thin man said. "The queen and her brother."

The long-bearded man hunched forwards, drawing Haim's attention. He frowned and projected a serious air. "I never thought I'd support a queen," he said.

"Simon," Haim said. "What did Simon do at Ashkelon?"

"He raided it," the long-bearded man said with a look of surprise on his face. "The temple, I mean. He went in with the mercenaries and cleaned that temple out."

"I heard seventy took part," the thin man said.

"Eighty," said a portly man, speaking for the first time. "I have a nephew who was there. He counted."

"He took more than that to Ashkelon," the long-bearded man said. "Eighty was the number of women he crucified there." He locked eyes with Haim and nodded as though to punctuate the count.

"Women?" Haim asked.

"Priestesses," the long-bearded man said.

"Sorceresses," said the thin man.

"Witches," said the portly one.

The long-bearded man leaned back, and there was satisfaction on his face. "Simon cleaned out Ashkelon and good riddance to them. I'd say they were Philistine remnants. Should have been gone centuries ago."

"They killed a lot of dogs as well, so I heard," the thin man said. "Some kind of dogs the witches kept."

"Queen Salome got the Idumeans in hand with that raid," the long-bearded man said. "They were fit to revolt like the Itureans under Jannaeus, but she's shut that up pretty quick."

"It's not the same," the thin man countered. "Jannaeus deserved his rebellions. This queen deserves their loyalty."

"That's what I said."

"He means she's winning over people that under Jannaeus . . ."

Haim let the thread of conversation drift away from him again.

A day later at a settlement in western Samaria he sat with a scribe passing through who respected his Essene training. The old man showed Haim the scrolls he had in his possession, and Haim pored over them with interest, reading what he could decipher, quizzing the man about the words he did not know.

Leaving that place, he felt like someone followed him—a ghost of Arbel or one of the crucified priestesses of Ashkelon. There were many people on the road. Samaria was repopulating under Salome. As he looked around, none of the travellers here seemed to have any interest in Haim. Still, he felt uneasy.

The next day he stopped at an abandoned and overgrown field and practised with his sling, first on targets that were around twenty cubits away, then fifty, then eighty, and then a hundred, accepting declining degrees of accuracy with longer distances.

He went on then to Dora and sat outside the brothel there. It was the place where he had last seen Chaya. He did not look for her, for he believed that she was not here or anywhere else. He did not enter the place. He considered it but did not move from his perch.

He still had money from the men he had killed across the Jordan, and he wondered about the widow and her child. He thought about Ashkelon and its purge and about Qumran and his abandoned initiation and then about Arbel and the old scribe and yesterday's scribe, and he wondered why he was waiting outside this house of women in Dora.

He thought again about the three men he had killed and the similarities between them and those of Morta's gang. He thought of the queen and Manoach and Eli and then of Kalev and then again of Morta's brood, each in turn. Last, he thought about his mother and his sisters, and he knew now that he had not known them at all as he also had not been known. He had been a boy pursued by something unseen across all of Eretz-Israel, his own lost and discarded soul finding nothing but a maze from which he could not emerge.

Haim wanted someone to see him outside this house in Dora. He wanted a wise soul to come and lead him away and tell him where the ladders lay.

He waited in the street until it grew dark, and then he walked through the streets, through the gate, and left the city walking south, still carrying his old pack, the money, his water skin and weapons, and few other possessions. He walked in the dark as he had on so many other nights, but he did not wander. He took the road the old scribe had once taken to the widow's house. His mother's house. When he arrived, it was dark, and he did not investigate how over-grown the property was. He could tell it was abandoned, even in the dark. A light rain started. He found a dry place beneath a fallen and leaning roof that he did not recognize and wrapped his mantle about him and slept to the sound of rain and beyond it the imagined sound of goats and his long-gone and unknown family.

The next day he surveyed the property. Little that was movable remained. The goat pens were still present, the stone walls as sturdy as ever. The barn's roof had fallen, but there were salvageable materials here. He walked to the seashore and studied the place where the dye maker had harvested his shells. Haim breathed in the salt air. He had not recalled missing that scent until now.

Haim did not know if the dye maker's shellfish still lived in this water, and he did not know how to make dye. He knew he could no longer eat the creatures, but he wondered if a good Jew could still make a living as a dye maker, if it was the act of eating or merely touching that caused contamination. He did not know and did not know who to ask or if the question mattered anymore.

He looked at the overgrown fields, which would still be good grazing ground for goats, and inspected the well, which still bore cold and sweet water. He went to the house. The caved-in roof let in light, and plants grew within, even in the ashes of the old firepit. But the stone walls of the house were sound. The small farm was recoverable.

Haim worked for two days with no clear plan except to clear debris and stack usable materials in a flat area while waste he mounded for future fires. He no longer had the axe he had left with; it had disappeared with everything else Ashkelon had stripped from him.

On the third day, an old man came by. He spoke to Haim about his mother and his sisters, and it was some time before Haim recognized him as the distant neighbour he had once purchased seed from.

"Your sisters went to live with relatives," the neighbour said. "They're married now, from what I hear, living somewhere south of Jerusalem."

The old man went on to relate that Haim's mother was dead and that she had been gripped by madness at the end. She had left instructions with this neighbour and the little money she had. The neighbour had sold off the house's removable goods, as she had dictated, along with the meagre supply of tools that remained: a small wagon, a garden hoe, even the gate from the goat pen. The man gave Haim a small purse that held the proceeds from these sales. The property and the money were Haim's. The old man had waited for many years to see if the widow's son would return. Haim could not remember the old man's name.

"How did she die?" Haim asked.

"Madness," the old man said.

"But how?"

The old man was silent and seemed about to turn away, but then he pointed towards the sea. "She was found washed up on the shore."

After the old man left, Haim sat for a while in the shade. He had cleared the house, which was now also roofless and ready for creative labour to begin. He sat under an old tree that he could not remember from his youth.

Later that day, he took a portion of the money left by the old man, bound it in a rag, and placed it in his bag. The rest he left in the purse, wrapped the pouch in another rag, and buried it within the house. Then he went back to Dora, where he bought an axe with one blade and a round butt for pounding. He bought an iron boring tool and a length of good rope. He considered the few available nails, but the price was more than he wished to pay. He purchased a few other supplies, including a tent of the same simple type he had used in his days as a slinger. It would be some time before he had a roof in place, and the rains would continue for months yet.

When he returned to the house, there were new footprints in the soft ground of the yard. They were not his, nor were they the old neighbour's. He remembered that uneasy feeling of being followed through Samaria, then put the thought aside. For now, he needed to build.

The main beam of the roof was one of the salvageable pieces. Even though the roof had partially collapsed, it had taken a great deal of effort to remove the beam from the house, and now he studied how he might return it to its high place. To build the new frame for the roof, raise the ridge beam, and assemble its rafters—these were jobs for several men working together. It would keep him busy working alone. It would tax both his body and mind, but he felt something new within him as he contemplated the work.

When it grew dark, he set up the tent and made his bed within. He heard sounds that night, the usual sounds of a night breeze and the ocean and insects, but also quiet footsteps stepping lightly nearby. The footsteps were not the confident walk of a late-night traveller who had drifted off the path but rather those of someone investigating. Haim listened carefully and said nothing. He heard the steps grow closer, trying to be quiet and mostly succeeding in the soft ground, but the rain had stopped and the air was clean and clear. After a time, the footsteps retreated, and in the morning, though it had rained again overnight, Haim still found the faint outlines of the night-time walker. They were too blurred for him to tell if they were the same as those he had seen the previous afternoon, but it seemed to him that they were similar. They were not the footprints of a large man. This was a small man, perhaps a woman.

In the cool of the morning, Haim considered how he would raise the ridge beam and decided that he would have to build false frames to raise the beam in stages, one side at a time, until it was at the correct height. He would then make the true gables to fit the beam, anchor the beam in place, and install the central pillar that had survived the years. Then he could remove the false frame and redeploy its pieces as the rafters they had been once before. He would have to cut new rafters, for not all that survived were sound, but he had enough to begin the work. He did not know if this was the proper way, but it seemed to him that this was one way, and he thought that he could manage this way on his own.

He began by leaning all the rafter poles up against one wall. They stood nearly vertical, taller than the house, like the wall of a temporary wooden fort. He knew his labour was not efficient. He had pulled this wood from the house and stacked it away from the house. Now he had returned it to the house, standing it in a tall row against the walls. He would move it again soon to build the false frame. It was the inefficient practice of a novice builder trying to organize and inventory his supplies.

Haim was conscious that his experience with construction was limited. He had seen joints cut, and he knew how to use the boring tool. His experience with an axe, however, had been against men when the sling had failed him. He looked forward to cutting his first joints and seeing what kind of job he might make of it.

Beyond creating a better shelter than the tent, Haim felt that rebuilding his childhood home was an act of purification. It was something like what he had sought with the Essenes. When he completed the task, there would be the validation he had once sought from his mother's touch, from Chaya, from the women found in unsavoury houses. It would be something like what his friendships among the slingers could have been, or his relationships within the walls of Qumran would have been had he crossed that barrier. He could not go to Jerusalem or find a new home somewhere else until he had finished this work here.

He passed by the hedge of tall, leaning poles in the afternoon, knowing that he was embarking on a great adventure. The air was wet and it would rain again soon, but the clouds provided a brief respite, and sunshine streamed down upon the land in lines of separated light, bright patches lingering in the sky and on the ground and piercing through the cloud-cast shadows. He came to the edge of the line of tall wood when suddenly he grunted, was thrust sideways and backwards, and heard a solid thump beside him. He bucked against a leaning pole and the pole slid sideways and he heard himself roar as the arrow poking out of his side, its tip buried in the pole, was pulled entirely through him, torn through him as the pole slid and fell. He twisted in shock and horror as the feathered end of the arrow ripped through his insides and exited in a gout of gore and fell snapping to the ground, the pole bouncing off the earth and the glistening arrow shaft spraying the ground with red lines of wet colour. The other poles began to tilt and slide away from him. Haim reached for them and fell into them, and they continued to fall away, and soon his entire construction was bouncing and rolling, and Haim landed where they had been and tried to hold his wound closed, front and back, twisting about to find his attacker somewhere in the sky.

The archer was a boy, perhaps ten years younger than Haim. He came from behind a screen of bushes and high grass. He carried a bow in one hand and notched a second arrow, watching Haim carefully.

"You are Haim of Arbel," the boy said.

Haim stared at the boy, the young man.

"I stayed in that place a week," Haim said. "Maybe a month."

"You stayed in my father's stable, and my mother cooked for you."

Haim struggled to recognize the boy in the grown figure before him. This was the boy he had hunted with and had shown how to repair an axe.

"How?" Haim asked.

"How did I live?"

Haim held his wound front and back and could feel that the flow was thick in both directions. He stopped trying to stem the bleeding then, for he had seen men with wounds of this kind. None of those men had lived. They bled like Kalev, and if they survived that, the fever got them. If they lived long, they suffered greatly. They always died. It was only a question of dying soon or horribly.

"How did you live?" Haim asked.

"They took us out to see my father on his cross. I fainted when they cut my mother's throat. I woke up later in a pile of bodies, my mother and my sister among them. I did not go out to see my father again, to see if he still lived, to give him comfort that I lived. I did not seek him out for fear they would find me. And I could not see him like that again. I escaped and found my way back to Arbel, where a few survivors remained. The queen's brother was there. They had been down in the valley the day you came. They looked after me from then on."

Horses rode up as the boy talked, and the men riding were not locals but military men wearing clothes that Haim associated with the garrison at Jerusalem. At the head of the riders was a man that Haim had first seen at Arbel and later at Ragaba: Simon. The queen's brother. The Cleanser of Ashkelon's Temple.

The riders held their places in front of Haim, staring at him. They did not seem interested in the boy with his notched arrow until Simon finally sighed and turned to him.

"You were supposed to let us capture him," Simon said.

"You've killed other Sadducees in the streets," the boy said.

There was silence then, broken in Haim's ears only by his breathing. He was surprised at how much effort it took not to try to stop his bleeding. He put his hands in his lap. They were red to the wrists, and the sleeves of his shirt were wet as well. He felt a deep sickness in his stomach and wanted to vomit. He looked at the house he would not rebuild. He looked at the scattered poles and the tools and the axe and ropes and then out towards the sea, but he could not see it from here, not seated. He looked at the boy again, who seemed upset, and Haim registered then that an argument had developed. The boy wanted to be in the right, but Simon had wanted Haim to be crucified at Jerusalem. Haim clearly would not live that long.

Another figure then came into view. He was a tall man wearing a long white robe, and Haim understood then that his time was very short indeed. He nodded as though this fit some natural order of things he had previously understood and only recently forgotten. Death came as a priest.

Haim wanted to tell the boy that he was sorrowful about what had happened at Arbel, but he did not know what words to use. He wanted to explain, but an explanation did not seem right. He had no words to compensate for the events of that day. He thought then of a thing he could say and tried to say it, but his breath was short and it was hard to draw more. The clouds were darkening, and nausea overwhelmed him. He could tell by the change in the light that the shafts of sunlight were disappearing. The boy did not seem to notice. The boy continued to argue with the men from Jerusalem and with the priest now as well. Haim squeezed his eyes closed and tried to sit up straighter and tried to speak and to make sense of the change in the argument over him, for that was what it was, the newly arrived priest making the case that Haim was not who the boy and the Jerusalem soldiers believed him to be.

"He's the Betrayer of Arbel," Simon insisted.

"No, he's not," the priest said. And then Haim knew him. Haim tried to speak, but no sound came. The world was becoming faint in his ears, and his eyes kept slipping out of focus.

"I know him. He is one of us." Manoach. It was Manoach in this place.

There was shouting from Simon and the boy and some of the riders that Manoach silenced by ignoring them and striding the last few steps to where Haim lay.

Haim tried to speak, and he stared for some time before he realized he still had not spoken, and he discovered he was not staring at any definite object but only generally in Manoach's direction. His attention had drifted. He tried to focus. He tried to speak again and stiffened himself for one more effort and then felt that his body was moving of its own accord, and then Manoach put his hands on him.

"Be still, my friend," Manoach said. He put his face close to Haim's, pressed his forehead against Haim's cheek, and then against his chest and then his forehead. "Be still." He turned then to the boy and the riders. "You've killed the wrong man," Manoach said. "This one is a priest of Qumran. He's my brother." Haim felt his body jerk then, and then it rhythmically moved again and then again, and his heart was racing, and Manoach held him closer, and the air was thick, and his eyes were sightless, and he did not—

In Jerusalem, there was a trial for the captain who had led the raids throughout Samaria and Galilee, collecting victims for Jannaeus's crucifixion of eight hundred and for the execution of those thousands more who had bled out before the crosses. The Sanhedrin at Jerusalem oversaw the trial. The queen was not present, for unlike her husband and the kings of his family before him, she had separated the high priesthood and the crown. She wore the crown. Her son served as the high priest.

The queen was not present at the captain's trial, but her unspoken opinion swayed the Sanhedrin, which was more Pharisee now than Sadducee. Very few Sadducees stayed in Jerusalem. The Sanhedrin banished the captain to Ragaba, the closest city of refuge for the Sadducees. There he retired in gratitude and fear. Peace remained in the land. There were few from Arbel or any other place to protest the queen's mercy. War was given no further excuse in the land.

❧

At Qumran, the priests buried a body beside Kalev. It was the second body buried at Qumran that did not belong, but Manoach insisted, and there was a will in that place to break their rule a second time.

Several years later, Elazar sat with a junior scribe who was hovering over his scroll, awaiting Elazar's next words. Elazar was here to record the history of a queen, but he couldn't help remembering one young man—a failed acolyte who had touched and in that way polluted a basalt millstone. That had been the young man's introduction to Qumran. The queen's story only made sense when contrasted with the acolyte's lost path. It was the horror before this queen that was the ever-present context for her reign.

The junior scribe shifted and made a small clicking noise with his tongue to attract Elazar's attention.

Elazar shook his head and focused on the scene before him. This was the queen's history and not a record of her husband's reign before her. Nor the story of the acolyte.

"In the days of Salome Alexandra," he started, "the rains always fell only on the eve of the Sabbath and stayed until the morning following the Sabbath. It was done so by God that all could rest on the holy day and that no work would be lost due to rain during the rest of the week. The produce of those rains made the grains of wheat and barley like olives and the lentils like gold coins. There was peace in the land and plenty."

"Is that all?" the scribe asked. It was dark outside, and he had been writing since the evening meal had concluded.

"No. No, that is not all." Elazar looked out the Qumran window, across the courtyard, beyond the wall to where the dead were buried. "There will be more. The full story of our queen has not yet been told."

In the far north, in what remained of the Seleucid Empire, far beyond the borders of Eretz-Israel, the Orontes River entered the Great Sea as a slow spillage. This occurred west of the Paradise of Daphne, downstream from that place of temple revelry. Here, at the seashore, it was quiet. There was only the sound of the water as it met and flowed into the sea and the sound of foreign winds that came from across the Great Sea and stirred the leaves of trees along the rocky shoreline. There were no birds, but there was loneliness. Occasionally, waste from the temple floated down to this place.

A calm heaviness suppressed the soul here—were a soul to come upon this place—and even the wind softened its advance when it approached. The clouds rolled up to the land, careful with rain, careful with sun, for it was a place for the discarding of memories into the flow to be drowned in deeper water. It was an empty joining of land and water, unmarked and unvisited, a secret place unremembered in tales north or south. Here rested solitude. Here, nameless-ness. Here a young and emptied body floated where fresh water intermingled with the salt, her hair a great fan to clothe her, and then she began to sink, fresh water sliding beneath the salt, the snake tattoo at her wrist sinking into the darkness below, the land above left wordless and without life.

A Note from the Author

Keziah and Joazar from my first novel, *Keziah's Song*, could have turned out like Haim and Chaya, but they did not. They had their community in Cana. Not every soul finds their Cana in time. Chaya did not. Haim found his only at the end, after it was too late.

A Review Request:

If you enjoyed *Blind Man's Labyrinth*, please consider taking a minute to leave a review wherever you buy books. Reviews help other readers find my work, and it would mean a great deal to me if you took a moment to tell others about your experience.

To Experience More:

If you would like to learn more about the creative process behind *Keziah's Song* and *Blind Man's Labyrinth*, read my commentary, ask me a question, sign up for my newsletter, or find out about upcoming publications, please visit my website at:

darylpotter.com

May you find your Kalev and Manoach early in life, and if not early, then soon. And may you also be a Kalev or Manoach to someone else. We all need friends. Even the quiet ones among us.

Daryl Potter
January 10, 2021
Oakville, Ontario, Canada

Acknowledgements

This novel flowed naturally out of my first novel, *Keziah's Song*. While separated by time and geography, the stories of Keziah and Haim are related. Their circumstances early in life were similar: orphans thrown into a world at war. The difference between the two was that Keziah had the gentile shopkeeper, the Iturean, and the Galileans. Haim had no one similar. He found Chaya, but they each needed supports that they could not be for each other.

As with my first book, writing *Blind Man's Labyrinth* managed to be both an exploration of ancient history and an intensely personal project, from beginning to end. I am pleased to have been able to share it with you.

Amelia Wiens was the editor for this work and once again she performed editorial works of both magic and hard work. From fact checking botany and geography to challenging timeline continuity both within the novel itself and against *Keziah's Song* details to the specifics of grammar and word choices, she was a joy to work with. Above all, I appreciate her efforts to help me be clear while allowing me to maintain what I hope is a poetic quality throughout the prose.

As with *Keziah's Song*, S. Robin Larin went above and beyond, catching the tiniest irregularities and offering insights that helped to polish this manuscript for its final delivery to the printer. She is a meticulous match for my ideal proofreader and a true pleasure to work with.

The folks at Damonza did another outstanding job with both the cover design and typeset. I am grateful for their creativity, professionalism, and patience as we worked through various ideas and changes.

My research for *Keziah's Song* was equally important to *Blind Man's Labyrinth*, including the works of Flavius Josephus, the first-century CE Jewish historian. While I studied many different sources in my pursuit for historical accuracy, *The Archaeology of Qumran and the Dead Sea Scrolls* by Jodi Magness was by far the most insightful resource I found. Her work was both thorough and easily digestible. I'm grateful that such resources have been made readily available to the general public. Numerous other sources gave incredibly helpful insight into ancient religions outside of the Judeo-Christian tradition, including *Religions of the Ancient World: A Guide*, edited by Sarah Iles Johnston; *Myths from Mesopotamia: Creation, The Flood, Gilgamesh, and Others*, translated by Stephanie Dalley; and *Classical Mythology* by Mark Morford, Robert J. Lenardon, and Michael Sham. Among other works on the ancient geography of the region, I found *Settlement and History in Hellenistic, Roman, and Byzantine Galilee* by Mohr Siebeck to very useful. An Essene work from the period, *The Manual of Discipline*, was one of the many documents discovered in the Dead Sea Scrolls and was a foundational resource for the Qumran arc of this novel. The document is widely available online, and you can find it at *https://www.essene.com/History&Essenes/md.htm*.

I would like to again thank Dr. Douglas Jacoby, an adjunct professor at Lincoln Christian University. Dr. Jacoby led trips through Turkey, Greece, Egypt, and Israel, which were educational and experiential milestones that helped make *Blind Man's Labyrinth* and *Keziah's Song* possible. Mike Luzine, who organized my participation in these trips, climbed all over Qumran when we visited there, and looking back, I deeply regret a stomach bug that kept me near sea level while my companions hiked into places that Haim, Kalev, and Manoach would have explored at length.

Lastly, I would like to thank my family, whose continual support and acceptance of this rather time-consuming project makes these books possible. As long as the stories continue to come, I will continue to write them down. I hope they mean as much to you as they do to me.

www.ingramcontent.com/pod-product-compliance
Lightning Source LLC
Chambersburg PA
CBHW051158190726
48288CB00006B/1706